A Death in Vienna

Also by Frank Tallis

A Death in Vienna

Frank Tallis

GROVE PRESS
New York

First published in the United Kingdom in 2005 by Century
The Random House Group Limited, London

Printed in the United States of America

Library of Congress Cataloging-in-Publication Data

Tallis, Frank.
[Mortal mischief]
A death in Vienna / Frank Tallis.
p. cm.
Originally published: London : Century, 2005, in series: The Liebermann papers.

ISBN 978-0-8021-2338-1
eISBN 978-0-8021-9164-9

1. Forensic psychiatrists—Fiction. 2. Women mediums—Crimes against—
Fiction. 3. Police—Austria—Vienna—Fiction. 4. Vienna (Austria)—Fiction.
I. Title.
PR6120.A44M67 2006
823'.92—dc22   2005050318

Grove Press
an imprint of Grove/Atlantic, Inc.
154 West 14th Street
New York, NY 10011

Part One

The God of Storms

I

It was the day of the great storm. I remember it well because my
father — Mendel Liebermann — had suggested that we meet for
coffee at The Imperial. I had a strong suspicion that something
was on his mind . . .

A ROILING MASS OF BLACK cloud had risen from behind the Opera
House like a volcanic eruption of sulphurous smoke and ash. Its
dimensions suggested impending doom — an epic catastrophe on the
scale of Pompeii. In the strange amber light, the surrounding buildings
had become jaundiced. Perched on the rooftops, the decorative
statuary — classical figures and triumphal eagles — seemed to have
been carved from brimstone. A fork of lightning flowed down the
mountain of cloud like a river of molten iron. The earth trembled and
the air stirred, yet still there was no rain. The coming storm seemed to
be saving itself — building its reserves of power in preparation for an
apocalyptic deluge.

The tram bell sounded, rousing Liebermann from his reverie and
dispersing a group of horse-drawn carriages on the lines.

As the tram rolled forwards, Liebermann wondered why his father
had wanted to see him. It wasn't that such a meeting was unusual; they
often met for coffee. Rather, it was something about the manner in
which the invitation had been issued. Mendel's voice had been
curiously strained — reedy and equivocal. Moreover, his nonchalance

had been unconvincing, suggesting to Liebermann the concealment of an ulterior — or perhaps even unconscious — motive. But what might that be?

The tram slowed in the heavy traffic of the Karntner Ring and Liebermann jumped off before the vehicle had reached its stop. He raised the collar of his astrakhan coat against the wind and hurried towards his destination.

Even though lunch had already been served, The Imperial was seething with activity. Waiters, with silver trays held high, were dodging each other between crowded tables, and the air was filled with animated conversation. At the back of the café, a pianist was playing a Chopin mazurka. Liebermann wiped the condensation off his spectacles with a handkerchief and hung his coat on the stand.

'Good afternoon, Herr Doctor.'

Liebermann recognised the voice and without turning replied: 'Good afternoon, Bruno. I trust you are well?'

'I am, sir. Very well indeed.'

When Liebermann turned, the waiter continued: 'If you'd like to come this way, sir. Your father is already here.'

Bruno beckoned, and guided Liebermann through the hectic room. They arrived at a table near the back, where Mendel was concealed behind the densely printed sheets of the *Weiner Zeitung*.

'Herr Liebermann?' said Bruno. Mendel folded his paper. He was a thickset man with a substantial beard and bushy eyebrows. His expression was somewhat severe — although softened by a liberal network of laughter lines. The waiter added: 'Your son.'

'Ahh, Maxim!' said the old man. 'There you are!' He sounded a little irritated, as though he had been kept waiting.

After a moment's hesitation, Liebermann replied: 'But I'm early, father.'

Mendel consulted his pocket watch.

'So you are. Well, sit down, sit down. Another *Pharisäer* for me and ... Max?' He invited his son to order.

'A *Schwarzer*, please, Bruno.'

The waiter executed a modest bow and was gone.

'So,' said Mendel. 'How are you, my boy?'

'Very well, father.'

'You're looking a bit thinner than usual.'

'Am I?'

'Yes. Drawn.'

'I hadn't noticed.'

'Are you eating properly?'

Liebermann laughed: 'Very well, as it happens. And how are you, father?'

Mendel grimaced.

'Achh! Good days and bad days, you know how it is. I'm seeing that specialist you recommended, Pintsch. And there is some improvement, I suppose. But my back isn't much better.'

'Oh, I'm sorry to hear that.'

Mendel dismissed his son's remark with a wave of his hand.

'Do you want something to eat?' Mendel pushed the menu across the table. 'You look like you need it. I think I'll have the *Topfenstrudel*.'

Liebermann studied the extensive cake-list: *Apfeltorte*, *Cremeschnitte*, *Truffeltorte*, *Apfelstrudel*. It ran on over several pages.

'Your mother sends her love,' said Mendel, 'and would like to know when she can expect to see you again.' His expression hovered somewhere between sympathy and reprimand.

'I'm sorry, father,' said Liebermann. 'I've been very busy. Too many patients ... Tell mother I'll try to see her next week. Friday, perhaps?'

'Then you must come to dinner.'

'Yes,' said Liebermann, suddenly feeling that he had already committed himself more than he really wanted. 'Yes. Thank you.' He looked down at the menu again: *Dobostorte, Gugelhupf, Linzertorte.* The Chopin mazurka ended on a loud minor chord, and a ripple of applause passed through the café audience. Encouraged, the pianist played a glittering arpeggio figure on the upper keys, under which he introduced the melody of a popular waltz. A group of people seated near the window began another round of appreciative clapping.

Bruno returned with the coffees and stood to attention with his pencil and notepad.

'The *Topfenstrudel*,' said Mendel.

'The *Rehrücken*, please,' said Liebermann.

Mendel stirred the cream into his *Pharisäer* — which came with a tot of rum — and immediately started to talk about the family textile business. This was not unusual. Indeed, it had become something of a tradition. Profits had risen, and Mendel was thinking of expanding the enterprise: another factory, or even a shop, perhaps. Now that the meddling bureaucrats had lifted the ban on department stores, he could see a future in retail — new opportunities. His old friend Blomberg had already opened a successful department store and had suggested that they might go into partnership. Throughout, Mendel's expression was eager and clearly mindful of his son's reactions.

Liebermann understood why his father kept him so well informed. Although he was proud of Liebermann's academic achievements, he still hoped that one day young Max would step into his shoes.

Mendel's voice slowed when he noticed his son's hand. The fingers seemed to be following the pianist's melody — treating the edge of the table like a keyboard.

'Are you listening?' said Mendel.

'Yes. Of course I'm listening,' Liebermann replied. He had become accustomed to such questioning and could no longer be caught out, as was once the case. 'You're thinking of going into business with Herr Blomberg.'

Liebermann assumed a characteristic position. His right hand — shaped like a gun — pressed against his cheek, the index finger resting gently against the right temple. It was a 'listening' position favoured by many psychiatrists.

'So — what do you think? A good idea?' asked Mendel.

'Well, if the existing department store is profitable, that sounds reasonable enough.'

'It's a considerable investment.'

'I'm sure it is.'

The old man stroked his beard. 'You don't seem to be very keen on the idea.'

'Father, does it matter what I think?'

Mendel sighed.

'No. I suppose not.' His disappointment was palpable.

Liebermann looked away. He took no joy in disappointing his father and now felt guilty. The old man's motives were entirely laudable and Liebermann was perfectly aware that his comfortable standard of living was sustained — at least in part — by Mendel's exemplary management of the family business. Yet he couldn't ever imagine himself running a factory or managing a department store. The idea was ludicrous.

As these thoughts were passing through his mind, Liebermann noticed the arrival of a gentleman in his middle years. On entering the café, the man removed his hat and surveyed the scene. His hair was combed to the side, creating a deep side parting, and his neatly trimmed moustache and beard were almost entirely grey. He received a warm welcome from the head waiter who helped him to take his coat off. He was immaculately dressed in pinstriped trousers, a wide-lapelled jacket and a 'showy' waistcoat.

He must have made a quip, because the head waiter suddenly began laughing. The man seemed in no hurry to find a seat and stood by the door, listening intently to the waiter, who now appeared — Liebermann thought — to have started to tell a story.

Mendel saw that his son had become distracted.

'Know him, do you?'

Liebermann turned.

'I'm sorry?'

'Doctor Freud,' said Mendel in a flat voice.

Liebermann was astonished that his father knew the man's identity.

'Yes, I do know him. And it's *Professor* Freud, actually.'

'Professor Freud, then,' said Mendel. 'But he hasn't been a professor for very long, has he?'

'A few months,' said Liebermann, raising his eyebrows. 'How did you know that?'

'He comes to the lodge.'

'What lodge?'

Mendel scowled.

'B'nai B'rith.'

'Oh yes, of course.'

'Although God knows why. I'm not sure what sort of a Jew he's supposed to be. He doesn't seem to believe in anything. And as for his ideas . . .' Mendel shook his head. 'He gave us a talk last year. Scandalous. How well do you know him?'

'Quite well . . . We meet occasionally to discuss his work.'

'What? You think there's something in it?'

'The book he wrote with Breuer on hysteria was excellent and *The Interpretation of Dreams* is . . . well, a masterpiece. Of course, I don't agree with everything he says. Even so, I've found his treatment suggestions very useful.'

'Then you must be in a minority.'

'Undoubtedly. But I am convinced that Professor Freud's system — a system that he calls psychoanalysis — will become more widely accepted.'

'Not in Vienna.'

'I don't know. One or two of my colleagues, other junior psychiatrists, are very interested in Professor Freud's ideas.'

Mendel's brow furrowed: 'Some of the things he said last year were obscene. I pity those in his care.'

'I would be the first to admit,' said Liebermann, 'that he has become somewhat preoccupied — of late — with the erotic life of his patients. However, his understanding of the human mind extends well beyond our animal instincts.'

The professor was still standing by the door with the head waiter. He suddenly burst out laughing and slapped his companion on the back. It was clear that the head waiter had just told him a joke.

'Dear God,' said Mendel under his breath, 'I hope he doesn't come this way.' Then he sighed with relief as Professor Freud was ushered to a table beyond their view. Mendel was about to say something else but stopped when Bruno arrived with the cakes.

'*Topfenstrudel* for Herr Liebermann and *Rehrücken* for Herr Doctor Liebermann. More coffee?' Bruno gestured towards Mendel's empty glass.

'Yes, why not? A *Mélange* and another *Schwarzer* for my son.'

Mendel looked enviously at his son's gateau, a large glazed chocolate sponge cake shaped like a saddle of deer, filled with apricot jam and studded with almonds. His own order was less arresting, being a simple pastry filled with sweet curd cheese.

Liebermann noticed his father's lingering gaze.

'You should have ordered one too.'

Mendel shook his head: 'Pitsch told me I must lose weight.'

'Well, you won't lose weight eating *Topfenstrudel*.'

Mendel shrugged and took a mouthful of pastry but stopped chewing when a loud thunderclap shook the building. 'It's going to be a bad one,' said Mendel, nodding towards the window. Outside, Vienna had succumbed to a preternatural twilight.

'Maxim,' Mendel continued, 'I wanted to see you today for a reason. A specific reason.'

At *last*, thought Liebermann. Finally, he was about to discover the true purpose of their meeting. Liebermann braced himself mentally, still unsure of what to expect.

'You probably think it's nothing to do with me,' Mendel added. 'But—' He stopped abruptly and pushed the severed corner of his *Topfenstrudel* around the plate with his fork.

'What is it, father?'

'I was speaking to Herr Weiss the other day and . . .' Again his sentence tailed off. 'Maxim.' This time he returned to his task with greater determination. 'You and Clara seem to be getting along well enough and — understandably, I think — Herr Weiss is anxious to know of your intentions.'

'My intentions?'

'Yes,' said Mendel, looking at his son. 'Your intentions.' He carried on eating his cake.

'I see,' said Liebermann, somewhat taken aback. Although he had considered many subjects that his father might wish to discuss, his relationship with Clara Weiss had not been one of them. Yet now the omission seemed obvious.

'Well,' replied Liebermann. 'What can I say? I like Clara very much.'

Mendel wiped his mouth with a napkin and leaned forwards.

'And?'

'And . . .' Liebermann looked into his father's censorious eyes.

'And . . . I suppose that my intention is, in the fullness of time to—'
(Now it was his turn to hesitate.)

'Yes?'

'To marry her. That is — if she'll have me.'

Mendel relaxed back in his chair. He was clearly relieved and a
broad smile lifted his grave features.

'Of course she'll marry you. Why shouldn't she?'

'Sometimes we seem to be . . . well, just good friends.' In all areas of
life, Liebermann was entirely confident of his powers of perception;
however, where Clara was concerned, he was never entirely sure if her
affectionate gestures were tokens of love or merely of flirtation. Desire
had blunted his clinical acumen. 'It isn't always clear what—'

'You have nothing to worry about,' Mendel interrupted, inclining
his hand in a courtly gesture. 'Believe me.' He leaned forward again,
and squeezed his son's arm: 'Nothing to worry about at all. Now eat
your *Rehrücken!*'

But Liebermann had no desire to eat. Clara had obviously told her
father that she would accept a proposal of marriage. He had *nothing to
worry about*. Liebermann thought of her delicate features: her expressive
eyes, small nose, and rose-petal lips — her straight back and slender
waist. She was going to be his wife. She was going to be *his* Clara.

'I won't tell your mother,' continued Mendel. 'I'll leave that to you.
She'll be delighted, of course. Delighted. As you know, she's very fond
of Clara. In fact, she was saying only the other day how pretty Clara's
become. And they're a good family, the Weisses. Good people. Jacob
and I go back many, many years. We went to the same school, you
know, in Leopoldstadt. And his father helped my father — that's your
grandfather — into the trade. They shared a market stall together.'

Liebermann had been told this more times than he cared to
remember. Even so, he knew that his father took immense pleasure in
reiterating family history, and simulated interest as well as he could.

Mendel warmed to his theme, and continued to expound upon the several other links that existed between the Weiss and Liebermann families. The *Rehrücken* helped Liebermann to survive the repetition. Eventually, when Mendel had exhausted the topic, he attracted Bruno's attention and ordered more coffee and cigars.

'You know, Maxim,' said Mendel, 'with marriage comes much responsibility.'

'Of course.'

'You have to think about the future.'

'Clearly.'

'Now tell me, will you really be able to provide for a young family on that salary of yours?'

Liebermann smiled at his father. It was extraordinary how Mendel never missed an opportunity.

'Yes,' Liebermann replied patiently. 'In due course, I think I will.'

Mendel shrugged.

'We'll see . . .'

The old man managed to sustain his stern expression for a few seconds longer before allowing himself a burst of laughter. Again, he reached over the table, and patted his son on the shoulder.

'Congratulations, my boy.'

The gesture was curiously affecting, and Liebermann recognised that — in spite of their differences — the relationship they shared was predicated on love. His throat felt tight and his eyes prickled. The bustle of the café faded as the two men stared at each other, suspended in a rare and vivid moment of mutual understanding.

'Excuse me,' said Mendel, rising precipitately and setting off towards the cloakroom. But the old man had been too slow. Liebermann had already observed a tear in his eye.

*

Liebermann watched his father disappear into the bustling Ringstrasse crowd. A gust of wind reminded him that — unlike Mendel — he was not carrying an umbrella. Fortunately, a cab was waiting just outside The Imperial. There was another rumble of thunder — the growl of a discontented minor god. It made the cab horse toss its head, jangle its bridle, and stroke the cobbles with a nervous hoof.

'Easy now,' called out the driver — his voice barely audible above the rattling of the carriages. Across the road a loose café awning snapped like a sail.

Liebermann looked up at the livid millstone sky. Ragged tatters of cloud blew above the pediment of The Imperial like the petticoats of a ravished angel. The air smelled strange — an odd, metallic smell.

Liebermann raised his hand to catch the cab driver's attention but was distracted by a familiar voice.

'Max!'

Turning, he caught sight of a sturdy man approaching. His coat was undone and flapping around his body as he walked into the wind — a precautionary hand kept his hat from flying off his head. Liebermann immediately recognised his good friend Inspector Oskar Rheinhardt, and smiled broadly.

'Oskar!'

The two men shook hands.

'Max, you will think this a dreadful impertinence, I know,' said Rheinhardt, pausing to recover his breath. 'But would you mind awfully if I took your cab?'

The Inspector possessed a face that suggested weariness. The skin under his eyes sagged into discoloured catenated pouches. Yet he had grown a miraculously trim moustache, the turned-up extremities of which tapered to form two sharp points.

'An incident?' asked Liebermann.

'Indeed,' said Rheinhardt, puffing. 'A matter of some urgency, in fact.'

'Then please be my guest.'

'Thank you, my friend. I am much indebted.'

Rheinhardt opened the door of the cab and as he climbed up, called out to the driver: 'The market square — Leopoldstadt.' The driver responded by touching his forelock with a gloved finger. Before closing the cab door, Rheinhardt addressed Liebermann again: 'Oh, and by the way, the Hugo Wolf songs are coming along nicely.'

'Until Saturday, then?'

'Until Saturday.'

With that, Rheinhardt pulled the door shut and the cab edged out into the noisy traffic.

A sheet of white lightning transformed the Ringstrasse into a glaring monochrome vision. Moments later a great ripping sound opened the heavens, and the first heavy drops of rain detonated on the paving stones.

Liebermann looked around for another cab — knowing already that the attempt would be futile. He sighed, good-naturedly cursed Rheinhardt, and stomped towards the nearest tram stop.

2

RHEINHARDT PRESSED HIS shoulder against the locked door and pushed. It didn't budge.

A blast of wind rattled the windows and unholy-sounding voices wailed in the chimney flues. A shutter was banging — again and again — like an impatient revenant demanding entry, and all around was the inescapable sound of rain: a relentless artillery. Teeming, drenching, torrential. Drumming on the roof, splashing from the gutters and gurgling out of drains. The deluge had finally come.

Rheinhardt sighed, turned, and looked directly at the young woman sitting in the dingy hallway. She was slight, wore an apron over a plain dress, and was very nervous. Her fingers fidgeted on her lap, a mannerism that reminded him of his daughter Mitzi. The young woman stood up as Rheinhardt approached.

'Please,' said Rheinhardt, 'stay seated if you wish.'

She shook her head. 'Thank you very much, sir, but I think I'd rather stand.' Her voice shook a little.

'I'd like to ask you a few questions, if I may?'

She mouthed the words 'Yes, Sir' — but no sound escaped.

Having determined the girl's name — Rosa Sucher — Rheinhardt asked: 'What time did you arrive today?'

'My usual time, sir. Nine o' clock.'

'And is Fräulein Löwenstein usually up by then?'

'Usually, but not always. As you can see — the bedroom door is open.' Rheinhardt responded politely by looking across the hallway. The corner of a drab counterpane was just visible. 'The bed had not been slept in, so I—' She broke off, her face suddenly flushing with embarrassment.

'Naturally you assumed that your mistress had not spent the night at home.'

'Yes. That's right, sir.'

'And what did you do then?'

'Well, sir, I got on with my duties . . . but I found that I couldn't get into the sitting room. The door had been locked — and I didn't know what to do. So I carried on cleaning, thinking my mistress would eventually return . . . but she didn't. And today is Thursday. My mistress always sends me to the shops on Thursdays, to get things. Things for her guests. Pastries, flowers—'

'Guests?'

'Yes, sir. Fräulein Löwenstein is a famous medium.' The young woman said this with some pride. 'She has a meeting here, every Thursday at eight.'

Rheinhardt felt obliged to look impressed.

'Famous, you say?'

'Yes. Very famous. She was once consulted by a Russian prince who travelled all the way from St Petersburg.'

The downpour intensified and the unfastened shutter banged with even greater violence. Rosa Sucher looked towards the sitting-room door.

'Please, do go on,' said Rheinhardt.

'I waited until the afternoon — and still my mistress hadn't come home. I began to worry . . . finally I went to Café Zilbergeld.'

'On Haidgasse?'

'Yes. I know Herr Zilbergeld, I worked for him last summer. I told him that my mistress had not returned, and he asked me if this had ever happened before? I told him that it hadn't, and he said that I should call the police. So I ran around the corner, to the police station on Grosse Sperlgasse.'

The young woman pulled a handkerchief from her sleeve and blew her nose. She was clearly about to start crying.

'Thank you, Rosa,' said Rheinhardt. 'You have been very helpful.'

The young woman curtsied and sat down, steadying herself by touching a small rosewood table.

Rheinhardt walked up the hallway, peering into the various rooms. The apartment was not very large: a bedroom, a drawing room, a bathroom and a kitchen — which also housed the closet. The maid watched him: a large man in a dark blue coat, apparently deep in thought. He paused, and twisted the right horn of his moustache into an even sharper point. Returning to the locked door, he crouched and looked through the keyhole.

He could see nothing. It had obviously been locked from the inside, suggesting that the room was still occupied. The occupant, however, had not moved, nor spoken a word since Rosa Sucher's arrival in the morning.

Rheinhardt could hear his assistant, Haussmann, and the constable from the Grosse Sperlgasse police station running up the stairs. Within seconds they appeared at the end of the hallway.

'Well?' Rheinhardt asked, slowly straightening up. He was a stout man, and pressed the palms of his hands down on his thighs to gain extra lift.

The two men marched towards him, leaving a trail of wet footprints in their wake.

'All the shutters are bolted,' said Haussman, 'except for one. It's difficult to see the window in the rain . . . but I think it's closed. The sitting room is completely inaccessible from outside.'

'Even with a ladder?'

'Well, a very long ladder would do it, sir.'

The two young men came to an abrupt halt in front of Rheinhardt. Even though they were thoroughly soaked, their expressions suggested a kind of canine enthusiasm — the controlled agitation of a retriever as a stick is about to be thrown. Beyond them, the pathetic figure of Rosa Sucher sat biting her nails.

'Constable,' said Rheinhardt, 'would you escort Fräulein Sucher downstairs?'

'Downstairs, sir?'

'Yes, to the foyer. I'll follow shortly.'

'Very good, sir,' said the constable, turning swiftly on his heels.

Rheinhardt clapped a restraining hand on the officer's shoulder before he could spring forward. 'Gently now,' said Rheinhardt close to his ear. 'The young woman is upset.'

Rheinhardt released his grip, allowing the constable to approach Rosa Sucher. He did so with the exaggerated slowness of an undertaker. Rheinhardt rolled his eyes at the ceiling, and turned to face Haussmann.

'I don't think we should waste any more time. It's a strong old door but we should be able to do it.' Haussmann removed his sopping cap and twisted it in his hands. Rainwater dripped to the floor, creating a small puddle between his feet. When he had finished wringing the cap he placed it back on his head.

'You'll catch a cold,' said Rheinhardt. Haussmann looked at his superior, unsure how to react. 'Why don't you take it off?'

Haussmann obediently removed his cap and stuffed it into his coat pocket.

They positioned themselves on the opposite side of the hallway.

'Ready?' asked Rheinhardt.

'Yes, sir.'

Running towards the door, they threw their shoulders against it. There was a dull thud, and the sound of air being forced from their lungs. Haussmann stepped back, grimaced, and rubbed his shoulder.

'That hurt.'

'You'll live,' said Rheinhardt. At the end of the hallway, the constable was holding the front door open for Rosa Sucher. For a brief moment she looked back before hurrying out, ducking beneath the policeman's arm.

'Now, let's try again,' said Rheinhardt.

They returned to their former positions and repeated the procedure. This time, however, when their shoulders made contact, the frame split and the door burst open with a loud *crack*. The two men struggled to keep their balance as they fell forward into the room beyond.

It took a few seconds for Rheinhardt's eyes to adjust. The curtains were drawn and the light was poor. Even so, the unpleasant smell was enough to confirm his worst fears.

'God in heaven . . .' The timbre of Haussmann's voice suggested a combination of reverence and horror.

The room was large, with a high bas-relief ceiling of garlands and floating cherubs; however, Rheinhardt's attention was drawn to a massive circular table, around which ten sturdy chairs were evenly spaced. In the middle of the table stood a gaudy silver candelabra. The candles had burned down, and long wax icicles hung from excessively elaborate arms.

Gradually more shapes began to emerge from the gloom, one of which was a chaise longue located on the other side of the room. The couch was not empty but was occupied by a shadowy form that swiftly resolved itself into a reclining female figure.

'Haussman,' said Rheinhardt. 'The curtains, please.'

His assistant did not respond but stood very still, staring.

Rheinhardt raised his voice: 'Haussman?'

'Sir?'

'The curtains, please,' he repeated.

'Yes, sir.'

Haussman walked around the table, keeping his gaze fixed on the body. He pulled one of the curtains aside, which filled the room with a weak light. As he reached for the second curtain Rheinhardt called out: 'No, that's enough.' It seemed improper, or disrespectful, to expose the body further.

Rheinhardt advanced, stepping carefully across the threadbare Persian rug, and stopped next to the chaise longue.

The woman was in her late twenties and very pretty. Long blonde tresses fell in ringlets to her slim shoulders. Her dress was of blue silk — its neckline tested the limits of decency — and a double string of pearls rested on an ample alabaster bosom. She might have looked asleep had it not been for the dark stain that had spread from her décolletage and the coagulated blood that had crusted around the jagged hole over her ruined heart.

There was something odd — almost affected — about her posture, like that of an artist's model. One arm lay by her side, while the other was placed neatly behind her head.

'Sir?'

Haussman was pointing at something.

On the table was a sheet of writing paper. Rheinhardt walked over and examined the note. It was written in a florid hand: *God forgive me for what I have done. There is such a thing as forbidden knowledge. He will take me to hell — and there is no hope of redemption.*

It appeared that the writer had been jolted, just as the final word was finished. A line of ink traced an arc that left the page just above the bottom right-hand corner. On closer inspection, Rheinhardt also noted that the writer had made a mistake in the final sentence. A word that she'd obviously decided against had been crossed out — before the *me* in *He will take me to hell.*

'Suicide,' said Haussmann.

Rheinhardt said nothing in response. Haussmann shrugged and walked around the table to the chaise longue. 'She's very beautiful.'

'Indeed,' said Rheinhardt. 'Strikingly so.'

'Fräulein Löwenstein?'

'Very probably. I suppose we should get Rosa Sucher back up here to identify the body. Though she was so upset — perhaps that's not such a good idea.'

'It might save us some legwork, sir.'

'True. But being a good policeman isn't only about making expedient decisions, Haussman.' His assistant looked slightly hurt, forcing Rheinhardt to amend his reprimand with a conciliatory smile. 'Besides,' Rheinhardt added, 'Fräulein Löwenstein was expecting some guests tonight — perhaps there will be a gentleman among the company who may be willing to assist us.'

Although the room had at first appeared rather grand, closer inspection soon revealed that this was an illusion. The paintwork was chipped, the floorboards scuffed, and a brown stain under one of the windows suggested damp. At one end of the room was an austere marble fireplace, above which an ornate Venetian-style mirror had been hung. Rheinhardt suspected that it was a copy. Recesses on either side of the fireplace contained shelves on which an array of items had been placed: a cheap porcelain figure of a shepherdess, an empty bowl, two vases, and a ceramic hand (displaying the chief lines of the palm). The other end of the room was occupied by a large embroidered screen. The total effect of the room was somewhat depressing, moth-eaten and shabby.

'We're going to need a floor plan for the file — can you do that, Haussmann?'

'Yes, sir.'

'And an inventory of items?'

'Yes, sir.'

Rheinhardt continued to scan the room.

The rain lashed against the windows, running in streams down the casement. Outside, the shutter continued to bang against the wall. Rheinhardt unlocked the offending window, opened it, and peered out. A blast of cold air scoured his face and the curtains billowed inwards. The road had become a river in spate — a rushing, tumbling flood. Peering over the ledge, the Inspector looked downwards. It was a sheer drop.

Rheinhardt fixed the loose shutter and closed the window. He wiped the rain from his face with a handkerchief and examined his reflection, making some minor adjustments to his moustache. His satisfied exhalation fogged the glass.

'Sir?'

The young man's voice was slightly edgy — uncertain. The room trembled as the celestial cannonade continued.

'Yes?'

'You'd better take a look at this.'

Behind the screen was a large lacquered box, decorated with Japanese figures. Rheinhardt tried to lift the lid but discovered that it was locked.

'Shall we force it open?'

'That won't be necessary. You can ask Rosa Sucher where her mistress kept the key.'

'Shall I do that now, sir?'

'No. Not yet, Haussmann. Let's just think a little, eh?'

Haussmann nodded, and assumed what he hoped the Inspector would recognise as a contemplative expression.

Rheinhardt's attention was drawn again to the body. Slowly, he advanced towards the sofa and knelt to inspect the wound. As he did so, he accidentally brushed against the woman's delicate but unyielding fingers. Her frozen touch made him shudder. He instinctively wanted to apologise but managed to stop himself. Rheinhardt used the damp handkerchief to cover his mouth and nose. Close up, the smell of stale urine and the beginnings of decomposition became deeply unpleasant. There was a double flash of lightning, and the crystals of dried blood around the wound glowed like garnets.

'Impossible.' He whispered the word almost unconsciously.

'I'm sorry, sir?'

The thunder roared like a captive giant.

Rheinhardt stood up and looked around the room, unnerved by the evidence of his own senses.

'Sir?' Haussmann sounded anxious.

Rheinhardt walked over to the door and checked that the key was still in the lock. It was — a large black key. He wheeled around. Haussman was staring at him, his head tilted to one side.

'What do you think happened here?' asked Rheinhardt.

Haussman swallowed: 'The Fräulein has committed suicide, sir.'

'Very well. Reconstruct events — tell me how she did it.'

Haussmann looked confused.

'She shot herself, sir.'

'Clearly — but from the beginning.'

'The Fräulein must have come into this room last night — well, that's what I would assume, given the way she's dressed. She locked the door and then sat at this table, where she began to compose a suicide note. She was evidently in a distressed state of mind, and gave up on the task after completing only a few lines.'

'And what do you make of those lines?'

Haussmann took a step towards the table and looked down at the note before continuing: 'They're a confession of some kind. She felt that she had done something wrong and should therefore make reparation by taking her own life.'

'Go on.'

'Then, perhaps after further deliberation — who can say? — the Fräulein sat on the chaise longue, lay back, and shot herself in the heart.'

'I see,' said Rheinhardt. And waited.

Haussmann pursed his lips and walked over to the couch. He looked at the Fräulein's wound, and then followed the line of her arm and hand. Kneeling on the floor, he looked under the couch and then said: 'Sir ...'

'Quite,' said Rheinhardt. 'There's no weapon.'

'But there must be.'

Haussmann got up and opened a drawer in the table.

'What are you doing?' asked Rheinhardt.

'Looking for the gun.'

'Haussmann,' said Rheinhardt patiently. 'The Fräulein has been shot through the heart. Do you really think that after sustaining such an injury she would have had sufficient time, firstly, to conceal a weapon, and secondly, to recover her position on the chaise longue?'

'She might have fallen back, perhaps?'

Rheinhardt shook his head: 'I don't think so.'

'But the door,' said Haussmann, almost petulantly, pointing to the broken frame. 'It was locked from the inside. The gun must be here somewhere!'

Rheinhardt pulled the remaining curtains aside.

'All of the windows were locked. And anyway, who in their right mind would choose to make an escape from up here?'

Through the streaming rainwater, Rheinhardt saw the blurred image of a solitary cab struggling up the road, its driver hunched up beneath a waterproof cape.

'In which case . . .' Haussmann started enthusiastically, but then smiled sheepishly and let his sentence trail off.

'Yes? What were you going to say?'

His assistant shook his head: 'Nothing, sir, it's ridiculous.'

Rheinhardt frowned at his young companion.

'Very well, sir,' said Haussmann, 'But it's only a thought, you understand?'

'Of course.'

'Fräulein Löwenstein. Her note . . .'

'What about it?'

'Forbidden knowledge?'

Rheinhardt shook his head: 'Haussmann, are you suggesting some kind of supernatural explanation?'

His assistant raised his hands: 'I did say it was only a thought.'

Rheinhardt gave an involuntary shiver. He picked up Fräulein Löwenstein's note.

He will take me to hell — and there is no hope of redemption.

Although Rheinhardt was still tutting and shaking his head, try as he might he could not think of a single alternative to Haussmann's suggestion. As far as Rheinhardt could see, Fräulein Löwenstein had indeed been murdered by someone — or some*thing* — that could pass through walls.

3

THE DOOR OPENED and the hospital porter wheeled in the subject of Professor Wolfgang Gruner's demonstration. She was dressed in a plain white hospital gown and wore no shoes. Her head was bowed, and her long dark hair had fallen in front of her face. The doctors — numbering over fifty and assembled on tiered benches around Professor Gruner — began to murmur.

Liebermann sighed loudly, slouched, and folded his arms.

'Max?'

He looked up at his friend and colleague, Doctor Stefan Kanner.

'What?'

Kanner pulled the cuffs of his shirt down to expose his gold cuff links and then adjusted his bow tie. He was wearing a particularly sweet cologne.

'Don't start, Max.'

'Stefan, I don't think I can watch another one of these.'

He began to rise, but Kanner grabbed him by the arm and pulled him down again.

'Maxim!'

Liebermann shook his head and under his breath declared: 'This is a circus.' The man occupying the bench directly in front of Liebermann glanced back over his shoulder and rebuked him with a scolding stare.

'Enough,' Kanner hissed, digging a pointed elbow into Liebermann's ribs. 'He's probably one of Gruner's friends!'

'Gruner is already acquainted with my views.'

'Indeed, so well acquainted is he that your position here becomes more uncertain day by day.'

The porter parked the rickety wheelchair close to Professor Gruner. Together, they lifted the woman up onto the modest stage where she was carried the short distance to a large wooden throne-like chair. There she was seated and her limbs arranged. The professor then slid a metal plate under the woman's feet. As he was doing this, the porter removed the wheelchair and assumed the stance of a guard by the door.

'Gentlemen,' declared the professor, his resonant voice filling the large room. The thrum of background conversation stopped dead. Outside, the storm had abated and the ferocious drumming of the rain had been replaced by a gentle pitter-patter.

Gruner was a tall, imposing figure, with a long brindled beard and an unruly mass of receding grizzled hair. The expression that he habitually wore was one of mild but constant disgruntlement, to the extent that a permanent vertical crease divided the professor's high forehead.

'Gentlemen,' the professor repeated. 'May I introduce Signora Locatelli?'

The woman stirred, and brushed the hair from her face. Liebermann judged her to be in her mid-twenties, and if she was not beautiful she was certainly striking. Her eyes were dark, and deeply set above sharp features. She surveyed the audience, and then looked towards Gruner, who inclined his head and smiled — but for no more than a fraction of a second.

'The signora,' continued Gruner, 'is the wife of an Italian diplomat. Some three to four months ago, she began to develop symptoms suggestive of a hysterical illness and was subsequently diagnosed by a local physician. She became increasingly infirm, anorexic, and now suffers from an apparent and seemingly total paralysis of both legs. On examination, we find no evidence of traumatic injury or disease.'

Turning towards his subject, Gruner addressed her directly.

'Signora. You cannot walk, is that correct?'

The woman nodded.

'I beg your pardon?' said Gruner. 'I am afraid I did not hear your reply.'

The woman swallowed, and in slightly accented German responded: 'No. I cannot walk.'

'Do you ever experience pain in your legs?'

'I experience nothing. They are . . .' Her face twisted in anguish. 'Dead.'

Gruner addressed the audience again.

'Sadly, at this time, and in Vienna especially, there is a pernicious trend in our profession towards psychological explanations of hysteria.' Gruner's head turned slowly until he was looking directly at Liebermann, who sat perfectly still. Liebermann knew that he was expected to shift uncomfortably and cower. Instead, he proudly held the professor's minatory gaze, and even dared to let the ghost of a smile animate his features. Gruner continued: 'Gentlemen, I would urge you most strongly to question the legitimacy of this approach, and the judgement of all those who endorse it. Hysteria is a medical condition, caused by a constitutional weakness of the nerves. A weakness that can be easily and swiftly corrected by electrotherapy.' Gruner gestured towards the apparatus that stood on the table next to Signora Locatelli.

'Today I will be demonstrating an instrument from the United States of America. My initial impression is that it is superior to those of local manufacture.'

Liebermann was familiar with Gruner's 'instruments', all of which were very similar in appearance. This one, however, was notable on account of its size — being much bigger than the others he had seen to date. Gruner moved to the table and caressed the polished surface of a large teak box. He released two brass hasps and gently lifted the lid, the underside of which was lined with red leather that was embossed in gold lettering: *The Galvanic and Faradic Battery Company of Chicago, Ill. USA.* Inside the box was an arrangement of knobs, rollers and dials. Gruner removed two bright metal rods with wooden handles, which were attached to the assembly by long leads.

'For those interested in the technical specifications of this instrument, it is of standard design. It is powered by six-volt dry batteries which are both safe and easy to maintain. The output voltage can be varied by adjusting a simple metal cylinder that slides over the core of the induction coil.'

Gruner flicked a switch and the room immediately filled with a loud buzzing. He then invited one of the assembly to assist. A middle-aged man rose from his seat.

'Thank you, Herr Doctor,' said Gruner. 'If you would position yourself on the other side of the patient?' The man walked across the bare wooden floor boards, stepped up on to the stage, and stood to attention beside the diplomat's wife.

'Signora Locatelli,' continued Gruner. 'Could I prevail upon you to raise your gown?'

The woman gathered up the material of the skirt of her gown in her hands and, as she did so, the hem began to lift, revealing her slim ankles and calves.

'Signora,' continued Gruner, 'it will be necessary to raise your gown to a level above the knee.' The woman blushed and, gripping more material in her hands, exposed her legs completely. Liebermann turned away and looked disdainfully at his colleagues, most of whom had leaned forward. Sensing his friend's movement, Kanner delivered another elbow jab and nodded towards the demonstration.

Gruner stepped forward and passed the metal rods over Signora Locatelli's legs.

'Do you feel anything?'

'No.'

'Nothing — not even a tickling sensation?'

'No.'

Gruner addressed the audience. 'I will now increase the charge.'

He took both rods in one hand and reached into the box, adjusting the dials and cylinders. The pitch of the buzzing ascended an octave. Gruner then returned to his patient and passed the metal rods over her legs a second time. She did not move, and her gaze remained fixed on some elevated point at the back of the room. Liebermann saw that she was staring at the bust of some long-forgotten medical luminary.

'Signora,' said Gruner. 'You must feel something now. Perhaps pins and needles?'

Without moving her head to make eye contact, the diplomat's wife simply continued staring.

'Signora?' Gruner said tetchily. 'What do you feel?'

'I feel . . .' The woman paused before saying: 'That there is no hope.'

Gruner shook his head: 'Signora, please refrain from obtuse answers. Do you feel any sensations in your legs?'

Still without moving, she said softly: 'No. I feel nothing . . .' And then, after another pause, she added: 'In my legs.'

'Very well,' said Gruner. He passed both rods to his assistant and then plunged his hands into the electrical apparatus. The buzzing became louder: a horrible glissando ascending to a pitch that made Liebermann's ears ache. Gruner then took back the rods.

It was clear that Gruner had increased the charge considerably and the room was tense with expectation. Even Liebermann found himself attending more closely, drawn into the drama by the woman's declaration that there was no hope — a statement that he felt resonated with many meanings.

Gruner extended his arms and then, after the briefest of hesitations, prodded Signora Locatelli's legs. She opened her mouth and let out a cry, not of pain but of anguish. It was not particularly loud, yet it was deeply disturbing to Liebermann. It reminded him of an operatic sob, full of despair and melancholy. At the same time, the woman's right leg moved forward.

'Good,' said Gruner. He applied the rods again.

The woman's legs began to shake.

'Stand up, Signora.'

The shaking became more pronounced.

'Stand up!' Gruner commanded.

Grimacing, Signora Locatelli pressed her hands down hard on the arms of the wooden throne and a moment later she was standing up, her whole body trembling. Gruner stepped back so that every member of the audience could see and appreciate his achievement. He held the metal rods up like trophies.

'Observe, gentlemen. See how the subject stands. If hysteria were a psychological illness, then what you are now witnessing would not be possible.'

To Liebermann, Signora Locatelli's balance looked precarious. Her arms were extended outwards, a little like an acrobat standing on a high wire. She did not appear to be pleased or surprised by her accomplishment. Instead, her features seemed to be contorted by fear and confusion.

'Signora,' said Gruner. 'Perhaps you would care to venture a step or two?'

Her upper body swayed and wobbled above legs that refused to respond. It was as though the patient's feet were fixed to the floor.

'Come now, Signora. Just one step.'

Using all her strength, the diplomat's wife cried out as she forced her left leg forward. But as she did so she finally lost her balance and fell. The assisting doctor caught Signora Locatelli under the arms and lowered her gently onto the chair, where she lay back, breathing heavily, her forehead beaded with sweat.

Gruner placed the rods in the box and switched off his machine. The buzzing stopped, creating a strangely solid silence that was broken only by Signora Locatelli's loud exhalations.

A smattering of applause, which then became more vigorous as others joined in, passed through the audience. The man sitting in front of Liebermann suddenly stood up and cried out: 'Bravo, Herr Professor.'

Liebermann turned towards Kanner, raising his voice above the applause.

'I'm never going to sit through one of these absurd, barbaric and humiliating demonstrations again.'

Kanner leaned towards his friend and spoke directly into his ear.

'You'll be dismissed.'

'So be it.'

Kanner shrugged: 'Well, don't say I didn't warn you.'

4

THE CENTRAL PATHWAY was flanked by eight muses and ascended to the lower cascade: a giant stone shell, supported by a team of tritons and sea nymphs. The balustrades lining the steps on either side of the fountain were populated by chubby putti, and beyond was the first of the Belvedere's celebrated sphinxes.

'Did the storm frighten you?'

'Max, I'm not a child. Of course it didn't frighten me.'

The ground was still wet, and Liebermann had to guide Clara through an archipelago of puddles. He couldn't help noticing her boots — so small and elegant.

'Although Rachel made a fuss.'

'Did she?'

'Oh yes, she knocked on my door and insisted that I let her in.'

'And did you?'

'Of course I did. I told her that there was nothing to be frightened of — and that the storm would pass. But it didn't seem to do much good. She simply crawled into my bed and pulled the covers over her head.'

'How long did she stay like that?'

'Until it stopped.'

Once they had negotiated the puddles, Liebermann offered Clara his arm, which she took without hesitation.

'What was Rachel frightened of? What did she think was going to happen?'

'I don't know. Perhaps you should *analyse* her — although it wouldn't do any good. Rachel wouldn't listen to anything you said.'

Liebermann had explained to Clara that psychoanalysis was more about listening than 'telling', but resisted the urge to correct her. 'True. But neither do you!'

Clara broke away, laughing. She turned and, facing Liebermann, started walking backwards.

'Be careful,' said Liebermann. 'You might stumble.'

'No, I won't. It's better this way — I'm enjoying the view.'

Clara was wearing a long coat with a fur collar and a Cossack-style hat. The ensemble emphasised the delicacy of her features. Her little face, peering out from its bed of sable, appeared curiously feral.

Was this the right moment?

Since meeting with Mendel in The Imperial, Liebermann had thought of nothing else but this walk. He had been looking forward to it with fervid impatience. Every intervening second had passed slowly — particularly those spent at Gruner's demonstration — stretching the minutes into refractory hours. For much of the afternoon the storm had threatened to scupper his plan, but now nothing stood in his way. He cleared his throat, ready to speak.

'Do you know what my father said this morning?' asked Clara.

The opportunity vanished as swiftly as it had appeared.

'No. What did he say?'

'He said that we're going to Meran in the summer.'

'Really? For how long?'

'A month or two . . . He thinks it will help Rachel's asthma.'

'I'm sure it will. The Tyrol air is very good for bronchial problems.'

Clara stopped, turned again, and extended her arm, allowing Liebermann to take it as he advanced.

'Have you ever been there, Max?'

'Yes,' Liebermann replied. 'I worked in Meran when I was a

student. Let me offer you a piece of very useful advice. Avoid anything that's supposed to have medicinal properties — particularly the *whey cure*.'

'What's that?'

'A local remedy, much favoured by the good people of Meran. It consists of coagulated milk with white wine, strained from the curd and sweetened with sugar.'

Clara screwed up her face.

'Oh, that sounds utterly disgusting.'

'It is — but the locals swear by it. However, if you're going in the summer you might be all right. I think it's a seasonal delight, served mostly in the spring.'

A cold gust of wind blew in from the east, and they instinctively drew closer together.

'Will I get bored, do you think?'

'A little, perhaps. But there are fairs and market days. And there are so many Viennese there — you're bound to bump into someone you know . . .'

Ahead of them the detail of the baroque palace was becoming clearer. It was an enormous building of white stucco that extended between two octagonal domed pavilions; however, it looked as though a garrison of Turks had pitched a line of green tents on the roof. This was, of course, an architectural conceit, intended to remind onlookers of the great siege.

Clara squeezed Liebermann's arm in the crook of her elbow.

Again, Liebermann wondered whether the moment had arrived. Whether he should stop walking, take Clara in his arms, and ask her to be his wife.

'Herr Donner came today.'

The sound of her voice brought him out of his reverie.

'I'm sorry?'

'Herr Donner, my piano teacher.'

'Of course . . . and what did he teach you?'

'We played a duet by Brahms. A waltz.'

'Which one?'

'I don't know. I've forgotten.'

'Then how does it go?'

Clara attempted to sing the melody, but quickly lost her way in a succession of chaotic key changes. 'No,' she said. 'It didn't go like that at all.' She tried again, this time managing to hum a lilting tune that sounded more like a lullaby.

'I know that. It's one of the Opus 39 waltzes. Number fifteen, I think. Perhaps we should try it when we get back?'

'Oh good heavens, no. It's too difficult . . . I need more practice.'

Clara continued describing her day: a trip to Blomberg's with her mother; the purchase of curtains for the sitting room; the shortcomings of the new maid. Liebermann had little interest in the Weisses' domestic arrangements, yet he derived enormous pleasure from listening to the familiar cadences of Clara's speech and her musical laughter. And most of all he enjoyed being close to her, feeling the warmth of her body and inhaling the subtle fragrance of her perfume.

There was something hypnotic about their slow ascent, the pleasing regularity of their step, accompanied by the satisfying scrunch of damp gravel underfoot. Indeed, it seemed that this gentle rhythm had assisted their transition between worlds. They had passed into a kind of waking sleep and had entered the landscape of a dream.

Liebermann looked over his shoulder. They were totally alone in the gardens, having no other company except for the sphinxes. The inclement weather had obviously deterred other visitors. After ascending the final incline, they paused to enjoy the view.

At the foot of the slope, beyond the sunken hedge gardens, fountains and statuary, was the relatively modest lower palace.

Further out, the spires, domes and mansions of the city dispersed and dissolved into an elevated horizon of blue hills. A subtle mist softened the panorama and intensified an opaque silence. The proud capital looked spectral — even oddly transparent.

'It's beautiful, isn't it?' said Clara.

'Yes,' said Liebermann. 'Very beautiful.'

He knew, at last, that the moment had arrived. He had been rehearsing lines in his head all day: poetic set pieces of increasing power that culminated in dramatic declarations of love. But suddenly all these words seemed redundant. Forged endearments. Corpulent language, bloated with insincere affectation.

'Clara.' He spoke the words quietly and clearly: 'I love you very much. Will you marry me?'

Taking her small gloved hand in his, he raised it to his lips.

'Please say yes.'

Clara's expression trembled with uncertainty, oscillating between emotions. Then, finally, she produced a hushed and breathless response — a mere whisper: 'Yes, Maxim. I'll marry you.'

Liebermann gently raised her chin and tested her lips with the briefest of kisses. She closed her eyes and he embraced her, pulling her suddenly limp body close to his.

When they drew apart, she was smiling. But her eyes had become glassy. She sniffed, and the first of many tears spilled down her glowing face.

Liebermann had never seen her cry before, and his eyes narrowed with concern.

'It's all right,' said Clara. 'Really. I'm just so happy.'

5

Karl Uberhorst looked up at the Inspector through the oval lenses of his silver pince-nez. He was a small man with short brown hair and a thick moustache combed down to cover his upper lip. Rheinhardt had noticed that it was the habit of most small men to counter their diminutive stature by standing erect. This was not the case with Uberhorst, who allowed his shoulders to slope, his spine to curve, and his head to project forward. There was something about his appearance that reminded Rheinhardt, in some vague way, of a tortoise. Uberhorst was probably in his thirties, yet his stoop and his conservative dress made him look much older.

Uberhorst was the second 'guest' to arrive. The first had been a young woman called Natalie Heck: an attractive girl, with large dark eyes. She was now sitting on the chair by the rosewood table — the one previously occupied by Rosa Sucher.

'The others will be here shortly,' said Uberhorst. 'They're usually very punctual.'

It was obvious that the little man was reluctant to view the body, but Rheinhardt could not justify a further delay. Looking towards Haussmann he said: 'Perhaps you should take Fräulein Heck into the drawing room?'

The young woman rose and adjusted her shawl — which had been beautifully embroidered. It looked, thought Rheinhardt, to be a more expensive item of clothing than a girl with her accent should have been able to afford. Her lustrous black hair had been arranged so as to reveal only one ear, from which a large glass earring dangled. She looked like a little gypsy.

'She's not in there — is she?' said the girl, pointing towards the drawing-room door, her voice quivering.

'No,' said Rheinhardt. 'The body is in the sitting room. Herr Uberhorst will make the identification.'

The woman sighed with relief.

Haussmann guided Fräulein Heck towards the drawing room and Rheinhardt observed — with some satisfaction — that his assistant had already taken out his notebook. He could be trusted to undertake the preliminary interview.

'This way, please,' said Rheinhardt to Uberhorst.

The light in the sitting room was no better than when the storm had been raging. It emanated from a single paraffin lamp that had been placed on the massive circular table. As they entered, the police photographer crouched next to his tripod and pulled a large black cloth over his head. The apprentice, a gangly, doleful-looking adolescent, struck a match and a moment later a strip of magnesium ribbon flared. Suddenly the body was illuminated by a harsh, petrifying light. Its cruel brilliance made the blue dress and bloodstains burn with a terrible intensity.

'Well?' asked Rheinhardt.

'Yes,' said Uberhorst. 'That is Fräulein Löwenstein.'

'Fräulein Charlotte Löwenstein?'

'Yes.'

'Thank you.'

The already fetid air thickened with smoke and chemical fumes from the burning metal ribbon.

Rheinhardt touched the little man's arm. He seemed mesmerised by the hellish vision.

'Herr Uberhorst?'

He shook his head and allowed the Inspector to guide him, like a sleepy child, through the broken door frame.

Once in the hallway, Uberhorst rushed towards the chair by the rosewood table. He collapsed on to it, placing his head in his hands. Within moments his whole body was convulsing. Rheinhardt waited patiently until the sobbing had begun to subside.

Uberhorst sat up, took a deep breath, and removed his pince-nez. Taking a neatly pressed handkerchief from his pocket, he unfolded it, dabbed at his eyes and finally blew his nose loudly.

'I'm sorry, Inspector.'

'I understand,' said Rheinhardt.

'I'm a locksmith. I've never—' His sentence was interrupted by another sob. Uberhorst stuffed the soggy handkerchief back into his pocket and began to rock, ever so slightly, backwards and forwards. After some time, he said, 'I can't believe it,' and after another long pause he asked, 'What happened?'

'We don't know yet,' said Rheinhardt.

Uberhorst sniffed, and shook his head.

'It's unbelievable. Unbelievable ...'

'Herr Uberhorst, who else is expected this evening?'

'The regular members of the circle.'

Rheinhardt produced a notebook and waited, his pencil poised.

Uberhorst suddenly realised that the Inspector had anticipated a more comprehensive answer.

'Oh, I see. You want names. We are also expecting Otto Braun, Heinrich Hölderlin and his wife Juno. Hans Bruckmüller ... and the Count.'

'The Count?'

'Zoltán Záborszky — he's from Hungary.'

Another magnesium ribbon flared, spilling its merciless mineral light into the hallway.

'Herr Uberhorst, how long have you been attending Fräulein Löwenstein's meetings?'

'For about four months.'

'And how did you come to join her circle?'

'By chance. I met her one day on the Prater and she invited me.'

A constable appeared from behind the front door.

'Two more gentlemen, sir.'

'Let them through.'

The door opened fully, revealing a somewhat overweight man in a camel-hair coat. He removed his bowler hat and walked briskly down the hallway. His moustache was similar to Rheinhardt's, turned up at the ends — but perhaps less finely groomed. He was followed by another man, whose flamboyant but shabby dress gave him the appearance of a down-at-heel impresario.

The first man stopped beside Uberhorst.

'Karl? Is it true? Lotte?'

His voice was a rich bass — deep and resonant.

Uberhorst nodded and whined: 'Yes. It's true. She's dead.'

'My God!' the big man boomed. Then, looking towards Rheinhardt, he added: 'I beg your pardon . . . Inspector?'

'Rheinhardt.'

'Inspector Rheinhardt. My name is Bruckmüller. Hans Bruckmüller.' He removed a calfskin glove and extended his hand. Rheinhardt was surprised by the strength of his grip. 'The young constables downstairs said —' Bruckmüller made an unsuccessful attempt at lowering his voice, '— that Fräulein Löwenstein has been shot?'

'Yes,' said Rheinhardt. 'She has.'

'When? When did it happen?'

'Some time late last night, or in the early hours of the morning.'

'Extraordinary.'

Bruckmüller began walking down the hall.

'Herr Bruckmüller!' Uberhorst called out. The cry was loud and distraught.

Bruckmüller stopped and looked back

'Don't go in there,' said Uberhorst. 'It's terrible. The stuff of nightmares.'

Bruckmüller caught Rheinhardt's eye.

'I see,' said Bruckmüller. Then gesturing to the door he added. 'If it would help, Inspector . . . I would be willing to—'

'No,' said Rheinhardt. 'That won't be necessary. The body has already been identified.'

Bruckmüller walked over to Uberhorst and rested a fat hand on the little man's shoulder.

'Good fellow,' he said, and squeezed.

Uberhorst winced.

Rheinhardt turned towards the other man, the 'impresario', who had positioned himself by the bedroom door. He wore a moth-eaten fur coat over a tired pongee suit, his necktie was made of red silk, and a monocle — attached to a length of black ribbon — dangled from his waistcoat. In his hand he carried a walking cane. His features were broad, suggesting a trickle of Mongolian blood in his veins. This general impression of foreignness was exaggerated by an oriental moustache, which hung down to his chin, and a small goatee beard. He did not react but stood stock-still, impassively accepting Rheinhardt's scrutiny.

'Forgive me, Inspector' said Bruckmüller, his stentorian declaration filling the hallway. 'May I introduce Count Zoltán Záborszky?' Then, feeling that further explanation was necessary, he added: 'We arrived at the same time — outside.' It was as though Bruckmüller wanted to clarify the nature of their relationship by stressing that they had not come together. They were companions by coincidence rather than choice.

The Count inclined his head slightly and raised his cane, the top of which was a small gold likeness of a jaguar's head baring its teeth. He moved forward — an unhurried, swaying swagger.

'The body is in the sitting room?' His German had a distinctive Magyar accent.

'Yes,' replied Rheinhardt.

'I must see it.'

It was clear that the Count had no intention of asking Rheinhardt for permission. He simply sashayed towards the sitting-room door, barely acknowledging the Inspector's presence. Although tempted to assert his authority, Rheinhardt was also curious to see how this odd man would react and followed in his scented wake — the fragrance was like stale pot-pourri.

The Count stepped through the broken door frame and positioned himself by the large circular table. He peered through the gloom, which was immediately dispersed by another magnesium flash. Fräulein Löwenstein's corpse leapt out of the darkness.

The Count's nostrils flared.

'Evil,' he whispered softly. 'I smell evil.' His face was entirely without emotion — an inscrutable blankness. Taking a small ivory crucifix from his waistcoat pocket, he kissed the figure of Christ and placed it on the table. 'God protect us,' he whispered.

His eyes flicked from side to side, as though trying to locate a concealed demon.

6

THE PUBLIC HOUSE — a gloomy cellar, illuminated by flickering gas lights and the red glow from a squat cast-iron stove — was situated in the working-class suburb of Meidling. A beggar sat in the corner, scraping tunelessly at his violin, while three old men, seated at a central table, argued loudly. The atmosphere was dense with pipe smoke. At the bar a woman with yellow skin was picking at a plate of sliced cucumber and chewing on a black rusk.

Otto Braun emptied the last drops of vodka into his glass and ran a hand through his hair. It was long and kept on falling into his eyes.

One of the old men called out: 'Gergo! Gergo, where the hell are you?'

Braun tilted his head back and swallowed. The alcohol was finally beginning to work, making him feel pleasantly detached.

Beyond the bar, two boots (with red trim) appeared on the staircase, followed by a heavily built Ruthenian who called out: 'All right, all right . . .' He was wearing loose trousers and a greasy satin waistcoat.

'Well, well.' The voice floated into Braun's consciousness. 'Haven't seen you here before.'

Braun looked up. The woman from the bar was standing by his table.

'I've been watching you,' she said, taking the seat next to him.

'Have you?'

'Oh yes. And I've been thinking, there's a man who could do with some company.'

Before Braun could answer, the woman had caught the landlord's arm. 'Gergo?'

'What?'

She held up the empty vodka bottle.

'The gentleman's finished.'

The landlord looked from the bottle to Braun.

'You want another?'

Braun looked at the woman and inspected her features. Although her skin was sallow, her eyes had retained a suggestion of former beauty.

'Yes,' said Braun. 'Why not?'

The woman smiled, and a network of creases tessellated her face.

Perhaps Braun had overreacted. It was inevitable that the police would be involved. Crossing the deserted square, he had seen the two officers outside the main entrance to Lotte's apartment building: constables, in long blue coats and spiked helmets — and armed with sabres. He had hidden himself behind an abandoned market stall in order to observe what was happening. Herr Bruckmüller and the Count had arrived at the same time, and after some questioning had been allowed in. Not long after, Hölderlin and his irritating wife had arrived. Braun had acted instinctively, turning away without thought and keeping close to the wall as he crept back the way he had come. He had responded like an animal. It was probably the wrong thing to do but it would give him an extra day or two — and sometimes an extra day or two made all the difference.

The landlord returned with another bottle of vodka and banged it down in the middle of the table.

'So,' said the woman. 'What's your name, then?'

'Felix,' said Otto.

'Mine's Lili.'

Otto lifted the bottle and tilted the neck over his glass. He had tipped it too steeply, and the clear liquid began to splash out, over the rim and onto the deeply scored table top.

'Hey, hey,' said Lili, straightening his hand. 'Take it easy, Felix.'

She guided the bottle back to its upright position, letting her hand linger on Otto's. One of the old men was shouting something about the battle of Solferino, and the fiddler suddenly burst into a discordant but recognisable gypsy folk melody. Otto picked up the glass and poured the contents down his throat. The cheap vodka was rough and excoriating.

An image entered his mind, uninvited and vivid.

Lotte. Her blonde hair — like spun gold in the candlelight. Her green eyes incandescent with rage.

He shouldn't have asked her for more money and he certainly shouldn't have hit her. But the argument had escalated. And suddenly there she was, framed in the doorway, brandishing a kitchen knife. Otto shook his head, and made a gesture — as though trying to push the memory out of his mind.

'What's the matter?' said Lili.

'Nothing,' Otto replied. He turned to look at the violinist who, except for a pair of cloudy white irises, was almost invisible in his shadowy recess. The vagrant was sawing his bow with a crude violence. The sound he created was diabolical — as were his mephitic exhalations.

Lili poured another drink and, without looking to Otto for approval, drained the glass herself. She then caressed the arm of his jacket.

'Very nice,' she said. 'Velvet. And so well cut.'

She leaned back and looked at Otto more carefully, inspecting his clothes and estimating their value. Although somewhat dishevelled, he was a handsome young man. His long dark hair and the squareness of his jaw gave him the look of a Romantic poet.

'So what do you do, eh?'

Otto didn't reply.

'An artist?'

He pushed his fringe back, plastering the hair over his crown with the sweat from his forehead.

'Of a kind.'

'How d'you mean?'

Otto took Lili's hand and deftly removed a paste ring from one of her fingers.

'Oi!'

'Quiet,' said Otto. 'Watch.'

He then presented Lili with two closed fists.

'Which hand is it in?'

Lili smiled and touched his left. Otto showed her that it was empty. She then touched his right — which also proved empty.

'Very clever! I'll have it back now!'

Otto pointed at the vodka bottle.

Lili leaned forward, and said softly: 'Well, I never . . .' Her ring was inside — where it had apparently floated to the bottom.

'Now we'll have to drink the whole lot to get it out,' said Otto.

Lili laughed loudly — like a rattle. She edged closer, and as she did so Otto felt her hand slide across his thigh.

'Show me another one,' said Lili. 'Go on.'

'All right,' said Otto. He took the last three coins from his pocket and laid them out in a row. 'I want you to watch very, very carefully . . .'

7

THE MORGUE WAS cavernous and cold. A large electric light suspended at the end of a long cord hung several feet above the body. Its wide conical shade created a pool of illumination beyond which it was difficult to see anything but shadow.

Professor Mathias peeled back one of the mortuary sheets and examined Fräulein Löwenstein's face. Her skin was without blemish and under the close light her hair shone brighter than ever. Although her lips were no longer red but a curious blue, she was still very beautiful. Indeed, the strange colouring of her lips seemed to add a further dimension to her unnatural perfection. She looked, to Rheinhardt, like an exotic doll.

'Forgive me,' said Mathias. 'What did you say her name was?'

'Does it matter, Herr Professor?'

Mathias looked over his glasses

'Of course it matters, Inspector.'

Rheinhardt shrugged.

'Her name was Charlotte Löwenstein.'

Mathias looked down at the woman's angelic face and repositioned a spiral of her hair. Then, after a few moments' silence, he rested his knuckles against her cheek and began to intone: 'Lotte! Lotte! Just one more word! Just a word of farewell! Farewell, Lotte! For ever adieu!'

'Goethe,' said Rheinhardt.

'Well done, Inspector. *The Sorrows*, of course.'

Mathias did not remove his hand. Instead, he stared at the corpse, his face brimming with compassion.

Rheinhardt coughed, somewhat disconcerted by the professor's eccentricities.

'Professor. If we could proceed . . .'

Mathias sniffed in disapproval.

'When you work with the dead, Rheinhardt, you learn to take things slowly.' He continued to gaze at the Fräulein's face, and as he did so he sighed, his breath clouding the air. Mathias turned to look at Rheinhardt, his head descending and rising with almost bovine slowness. His rheumy eyes swam behind thick magnifying lenses. 'Do the dead make you uncomfortable, Rheinhardt?'

'Actually, Professor, they do.'

'Be that as it may,' said Mathias, 'it is my belief that the dead are still deserving of small courtesies.' Saying that, the professor covered Fräulein Löwenstein's face, and under his breath continued to quote from *The Sorrows of Young Werther*: 'Be of peaceful heart . . .'

Rheinhardt was relieved when Mathias finally snapped out of his abstracted state and began to show signs of industry. The professor rolled up his shirtsleeves, tied his apron, and began to arrange the tools of his trade on a white metal trolley: knives, saws, chisels, small metal mallets, and a drill. The professor was clearly unhappy with the arrangement and began tinkering with the positions of several objects. Rheinhardt could see no obvious reason for these trivial changes, and suspected that Mathias was engaging in some obscure superstitious ritual. After a few minutes of deliberation, the professor nodded, and his expression changed from mild anxiety to satisfaction.

'Let us begin,' he said.

Mathias picked up an oversized pair of scissors and began cutting the corpse's dress. He began in the middle of the décolletage and proceeded down to the waist. When the cut was complete, he tugged gently at the material: dried blood had made it adhere to the corpse's skin. The material came away gradually, revealing Charlotte Löwenstein's naked breasts and torso.

'No corset,' commented Mathias.

He pulled at the sheets, covering the body so that nothing was exposed except the blood-encrusted crater over Fräulein Löwenstein's heart. When one of the dead woman's nipples threatened to reappear, Mathias repositioned the sheet to protect her modesty.

'I beg your pardon,' he said softly.

Rheinhardt was finding Mathias's sympathy for the dead both tiresome and macabre.

The old man probed gently around the wound with the tips of his fingers. As he did so, he started to hum a tune. Rheinhardt listened to the first verse and wondered whether he was being tested again. He found it impossible not to rise to such easy bait.

'Schubert.'

The professor stopped, ending his impromptu recital on a wheezy, unsteady note. The sound called to mind a set of ancient bellows closing.

'Is it? The tune just came into my head. I don't know what it is.'

'It's Schubert. Das Wandern . . .'

'Ah yes, I remember now. You sing a little, don't you?'

'A little . . .'

'Das Wandern, eh?'

'Without a doubt.'

Mathias began to hum again and continued probing the wound. He then took a magnifying glass from his trolley and lowered his head to get a closer look. The professor suddenly stopped humming mid-phrase, and gasped. After a moment's silence, he said in a dramatic stage whisper, 'Ahh, yes.'

'What is it?' asked Rheinhardt.

'She's been shot,' replied Mathias.

Rheinhardt sighed.

'I thought we had already established that, Professor.'

Mathias shook his head.

'I have always been a great believer, Rheinhardt, in the Roman dictum: *festina lente*. More haste, less speed.'

'You know,' said Rheinhardt, 'I can't say that surprises me.'

The professor ignored Rheinhardt's pointed remark and continued his leisurely inspection. Closing one eye, the old man altered the focal length of the magnifying glass and nodded. Then, speaking more to himself than to Rheinhardt, he said: 'A direct shot — into the heart, at close range. There are the powder burns and . . . yes, I see some muzzle bruising.'

Rheinhardt's fingers were going numb, and he was beginning to regret seeking Professor Mathias's assistance. Mathias returned the magnifying glass to its special position on the trolley and picked up a medium-sized silver knife. He then made a deep cut in Fräulein Löwenstein's white flesh, which opened with the slow grace of a scallop shell, exposing the pulpy redness within. Rheinhardt had attended many autopsies but he still found them highly disturbing.

'Excuse me, Herr Professor,' Rheinhardt took a step backwards. 'I think I'll leave you to it.'

'As you wish, Inspector,' said Mathias, clearly becoming more absorbed in his task.

Rheinhardt walked around the autopsy table and out into the darkness. Behind him he could hear Mathias sorting through his tools. First he heard some tapping, and then the grating of a saw. Rheinhardt assumed that Mathias was removing a rib. As Mathias worked, he began to hum the Schubert tune again. His performance was slow, and many of the notes were cracked or unsteady. Yet his old voice, and the lingering quality of each phrase, imbued Schubert's joyful walking tune with infinite pathos.

As his eyes adjusted to the darkness, Rheinhardt found that he was standing next to a bank of square metal doors. He knew that most of the chambers behind them were, in all probability, occupied by corpses. The frozen dead.

He turned and looked back at the strange little man who was hunched over Fräulein Löwenstein's body like a goblin or dwarf, something from a fairy tale by the brothers Grimm. Under the bright light, Mathias's breath had condensed in the cold air and collected over the table as a fine, luminous mist. Rheinhardt blew into his cupped fists and rubbed his hands together. The mortuary chill was seeping into the marrow of his bones.

Making his way back to the autopsy table, Rheinhardt stopped to examine Professor Mathias's tools, attempting to ignore a sound that reminded him of the leg being pulled from a roast chicken.

Suddenly the lights went out and the morgue was plunged into total darkness: an expanse of impenetrable pitch.

Professor Mathias was still quietly humming the Schubert song and Rheinhardt, already unnerved by the eerie ambience, was conscious that his heart was beating a little too fast. Count Záborszky's words — like an auditory hallucination — entered his mind: *I smell evil.*

'Professor?' Rheinhardt called into the void.

The humming stopped.

'Oh, it's all right, Inspector, the light usually comes on again after a few minutes — probably something to do with today's storm. Personally, I think we should have stuck to gas.'

There was a small movement, and the clatter of metal on tiles. Rheinhardt felt something hit his foot.

'Oh dear,' said Mathias. 'I seem to have disturbed one of my instruments.'

There was a loud click, and suddenly the light came on again.

'There we are,' said the professor. 'Told you so.'

Rheinhardt looked down and saw a scalpel on the floor by his foot. He crouched down and picked it up.

'Your scalpel, Professor?'

'Just put it back on the trolley for the moment — not with the others, though. Bottom shelf, in the glass retort.' As he said this, Mathias was removing a large piece of bloody matter from Fräulein Löwenstein's chest. Rheinhardt quickly looked away, bowing his head. To distract himself, he turned the blade idly in his hands and let it flash a few times as it caught the light. Rheinhardt noticed that the scalpel was engraved with a cursive script: *Hans Bruckmüller and Co.*

'Professor?'

'Yes, what is it?'

'Does the name Hans Bruckmüller mean anything to you?'

'Yes, of course. Bruckmüller's. It's the surgical-instrument shop near the university.'

'Do you know Herr Bruckmüller?'

'No. Why do you ask?'

'He was an acquaintance of Fräulein Löwenstein.'

'Really?' said the professor — although it was clear that he wasn't paying much attention. Rheinhardt placed the scalpel in the glass retort. It rang like a bell.

As Rheinhardt stood behind Mathias, he couldn't help but notice that, in spite of the old man's earlier exhortations concerning haste, he was working much faster now. He was employing different instruments, one after the other, and tutting loudly. Indeed, he was looking increasingly agitated — if not actually annoyed. Rheinhardt thought it best not to interfere and waited patiently.

After several minutes Mathias wiped the blood from a long pair of tweezers and, displaying an uncharacteristic lack of care, tossed them on to the trolley. Rheinhardt was startled. The old man then stared directly at Rheinhardt, saying nothing. His expression was far from friendly.

'Professor?' ventured Rheinhardt.

'What is the meaning of this?' asked Mathias, gesturing towards the corpse.

'I beg your pardon, Professor?'

'Was it Orlov? Or was it Humboldt? Did they put you up to this?' Rheinhardt raised his hands.

'I'm sorry, Herr Professor, but I haven't a clue what you're talking about.'

Mathias grunted, took off his spectacles, and rubbed his eyes. Rheinhardt wondered whether Mathias's eccentricity wasn't, after all, something very close to madness. The old man replaced his spectacles and undid his apron with a decisive tug. He lifted the collar over his head, rolled the apron up, and placed it on the bottom shelf of the trolley. He then began to fidget with his instruments, moving them around as though they were the pieces in a bizarre chess game.

'Professor,' said Rheinhardt. 'I would be most grateful if you would explain yourself.'

Mathias looked up from his instruments. Again, he stared at Rheinhardt, his enlarged eyes swimming behind their lenses. Rheinhardt endured the silence for as long as he could before finally losing his patience.

'Herr Professor, I have had a long and difficult day. I have not eaten since this morning, and I am tired. I would very much like to go home. Now, for the last time, I would be most grateful if you would explain yourself!'

The professor snorted, but a fog of doubt passed across his face, softening his angry pout.

'This isn't a joke?' he said in a neutral voice.

Rheinhardt shook his head.

'No, Professor, this isn't a joke.'

'Very well,' said Mathias warily. 'I will explain my findings, and if you can make any sense of them, you're a better pathologist than I am.' The old man paused before turning to face the corpse. Pointing at the gaping hole in Fräulein Löwenstein's chest, he continued: 'This woman has been shot. Here is the point where the bullet entered her body. The heart has been torn open, as one would expect.' He poked his finger into her chest and lifted a flap of skin. Rheinhardt felt a little sick. 'See here,' said the professor. 'This is where the bullet ripped through the left ventricle. Everything is consistent with a gunshot wound.'

'Yes,' said Rheinhardt. 'I can see that.'

'But,' said Mathias, 'there is no bullet.'

'I beg your pardon, Herr Professor?'

Mathias said again: 'There is no bullet.'

Rheinhardt nodded.

'It passed through her body?'

'No,' replied Mathias. 'The entry canal had a definite terminus. Nothing came out the other side of her body.'

'Then what are you saying?' asked Rheinhardt. 'That the bullet was . . . removed?'

'No. The bullet has not been removed.'

'You're absolutely sure?'

'Absolutely.'

'Then how can you explain . . .'

Rheinhardt's words trailed off into silence. The electric-light system began to buzz, and the lights blinked out again for a second or two.

'I can't explain this,' said Mathias, flicking the flap of skin back like the lid of a jewellery box. 'Rheinhardt, you have brought me a physical impossibility. That is why it is my belief that I — or perhaps both of us — are the victims of a tedious prank. Goodnight, Inspector.'

Mathias wiped his bloody fingers on a white towel. He then walked towards the door, his metal-tipped shoes sparking on the flagstones as he dragged his heavy heels.

8

Heinrich and Juno Hölderlin were seated in the spacious breakfast room of their Hietzing villa. Two housemaids were clearing the plates — and as they did so they exchanged surreptitious, knowing glances: the master and mistress of the household were clearly not very hungry. A slab of gleaming yellow butter had been scraped no more than a few times and the breadbasket was still piled high with freshly baked rolls. The bacon and boiled eggs had hardly been touched.

Hölderlin rang the table bell to summon the steward, who swiftly materialised with the coffee. He was immaculately turned out in white gloves and a brick-red coat with a black velvet collar.

'Thank you, Klaus,' said Juno, as the decorous manservant deposited a large silver pot and tray on the table.

'Cook will be preparing suckling pig and artichokes for supper — and wanted to know whether sir would like pineapple mousse or ice cream to follow.'

Hölderlin looked briefly at his wife.

'The mousse?'

'Yes,' said Juno. 'The mousse.'

The steward bowed, clicked his heels, and marched out of the room, pursued by the heavily burdened housemaids. Hölderlin picked up his copy of the *Wiener Zeitung* and turned to the financial pages.

'What does it say?' asked Juno nervously.

The polished dome of her husband's pate rose above the newspaper's horizon like the dawn sun.

'About Fräulein Löwenstein?'

Juno nodded, eyelids flickering rapidly.

'Nothing, of course. It's too early.'

Juno poured a cup of coffee for her husband, and then for herself.

'Who would do such a thing? It's such a terrible business,' she said quietly.

'No one would disagree with you there,' said Hölderlin, turning a page.

'I couldn't sleep.'

'Nor me.'

Juno looked around the room and made an impromptu inspection of her house plants. She thought that the aspidistra was looking a little withered, and made a mental note that it should be given extra water. Next to the aspidistra was a framed picture of her beloved sister, Sieglinde.

Sieglinde had died (or, as Juno preferred to say, had 'departed') in the autumn of the previous year after a long and painful illness. The doctors had done little to ease her suffering, and it had been with mixed feelings that Juno had buried her sister in the Zentralfriedhof. Juno had known that she would feel her sister's absence like the loss of a limb — but watching Sieglinde coughing up dark clots of blood and writhing in agony had been intolerable.

Throughout the winter months, even when it had been snowing, Juno had journeyed from Hietzing to the Zentralfriedhof to lay flowers on her sister's grave. Then, one bleak December morning while leaving the cemetery, she had fallen into conversation with another mourner, a handsome young man by the name of Otto Braun. He had explained how, after the loss of his own dear mother, the desolation of his grief had been relieved by a talented medium in Leopoldstadt. Juno begged Heinrich to accompany her. The woman, Fräulein Löwenstein, held meetings every Thursday evening and Juno did not want to venture into Leopoldstadt on her own. After only one sitting, Juno was convinced that the woman was no charlatan. Heinrich had been sceptical at first — but even he was forced to change his mind when his father 'came through'.

Yes, Fräulein Löwenstein had been special.

'Do you think the Inspector will call today?'

'I have no idea.'

'What was his name? I've forgotten it.'

'Rheinhardt — Inspector Rheinhardt.'

'He said that he would, didn't he?'

Hölderlin looked at his wife. The rate of her blinking had increased.

'He said that he would like to interview us again, yes,' said Hölderlin, 'But I don't think he said that it would be today, specifically.' He raised the newspaper. 'Well, that wasn't my impression, anyway.'

'Why does he want to ask us more questions?'

'I don't know.'

'Surely . . . surely he doesn't suspect us. Surely he doesn't think that we—'

'Of course not!' said Hölderlin, raising his voice. 'Don't be so ridiculous! Of course he knows it's got nothing to do with us!' He turned the page angrily.

Juno lifted the coffee cup to her lips but did not drink. 'I do hope so,' she said more calmly. 'He seemed a sensible man.'

'Yes,' Hölderlin replied gruffly. 'Very sensible.'

Juno took a minute sip of coffee. 'The little locksmith,' she said. 'He was so upset. Devastated.'

From behind the paper Hölderlin replied: 'Herr Uberhorst is a very sensitive fellow.'

'Yes, he is,' said Juno. 'I believe he still has one of my books. I lent him my Madame Blavatsky. Perhaps you could get it back from him, my dear — if you're passing?'

'Yes ... yes.'

'He *is* a sensitive fellow. But there was more to it, don't you think?'

Hölderlin did not reply.

'The way he used to look at her ...'

Hölderlin lowered his paper with evident impatience.

'What?'

'Didn't you ever notice?'

'Notice what?' Hölderlin asked irritably.

Juno blinked at her husband.

'The way Herr Uberhorst used to look at Fräulein Löwenstein. The way he would hang on her every word.'

Hölderlin shook his shiny head and continued reading.

'He was like a schoolboy,' Juno continued. 'Mind, he wasn't the only one, of course. She seemed to have, how can one put it, an influence over men. Wouldn't you say? If you ask me, the Count was besotted too — as was that young fellow Braun. There's no denying her gift, of course. She was very talented. Blessed, one might say. Strange, isn't it? That such a — would it be fair to say this, I don't know — that such a vain woman who was so very particular in matters of appearance should possess such a gift. Still, who am I to question the Lord's will? Such a gift is God-given — of that I'm sure.'

When she had finished speaking, the silence was crushing.

'Heinrich?'

Her husband said nothing.

Juno allowed her coffee cup to drop loudly into its saucer.

'Heinrich?' she said again, somewhat louder. 'You're not listening, are you?'

Behind the protective cover of his newspaper, Heinrich Hölderlin was sitting with eyes wide, staring blankly at an advert for Kalodont toothpaste: *Indispensable*. He had heard every word, and his mouth had gone wholly dry — as though packed with sawdust. Hölderlin swallowed to relieve the uncomfortable sensation, but to no effect.

9

Her hair was pulled back tightly from her face and the cast of her features, set in a permanent half-frown, suggested habitual seriousness. Although young, there was nothing about her that suggested naivety or insouciance.

Beyond the confines of the examination room, Liebermann could hear a man screaming. He was accustomed to such sounds in the hospital; however, he was concerned that these anguished cries — suggesting the practice of some medieval torture — would upset his new patient.

The woman raised her left hand to stifle a repetitive cough. Her right hand remained conspicuously still — the palm and fingers curled upwards on her lap like the petals of a dying flower.

The screaming stopped.

'If I may,' said Liebermann, 'I would like to examine your arm, Miss Lydgate.'

'Of course.' Her voice was soft, but serrated with a certain huskiness: a consequence, no doubt, of her incessant coughing.

Liebermann rolled up the right sleeve of her gown. Her arm was slender, almost emaciated, and beneath the crêpe-paper transparency of her skin a network of branching veins was clearly visible.

'Could you close your eyes, please? Now, tell me if you feel anything.'

Liebermann tapped the woman's palm, wrist and forearm with his pencil, to none of which was there any response. When he reached a point close to her shoulder, she suddenly flinched, saying: 'Yes, I feel something there.' By continuous tapping in this region, Liebermann was able to establish that the woman's paralysis had begun quite suddenly. It was as though an amulet encircled her upper arm, below which the sensory apparatus was no longer functioning. Such a decisive boundary did not correspond with the underlying continuities of the nervous system. The phenomenon was a physical impossibility and a cardinal symptom of hysteria.

'Thank you, Miss Lydgate, you can open your eyes now. When did you first notice the paralysis?'

'Last week.'

'Had you ever had problems of this kind before?'

'No.'

'Did the paralysis develop suddenly or gradually?'

'Suddenly. When I woke up, I could no longer move my arm.'

'Not even the fingers?'

'No.'

'Is the paralysis continuous, or do you get the feeling back sometimes?'

'It is continuous.'

Liebermann let Miss Lydgate's sleeve down and somewhat pedantically positioned the fringe of her cuff along the crease-lines of her wrist.

'Did the cough begin at the same time?'

'Yes.'

'Did anything significant happen — last week?'

'No. Not really.'

'Do you suffer from any other problems?'

She paused and took a deep breath.

'Amenorrhoea.'

'I see,' said Liebermann, attempting to gloss over her embarrassment with workaday efficiency. 'And when was the last time you menstruated?'

Miss Lydgate's cheeks coloured as though they'd been sprinkled with a pinch of ochre.

'Three months ago.'

'I imagine your appetite hasn't been very good lately.'

'No, that's right. It hasn't.'

Liebermann opened his notebook and began scribbling.

'Your German is remarkably good, Miss Lydgate.'

A smile began to flicker into existence, but failed to ignite: the half-frown quickly reasserted itself.

'Well, it isn't *so* remarkable. My grandfather was German — and my mother spoke to me in German when I was a child.'

Liebermann turned to a fresh page and proceeded to ask Miss Lydgate several questions about her circumstances. He discovered that she lived with distant relatives: Herr Schelling (a Christian-Social parliamentary minister), Frau Schelling, and their two children Edward and Adele. Herr Schelling had agreed to provide Miss Lydgate with a room and a monthly stipend, contingent upon her performing the duties of a governess; however, in reality her only significant task was to provide Edward and Adele with instruction in written and spoken English.

'How long do you intend to stay in Vienna?' asked Liebermann.

'For some time,' replied Miss Lydgate. 'Years, perhaps.'

'The Schellings have agreed to this?'

'That isn't necessary,' she replied. 'I do not wish to retain my position as the Schellings' governess.'

'No?'

She shook her head, and continued: 'No. I want to study medicine.'

'Here?' asked Liebermann, raising his eyebrows. 'In Vienna?'

'Yes,' replied Miss Lydgate. 'The university department has recently started accepting female students.'

'Indeed,' said Liebermann. 'But why here? Surely, if you wish to study medicine it would be more convenient for you to study in London?'

'I came to Vienna because of Doctor Landsteiner. You see, I am interested . . .' She paused before beginning her sentence again: 'I am interested in blood.'

Her eyes were an unusual colour, neither blue nor grey but something in between: a blend that reminded Liebermann of pewter. They had an arresting depth, enhanced by a subtle darkening at the edges of each iris. She could see that Liebermann required further explanation.

'My grandfather was a physician, and wrote extensively on diseases of the blood. He was also greatly fascinated by the virtuosi of the British Enlightenment — particularly those who had experimented with transfusion. I became interested in the subject after reading my grandfather's journal, which contains a detailed record of his thoughts and observations. By mixing blood samples and examining them under the microscope, he established that blood is not a singular substance but one that can be classified according to type — and he subsequently proposed that incompatibility of bloods was the principal reason why early and subsequent attempts at transfusion have failed. Thus, my grandfather seems to have anticipated Landsteiner's recent discovery by over half a century. I corresponded with Doctor Landsteiner when I was still living in England, and when I arrived in Vienna he invited me to attend some meetings at the Pathological Institute.'

'To discuss your grandfather's work?'

'Yes, and . . .' She paused again before continuing: 'And to review some ideas of my own. Doctor Landsteiner has since promised that if I am accepted by the university I can also work in his laboratory.'

'He must have been very impressed.'

She looked down at her feet, discomfited by Liebermann's compliment.

Liebermann encouraged Miss Lydgate to talk in greater detail about her grandfather and his journal. Although his patient was a little reticent at first, she was soon speaking with considerable fluency and enthusiasm. Doctor Ludwig Buchbinder had moved to England at the request of none other than Prince Albert. He was appointed Physician-in-Ordinary by Queen Victoria, but his duties extended well beyond the practice of medicine. He was the Prince Consort's confidant and played a significant role in the planning and organisation of the Great Exhibition. He was also one of a relatively small group of doctors who championed the use of the stethoscope (an instrument viewed with considerable suspicion by most British physicians on account of its Continental provenance). Although there were considerable demands on his time, Buchbinder still managed to indulge his passion for medical history and in due course came across several accounts of transfusion experiments conducted in the seventeenth century under the aegis of the Royal Society. Buchbinder settled in London — marrying late. He and his wife produced two daughters, the youngest of whom was Greta (Miss Lydgate's mother). In later life Buchbinder continued to speculate on many practical issues, including the analgesic properties of plants. Among his list of candidates was *Salix Alba* — the white willow tree (a derivative of which had been introduced into medical practice as aspirin by Hoffmann only three years earlier).

'Fascinating,' said Liebermann. 'He sounds like a truly remarkable man.'

'Indeed,' replied Miss Lydgate. 'Doctor Landsteiner believes that my grandfather's journal should be edited for publication.'

'Would you be willing to undertake such a task?'

'When I am better, yes.'

'And what of the rest of your family?'

Miss Lydgate progressed from the topic of her illustrious grand-father to her mother, whom she described with great affection. She then spoke of her father, Samuel Lydgate, a science master and a gentleman with distinctly progressive sympathies. He believed that modern women should have the same opportunities and rights as men, and had treated his daughter accordingly. Miss Lydgate was an only child, and Liebermann wondered whether her upbringing would have been different had Greta Lydgate provided her husband with more than one child on whom to practise his pedagogic theories. Liebermann could see that Miss Lydgate was the beneficiary — or victim — of a singularly taxing education.

The Lydgates lived a few miles north of the capital. Liebermann had visited London many times but had never heard of Highgate. Miss Lydgate's description called to mind a kind of English Grinzing: a village built on a natural eminence, from which at night an observer could enjoy the glittering spectacle of the city lights below.

After Liebermann had gained enough background information he drew a line under his notes and looked up. He was again surprised by the intensity of his patient's expression: the way her pewter eyes glowed beneath her troubled forehead, the tightness with which her hair had been pulled back. Liebermann smiled, inviting her to reciprocate — but Miss Lydgate simply tilted her head to one side (almost as though she was puzzled by his behaviour). Then, unexpectedly, she said: 'Is that a battery, Doctor Liebermann?'

Liebermann turned and looked across the room. In the corner a large wooden box sat on the top shelf of a hospital trolley.

'Yes, it is.'

'Will my course of electrotherapy begin today?'

She spoke these words evenly, without emotion.

'No,' replied Liebermann.

'Tomorrow, then?' She stifled a nervous cough.

'Perhaps.'

'I was told by Professor Gruner that—'

'Miss Lydgate,' Liebermann interrupted. 'For the moment, I think we should just talk.'

'What about?'

Liebermann formed a steeple with his fingers.

'About you. And your symptoms, of course.'

'But what good will that do?'

Before he could answer there was a knock on the door.

Stefan Kanner entered. He glanced briefly at Miss Lydgate and then spoke quietly to Liebermann.

'I'm sorry, Max, but I think you walked off with the keys to the storeroom.'

Liebermann stood up and pulled three bunches of keys from his pocket: his apartment keys, the hospital keys and, finally, the keys to the storeroom.

'Ah yes, how foolish of me.'

Before Kanner could take them, both men were distracted by Miss Lydgate. She had begun to cough with considerable violence — an ugly, rasping bark. Without warning she bent forward and started to retch. The vertebrae of her spine and the sharp edges of her shoulder blades showed clearly through the hospital gown. It looked as if some strange marine creature, with massive gills and a long segmented tail had attached itself to her body — and was in the process of shaking her to death.

Kanner was nearest to the sink, under which stood an old tin pail. He acted swiftly, picking it up and placing it on the floor in front of the woman's chair. As he did so, he laid a comforting hand on her back.

What happened next also happened very quickly but it left a lasting impression on Liebermann.

The young woman's body twisted — as though Kanner had pressed a white-hot branding iron between her shoulder blades. She squirmed at his touch, her spine warping sinuously to escape his fingers.

Miss Lydgate had undergone an extraordinary transformation. The softly spoken Englishwoman had been possessed by something demonic, and her expression had become hateful and venomous. Her bloodshot eyes bulged from their sockets and a thick blue vein had risen on her forehead — a livid weal against the paleness of her skin. She was sneering, scowling, animated by an inhuman anger. Kanner could not move — he stood, watching, in a state of utter shock. But it was not Miss Lydgate's fiendish expression that had caught Liebermann's attention. Something far more significant was happening: her hitherto dead hand had come to life, and was twitching furiously.

10

ABOVE THE HEAD of Commissioner Manfred Brügel hung a huge picture of the Emperor, Franz Josef. It was a portrait that could be found in most homes and in virtually every public building. The imperial patriarch, seemingly eternal, was an inescapable and watchful presence. Like many senior officials, Brügel had chosen to affirm his support for the Habsburgs by growing an exact copy of the monarch's oversized mutton-chop whiskers.

Brügel examined the first of several photographs: Fräulein Löwenstein, reclining on the chaise longue, the bloodstain clearly visible over her heart.

'Pretty girl.'

'Yes, sir,' said Rheinhardt.

'Do you have any idea what happened to the bullet?'

'No, sir.'

'Well, do you have any theories?'

'None as yet, sir.'

'What about Mathias? What does he think?'

'Professor Mathias could not explain his findings.'

Brügel dropped the first photograph and picked up a second: a head-and-shoulders portrait of the victim. She looked like a sleeping Venus.

'Very pretty,' Brügel repeated. After further contemplation of Charlotte Löwenstein's image, the Commissioner raised his blockish head and fixed his subordinate with a sullen stare.

'Do you believe in the supernatural, Rheinhardt?'

The Inspector hesitated.

'Well?'

'I believe,' said Rheinhardt, selecting his words with utmost care, 'we should only consider a supernatural explanation when all other explanations have been eliminated.'

'Indeed . . . but I asked whether or not you believed in the supernatural?'

Rheinhardt changed his position to ease the discomfort of the Commissioner's scrutiny.

'It would be presumptuous to suppose that we have a complete understanding of the world in which we live. I dare say there are many phenomena that have not ceded their secrets to science. But with the greatest respect, sir . . . I'm a policeman, not a philosopher.'

Brügel smiled: an enigmatic half-smile — opaque and saline.

'This business is going to attract a lot of attention, Rheinhardt. You do realise that, don't you?'

'The facts of the case that we have gathered to date are . . . intriguing.'

'Intriguing?' The Commissioner puffed as though the word was goose down and he was trying to dislodge it from his upper lip. 'The facts are not *intriguing*, Rheinhardt — they are extraordinary! I imagine our friends at the *Zeitung* will sensationalise every detail. And do you know what that means, Rheinhardt?' The Commissioner's question was rhetorical. 'Expectations!'

Brügel picked up the third photograph: a close-up of the bullet wound. Next to the ragged crater was a metal ruler. The hand of whoever was holding the ruler appeared in the bottom right-hand corner.

'Such cases shape public opinion, Rheinhardt,' continued Brügel. 'Solve a mystery like this and the Viennese security office will be lauded from here to the furthest outposts of His Majesty's Empire.' As he said this, his thumb jerked back at the painting of Franz Josef. 'Fail, and . . .' The Commissioner paused. 'Fail . . . and we run the risk of becoming a laughing stock. I can see the headline now: *Leopoldstadt Demon Foils Viennese Detectives*. We don't want that, now, do we, Rheinhardt?'

'No, sir.'

Brügel pushed the photographs of Charlotte Löwenstein across the table.

'Keep me informed, Rheinhardt.'

The interview was over.

II

WHILE OSKAR RHEINHARDT turned the pages of his songbook, Liebermann amused himself by improvising a simple chord sequence on the Bösendorfer. On repeating the sequence, he realised that he had unconsciously chosen the basic harmonies of Mendelssohn's bridal march. Looking up at Rheinhardt — the happiest of husbands — he experienced a curious sense of camaraderie. Soon, he too would be joining the fraternity of married men. Liebermann was impatient to share the news of his engagement with Rheinhardt, but recognised that it would be somewhat improper to inform his friend before he had told his own family.

'Oskar? It's your wedding anniversary soon — isn't it?'

'Yes,' said Rheinhardt. 'Next month.'

'The nineteenth?'

'That's right.'

'Have you bought Else a present yet?"

'I've been having clandestine meetings with Maria, her dress-maker.'

'Ah,' said Liebermann, letting his hands fall on an ominous-sounding chord at the lower end of the keyboard.

'It's a complicated business, dressmaking,' said Rheinhardt. 'More complicated than you'd imagine.'

'I dare say that's true.'

'Maria has been recommending all sorts — you know, materials, patterns . . . said that she could imitate a design she saw in Bertha Fürst's boutique — the fashionable one on Stumpergasse . . . Hope I've done the right thing.'

'Oh, I'm sure you have. What colour did you choose?'

Liebermann began playing a chromatic scale, in thirds, but stopped when he realised that his friend hadn't answered. Raising his head, he saw that Rheinhardt appeared a little uncomfortable. His immaculately groomed moustache was shifting from side to side as his expression changed to reflect increasing degrees of mental exertion.

'What is it, Oskar?' asked Liebermann.

'You know,' replied Rheinhardt. 'I'm not sure what we decided on in the end. There was so much talk — and so many colours. Was it a shade of green? You know, I can't remember.'

Liebermann shrugged.

'Don't try so hard — it'll come to mind soon enough.'

Seeing that his friend had taken little heed of his advice, Liebermann tapped the tower of song books by the music stand and asked: 'Well, what shall we finish with?'

'Nothing else in here . . .' Rheinhardt put the volume he was holding down. 'How about some Schubert?'

'Excellent.'

'*Das Wandern?*'

Liebermann ran a finger down the scores' spines and pulled *Die Schöne Müllerin* from the pile. He opened the volume at the first page and, when Rheinhardt was ready, launched into the repetitive figure of the accompaniment. The Bösendorfer was sounding particularly full-bodied, and Liebermann pounded the keys with relish.

Unexpectedly, Rheinhardt held up his hand.

'No, Max.'

Liebermann stopped playing and looked inquisitively at his friend.

'I was wondering,' continued Rheinhardt. 'Could we try it a little slower?'

'Of course.'

Liebermann began again, this time, playing the accompaniment to suggest a gentle amble rather than a brisk march. After a few bars, Rheinhardt opened his mouth and filled the room with his sweet, lyrical baritone.

'*Das Wandern is des Müllers Lust, Das Wandern!*'

The walking song — evoking a rural idyll of open roads, babbling brooks, and mill wheels turning.

'*Das Wandern! Das Wandern!*'

Rheinhardt lingered on every word, savouring the shape of each phrase, and Liebermann responded, labouring the accompaniment. The musical effect suggested effort. A tired walker, sapped of strength, struggling towards his destination. The performance was strangely elegiac. After the last bar, both men were silent, lulled into states of meditative reflection.

'Enchanting,' said Liebermann. 'Not the standard interpretation, of course, but enchanting nevertheless.'

He closed the music book.

'Ah,' said Rheinhardt, as though he had been suddenly startled.

'What?'

'The colour of Else's dress. It was blue! A blue evening dress.'

'There you are,' said Liebermann. 'I told you it would come.'

Liebermann placed *Die Schöne Müllerin* on top of the book pile, folded the music stand and closed the piano lid. He couldn't resist stroking the shiny surface of the instrument as he stood up.

The music room was large and decorated in a modern style. The chairs were matt black and upholstered with a fabric of Spartan design — red lines on a buff background. The rug, too, had little detail — nothing more than a border of small blue and red squares. Rheinhardt did not share his friend's modern taste. In fact, it mystified him. Rheinhardt felt much more comfortable when Liebermann opened the double doors, revealing the panelled smoking room beyond: leather armchairs, a roaring fire and a table on which the servant had placed a decanter of brandy, crystal glasses and two freshly cut fat cigars.

Rheinhardt lowered himself into the right-hand chair, the one he always chose, and surrendered his awareness to the flames of the fire. He could hear Liebermann pouring the brandy but did not look up until his friend offered him a cigar. When they were both settled, Liebermann was the first to speak.

'Well, Oskar, you are about to tell me of a murder investigation. And if I'm not mistaken, you'll be wanting my help.'

Rheinhardt laughed: 'Is it that obvious?'

'Yes,' said Liebermann. 'The body was discovered on Thursday afternoon and you had to break down a door to enter the apartment. The victim was a young woman in her twenties — and quite attractive. She had lost a considerable amount of blood, which had gushed from a fatal wound, staining her . . . let me think: was it a blue dress?' Liebermann took a sip of brandy and smiled at his friend: 'This is good, try some.'

Rheinhardt responded to Liebermann's invitation and nodded with approval before saying, 'So, how did I give myself away this time?'

'Earlier this evening' began Liebermann, 'we were discussing Schubert and you unintentionally confused the *Death and the Maiden* string quartet with *The Trout* quintet! Now I know for a fact that you are very familiar with the Schubert repertoire. So I considered that the mistake, this slip of the tongue, was significant. Being, as you are, a detective inspector, the kind of death that naturally preoccupies you most, is murder. The term "maiden" implies youth and beauty . . . Putting all this together, I inferred the influence of an unconscious memory. An unconscious memory of a murdered young woman.'

Rheinhardt shook his head in disbelief.

'All right. But what about the blood — the blood on the blue dress? How did you work that out?'

'When we were performing the Hugo Wolf song — *Auf dem See* — you stumbled over the word "blood" on both renditions. I took this to be confirmation of my earlier speculation. When I asked you just now what you intended to buy your wife on your wedding anniversary, you said a dress. But you couldn't, at first, remember the colour of the material that her dressmaker had recommended; however, some time later, you were able to say that it was blue. I took this to mean that the idea of a blue dress was being repressed.'

Liebermann flicked his cigar, letting a cylinder of ash fall into the tray.

'And the date of the investigation? How did you know it was Thursday?'

'We bumped into each other outside The Imperial — remember?'

'Yes, of course, but—'

'You were in a terrible rush. I made an educated guess — nothing more psychological than that, I'm afraid.'

Rheinhardt leaned towards his friend.

'Incidentally, thank you again for allowing me to requisition your cab. Did you get very wet?'

'Yes. Very.'

'Oh, I am sorry . . .'

Rheinhardt looked inordinately pained — his sagging, melancholy eyes expressed considerable anguish and pity.

'It really wasn't that bad, Oskar,' said Liebermann, embarrassed by his friend's contrition.

Rheinhardt smiled weakly and continued to puzzle over Liebermann's deductions: 'Max, you said that I had to break a door down — to get into the apartment. Did you guess that, too?'

'No. You've been rubbing your right shoulder in a distracted fashion for most of the evening. You always do that after you've broken a door down. I expect it's quite bruised. Might I recommend that you use your foot next time?'

Rheinhardt paused for a few moments before allowing himself to laugh. 'Remarkable. That really was very perceptive, Max.'

Liebermann leaned back in his chair and drew on his cigar. 'But,' he added, 'what I haven't been able to work out is why you need my help? There must be something different — or special — about this case?'

Rheinhardt's expression darkened.

'Yes. There is.'

Liebermann turned to face his friend.

'Go on ...'

'The victim,' said Rheinhardt, 'was a spiritualist, a medium called Charlotte Löwenstein. We discovered her body on Thursday afternoon in an apartment in Leopoldstadt, overlooking the market square.'

Liebermann assumed his listening position, his right hand pressed to his cheek, index finger flat against his temple.

'Apparently,' Rheinhardt continued, 'she had been shot through the heart. However, the room in which we found her body had been locked from the inside and there was no murder weapon. There was also no means of escape.'

'You're quite sure?'

'In the annals of detection, there have been a number of cases of this kind — a body found in a locked room. Usually, the effect is achieved through concealment. The murderer waits in a secret compartment, and then leaves when the door is finally opened. The walls of Fräulein Löwenstein's apartment were completely solid and the floor was sound.' Rheinhardt exhaled a billowy cloud of cigar smoke before continuing. 'Moreover, when Professor Mathias conducted a post-mortem examination, he was unable to find a bullet. There was no secondary wound — showing where the bullet might have exited from her body — nor any evidence to suggest that a bullet had been removed.'

Rheinhardt paused to gauge Liebermann's reaction, and recognised in the narrowing of the young doctor's eyes the suspicion he had expected. Liebermann's index finger tapped against his temple.

'It's a trick — isn't it? An illusion.'

'I suppose it must be.'

'Why suppose? How fascinating, that someone should go to so much trouble . . . I mean, what sort of a person would—'

'There's more, Max,' Rheinhardt cut in. 'We found this by the body.'

Reaching into his pocket, Rheinhardt produced Fräulein Löwenstein's note and handed it to Liebermann.

'*God forgive me,*' Liebermann began reading, '*for what I have done. There is such a thing as forbidden knowledge. He will take me to hell — and there is no hope of redemption.*' His voice was steady and without inflection.

'Well,' said Rheinhardt. 'What do you make of that?'

Liebermann inspected the note closely before answering.

'Clearly, this is the rather pleasing hand of a woman. I've never seen a man's handwriting in which dots are executed as small circles.' Liebermann then turned the note over and looked at the reverse side. 'She was extremely tense when this was written. The nib of the pen was pressed hard into the paper. She paused when she had completed the final word. I know this because the paper has absorbed more ink here.' He pointed to a specific area. 'Then, I imagine, she got up in a hurry, producing the arc that runs off the page . . .' Liebermann's eyes glinted in the firelight. 'But what I'd really like to know,' he continued 'is the identity of the third person.'

Rheinhardt almost choked on his brandy.

'Third person? What do you mean, third person?'

Liebermann gave a sly smile.

'When this note was written there were three people in the room. Fräulein Löwenstein, her murderer, and a third person who — we must assume — accompanied her on her journey to hell.'

Rheinhardt shook his head.

'That's preposterous, Max! How can you possibly know such a thing just by looking at that note?'

Liebermann rose from his chair, and after a swift examination of his bookcase returned with a volume that he held out for Rheinhardt to inspect.

'*The Psychopathology of Everyday Life*,' read Rheinhardt. 'By Doctor Sigmund Freud.'

'Yes,' said Liebermann, sitting down again. 'I can't recommend it strongly enough. As you know, Freud suggests that mistakes such as slips of the tongue can be very revealing. But so can inadvertent actions, such as slips of the pen while writing. Now, take a look at Fräulein Löwenstein's note.' He handed it back to Rheinhardt. 'Do you see anything interesting?'

'You are, of course, referring to this crossing-out before the word *me*.'

'Exactly. Look at it closely — what word do you think she started to write before she crossed it out? Hold the note up in front of the fire — the ink becomes more transparent.'

Rheinhardt did as he was instructed.

'It's difficult to say . . . but I think — I think she started to write the word *us*.'

Liebermann smiled.

'Exactly. She had started to write *He will take us to hell* when she meant to write *He will take me to hell*. Now, why should she make a mistake like that?'

Rheinhardt looked somewhat disappointed.

'You know, Max, sometimes, a mistake is just a mistake.'

Liebermann executed a silent scale on the arm of his chair and began to chuckle.

'Yes, you're probably right, Oskar. Like many who enjoy Freud's work, I am inclined to spoil things by going just a little too far.'

12

As Natalie Heck passed the brightly coloured marquees of the Volksprater, she found herself stopping, yet again, to look up at the Riesenrad. It was a miracle of engineering. The circumference of the wheel was an approximate circle, achieved by the continuous linkage of bolted iron girders, while the space inside the circle was filled with a reinforcing webbing of immense metal cables. Natalie imagined a Titan's hand, strumming them like the strings of a giant harp. The most eye-catching feature of the Riesenrad, however, was its fleet of red gondolas, each the size of a tram and each carrying a fragile human cargo high above the city.

Natalie's friend Lena had actually ridden on the Riesenrad. She had been taken by her father four years earlier in 1898. Natalie knew the exact date because the wheel had been erected to commemorate Emperor Franz Josef's golden jubilee and Lena had been among the first to step into one of its gondolas. Lena's description of the ride had frightened Natalie. The juddering ascent, the gasps of the passengers, the groaning and creaking of the stressed metal cables. And worst of all, the terrible moment of suspension at the highest point, where the wind had buffeted Lena's gondala — making it tremble and rock like a cradle. Apparently, another young woman had swooned.

Lena was lucky — *her* father was still alive. Natalie's father had died three years before the Emperor's golden jubilee, so there had been no one to take her on the Riesenrad even if she had wanted. Natalie had adored her father. After his death, she would talk to him in the moments before sleep, addressing the darkness and imagining his replies. She often needed advice, but could turn to no one. Her mother had become cold and distant.

The aching sense of loss that Natalie felt persisted for years, and would have continued had she not made the acquaintance of the woman whom the stallholders (particularly the men) called 'The Princess' — an elegant, graceful woman who spoke so very nicely.

The Princess was particularly fond of Natalie's table, which always displayed a fine selection of embroidered shawls. She had introduced herself as Fräulein Charlotte Löwenstein, and Natalie was genuinely surprised that the woman did not possess an aristocratic title. Friendly exchanges became conversations, and when Fräulein Löwenstein learned of Natalie's loss she immediately invited the 'poor girl' for tea in her apartment, which was situated just across the road. It was while taking tea with Fräulein Löwenstein that Natalie Heck had learned of the woman's strange gift. The following Thursday evening, Natalie arrived at Fräulein Löwenstein's door at eight o'clock precisely. Three hours later, Natalie was hugging herself in bed, weeping with joy.

But since that time her relationship with Fräulein Löwenstein had become increasingly complicated — her feelings more confused . . .

The wheel's progress was slow, and Natalie had to watch it very carefully to detect any movement. Although the prospect of a ride on the Riesenrad made Natalie's breath quicken so that her chest pressed against the restraining whalebone cage of her corset, the emotions she felt were not straightforward. She was both frightened and excited at the same time.

Natalie drew her shawl closer around her shoulders and hurried along. It was a very attractive shawl — but then, everything she made was attractive. She was nothing if not industrious.

Fräulein Löwenstein is dead.

Like the Riesenrad, the thought evoked both fear and excitement. Natalie's conscience was perturbed by a subtle eddy of guilt as she dared to believe that now things might change for the better.

On entering Leopoldstadt, Natalie chose a circuitous route in order to avoid going anywhere near Fräulein Löwenstein's apartment. Last Thursday evening was still fresh in her memory: the police with their notebooks, hushed voices, the sound of Herr Uberhorst sobbing and all the time knowing that *she* was still in the next room. Natalie had been unable to dismiss disturbing mental pictures — macabre imaginings — of Charlotte Löwenstein's corpse either sprawled out on the floor or draped across the chaise longue like an ill-fated Romantic heroine.

Fräulein Löwenstein was — or, rather, had been — a beautiful woman. So beautiful that Natalie had never attempted to compete with her. She had never bothered to pin her hair up, powder her face or wear a revealing dress in her presence. It was not that Natalie was unattractive. Indeed, quite the opposite. She was young, shapely and had dark eyes that — in recent years — had invited many compliments. However, she knew as well as anyone that Charlotte Löwenstein was an unassailable rival in matters of the heart. During a seance, in the flickering candlelight, when her full lips parted to produce a radiant smile, her beauty was uncanny.

When Natalie had confessed her secret (and her despair) to Lena, her friend had said that a woman like Fräulein Löwenstein must be in league with the devil. It had been said in jest, but Natalie now wondered if such a thing were possible. The police had asked her some very strange questions...

Although the main thoroughfares of Leopoldstadt were respectable, the back streets were still run-down and shabby. The dreary old buildings were tall and blocked out most of the sky. Natalie quickened her pace, slipped, and had to grab a lamp-post to stop herself from falling.

She was getting closer to where he lived.

A large black rat ran out from under a pile of rubbish and scurried down the street ahead of her. Natalie shuddered and slowed to a halt. She decided to take a detour. Turning a corner, she progressed further into the dismal labyrinth.

It was so unfair, thought Natalie, that a man of his class and talent should be reduced to such circumstances through no fault of his own. He had been cheated out of an inheritance by his contemptible older brother Felix and now had to eke out an impecunious existence as an artist. He was always struggling to find the money to pay his rent, and Natalie had got into the habit of lending him small amounts to prevent his eviction. As their friendship had deepened, Natalie had repeatedly taken coins from her savings box, which she kept beneath a loose floorboard in her bedroom. Over time these small amounts had added up and now the box was almost empty.

Even so, it was worth it. Only a month ago, they had been walking on the green open spaces of the Prater, watching the deer, and talking of his plans for the future — a large exhibition in the new Secession building with the likes of Gustav Klimt. He had thanked her for her assistance, calling her his 'saviour', his 'angel'. Then, without warning, he had leaned forward to plant a kiss on her cheek. It had been improper but she had not protested: the strange combination of fear and excitement had been dizzying.

Natalie raised a hand to her face, in order to feel the place where his lips had touched her skin.

Beauty isn't everything, she thought. *There is also kindness.*

But again an image of Fräulein Löwenstein invaded her mind — made even more striking by her recent acquisitions: her pearl necklace, her diamond earrings, and her exquisite butterfly brooch (supposed to be the work of Peter Breithut). Thus adorned, Löwenstein's perfection had mocked the seamstress's worthy sentiment.

When Natalie arrived at his apartment building she found the main door open. It was hanging off the frame on only one hinge. Natalie eased through the gap and found herself in a dank, lightless hallway. The stale air smelled of boiled cabbage and urine. She could hear a baby crying, but no adult voices. The walls were streaked with damp and in one or two places lumps of plaster had fallen away. Natalie shivered, ran up the steep stairs, crossed the landing and gently knocked on his door.

'Otto,' she said. 'Otto, it's me. Natalie.'

There was no response.

She knocked again, this time a little harder.

'Otto' she said. 'Are you in there?'

As she pressed her ear against the door, she became dimly aware of a movement in the shadows. Before she could turn, a large gloved hand came down heavily on her shoulder.

13

It was Sunday afternoon and Rheinhardt was sitting in the parlour, smoking an after-dinner cigar. In his lap was the first volume of the *Handbook for Magistrates* by Professor Hans Gross, the definitive work on the subject of criminology. Rheinhardt was perusing a passage that exhorted the investigator to seek out men with specialist skills: *With such men at his disposal*, proclaimed the authoritative voice of Gross, *much labour and trouble and many mistakes may be obviated.*

Yes, thought Rheinhardt. *That makes perfect sense.* And congratulated himself for consulting his friend Liebermann the previous evening.

Rheinhardt raised his head and looked around the room. Seated at the table was his wife Else, sewing a silver button back onto his old tweed jacket. Fifteen years of marriage had not diminished the pleasure he experienced just looking at her. She had the kindest face, and a mouth the curve of which — even in repose — suggested a certain readiness for laughter. On the sofa sat his two daughters, Therese — who was just thirteen — and little Mitzi, aged eleven. The older girl was entertaining the younger by reading stories from a book of folk tales. Rheinhardt sighed with pleasure, and turned to another section of the *Handbook*. It dealt with the dangers of preconceived theories . . . As he tried to follow the professor's line of reasoning, his attention wandered back to the girls.

'Another one?'

'Yes, please.'

'Are you sure, Mitzi?'

'Yes.'

'Oh, very well then.'

Therese cleared her throat like an orator and began reading.

'High up in the Böhmerwald — the mountain range that lies between Austria, Bavaria and Bohemia, is the ancient city of Kasperske Hory. As you approach the city, you must be very careful, because nearby lives the old hag Swiza. She is not like other old women, not like your grandmother, or even your great-grandmother. If you saw her your blood would run cold. Swiza has the antlers of a deer and wears the fur of a wolf. She has lived near Kasperske Hory for longer than anyone can remember. No one knows who she is, or where she comes from, or why she is there. Some say that she is a witch. When travellers arrive at the tavern, claiming to have seen the old hag, men stop talking and the women pray. For whenever Swiza is seen, misfortune must follow . . .'

Rheinhardt looked over at his wife. She too had stopped working and was listening to the story.

'Many years ago,' continued Therese, 'a man from Zda . . . Zdan—'

'Zdanov,' Else called out.

'Oh yes, Zdanov — a man from Zdanov was riding into Kaperske Hory and met Swiza. He knew who she was and tried to escape, but the old hag ordered him to stay and worship her. The man from Zdanov was a Christian and did not wish to do so. As a punishment, Swiza turned him to stone.'

'Therese,' said Rheinhardt. 'Must you read your sister such stories? You'll frighten her.'

'I'm not frightened,' piped the younger girl.

'Well, you say that now, Mitzi, but you won't say that at bedtime.'

'I like these stories.'

Rheinhardt sighed and looked to his wife for guidance.

'I like them too,' said Else, her eyes sparkling with good humour.

Accustomed to making concessions when confronted with female solidarity, Rheinhardt grumbled: 'Then carry on . . . but if Mitzi has nightmares don't come running to me.'

He buried his nose back between the pages of Gross's tome.

'Father?'

It was Mitzi.

'Yes.' The syllable was extended and dipped a little in the middle, signalling mild irritation.

'Do you believe in witches?'

'No.' He spoke the word loudly, as if by denying the existence of witches he could deny the existence of all things supernatural.

14

'SHE WAS FOUND THERE,' said Rheinhardt, pointing at the chaise longue.

Liebermann's gaze wandered from corner to corner, and once or twice ventured up the walls to the cracked bas-relief ceiling.

'She was reclining,' Rheinhardt continued, 'with one hand behind her head, and the other at her side.'

'It struck you as odd?'

'Of course. She looked like she was relaxing. Not what you'd expect, given the circumstances.'

Liebermann crouched beside the open door and examined the lock. It was still working, and he turned the key a few times to test it. The lock worked perfectly. Liebermann allowed the thick metal bolt to slide out of its casing and press against his palm.

'So . . .' he said, thinking out loud. 'What are we supposed to believe? That Fräulein Löwenstein was expecting some form of supernatural retribution? She composed her note and, recognising that there would be no escape, lay back on the chaise longue where she patiently awaited her transport to hell. Like Faust, Fräulein Löwenstein had benefited from forbidden knowledge, the price of which was eternal damnation?'

Liebermann walked over to one of the windows and, reaching up, released the lock. He then opened the window and looked out — a blast of cold air made him wince. The apartment was high up, and there was no visible means of escape. Closing the window, he continued to think aloud.

'In due course, a spectral assassin did arrive, armed with a ghost gun, the chamber of which was loaded with an ectoplasmic bullet. Apparently, our demonic friend then promptly dispatched Fräulein Löwenstein and sailed away through a locked door — or through one of the windows, perhaps — presumably dragging the doomed soul of the unfortunate Fräulein Löwenstein behind him.'

It was clear from Liebermann's tone that he found the idea entirely ridiculous.

'Yes,' said Rheinhardt. 'It is absurd — but unfortunately there are no alternative explanations.'

Liebermann walked over to the shelves and picked up the ceramic hand, showing palpable disdain.

'Do you have any suspects?'

Rheinhardt threw his arms up in the air and looked despairingly around him.

'Suspects? Do impossible murders have suspects? To be honest, Max, I haven't really given the matter of suspects much consideration.'

'Which, of course,' said Liebermann, 'was the intention. The picture you paint of the crime scene is so bizarre that all of our mental resources are expended on the task of working out how the murder was accomplished. We become so preoccupied with this question, we don't even think to ask the more *important* question: who killed Fräulein Löwenstein? Further, I imagine that even if you were to arrest a particular individual on suspicion of murder, at present there would be little prospect of a satisfactory prosecution. How can you try someone for an impossible crime! It's all very clever. The man — or woman — you are looking for is certainly very intelligent and highly imaginative.'

'So, how do you think we should proceed Max?'

'Don't be fooled by the illusion. Forget demons, visitations, and Faustian pacts. Just go about your business as usual.'

'And you're convinced it's an illusion?'

'Of course it's an illusion!' exclaimed Liebermann, evidently appalled that his friend should ask such a question. 'Illusions are the stock-in-trade of these people — these spiritualists! I mean, take a look at this table.' Liebermann rapped it with his knuckles. 'Listen.' As his fist moved across the surface the quality of the sound changed. 'Parts of it are hollow. Look at the size of the thing! Open it up and you'll find all manner of trickery inside. Fräulein Löwenstein must have had accomplices who helped her to practise her deceptions. A locked room, a disappearing bullet — it all smacks of theatre to me. Stagecraft. Smoke and mirrors! Perhaps one of her accomplices killed her. And perhaps you should be consulting a stage magician rather than a psychiatrist!'

'Well, as it happens,' said Rheinhardt, 'I visited the Volksprater this morning and spoke to one Adolphus Farber, better known to circus patrons as The Great Magnifico. He makes people vanish after locking them inside cabinets.'

'And?'

'Although Herr Farber is reputed to be the finest of illusionists, when I told him the facts of the case he was unable to help.'

'What did he conclude?'

'He said that the murder must have been the result of a super-natural visitation.'

Liebermann shook his head in despair.

'This crime is an illusion, make no mistake, and if we fail to understand how it was accomplished this will only demonstrate the intellectual and creative superiority of our adversary, nothing more.'

Rheinhardt was heartened by his friend's confidence, but the extraordinary facts of the case still made him deeply uneasy.

'If,' said Liebermann, 'this murder was perpetrated by an accomplice, then he — or she — must be a member of Fräulein Löwenstein's spiritualist circle. Do you know much about them?'

Rheinhardt took out his notebook.

'There's a locksmith called Uberhorst. Hans Bruckmüller — a businessman — makes surgical instruments. A banker and his wife — Heinrich and Juno Hölderlin. Natalie Heck — a seamstress. And Zoltán Záborszky — a Hungarian aristocrat. I say aristocrat, but from his appearance I would guess that he has fallen on hard times. These people seem to represent the nucleus of her group. Oh, and there's another one — a young man called Otto Braun. He was expected on Thursday night as usual, but he didn't arrive. He hasn't been seen since.'

'Well, that's suspicious . . .'

'Indeed. Haussmann and I undertook some preliminary interviews with the circle — so we know a few things about him. What he looks like, where he lives . . .'

'What does he do?'

'He's an artist.'

'An artist? I've never heard of him,' said Liebermann.

Rheinhardt shrugged. 'It's possible that something might be going on between Braun and the seamstress — Natalie Heck. She visited Braun's apartment yesterday, and was surprised by one of our constables.'

'What about the locksmith? Did you discuss the door with him — the lock, I mean?'

'No. We haven't disclosed the unusual nature of the murder to anyone — as yet.'

'But you will eventually?'

'Of course.'

'What about the newspapers?'

'Yes, they'll be told everything in due course.'

'Why the delay?'

'Commissioner Brügel is concerned that if the newspapers are informed then the Löwenstein murder will attract a lot of interest. You know how the people of this city love anything sensational, and if we are unable to solve this mystery . . .'

'You'll appear incompetent?'

'Well, let's say it could certainly damage public confidence in the security office.'

Liebermann touched the door frame.

'One cannot help thinking that a locksmith might have the means to accomplish such an illusion — or at least this part of it, anyway.'

'But he was devastated. On Thursday he was absolutely consumed with grief.'

'Real grief?'

'That was my impression.'

'Why, though? Could it be that their relationship went beyond that of fortune-teller and client?'

'I couldn't imagine a more ill-matched couple!'

'Even so . . .'

Rheinhardt scribbled a memorandum in his notebook.

'What about the others?' Liebermann continued.

Rheinhardt pocketed his notebook and twirled his moustache.

'The Hungarian — Záborszky — was a strange fellow. He said something odd about being able to smell evil.'

'And that unsettled you?'

'If I'm honest, it did.'

'Perhaps that tells us more about you than about him,' said Liebermann, smiling broadly.

Rheinhardt looked puzzled.

'Oskar,' said Liebermann, resting a friendly hand on the Inspector's arm, 'it was an illusion! I assure you!'

Rheinhardt shifted his weight from one foot to the other. He was embarrassed. The young doctor had obviously detected in him an underlying seam of credulity — a latent willingness to accept the supernatural. The Inspector envied Liebermann's urban sensibility, his seeming immunity to the shadowy forces that every Middle European learned to respect before leaving the nursery. Somewhere in the darker recesses of Rheinhardt's troubled mind an old hag with antlers was cackling with glee — a dry, mocking laugh.

'What's in here?' It was Liebermann. He had disappeared behind the screen and was drumming on something that produced a hollow, wooden sound.

'Oh God!' said Rheinhardt under his breath.

'Oskar?'

Liebermann appeared again, carrying the Japanese box.

'I'd completely forgotten about that. Haussmann was supposed to be getting the key.'

Liebermann shook the chest a little.

'There's something in it.' He placed the box on the table, and the two men looked at each other.

'Well?' said Liebermann.

'I suppose we'd better open it,' said Rheinhardt. He walked to the door and called into the hall: 'Haussmann?'

A few moments later his assistant appeared. He entered the room and executed two small bows: 'Inspector. Herr Doctor.'

'Haussmann, did you find the key to this box?' asked Rheinhardt.

'No, sir,' replied Haussmann. 'Fräulein Sucher didn't have a key and she said she'd never seen the box opened.'

'That's probably because it contains some trickery,' said Liebermann.

Haussmann looked at Liebermann, not quite sure what to make of his statement.

Rheinhardt beckoned Haussmann to the table.

'Force it open.'

Haussmann took a penknife from his inside pocket and began to jemmy the lid. The thin lacquered wood splintered easily.

Liebermann stepped forward and opened the box. He could feel Rheinhardt and Haussman peering over his shoulders.

Inside, lying on a bed of velvet, was a small stone figure. It had a canine body, slanting eyes, square-tipped ears and a long curved snout. The most striking feature of the creature was its long forked tail.

'What on Earth is that?' asked Rheinhardt.

'I don't know,' said Liebermann. 'But it looks very old. An antiquity, I think.'

He reached in and lifted the effigy. It was quite heavy for its size. But as he did so he noticed a small key protruding from the container's edge. The creature had been locked in the box — from the inside.

15

'But why must I lie down?'

'Because I want you to relax.'

Miss Lydgate was seated on an examination table. She swung her legs around and leaned back slowly. When her head touched the pillow she began rolling it from side to side. She couldn't find a comfortable position because of the way she had pulled back her hair.

'Well, I can't relax like this . . .'

Her voice was slightly tetchy. She sat up again and after removing numerous pins, ribbons and a net she released her mane. It sprung out and tumbled down her back: a flaming mass, streaked with russet and flecks of copper. Liebermann was surprised that so much bulk had been so cleverly concealed. She lay back for the second time.

'That's better.'

'You may close your eyes if you wish.'

They remained open and rolled upward, searching for the speaker.

'Miss Lydgate,' Liebermann sighed. 'It is important that you do not try to look at me. You will strain your eyes.'

Miss Lydgate stared blankly at the ceiling and dragged her right arm across her stomach with her left hand.

'I do not feel comfortable lying here like this, with you behind me.'

'You will become accustomed to the procedure in time, I assure you.'

The young woman bit her lower lip, coughed into her left hand, and finally settled; however, her toes were curled with tension.

'Miss Lydgate,' Liebermann asked. 'Do you remember the last time you were in this room?'

'Yes.'

'Tell me what happened?'

'You examined me . . . and we discussed a number of topics. I seem to recall talking, at some length, about my grandfather.'

'Indeed. And what else did we discuss?'

'The Schellings, Doctor Landsteiner . . .'

She stopped and sighed.

'Please continue.'

'There is nothing wrong with my memory.'

'Of course. I am interested in your impressions of our last meeting.'

'I don't understand what you want me to say, Doctor Liebermann? Do you want me to repeat everything, word for word?'

'No. I just want you to tell me what happened.'

'Very well. I was escorted here by a nurse. You examined my arm. We then discussed how I acquired my position working for the Schelling family. I told you of my intention to study medicine, and I explained why I wanted to study here rather than in London. I told you about my grandfather's journal and something of his life. You then asked me about my family and our home. Shortly after, there was a knock on the door and one of your colleagues came in.'

'Doctor Kanner.'

'Is that his name?'

Liebermann nodded: 'And what happened then?'

'You talked together — for some time, I believe.'

'How long?'

'It must have been . . . it's difficult to say.'

'Five minutes, ten minutes? How long?'

'Long enough for me to fall asleep.'

'You can't remember anything else?'

'No. I assume that you thought it was in my best interests not to be disturbed and subsequently had me removed to the ward.'

Liebermann said nothing.

'Did—' Miss Lydgate was hesitant and her voice quivered slightly with anxiety. 'Did something happen, Doctor Liebermann? Something that I cannot remember?'

'Yes. Something did happen.'

'What?' Miss Lydgate shifted uncomfortably and squeezed her dead right hand with her left. 'Please tell me.'

'You became very agitated. It was a little like a seizure.'

'And I did something?'

'You really don't remember?'

'No!' Her voice rose in pitch, and she began to cough.

'You were extremely distressed and Doctor Kanner came to your assistance. You were going to be sick, so he placed a pail in front of your chair.'

'This cannot be true.'

'He tried to comfort you by resting a hand on your back. It was then that you threatened to kill him — before hitting him in the stomach with—' Liebermann broke off. The room was absolutely silent. Even Miss Lydgate's cough was subdued. Liebermann continued: 'With your right fist.'

Liebermann observed Miss Lydgate's chest, rising and falling as her breathing accelerated. She rocked her head from side to side, and her habitual half-frown melted into an expression of total disbelief.

16

Uberhorst stood in the middle of his small workshop. He was wearing a white apron smeared with oil; however, his hands were meticulously clean.

'You were very distressed, the evening her body was discovered?'

'Yes, Inspector — I still can't believe it happened. She was a dear friend.'

Uberhorst was clearly still struggling to manage his emotions.

'How well did you know her?'

'In some ways I didn't know her at all. If you were to ask me where she was born, who her parents were, or where she went to school, I couldn't answer. But I do know other things . . .'

Uberhorst could not maintain eye contact. He looked away and then all around the workshop, his abrupt birdlike movements suggesting anxiety.

'What things?' asked Rheinhardt.

'That she was a kind person — and brave.'

'Did you ever meet with Fräulein Löwenstein privately? On your own?'

'Yes. For readings.'

Uberhorst held up his palm and traced a crease with the forefinger of his left hand.

'She made predictions?'

'No, she never spoke of the future.'

'Then what was the point of the consultation?'

'She told me about . . . myself.'

'Was she accurate?'

'Very. It made me feel . . . understood. Less . . .' The little man's voice trailed off, and he looked up at an effigy of Christ on the cross that hung above a small bookcase. His lower lip trembled.

'Less what?' Rheinhardt pressed.

'Alone,' said Uberhorst. His eyes filled with tears.

'How much did Fräulein Löwenstein charge for these readings, Herr Uberhorst?'

'Nothing, but I was happy to make a voluntary contribution.'

'Which was how much?'

'Two krone.'

'You could have gone to the Court Opera for less.'

'But then I would never have benefited from her extraordinary powers.'

Uberhorst wiped his forearm across his cheek, attempting to conceal his tears. It was a pathetic gesture, like the pitiful attempt of a hurt child to maintain its dignity.

'Why did you say she was kind? And brave?'

'She had a difficult life, Inspector. Only a courageous soul could overcome such terrible adversity.'

'Oh? In what way was her life difficult?'

'Her mother and father died when she was very young — she was about ten or eleven, I think. She was sent to live with her uncle, her father's brother. He lived alone and Lotte had to cook and care for him. She did her best, but he was never satisfied. He would often beat her . . . and when she was older — when she was turning into a woman — he . . . He was a cruel man and . . .'

Uberhorst shuddered.

'What, Herr Uberhorst?'

'I believe he may have . . .'

'Taken advantage of her?'

Uberhorst nodded and adjusted his pince-nez, mutely confirming the Inspector's speculation.

'Why do you think Fräulein Löwenstein told you these things? They are very personal, are they not?'

'Perhaps she was lonely too.'

Rheinhardt considered this statement. Was it possible? That the beautiful Löwenstein and the diminutive Uberhorst were equally alienated? That an intimate friendship had developed between them? Rheinhardt pencilled the words 'loneliness' and 'disclosure' in his notebook, followed by three question marks.

'What happened then? After she went to live with her uncle?'

'She ran away . . .'

'To where?'

'I don't know.'

'And how did she live?'

'She found menial jobs — cleaning, running errands — and then I think she may have worked in the theatre. Inspector?'

'Yes?'

'What I just said — about her uncle? She told me these things in confidence.'

'Obviously.'

'The others — Bruckmüller, Záborszky, the Hölderlins — I would be grateful if you did not discuss these matters with them.'

'You have my word. Herr Uberhorst, when did Fräulein Löwenstein become a medium?'

'She was always sensitive — she always saw things.'

'Spirits?'

'Yes.'

'All right — when, then, did she become a professional medium?'

'I don't know. But she accepted her vocation after a vision.'

'What kind of vision?'

'She said that it could not be described — how can one describe communion with the infinite?'

'You think that she was instructed by a higher power?'

'Certainly.'

'I see.' Without pause or preparation Rheinhardt added: 'Do you remember what you were doing on Wednesday evening, Herr Uberhorst?'

'Yes.' There was a slight wavering in Uberhorst's voice.

'Where were you?'

'Please, I don't wish to be discourteous, Inspector, but I did tell your assistant who . . .'

Rheinhardt's brow furrowed, prompting Uberhorst to answer the question without further hesitation.

'I was here. I live upstairs.'

'And is there anyone who can confirm your story?'

'It isn't a story, Inspector. I was here — and no, I have no alibi. I rarely have visitors.'

Rheinhardt walked to the lathe, his shoes crunching on a carpet of metal shavings. Above it hung a framed mezzotint. It appeared to have little artistic merit, being only a diagrammatic representation of a mechanism, the parts of which were labelled with the letters of the alphabet.

'What is this?' asked Rheinhardt.

'It is a drawing of the detector lock designed by Jeremiah Chubb. It was patented in 1818. A masterpiece, I believe.'

Rheinhardt took a few steps and examined the titles that filled the bookcase. They were mostly bound journals and technical histories.

'You seem to be something of a connoisseur,' he said.

'I enjoy my work.'

Uberhorst joined Rheinhardt and pulled a volume from the top shelf. The spine was embossed in English, but Uberhorst translated: 'On the Construction of Locks and Keys — by Jeremiah Chubb. It is a first edition.' He caressed the cover and produced a weak, nervous smile.

Rheinhardt tried to look impressed and pointed to another volume.

'Locks of the Ancient World? I didn't realise they had them ...'

'Oh yes,' said Uberhorst, his eyes now shining with the special light generated by fanatical interest. 'The very earliest were made of wood, but metal examples — of a similar design — can be found dating back to the time of the Caesars. Roman keys are still being found today ... I have one in my possession, in fact. It was found when they were building the new Karlplatz station.'

Uberhorst slid Jeremiah Chubb's treatise back into its vacant slot.

'Herr Uberhorst, are you familiar with the locks in Fräulein Löwenstein's apartment?'

'I didn't give them any special attention. But I imagine, given the age of the building, they arc all some form of lever tumbler.'

'When we found her body,' Rheinhardt said casually, 'there was no weapon in the room, and the door had been locked from the inside. Do you have any idea how Fräulein Löwenstein's murderer accomplished this?'

'He must have locked the door and climbed out of the window.'

'I don't think so. The windows were locked too, and as you know the drop is quite considerable.'

Uberhorst thought for a moment.

'Then you must be mistaken, Inspector.'

'Why?'

'It's impossible.'

'Really? Even for a master locksmith?'

The little man touched his lower lip with his forefinger. His lip was no longer trembling, but his finger very clearly was.

17

It was late afternoon but the chandeliers of the Café Schwarzenberg were blazing. Outside, a thin, persistent rain had subdued the light. Looking out of the window and on to Scharzenberg Platz, Liebermann could see the large equestrian statue of Prince Karl von Schwarzenberg, a pallid, ghostly rider, emerging slowly from the fine mist. Beyond the spectral prince, just visible, was the spout of a fountain.

'I don't understand,' said Clara. 'If there's nothing wrong with her arm, why can't she move it?'

They were sitting in a cosy wood-panelled alcove. Even though the café's vaulted interior was almost full their seating felt private. They were also isolated by the peculiarly potent, almost tangible intimacy of lovers.

'The arm is paralysed,' said Liebermann.

'All right, if it's paralysed how is it that she was able to hit Doctor Kanner? Can't you see? She's just pretending, Maxim!'

Having offered her very definite opinion, Clara began to dissect her apfelstrudel. She broke the sugar-coated pastry case: large pieces of cooked apple and several raisins spilled across her plate. The sweet bouquet of cinnamon and cloves mingled with the aroma of coffee and cigar smoke. Fixing her fiancé with an ambiguous expression that vacillated between impertinence and amusement, Clara scooped a cube of aromatic apple into her mouth.

'In a way . . . you're right,' said Liebermann. His words were almost lost in the din of cutlery, conversation and piano music. 'She *is* pretending. But not to us. She's pretending to herself.'

Swallowing quickly, Clara retorted: 'Maxim, how can you pretend to yourself — you'd know you were pretending!'

'Well, that depends on how you think about the mind,' Liebermann replied. 'What if the mind is not one thing — but two? What if the mind has a conscious region and an unconscious region? Then it might be possible for memories in the unconscious to influence the body without the conscious mind knowing anything about those memories. If this is how the mind works, then when she says she can't move her arm, she's telling the truth. She really can't.'

'But she *can* move her arm!' said Clara again, a hint of genuine frustration entering her voice.

'No,' said Liebermann firmly, 'she can't. There is a part of her mind — the unconscious part — which can move her arm. But that is not the part of her mind that corresponds with her daily thoughts, emotions, and perceptions.'

'Oh, it all sounds so . . . so . . .' Clara waved a chunk of apple on the end of her pastry fork.

'Complicated?' said Liebermann.

'Yes.'

'Well, I suppose it is.'

Clara smirked and offered Liebermann the piece of impaled apple. Glancing around to ensure that no one was looking, he thrust his head forward and took the glistening fruit into his mouth. His indecorous behaviour seemed to make Clara absurdly happy. She beamed like a naughty child who had just escaped punishment.

'And how is Doctor Kanner now?'

'Oh, Stefan is in excellent health.'

'Is he still pursuing that singer — what's her name?'

'Cora. No.'

Clara lowered her head and looked up with doleful supplicatory eyes.

'She was very pretty . . .'

Liebermann knew that a diplomatic response was required, and suppressing the urge to laugh replied in an offhand manner: 'I did not find her especially attractive.'

His words had the desired effect. Clara's face beamed again and she promptly offered him another chunk of apple. This time he declined.

The rain continued to patter against the window with patient determination. A tram rattled by, arcing around the phantom horseman.

'She's English, you say?'

'Who?'

'This patient of yours.'

'Yes.'

'They're rather odd, don't you think, the English?'

'In what way?'

'Lacking in warmth.'

'Sometimes . . . but when you get to know them they're much the same as us. I made some very good friends while I was staying in London.'

'Frau Frischmuth employed an English nursemaid last year . . .'

'And?'

'They didn't get on at all.'

Liebermann shrugged.

At the far end of an adjacent road, the ornate green dome of the Karlskirche shimmered in the distance like a fairy-tale palace. The pianist, who had previously been playing some unsophisticated waltzes, began a rendition of Schumann's *Träumerei*. It was delightful: innocent, wistful, almost veering into sadness but somehow resisting at the last moment as each inventive chord melted into the next. The music floated in the air like incense, wafting and lulling the mind into an opiate languor. Liebermann's fingers automatically shadowed the melody on the marble table top.

Surfacing from his reverie, Liebermann became aware that Clara was pressing her knee against his. He looked at her, and for a moment her confidence stalled. She blushed and looked away, but then, recovering her sense of purpose, allowed his leg to slip between hers. They maintained contact for a few seconds, and then simultaneously disengaged.

'Do you know what this is?' asked Liebermann, smiling.

'Yes,' said Clara. 'It's the piece about dreaming . . . by Robert Schumann.'

'And what are you dreaming of?'

'Can't you guess, Maxim?'

The look she gave him was little short of indecent.

18

'So,' SAID PROFESSOR FREUD. 'Two Jews meet outside the bathhouse. *Have you taken a bath already?* asks one. *How come?* says the other. *Is one missing?*'

Liebermann laughed, although more at Professor Freud's delivery than at the joke itself. Freud had adopted a pronounced Yiddisher accent and had chosen to end the joke with a fixed gesture, hands raised, a grotesque parody of the mannerisms of Eastern Jewry.

'Let me tell you another,' said Freud. 'A young man goes to the matchmaker, and the matchmaker asks: *What kind of bride do you want?* The young man replies: *She must be beautiful, she must be rich, and she must be clever. Fine,* says the matchmaker. *But I make that three wives.*'

Freud stubbed out his cigar, and was unsuccessful in his attempt to stop a reticent smile from turning into a wheezy chuckle that continued for some time. He was looking very well, Liebermann thought. Indeed, Freud had been much happier since February — when, finally, after many years of unjustified delay he had been distinguished with the all-important title of Professor Extraordinarius. It was odd that a man whose advancement had been obstructed because of anti-Semitism should be so fond of Jewish jokes, many of which portrayed Jews in a less than flattering light. But then, Professor Freud was a complex man, and Liebermann was disinclined to analyse the father of psychoanalysis. There was only one individual equipped to embark on such a daunting enterprise, and that was Freud himself.

As Freud's chuckling petered out, he raised a finger.

'One more. Then I'll stop.'

'As you wish,' replied Liebermann.

'How do we know that Jesus was Jewish?' asked Freud.

'I don't know,' said Liebermann. 'How do we know that Jesus was Jewish?'

'He lived at home until he was thirty, he went into his father's business, and his mother thought he was God!'

This time Liebermann burst out into genuine laughter. 'Why have you started collecting jokes?' he asked.

'I haven't *started*. I've been collecting them for years. I'm thinking of writing a book about them.'

'Jokes?'

'Yes. Jokes. It is my belief that jokes, like dreams and slips of the tongue, reveal the operation of the unconscious.'

The professor lit another cigar. It was his third since Liebermann had arrived, and the study was thick with smoke. Some hung like a dense fog around the feet of the ancient figurines on Freud's desk. From Liebermann's point of view, Freud's collection looked like a mythic army emerging from a primal swamp.

'Are you sure I can't interest you in another?' asked Freud, pushing the box of cigars across the desktop. 'They're very good, you know. Cuban.'

'Thank you, Herr Professor. But one was quite enough.'

Freud looked at Liebermann as though his reluctance to take another cigar was completely beyond comprehension.

'My boy,' said Freud, 'I consider smoking to be one of the greatest — and cheapest — enjoyments in life.' He drew on the cigar, leaned back in his chair, and smiled blissfully.

'I see that your collection is growing,' said Liebermann, pointing at the figures. 'Every time I visit, you seem to have acquired another.'

'Indeed,' replied Freud. He reached out and stroked the head of a small marble ape, almost as though it were a real pet. 'This is my latest acquisition. It is the baboon of Thoth. Egyptian, of course, 30 BC — or thereabouts.'

Liebermann did not know a great deal about archaeology. Nor did he understand the aesthetic appeal of antiquities (his sympathies were decidedly modern). Even so, he did not want to offend the professor and so nodded his head appreciatively.

While Freud was admiring his collection, Liebermann seized the opportunity he had been waiting for.

'Actually, Herr Professor, I wondered whether I might consult you in your capacity as an archaeologist?'

Freud looked up and smiled, a little embarrassed.

'Archaeologist? Me? It's a hobby, that's all . . .'

Liebermann gestured at Freud's bookcase.

'Still, I don't know anybody who has read more on the subject.'

The professor nodded vigorously. 'That is true. You know, I'm ashamed to admit it but I've read more archaeology than psychology.'

'Perhaps you should have been an archaeologist?'

Freud blew a cloud of smoke over the desk.

'Ahh,' he said. 'But, in a way, I am. Don't you think?'

Liebermann tacitly accepted the professor's point. Then, reaching into his leather bag, he took out the statuette from Charlotte Löwenstein's apartment.

'Do you think that this is an authentic antiquity?' He showed it to Freud. 'And if so, do you have any idea what it's supposed to be?'

Freud placed his cigar in the ashtray and reached out — his expression becoming more intense and serious. He took the piece gently in his hands, and began to rotate it, inspecting every detail. The silence was disturbed by the sound of the professor's children, running and shouting upstairs. Freud raised his head, momentarily distracted by the noise, before falling once again into a state of total absorption. Liebermann was judging whether it would be considered impolite to remind the professor of his presence when Freud suddenly announced: 'It's Egyptian. Certainly looks genuine — but it's difficult to say. You'd have to get a dealer to confirm that.'

'And what's it supposed to be?'

Freud looked up and fixed Liebermann with his penetrating stare.

'There is only one deity with a snout and a forked tail. That is Set or Seth. The god of chaos — the god of storms and mischief.'

Liebermann appeared unperturbed, yet inside his head his thoughts were racing. The professor's words were like hammer blows: storms and mischief. He had always assumed that Fräulein Löwenstein's murder was a clever illusion. Nothing more than a sophisticated stage trick. Mischief, most certainly, but mortal mischief. For the first time Liebermann experienced doubt. What kind of illusionist could conjure a storm? Liebermann remembered Thursday's unseasonal deluge: massive forks of lightning — followed by apocalyptic thunder — and rain spilling from the gutter and crashing on to the pavement below like a waterfall.

'Where did you get this?' asked Freud.

'It belongs to a friend of mine,' answered Liebermann. 'He asked me to get it valued.'

'Ah,' said Freud, holding the piece up to the light. 'It won't be worth a great deal of money. Egyptian antiquities aren't very popular in Vienna. It's all Baroque and Biedermeier these days.'

'Is it?'

'Oh yes. But there are some good dealers on Wieblinger Strasse. You should take it there.'

'I will—'

'And,' Freud cut in very quickly, 'if your friend isn't satisfied with the offer, please let me know. I would be keen to add this little fellow to my collection.'

The professor placed the statuette on his desk, between the ape and a bronze of Horus. Then he patted the demon's head, saying: 'Handsome little fellow. Handsome.'

A spiral of smoke curled around the creature's legs and tail, evoking, once again, an impression of primeval power — the awakening of an ancient and frivolous malevolence.

Part Two

The Third Person

19

It was early evening, and the gaslights were low. Rheinhardt poured his *Türkische* coffee from a small copper pot and raised the cup to his lips. Dissatisfied, he added another half-teaspoon of sugar and took a second sip.

'That's better,' he said. 'How's yours?'

'Adequate,' replied Liebermann.

On the other side of the room, under the first of two low arches, the café proprietor was standing like a guardsman. With the exception of an old man in a kaftan, Liebermann and Rheinhardt were his only customers.

'Locks seem to have acquired a special significance for Herr Uberhorst.'

'In what way?'

'Well, he described one as . . . a masterpiece. He seems to approach lock mechanisms with the same degree of veneration that you or I might reserve for a Beethoven sonata. Now that I've actually interviewed him properly — and seen his shop — I have to admit that I am more suspicious . . . But . . .'

'You don't think him capable of murder.'

'Frankly, no.'

Liebermann detected a certain hesitancy — a telling pause between words.

'What is it Oskar?'

The Inspector frowned.

'I don't think he's capable of murder, but I'm not convinced that Herr Uberhorst is being candid.'

'Why do you say that?'

'He's so very nervous.'

'That might be his disposition.'

'It very probably is. Even so . . . call it a hunch.'

'Could he have used his skills to assist someone else? Someone temperamentally better fitted to the task of murder?'

'Braun? It's a possibility . . .'

Liebermann looked out of the window. Two hussars marched past. From within the shabby café, they looked like creatures from another world, birds of paradise with extravagant plumage. The uniform of the light cavalry was striking: a high busby, a heavily braided jacket, and the distinctive loose cloak that hung from the left shoulder. In a few seconds they were gone and the window became a vacant square of darkness again.

'May I see Fräulein Sucher's statement?' asked Liebermann.

'Yes, of course.'

Rheinhardt took two sheets of paper from his pocket and handed them to his friend.

'Is this her handwriting?'

'No, it's Haussmann's.'

'I thought as much.'

'The important information is on the second page. Just there,' said Rheinhardt, pointing.

Liebermann studied the paragraph.

'So, Braun was a frequent visitor.'

Rheinhardt nodded.

Liebermann began reading: '*Herr Braun visited my mistress's apartment when I was there. She entertained him in the sitting room. On several occasions I* heard raised voices, but I don't know what passed between them. It was none of my business.' Liebermann raised his eyebrows and sipped his *Schwarzer*.

'What? Don't you believe her?'

'A maid who doesn't eavesdrop?'

'It's possible,' said Rheinhardt, with just enough emphasis to arouse Liebermann's interest.

'Why do you say that?'

Rheinhardt's expression changed from indignation to embarrassment: 'All right, all right. She reminded me a little of Mitzi.'

'Ahh . . .' said Liebermann.

'Even so,' said Rheinhardt, 'I have the utmost confidence in Fräulein Sucher. She's a good girl, believe me.' Rheinhardt's use of the term 'good girl' only strengthened Liebermann's conviction that his friend had somehow conflated Fräulein Sucher and his daughter. 'To be honest, Max,' continued Rheinhardt, 'I'm not sure about this evening's enterprise. What else can we expect to learn? Fräulein Sucher has already told us all she knows.'

Liebermann pushed the statement back across the table. 'However, memory and knowledge are not the same thing.'

'And what's that supposed to mean?'

'Fräulein Sucher might be able to remember more than she knows.'

Rheinhardt twisted the corner of his moustache and was about to ask a further question when the clock began to chime.

'Eight o' clock,' said Liebermann. 'We should be going.'

Rheinhardt picked up Rosa Sucher's statement and dropped some hellers into a silver tray. Then, glancing around at the empty tables, he allowed a few more coins to fall as a gratuity. The old man in the kaftan looked up, his attention captured by the sound of falling coins.

'And you're always insisting that I'm extravagant,' said Liebermann quietly.

The proprietor bowed and clicked his heels as the two strangers collected their coats and left.

It had been raining again — a brief shower that had glazed the cobblestones. The air smelt of horse manure and coal dust.

Rheinhardt set off at a brisk pace, immediately turning along a narrow alley. It was so dark that Liebermann found himself instinctively reaching out to touch the wall. Rheinhardt forged ahead, incongruously whistling the introductory theme of Beethoven's *Pastoral Symphony*: a jaunty melody, supposed to represent the awakening of cheerful feelings on arriving in the countryside.

At the end of the alley, Rheinhardt stopped to get his bearings: 'Over there, I think.'

They were on a principal road again, although it was completely devoid of traffic and people. The street lights had been lit, and the dank air produced a haze of phosphorescence around the flickering lanterns.

Liebermann noticed a woman standing in a doorway on the opposite side of the road. She stepped out of the shadows as they approached, raising her skirt high enough to reveal lime-green stockings and her petticoats.

'Good evening, gents,' she said in a brassy voice.

Her face had been thickly powdered, giving it the vacant and slightly disturbing appearance of a Venetian mask.

'Good evening,' said Rheinhardt curtly.

The woman shrugged and walked away, providing unequivocal confirmation of her profession. She glanced back over her shoulder, still hopeful, before disappearing into the darkness of another alleyway. The sound of her footsteps pinking on the cobblestones faded into the night.

After walking another hundred yards or so, Rheinhardt stopped outside a large dilapidated apartment building.

'This is it.'

Liebermann looked up at the façade. It must have been beautiful once. The remains of statues could be seen in several alcoves, as could the ghosts of gilded relief work — thick cords and spectral foliation. The front door was massive and decorated with a rusting iron grid that suggested the portcullis of a medieval castle. Rheinhardt tested it with the palm of his hand and was surprised to feel little resistance. The hinges groaned and the door swung open.

Liebermann followed Rheinhardt into an austere hallway. The walls were featureless and the floor a crude checkerboard of black and white tiles, many of which were either cracked or missing. To their immediate right, a few steps led to a landing and the scuffed and dented door of Rosa Sucher's apartment. Rheinhardt took the iron knocker in his hand and tapped three times.

The door opened almost immediately.

'Good evening, Inspector.'

Rosa Sucher was exactly as Rheinhardt had remembered her: plain, polite, and timid.

'Good evening, Rosa. May I introduce my colleague, Doctor Max Liebermann.'

Rosa's eyes widened, suggesting a combination of surprise and respect. 'Please, come in, Herr Doctor.'

Rosa took their coats and hung them on the hallstand before ushering them into what served as the guest room. It was small and sparsely furnished; however, much effort had been expended on the arrangement of ornaments and cushions to create an illusion of homeliness. In the corner an old woman had risen to her feet and was wobbling precariously as she leaned on a walking stick.

'My grandmother,' said Rosa, before rushing over to help support her tiny frame.

'Fetch the gentlemen some schnapps,' croaked the old woman as she crouched and fell back into her seat. 'It's a cold night, they'll be wanting schnapps.'

'We don't have any, grandmother,' said Rosa quietly, glancing desperately at Rheinhardt.

The Inspector waved his hand in the air: 'Dear lady, thank you so much for your kind offer, but my colleague and I will have to decline.' Then, looking directly at Rosa, he added more tenderly, 'Thank you for agreeing to a further interview.'

The young woman blushed and performed a barely perceptible curtsy.

Rosa took some chairs from beneath a table and invited her guests to sit close to a pot-bellied stove. She then sat on a stool next to her grandmother, taking the old woman's hand in her own.

Rheinhardt made some small talk about the weather before thanking Rosa again. He then looked at his companion and said that the doctor wished to ask her a few questions.

Rosa smoothed the creases from her dress and looked nervously at Liebermann.

'Fräulein Sucher,' he began, 'are you familiar with the notion of hypnosis?'

20

THE PARAFFIN LAMP was turned down low and emitted only a miserly light. Rosa Sucher was completely still, her body laid out on an ottoman like a corpse in a casket. Liebermann sat at the head of the ottoman, out of Rosa's view but observing her intently.

'I want you to stare at a point on the ceiling — the beading near the curtain rail will do.'

Rosa did as she was instructed, rolling her head back to catch sight of the beading.

'As you concentrate,' continued Liebermann, 'your eyes may begin to feel tired — your eyelids will become heavy.'

Rheinhardt was surprised to see that Liebermann's words had an immediate effect. Rosa Sucher began to blink with increasing frequency, and in due course her eyelids were fluttering as though she was engaged in a struggle to stay awake. Liebermann modulated his voice, speaking in a persuasive monotone: 'Your arms feel heavy. Your legs feel heavy. Heavy and relaxed.' Rosa Sucher's hand slipped off her thigh, and hit the ottoman with a dull thud. 'See how your breathing is becoming shallow. Every time you breathe out, you relax a little more . . .'

The stove hissed as the scorched logs inside exuded a smoky fragrance.

'Your eyelids are becoming heavier and heavier,' murmured Liebermann. 'Heavier and heavier. You are sinking into a deep, deep, relaxing sleep.'

A detonation in the stove made Rheinhardt startle. His neck muscles had become slack, allowing his head to roll from side to side, and he was alarmed to discover that his breathing had acquired the limping rhythm that typically accompanies the mind's descent into oblivion. Rheinhardt bit his lower lip until the pain cleared the fog in his head, and then, to ensure continued wakefulness, he surreptitiously pinched himself.

'When I count to three,' said Liebermann, maintaining his languid delivery, 'your eyes will close, and you will enter a deep, dreamless sleep. However, this sleep will be very different from the ordinary sleep to which you are accustomed. While you are in *this* sleep, you will retain the ability to hear my voice, and you will be perfectly capable of answering questions. One. Two . . .' Rosa's eyelids began to close, continuing to flutter with the restless agitation of a butterfly. On the count of 'Three', however, she succumbed to sleep with the decisive swiftness of a falling guillotine. Her eyelids dropped, and in an instant her face had acquired the cherubic composure of a slumbering infant's.

Liebermann raised his head and smiled at Rheinhardt — clearly satisfied that the procedure had been successful. He then proceeded to ask Rosa a number of questions about the domestic duties she had been instructed by Fräulein Löwenstein to perform. The young woman's answers were perfectly intelligible, although her voice sounded somewhat flat as though she was under the influence of a powerful soporific. This form of questioning went on for some time. Indeed, Rheinhardt found himself becoming a little impatient, as Liebermann's interrogation progressed from one inconsequential matter to the next: flower arrangement, laundry, dusting, furniture polish, and so on. Rheinhardt became particularly exasperated when Liebermann seemed to get caught up in a protracted discussion on the subject of shopping lists and food.

'So, you ordered less coffee?'

'In February, yes.'

'And fewer eggs?'

'Mistress went off eggs.'

'But noodles appeared more frequently on the shopping list?'

'My mistress asked me to make her some *Schinken-fleckerin.*'

'For breakfast?'

'Yes, sir.'

'How many times.'

'Five, sir.'

'Did that strike you as unusual?'

'Yes, sir. Mistress rarely ate breakfast.'

'Tell me, did Fräulein Löwenstein ever ask you to purchase peppermint tea?'

'Yes. From a shop on Kärtner Strasse.'

'Recently?'

'In February.'

'Had she ever asked you to buy peppermint tea before?'

And so the peculiar conversation went on, touching upon one trivial topic after another. Eventually Liebermann abandoned his exhaustive investigation into the minutiae of Charlotte Löwenstein's domestic arrangements and raised the subject of Otto Braun. Rheinhardt sighed with relief, attracting Liebermann's attention, who turned to see if anything was wrong. Rheinhardt shook his head as if to say, 'Nothing.' Liebermann continued: 'How often did Herr Braun visit your mistress?'

'Very often, sir.'

'Every day?'

'No. Not every day.'

'Two or three times a week?'

'Yes, about that. Although not always. Sometimes he would not call for several weeks.'

'Why was that? Do you think he had to go away sometimes?'

'No. Because he always attended Fräulein Löwenstein's meetings.'

'Where did Fräulein Löwenstein entertain Herr Braun?'

'In the sitting room, sir.'

'And where were you? When they were together?'

'Sometimes I was in the kitchen . . . sometimes in the study . . . and sometimes—' Rosa's brow furrowed.

'Yes?' said Liebermann.

'Sometimes, Fräulein Löwenstein suggested that I should leave the apartment . . . for a few hours.'

'She wanted to be alone with Herr Braun?'

'I don't know.'

'That seems likely, don't you think?'

'I don't know.'

Rheinhardt found her loyalty touching. Even under hypnosis, she strived to protect her mistress's honour.

'Listen to me very carefully,' continued Liebermann. 'You must answer my questions honestly. I repeat: do you think your mistress wanted to be alone with Herr Braun?'

The corner of Rosa's mouth twitched.

'You must answer,' Liebermann pressed.

'Yes,' said Rosa, sighing heavily. 'Yes, I do think that.'

Liebermann glanced at Rheinhardt and then continued: 'Did they ever argue, Herr Braun and Fräulein Löwenstein?'

'Sometimes . . . sometimes I heard their voices. When I was in the kitchen. They sounded upset . . .'

'What were they saying?'

'I can't remember.'

Liebermann leaned forward.

'Rosa, imagine you are in Fräulein Löwenstein's kitchen. Picture it with your mind's eye. Every detail. The floor, the cupboards, the sink

... The curtains hanging in the window casement. Can you picture those things?'

'Yes.'

'The picture in your mind is so clear, so vivid, that it is almost real. It feels like you are in the kitchen again. It feels like you are there. Tell me, are you seated? Or are you standing?'

'Seated. Seated at the table.'

'What are you doing?'

'Sharpening knives.'

'Now listen. Listen very carefully ... You hear voices. It is Fräulein Löwenstein and Herr Braun. They are in the sitting room, and you can hear their voices. They sound upset ...'

'Yes. Upset and ...'

'What?'

'Angry.'

'Listen carefully now. What are they saying?'

'I can't hear them properly. They are too far away.'

'Try, Rosa. Concentrate. Listen to their voices. What are they saying?'

'It's nothing to do with me. It's none of my business.'

'But you cannot help yourself from hearing. They are shouting at each other. What are they saying, Rosa?'

'I can't hear them. They are too far away ...'

Liebermann leaned forward and placed his hands on either side of Rosa's head. Applying a gentle pressure to her temples with his fingertips, he continued in a low, persuasive purr: 'Listen, Rosa. Listen to the voices. As the pressure increases, so the voices become louder. Listen to them ... You are seated at the table, sharpening knives ... and in the sitting room Fräulein Löwenstein and Herr Braun are shouting at each other. What are they saying, Rosa? What are they saying?'

Suddenly, Rosa gasped.

'Get out . . .' Her voice was quite different. The dead tones of the trance state had been replaced by an eerie, emotionally charged stage whisper: 'Get out of here . . . you . . . you . . . disgust me . . . I need more money . . . You always need more money . . . Get out, get out or I'll—' Rosa's voice dropped to an agitated grumble: an odd, muffled sound that arose from the back of her throat. Before long, more fragments of language surfaced from the chaotic burble of tones: 'Theo . . . Never . . . last time, I swear I'll . . . God help me, I will—'

And then there was silence again. Silence, except for the gentle sibilance of the stove.

'Feel the pressure,' said Liebermann. 'The voices are becoming clearer — what can you hear?'

'There are no voices.'

'Are you sure?'

'A carriage is passing — passing in the street below . . . and a tinker is shouting . . . shoelaces — shoelaces for sale . . . shoelaces . . .'

Liebermann removed his hands from Rosa's head and sat back in his chair. The girl's face had once again assumed the expression of a sleeping child's.

21

THE AFTERNOON HAD been uneventful and the hospital ward was as peaceful as a lake in summer.

Sabina Rupius was a graduate of the prestigious Rudolfinerhaus — where only girls of 'good family' were admitted for a thorough education in nursing. The institution had a reputation for producing conscientious professionals. Yet her mind was adrift.

She was supposed to be preparing the medication trolley. But between checking the dosage of Frau Auerbach's gelatin chloral hydrate capsules and pouring Frau Bertram's mentholated linctus, she had become distracted by her own thoughts and was now fully immersed in a daydream, the subject of which was Doctor Stefan Kanner.

There was no doubting it — Doctor Kanner was an exceedingly handsome man. Sabina formed a mental picture of his face and contemplated the unnatural blueness of his eyes. Even thinking about them produced a curious sensation in the pit of her stomach and made her cheeks burn. He was so particular about his dress — so fastidious. And when he stood close, the fragrance of his cologne was intoxicating.

Nurse Rupius shook her head.

This won't do. This really won't do at all.

She forced herself to focus her attention on the pot of chloral hydrate capsules. Counting out Frau Auerbach's prescription again, she replaced the heavy lid with a sigh.

Frank Tallis

A strand of thick auburn hair fell from under Nurse Rupius's cap. She tutted, lifted it back into place, and secured it with a pin. Inspecting her reflection on the metal surface of the trolley, she admired her handiwork.

I have large eyes — and a delicate chin. I am not unattractive.

Looking up, she noticed that the English governess had walked over to Fräulein Dill's bed and the two women were engaged in polite conversation.

Nurse Rupius removed the cork from the dark green bottle of mentholated linctus and, measuring out two teaspoons, transferred the syrup into a small glass. Then, sitting down, she made a note on Frau Auerbach's and Frau Bertram's charts.

The young woman and the English governess continued to talk in subdued voices. Nurse Rupius had not yet recovered from her daydream, and the image of Doctor Kanner's face still haunted her imagination, interposing itself between her and the two patients. Through the transparent shadow of Kanner's benign visage, Rupius saw the Dill girl uncover her needlepoint.

Again, Sabina Rupius shook her head to dispel the image.

Dill held up her unfinished needlepoint for the English governess to inspect. Then she produced a small basket from which she took a ball of wool and a pair of scissors.

The English governess's smile vanished. It was a dramatic change, like the sun being swallowed by a cloud. Suddenly she looked fearful — troubled. Nurse Rupius watched as Fräulein Dill tried to comfort her, but the young woman's efforts had no effect. The governess had become completely unresponsive. Her face was locked in an attitude of terror, and her frozen stare was fixed on the wool and scissors.

'Nurse?' Fräulein Dill called out. 'Nurse, I think something's wrong.'

Nurse Rupius got up and went to Dill's bed.

{ 130 }

'What is it, Fräulein Dill?'

'We were talking,' said the young woman. 'And all of a sudden, the English Fräulein just stopped. She started looking at me in a funny way — as though she was scared.'

Sabina Rupius bent down and rested a hand on the governess's shoulder.

'Miss Lydgate?' She shook the Englishwoman a little. 'Miss Lydgate? What is the matter?'

The English governess did not reply. It was as though she was suffering from catalepsy; yet her left hand was gripping her right arm very tightly. So tightly, in fact, that the nails had broken the papery skin and bright beads of blood had begun to seep out.

'Nurse?' Sabina Rupius looked up to see that Miss Lydgate's rictus of terror was being mirrored on the face of Fräulein Dill.

'Nurse,' repeated the girl in a tremulous voice. 'Look at her lips. I think she's trying to say something.'

Sabina Rupius pressed her ear close to the governess's mouth. Miss Lydgate *was* saying something — but not in German. Nurse Rupius's command of English was not very good, yet she was able to recognise a few of the words and she made a determined effort to remember what the woman was saying.

'I'll do it, if you won't,' said the governess. 'I'll do it. I'll do it, if you won't . . .'

22

THE LOCK WAS HELD in place by two small vices. Only a single candle burned on the mantelpiece, but he did not need to see what he was doing. In his mind he held a mental picture of the mechanism, and his dexterous fingers responded to the slightest resistance as he manoeuvred the pick.

It was what he did to divert himself and he had been doing so for many years. Some might play chess or a musical instrument, or read poetry, but Karl Uberhorst picked locks. The task was so demanding that he could lose himself in the process and hence avoid thinking about those things that made his soul ache: his loneliness and regrets.

Sometimes it would take him months to work out (by trial and error) the exact sequence of the movements necessary to pick a particular lock. But for a man whose life was solitary and without any event save the routine, the duration of each project was largely irrelevant. His patience was infinite. Moreover, he felt that he had no right to claim an understanding of any lock mechanism unless he could master it.

Although a sensitive man, Uberhorst was not fanciful. Yet, on occasion, lock-picking would stir and awaken in him something close to poetic inspiration. Similes that were then transformed into colouful mental frescoes would suggest themselves. He was like a mystic, probing the mysteries of the universe; like a lover overcoming the resistance of a coy woman; like Oedipus discovering the secret of the sphinx. These similes, when they surfaced, influenced his technique. Some locks needed to be persuaded, seduced with subtle stratagems — while others needed to be stormed, requiring a kind of heroism.

The lock upon which he was working was a Chubb-style 'detector' that had recently been patented in America (a country that now seemed to be threatening the historical pre-eminence of the British). Such locks required great care, as the bolt would become trapped if any of the levers were raised too high. The lock would then have to be reset using the true key, and he would have to begin his labours afresh. Biting his lower lip, he insinuated the pick, testing each lever to establish which one secured the bolt.

In addition to recreation and analgesia, Uberhorst's singular hobby served another, less readily articulated purpose. Somewhere, in the darker recesses of his sombre mind, a germ of ambition had taken root. His comprehensive understanding of lock mechanisms would allow him, one day, to design a system that was truly invulnerable. In the moments before sleep, he was teased by a speculative vision, a hypothetical mechanism floating in the darkness: a pin-tumbler lock with a revolving cylinder ...

Uberhorst closed his eyes and raised the lever, feeling the slight resistance.

A little more ... a little more.

At this point, skill required the supplementary advantage of intuition. Uberhorst decided that he would take a risk.

Ever so gently ...

But he had gone too far. He had tripped the lever past the corner of the detecting spring.

The bolt was trapped.

He sighed, withdrew the pick, and considered the importance of his mistake. As he did so, his thoughts were interrupted by an image that had been invading his mind all week: the Inspector — sagging eyes and turned-up moustache, his large body filling the workshop, the final words of their conversation.

Then you must be mistaken, Inspector.

Why?

It's impossible.

Really? Even for a master locksmith?

If Uberhorst wasn't careful, he could find himself swinging from a rope.

23

When Liebermann had accepted his father's invitation to dinner he had felt slightly uneasy. The feeling had returned as he got out of the cab in Concordiaplatz, and when he discovered that in addition to his parents and younger sister Hannah, his elder sister Leah had been invited — with her husband Josef — and that little Daniel was also present his heart sank. Mendel had obviously decided to organise a family gathering around his son's visit, which meant that the old man would feel justified in celebrating the Sabbath.

With his wine cup conspicuously raised, Mendel stood at the head of the table, reciting *Kiddush* with the solemnity of an Old Testament prophet.

Mendel was perfectly aware that his son had virtually no attachment to Jewish tradition, but it was a fact that he was unwilling to accept. Indeed, at times it seemed to Liebermann that his father was conducting a war of attrition — always seeking to erode his resistance by subjecting him whenever possible to customs and rituals.

'Boruch Atoh Adonoi Eloheinu Melech Hoolom . . .'

Blessed are You, Lord, Our God, King of the Universe, who sanctifies us with his commandments, and has been pleased with us.

Across the table, beyond the Sabbath candles, Liebermann caught Hannah's eye and assumed an expression of exaggerated piety. His younger sister looked away, and Liebermann was gratified to see her shoulders shaking as she fought to conceal laughter. He found the ease with which he could provoke her only slightly less remarkable than the magnitude of his own immaturity.

'Kiy Vanu Vacharsa V'osanu Kidashta Mikol Haamim . . .'

Indeed, You have chosen us and made us holy among all people, and have willingly and lovingly given us Your holy Sabbath for an inheritance.

Liebermann filled the vessel for washing hands, and systematically poured a small quantity of water over his right hand, then his left, three times in succession. His actions reminded him of the superstitious rituals associated with obsessional neuroses. Before drying his hands he recited the next blessing.

Blessed are You, Lord our God, King of the Universe, who sanctifies us with his commandments, and commands us concerning washing of hands.

Leah, gifted with the uncanny prescience of watchful mothers, intercepted Daniel's chubby little fingers as they crawled towards the bread. Unperturbed, Mendel removed the shabbos deckle covering the loaves in preparation for the final blessing:

'Boruch Atoh Adonoi Eloheinu Melech Hoolom,'

Blessed are You, Lord, our God, King of the Universe,

'Hamoitzi Lechem Min Haaretz.'

Who brings forth bread from the earth.

Liebermann whispered an indifferent 'Amein' with the others, and winked at Hannah when she lifted her head. She was smiling — a broad, triumphal smile. Once again, she had survived the Sabbath ritual, in spite of her brother's efforts to embarrass her.

Mendel signalled to the head servant who had been patiently standing by the door and a few moments later the room was a hive of activity. A large tureen of chicken soup was deposited in the middle of the table, and several conversations began at once. Liebermann's mother — Rebecca — was fussing over Daniel, while Mendel questioned Josef on an abstruse point of contract law. The old man looked down the table at his son, willing him to join in, but Liebermann only smiled and turned towards Hannah.

'So,' he began. But before he could utter another word his mother was talking to him.

'Maxim, you'll never guess who I met the other day.'

'Who?'

'Frau Hirschfeld.'

'Really?'

'Yes. I haven't seen her for years. Apparently —' without pausing, Rebecca wiped a dribble of soup from Daniel's mouth and combed his hair with her fingers '— they've been living in Italy — the whole family — except for Martin, of course. Do you ever see Martin?'

'Very rarely.'

'He's been promoted, you know.' Rebecca passed more bread to Mendel. 'She was looking well, Frau Hirschfeld. She's put on a little weight, of course — but then, who doesn't when you get to our age.' With a swiftness that almost eluded detection, Rebecca adjusted the angle of the spoon in Leah's hand before it reached Daniel's mouth. 'Oh, and Rosamund — you remember Martin's sister Rosamund? She has two children now. She was the one who married the architect. What was his name?'

'Weisel. Hermann Weisel.'

'That's right. Herr Klein's cousin. Making a name for himself — so Frau Hischfeld says.'

'Herr Klein?'

'No, no. The architect.' Suddenly turning on her husband, she said: 'Mendel, let Josef eat. He hasn't touched his soup.'

Gesturing towards Rebecca's bowl, Mendel responded dryly: 'Neither have you, my dear.'

Rebecca shrugged and continued to fret and fidget.

'So,' said Liebermann, looking across the table at Hannah for the second time. 'What have you been up to?'

Hannah screwed up her face.

'Nothing, really.'

Liebermann shook his head.

'You must have done something, I haven't seen you for almost a month.'

'All right,' said Hannah, her adolescent moue softening to become a more adult pout, 'I've been to see Emelie. But that's all.'

'Really?'

'Yes, really.'

Liebermann felt sorry for his younger sister. Hannah was a late addition to the family, and since Leah's marriage she had had to live alone with their parents. At sixteen she had been marooned in a household that was beginning to feel frowsty and moribund.

'Then I suppose I should take you out, to cheer you up. How would you like that?'

Hannah's face brightened.

'I'd like that very much.'

'Where do you want to go?'

'I don't know.'

'Come on — you choose.'

'An exhibition?'

'Which one?'

'Any one.'

'Well, what about the Secession? Would you like to see that? It's in the new building. You know, the one that the philistines are calling the golden cabbage.'

'Will it be very . . .' She paused before adding, 'Modern?'

'Of course — but you'll love it, I promise you. Klimt has produced a massive frieze. Very controversial, apparently.'

'I'm not sure father would—'

Liebermann raised a finger to his lips. Checking to see that Mendel hadn't heard anything, he whispered: 'I'll send you a note. Sometime next week.'

The Liebermann family sustained a babble of conversation through several courses, flagging only after the arrival of dessert — a fragrant pool of plum compote in a wide silver dish. The cook brought it to the table personally, and was welcomed with a chorus of compliments.

When everyone had finished eating Liebermann stood up.

'Could I have your attention, please.'

The room fell silent.

'I'm glad you're all here — because I have an important announcement to make.'

'Announcement?' said Rebecca, more anxious than curious. 'What announcement?'

Mendel rested a pacifying hand on Rebecca's arm.

'I'm about to tell you, Mother,' said Liebermann.

He looked around the table. All of his family were looking at him with questioning eyes. Only Mendel seemed fully composed.

'Last Thursday,' Liebermann began, 'I proposed to Clara Weiss.' He paused, prolonging the suspense. 'And . . . I am delighted to report that she accepted my proposal. We are engaged to be married.'

A heartbeat of silence preceded an eruption of cries and applause. Rebecca rose from her chair and, rushing to her son, threw her arms around his neck. Leah and Hannah followed — and a few moments later Liebermann found himself in the middle of an affectionate, tearful scrum, being squeezed, kissed and congratulated. The frenzy was so sudden, and so loud, that it frightened little Daniel — who subsequently added to the hubbub by bawling. When Liebermann was finally released, he found that his father had risen too and was now standing directly in front of him. The old man opened his arms.

'Congratulations, my boy.'

'Thank you, Father.'

They embraced — for the first time in more years than Liebermann could remember.

24

THE INTERROGATION ROOM was sparsely furnished: a table and some simple wooden chairs. The Spartan emptiness was softened a little by a photographic portrait of the ubiquitous Franz Josef. The old Emperor looked down, radiating benevolence. From his elevated, almost god-like vantage point, he appeared content to wait aeons for a confession. The same, however, could not be said of Rheinhardt.

Once again, the Inspector found himself feeling somewhat irritated and bemused by his friend's roundabout questioning. Even Natalie Heck was showing signs of bewilderment. She had clearly been expecting a more demanding interview, perhaps anticipating being tricked by the 'doctor' into revealing more than she intended. Instead, Liebermann had spent an inordinate amount of time discussing the craft of dressmaking and now seemed wholly fixated on the seam-stress's knowledge of Fräulein Löwenstein's wardrobe. Rheinhardt had watched Fräulein Heck's expression pass from fear through relief to something that looked very much like confusion.

'There were three silk dresses?'

'Yes,' replied Natalie Heck, 'as far as I know. A red one — she bought it from Taubenrauch and Cie, the shop on Mariahilferstrasse — a green one, and a blue one — designed by Bertha Fürst. She would sometimes wear a wonderful butterfly brooch with the blue one.'

'And they were well made? Of good quality?'

'Of course. The silk was very expensive — Chinese, I think. And they were beautifully cut — particularly the Fürst — although not to everyone's taste.'

'Why do you say that?'

'Some would say they were immodest.'

'And what would you say?'

'I . . .' Natalie faltered before raising her chin and proudly declaring, 'I would not have been comfortable wearing such a dress.'

Rheinhardt stifled a yawn and consulted his pocket watch.

'So,' continued Liebermann, 'it was Fräulein Löwenstein's habit to wear one of these dresses every Thursday evening.'

'Yes.'

'She never wore any of the other dresses?'

'There was a black velvet ball gown — and an old satin one . . . but she stopped wearing them. Some time ago, in fact.'

'They were of inferior quality?'

'Yes. The cuff of the ball gown had frayed.'

'Tell me, did Fräulein Löwenstein exhibit an equal fondness for each of her silk dresses? Or did she like one more than the others?'

'She wore the blue one most — but that's because it was more comfortable.'

'And how do you know that?'

'Why,' said Natalie Heck, smiling, 'because she asked me to let it out. She said that it had always been too tight.'

Liebermann paused for a moment. He picked a hair off his trousers and disposed of it at arm's length. Then, returning his attention to Fräulein Heck, he asked: 'Didn't that strike you as odd?'

Natalie Heck did not understand the question. She pressed her lips together and stared blankly, her large dark eyes opened wide — two pools of Indian ink. 'Remarkable, don't you think?' continued Liebermann. 'That such a well-made dress should be too tight? Would someone like Frau Fürst — someone with such a fine reputation — make such an elementary mistake?'

Natalie Heck shrugged.

'These things happen. You can measure someone one day, and the next . . .' She held her hands out in front of her body and moved them apart.

Liebermann fell silent. He removed his spectacles and began cleaning the lenses with his handkerchief. When he had finished, he placed the handkerchief back in his pocket and inspected the lenses against the light. As he was doing this, he said, in the careless manner of an incidental observation or afterthought: 'Fräulein Heck, why were you visiting Herr Braun's apartment?'

Natalie Heck looked surprised as the interview veered — quite suddenly — into less comfortable territory. Rheinhardt stopped grooming his moustache and sat up straight.

'Herr Braun,' said Fraülein Heck, 'is my friend.'

Liebermann replaced his spectacles, and looked directly into the young woman's eyes. She looked away, and her cheeks flushed a little.

'Do you often visit Herr Braun's apartment?' After the smallest of pauses, he added: 'Alone?'

Natalie Heck shook her head: 'No, no. Herr Braun is my friend. We aren't . . .'

'Please,' Liebermann interrupted. 'Forgive me. It wasn't my intention to suggest any impropriety on your part.' Then, carefully selecting his words, he added: 'Any immodesty.'

Natalie Heck turned bright red. Flustered, she launched into a garbled defence.

'I've only been to Herr Braun's apartment a few times. He isn't a strong man — he's often sickly. On Sunday, when the constable stopped me — I was worried — I wanted to see if he was all right.'

'Do you have any idea where he is now?'

'Of course not.' She looked angrily towards Rheinhardt. 'Inspector, I told you the truth last week. There's nothing more to tell.'

'Indeed, Fräulein,' said Rheinhardt, 'and we are very grateful for your assistance.'

Natalie Heck turned to face Liebermann again. He continued as if the previous exchange hadn't happened.

'Do you think, Fräulein, that your friend Herr Braun was attracted to Fräulein Löwenstein?'

'I . . .' She struggled to regain her composure. 'I think he probably was. She was a very beautiful woman.'

'Did he ever talk about her?'

'No.'

'Then why do you think he was attracted to her?'

'Sometimes . . .' She tightened her richly coloured shawl around her shoulders as though a cold wind had passed through the room. 'Sometimes he would look at her in a certain way.'

Just as Rheinhardt thought that his friend had scented blood and was preparing his prey for the delivery of a fatal question, Liebermann simply smiled, leaned back in his chair, and said: 'Thank you, Fräulein Heck. You have been most helpful.' Then, turning to Rheinhardt, he added: 'I have no further questions, Inspector.'

'Are you sure, Herr Doctor?' said Rheinhardt.

'Yes, Inspector. Quite sure.'

Rheinhardt stood, somewhat reluctantly, wondering whether Liebermann was playing a psychological game and was craftily creating in Natalie Heck a false sense of security. But the young doctor showed no signs of further engagement.

'In which case,' said Rheinhardt, 'you are free to leave, Fräulein Heck.'

The seamstress rose from her chair and, frostily giving Liebermann a wide berth, left the room. Rheinhardt followed and Liebermann heard his friend instructing an officer to escort Fräulein Heck back to her home near the Prater.

When Rheinhardt returned, he sat in the chair previously occupied by the seamstress. For a moment the two men shared an uneasy silence. Finally Rheinhardt shook his head: 'That was a curious interview, Max.'

'Was it?'

'Yes. Why did you bring it to such a peremptory close? Just — or so it seemed to me — when things were starting to get interesting.'

'Fräulein Heck has told us all that she knows.'

'Then this hasn't been a very productive morning.'

'Well, I wouldn't say that.'

Rheinhardt frowned.

'All right: do we know anything now that we didn't know yesterday?'

'Yes — quite a lot, I think. We know that Natalie Heck was besotted with Otto Braun: her denial spoke volumes. We also have more evidence to suggest that Fräulein Löwenstein and Braun were lovers. Heck's despair was palpable. But more importantly, we now have confirmation of an earlier hypothesis.'

'We do?'

'Oh yes. You will recall that I speculated about the presence of a third person when Charlotte Löwenstein was murdered?'

'Indeed, but—'

Interrupting, Liebermann continued: 'We now know the identity of that third person.'

Liebermann paused and Rheinhardt, unable to restrain himself, stood up again. His movement was so abrupt his chair rocked back and almost toppled over.

'What?'

'The third person,' said Liebermann softly, 'was Fräulein

Löwenstein's unborn child. At the time of her murder, she was approximately three months pregnant.'

'But how on earth have you deduced that?' cried Rheinhardt. The door opened, and a junior officer poked his head in.

'Everything all right, sir?'

'Yes, yes,' said Rheinhardt impatiently, waving his hands in the air. The officer bowed apologetically, and closed the door.

'I'll explain in due course,' said Liebermann. 'I must get back to the hospital. But for the moment, Oskar, I would strongly urge you to compose a polite note to Professor Mathias, requesting the completion of Fräulein Löwenstein's interrupted autopsy — as soon as possible.'

'Of course.'

'Oh, and Oskar?'

'Yes.'

'I would like to attend as well — if I may?'

25

Zoltán Záborszky was sitting at his usual table in the garden of Csarda, a restaurant on the Prater. A cimbalom player and two violinists were performing 'Rákóczi's Lament', a folk song that Záborszky's nurse would sing to him when he had been a very small child. He closed his eyes, and for a moment it seemed to him that he could hear again the Tisza flowing through the park of the long-lost family estate. In his mind, he could see the imposing house with its battlements and round towers, perched on its steep, rocky bluff: those cavernous rooms, which in the summer had filled with a soft, slow light that rolled through the windows like honey. Who, he wondered, would now be availing himself of that well-stocked cellar, which, under blankets of spiders' silk, had contained bottles brought from the finest wine merchants in Paris?

Záborszky took a sip of his lifeless burgundy and winced, as though suffering from a toothache.

Had his father, the old Count, survived the final onslaught of tuberculosis he would very probably have risen from his bed with only one intention — to plant a bullet in his errant son's brain. Záborszky contemplated this imaginary scenario with some regularity, and more often than not regretted that it had not come to pass.

When the music stopped, he beckoned to the cimbalom player who immediately rested his mallets on the strings and came over to Záborszky's table.

'Yes, my dear Count?'

The musician could not suppress his reaction to Záborszky's appearance. He had acquired a sumptuous black eye. Swollen flesh had almost closed the socket, making the whites and the iris barely visible.

Záborszky noticed the musician flinching.

'An accident,' he said flatly.

'You must take better care of yourself, Count.'

'Indeed,' Záborszky folded a serviette before continuing. 'Tamás, please . . . no more of the old tunes.'

'Ahh, I understand,' the musician smiled sympathetically. 'The melancholy, is it?'

Záborszky nodded, his single visible eye becoming moist.

The musician bowed and marched back to his companions. When they started to play again, the air filled with a spare but spirited arrangement of Strauss's *Kaiser Waltz*.

Záborszky picked up his copy of the *Wiener Zeitung* and read the news — most of which did not interest him. Occasionally the text was interrupted by otherwise blank spaces bearing the single word 'Confiscated'. Copies of every paper were submitted each morning for approval by the censor — who was inclined to judge numerous articles unfit for public consumption. Záborszky was about to put the *Zeitung* down again, when his attention was drawn by a headline: *Leopoldstadt Murder Baffles Police.*

So: they had finally decided to publish the details. Záborszky wondered whether the delay was anything to do with the censor.

In his eagerness to read the article he skipped whole sentences.

Locked room . . . no bullet . . . a statuette of an ancient god . . .

Clever illusion . . . stagecraft.

A thin smile appeared on Záborszky's face.

Looking for a young man called Otto Braun.

Tamás, assuming that the Count was enjoying the Strauss, beat the strings of his cimbalom with greater vigour and encouraged his companions to play faster.

'That bumbling clown of an Inspector,' muttered Záborszky to himself. 'Completely out of his depth.'

Záborszky could picture them all: the constables with their ridiculous spiked helmets and sabres guarding the entrance, the Inspector's team floundering around her apartment, tapping the walls, looking for trapdoors and levers. They would discover nothing.

The Count closed his good eye again, and a distant memory floated to the surface of his already troubled mind: winter. Ravens, like tattered rags, caught on the branches of bare trees.

He had been hunting in the immense wood that covered the uplands of the estate: pools of fog churning in the hollows, clods of frozen earth kicked up by the horse.

The animal had been frightened. It sensed danger. An old crone was standing by the bridleway. She seemed to come from nowhere. The horse neighed and nervously swung its head. Záborszky did not know *who* she was — but he knew *what* she was.

The witch had spoken a taboo word. She had mentioned the *szépasszony* — The Fair Lady, the beautiful woman with long blonde hair who preyed on young men. The demonic seductress who emerged in storms and showers of hail . . .

The witch had cursed him.

She will get you, the witch had said.

26

FRÄULEIN LÖWENSTEIN'S BODY had been returned to the dissection table where it lay concealed under covers. The folds and creases of the material created a miniature landscape of mounds and ravines that all but disguised the human form underneath. The air was ripe with corruption — a noxious effluvium that might have been coughed up through a vent in the earth's crust.

Professor Mathias tugged gently at the top sheet. It slipped downward, revealing Fräulein Löwenstein's face. Rheinhardt had not expected her to be very much changed, but already her skin was discoloured and her features wasted. Her lips, previously blue in the early stages of death, were now almost black. There was something about her expression that suggested terror, as though her mouldering brain was still in possession of just enough sentience to generate a nightmare. Only Fräulein Löwenstein's hair had retained its incandescence. Her curls and tresses blazed defiantly beneath the merciless electric light.

Mathias placed a finger on her brow and pressed out a wrinkle.

'The grass withereth, and the flower thereof falleth away.'

Rheinhardt caught Liebermann's eye and assumed a hangdog expression — the old man's eccentricity was already beginning to pall. Mathias sighed and, slowly lifting his head, examined the young doctor who stood on the opposite side of the table.

'I will grant your request,' said Mathias with sudden firmness. 'But

I do so with some reluctance. I still suspect that we are all the victims of some dreadful practical joke. What you ask, Liebermann, is a kind of violation — you realise that, don't you? It is not a procedure that I undertake lightly.'

Liebermann had been forewarned of Mathias's peculiar affinity with the dead and was prompted to wonder why a man possessed of such sensitivities should choose to be a pathologist in the first place.

'Professor Mathias,' said Liebermann, 'permit me to assure you that I have given this matter the utmost consideration.'

'I hope so,' Mathias continued. 'Because if you are wrong and your psychological methods of deduction prove deficient, not only shall we all appear very foolish — yet again, I might add — but we shall also have performed an inexcusable act of violence against this poor, poor woman.'

Mathias's eyes bulged behind his thick lenses.

'Indeed,' said Liebermann. 'However, I am confident that the results of today's post-mortem examination will be in accordance with my prediction and of great value to my colleague.' He motioned towards Rheinhardt.

Mathias tilted his head a little.

'Where do you work, Liebermann?'

'In the psychiatry department of the General Hospital.'

'Under Professor Gruner?'

'Yes.'

'And what is your opinion of Professor Gruner?'

Liebermann replied with some hesitancy: 'I do not think it appropriate for me to comment on—'

'Come now — I am asking you a perfectly reasonable question!' Mathias snapped. 'What is your opinion of Professor Gruner?'

'I cannot claim any special knowledge of Professor Gruner as a man; however, as a doctor . . .'

'Yes?'

Liebermann took a deep breath: 'I disagree with his methods profoundly.'

'And why?'

'They are inhumane.'

Mathias grunted his assent.

'Precisely. The man's an idiot. Slowest student in my anatomy class — only got where he is today through nepotism and patronage!' Liebermann heard Rheinhardt releasing a little whistle of relief. 'Well, Herr Doctor,' continued Mathias, 'Perhaps you are not such a bad judge after all. Even though,' he added under his breath, 'you have decided to specialise in the most disreputable branch of medicine.'

Liebermann smiled politely and trapped his tongue between his teeth.

The old professor dragged his trolley closer to the table and began to arrange his collection of instruments. He moved a mallet a fraction of an inch to the left, but then nudged it back again. He then started lining up knives, only to give up halfway through in order to restart the operation from the very beginning. Liebermann was quick to recognise a very obvious case of obsessional neurosis.

Rheinhardt was growing impatient. Not only was he anxious for the professor to proceed but he was also finding the smell of the morgue intolerable. Fräulein Löwenstein's body was exuding fetid vapours that made his gorge rise. The air was thick with formaldehyde fumes and the stench of putrefaction. Rheinhardt took out a handkerchief and held it over his face, attracting the attention of Professor Mathias.

'Do you know,' the old man said, 'I can hardly smell a thing. I'm so used to it.' He placed a serrated blade next to a chisel and added: 'Might I suggest some cigars, gentlemen? Smoking makes the effluvium more tolerable — so I'm told.'

'Thank you, Herr Professor,' said Rheinhardt.

With quick, desperate movements the Inspector undid the top button of his jacket and pulled out a flat box of panatellas. He immediately lit a cigar and drew on it until his head almost disappeared in a cloud of pungent smoke. Rheinhardt's tense lineaments softened with pleasure as the fragrant tobacco neutralised the stench.

'Forgive me. Herr Doctor?' He offered his friend the box.

Liebermann felt that as a medical man he should be able to cope without smoking; however, he had not attended an autopsy for a long time and the rising miasma was making him feel quite sick.

'Thank you,' he said, taking the box.

Professor Mathias completed his preparatory ritual and proclaimed: 'If we do not find anything pleasant, at least we shall find something new.'

He then looked at his two companions, an expectant expression on his face.

'No? Very well, it was from *Candide*.' He then gently turned back the lower covers, revealing Fräulein Löwenstein's abdomen. Her stomach was bloated, the skin stretched taut by the gases in her gut. The sides of her back, pressed against the grey slab of the table, were marbled with streaks of maroon and violet. Mathias fussed with the canvas, ensuring that the dead woman's pudenda were properly covered.

'Herr Professor,' said Liebermann. 'Before you begin, may I see the bullet wound?' Mathias flashed a disapproving look in Liebermann's direction. 'Please,' Liebermann added hopefully.

Mathias lifted the upper sheet and dropped it again, offering Liebermann the briefest of glances.

'And you have no explanation?' Liebermann asked.

'None,' replied Mathias. The response was cool and dismissive.

The old man selected a small blade and began to make a series of incisions in Fräulein Löwenstein's abdomen. He peeled back the flesh, creating a large opening though which one could see the rounded, pink surface of the bladder. Behind it was the slightly darker mass of the uterus. Rheinhardt looked away.

'Well, well . . .' said Professor Mathias. He had become a little breathless and was wheezing slightly.

'What is it?' said Rheinhardt.

'The womb is engorged.'

Smoke from Rheinhardt's cigar rolled across Fräulein Löwenstein's body and collected inside the abdominal cavity. Mathias emitted a grunt of disapproval.

'Does that mean—'

'Patience, Inspector. How many times do I have to tell you!'

'*Festina lente?*'

'Of course. *Festina lente.*'

The old man wiped the gore from his blade, and then selected a large pair of scissors. He reached into Fräulein Löwenstein's body, made some cuts, and scooped the dead woman's bladder out of her abdomen with both hands. He deposited the limp sack into a jar of formaldehyde and paused to watch it sink. The organ descended, leaving stringy trails of brown viscosity in its wake. Mathias seemed deep in thought.

'Very interesting . . .' he said softly.

'What is?' asked Rheinhardt.

Mathias ignored the question. Instead, he briefly addressed Fräulein Löwenstein's head: 'Excuse me.' He then plunged his hands back into her body and pressed his palms against the straining balloon of her uterus.

'Yes,' he repeated. 'Very interesting indeed.'

After wiping a foul transparent residue from his fingers, Professor Mathias selected another knife and made two swift incisions. Liebermann had seen waiters in The Imperial make similar movements when preparing fruit. Mathias crouched over Fräulein Löwenstein's body and accompanied by the melodic inventions of his tired lungs, turned back the quarters of the segmented uterus with tender care.

When he had finished the operation he remained perfectly still. Neither Rheinhardt nor Liebermann could see what the old man had discovered. Mathias was bent over the corpse, his bloody hands still buried among Fräulein Löwenstein's innards.

Rheinhardt cleared his throat, hoping to attract the pathologist's attention.

There was no response.

'Herr Professor?

Mathias shook his head and whispered something inaudible.

Liebermann looked at Rheinhardt questioningly.

'Professor?' Rheinhardt repeated.

The old man took a step backwards and, gesturing towards Fräulein Löwenstein's exposed abdomen, said: 'Gentlemen . . .'

The Inspector and the doctor moved forwards.

Liebermann had considered himself beyond surprise. He was certain that Fräulein Löwenstein was pregnant and had already formed a mental image of what he was about to see.

But he was mistaken.

Suddenly all of his expectations were invalidated.

'Dear God,' said Rheinhardt.

In the raw and exposed shell of Fräulein Lowenstein's womb were two small bodies, each no bigger than a man's thumb but complete in every human detail. The tiny fingers and toes were fully formed, and the faces — with closed eyes — were a picture of serenity. A tangle of umbilical cord lay between them, like a serpent guardian. They looked snug in their rank puddle of amniotic fluid.

As the initial shock subsided, Liebermann was visited by a terrible sadness. He was moved to say a prayer, but in the absence of any religious instinct was forced to seek solace in the surrogate balm of poetry: 'Sleep is good, death is better; but of course, the best thing would be never to have been born at all.'

'Heinrich Heine,' said Professor Mathias, demonstrating again his peculiar fondness for quotations and their identification. '*Morphine*. I commend you on two counts, Herr Doctor: your powers of deduction and your choice of epitaph. We live in a wicked world. They will never be touched by evil or pain. Their innocent slumber will be eternal.'

Saying this, the professor anointed each tiny skull with the tip of his forefinger. Liebermann had never seen such a bizarre or macabre benediction.

Mathias wiped his fingers on his apron, leaving ruddy mucous trails. Looking at Rheinhardt, he added: 'Well, Inspector, it seems you are now investigating a triple murder.'

27

THE ROOM WAS quite small but was decorated like a sultan's palace. The curtains were dark blue, almost black, and embellished with a braided motif of gold. A pile of cushions decorated with silver thread and studded with tiny mirrors and pearls had tumbled off the divan and lay scattered across the floor. Three large candles, each as thick as a child's arm, burned in holders that were encrusted with gemstones: sardonyx, opal, sapphire and chrysoprase; and the air was dense with the heavy perfume of frankincense, a small heap of which was smouldering in a massive dish of polished granite.

Seated at a baize-covered card table was a substantial woman whose ample curves had been compressed between the solid arms of a large wooden throne. It possessed the primitive dignity of a medieval artefact — the high back-panel was festooned with crudely carved rosettes and serpentine creepers, among which were an odd company of raging gargoyles and winged seraphim.

Fräulein Löwenstein had been found dead in a locked room.

She had been shot through the heart — yet there was no bullet.

In the *Zeitung* they had tried to suggest that nothing strange had happened, that Braun might be responsible, that it was all an illusion — an elaborate stage trick. But what did *they* know?

Cosima von Rath cast her mind back to a strange meeting that had occurred two years earlier. She had travelled to New York with her father. At a society gathering hosted by the Decker family at which she and Ferdinand had been totally ignored by the Rothschilds (the snub still smarted), she had been introduced to a young English magus — Lord Boleskin, a handsome fellow — who had curiously ardent eyes. Boleskin was in New York trying to raise money for his own magical order, The Lamp of the Invisible Light. So persuasive was Boleskin that she had agreed to make a donation there and then, and had subsequently made several more in response to his letters. In return, Boleskin had sent her some volumes of poetry, which he had written himself under the unassuming name of Aleister Crowley. The most recent, *The Soul of Osiris*, lay on the table in front of her.

On the occasion of their first meeting Boleskin had rested a hand on Cosima von Rath's arm and leaning close — too close, perhaps — had whispered: *I know who you are. Forgive these fools.* Sweeping his hand around the room in an extravagant gesture, he had added: *They know nothing.*

Ushering her on to the balcony, from where they could see the Statue of Liberty in the distance, Boleskin had taken her into his confidence. He explained how he had been experimenting with a ritual that could make the celebrant invisible. A magus of Boleskin's stature — or someone even more skilled in the black arts — might enter a room, commit a murder, and simply wait for the locked door to be broken down, whereupon he could slip away unnoticed — right under the noses of the dim-witted investigators.

Reflecting on her hypothesis, Cosima congratulated herself, but she was troubled by its implications. Would Fräulein Löwenstein really have had the opportunity to mix in such exalted circles? She had been a talented medium, without doubt, but not someone versed in arcane law, that much was obvious. Hers had been a natural gift — raw and untutored. She had known virtually nothing of the Egyptian deities. When Cosima had mentioned Horus, Isis, and Hoor-Paar-Kraat (better known to the uninitiated as Seth), Charlotte Löwenstein had simply changed the subject, showing the unmistakable signs of embarrassment.

Cosima wriggled uncomfortably. The chair arms were pressing into the flesh that hung in loose folds around her stomach and hips. She picked up her well-worn set of tarot cards and flicked through the minor trumps, removing the four queens.

Which, she wondered, would best serve the purpose of representing Charlotte Löwenstein?

She touched each of the four suits and after some deliberation returned her stubby forefinger to the Queen of Cups, which she pushed out of the regal parade and towards a sphere of glass that rested in an ivory cradle on the card table.

Of course, there was still another possibility. Fraülein Löwenstein might have meddled with powers that she was ultimately unable to control. Lord Boleskin had spoken of 'The Operation of Abramelin' and other such rites: calling forth the four Great Princes of the world's evil — and their eight sub-princes . . . Charlotte Löwenstein's uncomplicated personality may have been a ruse, an expedient disguise, concealing a proud heart and more ambition than Cosima had at first suspected. If the silly girl had attempted to bargain with forces that she did not understand they would have exacted a terrible and unspeakable revenge.

Cosima stroked the diamond-encrusted ankh that hung from her neck, and stared into the crystal ball. An inverted world hung in its watery bubble, supporting no life except a deformed homunculus with bulging eyes. Cosima had sat like this for many hours, on many occasions, staring at her own distorted reflection, and not once had the ball become milky, not once had its interior clouded with prescient visions.

'Mistress . . . mistress.'

A tremulous voice was calling from the other side of the door.

Oh, that idiotic child.

'What is it, Friederike? I told you never to disturb me when I'm in here.'

The voice continued.

'Mistress. Herr Bruckmüller is here to see you.'

'Oh,' said Cosima, the tone of her voice changing from irritation to mild surprise.

'Shall I tell him to go away?'

'No,' Cosima shouted out. 'No, of course not, you foolish child. Bring him up at once.'

The maid scurried down the stairs and Cosima returned to her musings.

The police were ill-equipped to undertake such an investigation. They had equated Braun's absence with guilt. But what if he had been party to Fräulein Löwenstein's quest for power? The dark forces that had engineered the medium's extraordinary demise would be perfectly capable of spiriting away a young artist.

The rumble of Bruckmüller's basso profundo could be heard long before his heavy tread on the stairs. Why he bothered to make small talk with the servants was beyond Cosima's comprehension.

There was a soft knock on the door.

'Come in.'

The door opened and Friederike announced: 'Herr Bruckmüller.'

'Thank you, Friederike. That will be all.'

The big man smiled and advanced towards the wooden throne.

'My darling Cosima,' he bellowed. 'You look radiant.'

Cosima was at once delighted with — and embarrassed by — the compliment. She extended a chubby hand and allowed Bruckmüller to plant his lips on her dimpled knuckles. His bristly moustache was surprisingly sharp.

'Hans, my dear. Did you see the *Zeitung*?'

'I did. Extraordinary! Quite extraordinary!'

'She was visited by a higher power.'

'You think so?'

'Of course. The silly girl was playing with fire . . . dabbling in arts which she did not have the knowledge to practise safely.'

Bruckmüller sat on the divan and shook his head.

'It must have been terrible.'

'Indeed. It is difficult to imagine what perturbations of the soul she suffered that night. I shudder at the thought.'

Bruckmüller's expression suddenly changed: 'However . . .'

'What?' said Cosima.

'There is the matter of Braun. Where is he? Why has he absconded?'

'*Has* he absconded? That is what the police imply. But there could be another explanation. He might have been *removed*.'

'What? You mean by the same higher power?'

'I fear that the police will never have an opportunity to interview him.'

'But why?' asked Bruckmüller, his voice booming. 'Why Braun?'

'That is a question which I mean to answer,' Cosima replied, clutching her ankh and affecting an expression intended to be both alluring and mysterious. 'Very, very soon.'

28

LIEBERMANN PLACED HIS pen on the desk and applied a large square of blotting paper to his notebook. When he was satisfied that the ink was dry he reviewed his case summaries and placed the notebook back in the drawer. As he did so, there was a knock on the door. It was Kanner.

'Hello, Max. Can you spare a minute?'

'A minute — but not much longer. Mahler's conducting a Beethoven and Wagner programme at the Philharmonic. It starts at seven.'

'I won't keep you long,' said Kanner, taking a seat. 'Have you seen Miss Lydgate today?'

'No.'

'Max, she's had another one of those . . .' He paused for a moment before continuing: 'Fits.'

'Oh,' said Liebermann, his face creasing with concern.

'It was just like the previous fit,' continued Kanner. 'Apparently, Miss Lydgate had been well for much of the day — chatting to the nurses and reading. I was doing a round and went to say hello — and . . .' Kanner smiled apologetically and shrugged. 'I seemed to set her off again. As soon as I appeared she started to cough, and within seconds she was screaming at me . . . I just don't understand it.'

'Did her right hand—'

'Oh yes,' said Kanner, nodding vigorously. 'She threw a punch but, being better prepared this time, I managed to get out of the way. She was restrained by the porters until she calmed down.'

'Did she say anything else?'

'I don't know — I thought it best to leave. I didn't want to make the situation any worse. I understand that she fell asleep again and woke up two hours later with no recollection of what had transpired. I'm sorry, Max, I didn't mean to—'

'Please,' said Liebermann, raising a hand to silence his friend. 'It isn't your fault, Stefan.'

'Probably not, but I still feel responsible.'

Liebermann picked up his pen and slipped it into his jacket pocket.

'Oh, and there's another thing,' added Kanner. 'On Friday afternoon, Miss Lydgate was sitting with Katia Dill — you know, the young girl from Baden? Anyway, as they were talking, Katia showed Miss Lydgate her embroidery. A few seconds later Miss Lydgate became extremely agitated.'

'In what way?'

'Distracted — unable to concentrate. She might even have suffered an absence. Apparently she started mumbling something or other in English. I don't know what exactly, I wasn't there. I heard this from Sabina.'

Liebermann looked puzzled.

'Nurse Rupius,' continued Kanner. 'You know, the pretty one with the big brown eyes. Surely you must have—'

'Stefan!'

'Sorry, Max.' Kanner tried to recover some of his professional credibility before continuing. 'Perhaps you should have a word with Nurse Rupius — before you see Miss Lydgate next.'

'Yes, I'll do that.'

Liebermann looked at his wristwatch and stood up.

'I've really got to go, Stefan — and thank you.'

'Not at all.'

Liebermann opened the door to let Kanner out.

'Max?' Kanner looked uncomfortable.

'Yes.'

'Miss Lydgate is supposed to be receiving a course of electrotherapy.'

'Yes, I know.'

'What are you going to say to Professor Gruner when he demands an explanation?'

Liebermann sighed: 'I haven't really thought about it.'

'In which case,' said Kanner, resting a solicitous hand on Liebermann's shoulder, 'I think you'd better start.'

29

Everything in the concert hall seemed to have been cast from gold: the baroque ceiling, the carved friezes, and the elegant, gilded caryatids — the housing for the pipe organ — its tympanum and entablature. The effect was dazzling. A blaze of bullion.

Above the audience, massive crystal chandeliers sparkled with a restless light, and each starburst was answered by waves of coruscation below. Amid the sea of faces in the stalls an abundance of diamond brooches flashed and shimmered. The Grosser Saal was like an Aladdin's cave — scintillating with the tokens of bourgeois prosperity.

'Ah, there you are.'

Liebermann turned to see Rheinhardt negotiating — with some difficulty — the narrow aisle. 'What a rush,' he grumbled. 'I barely had time to change.' He slumped down in the seat beside Liebermann, caught his breath and, puffing a little, said, 'I've been completing my report on the second autopsy.'

Liebermann peered over the balcony.

'I was very lucky to get these seats, you know, particularly at such late notice. As far as I'm concerned, when Mahler's conducting it's not worth sitting anywhere else. You have to see his face — such humanity.'

Ignoring Liebermann's unconventional and somewhat inappropriate welcome, Rheinhardt lowered his voice and leaned closer to his friend: 'You know, I had to record that the second autopsy was initiated after seeking medical advice — that is, *your* advice. However, you still haven't told me how you did it. How did you work it out?'

A group of violinists and a few members of the woodwind section emerged from the wings and wandered onto the stage.

'Oh, it really wasn't that difficult, Oskar,' said Liebermann, seemingly more interested in the musicians. 'Rosa Sucher had described changes in Fräulein Löwenstein's eating habits. Fräulein Löwenstein was also drinking less coffee and had started taking peppermint tea. Now, surely, as a father of two, you must appreciate the significance of these facts.'

Rheinhardt scratched his head.

'Cravings? Yes. When Else was carrying Mitzi I had to get up at the crack of dawn to get strawberries from the Naschmarkt. She wouldn't eat anything else for weeks! But I'm afraid the significance of the coffee and peppermint tea escapes me entirely.'

Liebermann continued to monitor the arrival of the orchestra.

'Most women find coffee less palatable in the early stages of pregnancy.'

'Do they? I can't remember Else—'

'Would you have noticed?'

'Perhaps not.'

'And as for peppermint tea — it's an old cure for morning sickness. Quite effective, too.'

Rheinhardt grunted approvingly.

'Once this information was in my possession,' continued Liebermann, 'I wondered whether Natalie Heck, being a seamstress, and therefore perhaps more observant of Fräulein Löwenstein's wardrobe, might have noticed any changes in Charlotte Löwenstein's dress. Had she, for example, purchased any new and more generously proportioned garments? Clearly, Fräulein Heck exceeded all expectations when she confessed to having altered Fräulein Löwenstein's blue silk dress herself. Subsequently, I was minded to review my earlier interpretation of that tantalising error in Fräulein Löwenstein's death-note. The meaning of *He will take us to Hell* became wholly transparent.'

'This also explains something else,' said Rheinhardt. 'Something I thought inconsequential at the first autopsy. Fräulein Löwenstein was not wearing a corset.'

'Indeed, to do so would have involved considerable discomfort.'

Representatives from each section of the orchestra had now made their way onto the stage, and the horn players had begun to warm their instruments with a few muted scales.

'Well,' said Rheinhardt, 'once again, I am indebted to you, Herr Doctor.'

'That remains to be seen,' said Liebermann. 'Fräulein Löwenstein's pregnancy certainly introduces a new element into our mystery. But as to its significance, who can say?'

'True. But we've made some progress. And I have a hunch that Fräulein Löwenstein's pregnancy will play some part in the unravelling of a motive for her murder.'

'Possibly,' said Liebermann. But before he could elaborate, he was distracted by a group of finely dressed men who were processing in a halting fashion up the furthest aisle of the stalls. Several were dressed in a kind of uniform — green tailcoat, black velvet cuffs, and yellow buttons. Their slow advance created a swell of agitation in the audience: the familiar impassive drone became an excited susurration. Heads turned, and some people even pointed. Every few rows, a distinguished Viennese burgher or lady would rise to greet the company.

'Oskar?' Liebermann nodded towards the back of the Grosser Saal. 'What's going on down there? Do you recognise any of those men?'

Rheinhardt rested his hands on the balcony and shifted forward.

At the centre of the group a well-groomed gentleman wearing a dark grey suit was kissing the hand of an aristocratic-looking dowager.

'Good heavens — it's the Mayor.'

'What's he doing here?' exclaimed Liebermann. 'Damned hypocrite.'

A few years earlier the Mayor had affronted Mahler by inviting a different conductor to perform at a special Philharmonic charity concert. Knowing the Mayor's politics, Liebermann realised that his motive had been quite clear. The Mayor's supporters in the anti-Semitic Reform Union would have been delighted. The orchestra's members, however, had been furious and had complained bitterly.

'Not so loud, Max.'

Liebermann snorted and folded his arms.

'And ...' Rheinhardt's eyes narrowed. 'I don't believe it — there's Bruckmüller.'

'Who?'

'Hans Bruckmüller — remember? He attended Fräulein Löwenstein's meetings. You see that man there?' Rheinhardt pointed discreetly. 'The big chap — with the red carnation in his buttonhole.'

'Ah yes.'

'I didn't know he was one of Lueger's cronies ...'

'Well, you do now.'

As soon as the orchestra was assembled, the first violin made a brisk entry — accompanied by much appreciative clapping. He sat down, played an 'A' for his colleagues, and a chaos of different pitches gradually coalesced and unified around his lead. Lueger and his companions were still ambling up the aisle when Gustav Mahler appeared.

The audience unleashed a storm of applause.

Mahler leaped on to the podium and made a low bow. Liebermann thought that he saw the conductor's neutral expression shadow with irritation when he caught sight of Lueger's party — who had disturbed a row of settled patrons in order to get to their centrally placed seats.

The applause gradually subsided and the house lights dimmed. Mahler turned on his heels and faced the orchestra. He did not need to consult a score because he had memorised the entire programme. Raising his baton, he paused for a moment before lunging forward, liberating the majesty of Beethoven's genius.

Slender, nervous, and agile, the conductor clutched at the cellos and basses with his right hand. Drawing out a crescendo, his clenched fist rose up and shook at the sky — like a challenge to the gods. Here was the leaping, thrashing, strangling and jerking routinely vilified by critics who abhorred the director's flamboyant style. Here were all the 'ugly excesses' that had been ridiculed by cartoonists and commentators — 'St Vitus' Dance', 'delirium tremens', 'demonic possession'. All true. Yet the Philharmonic had never sounded more powerful, or a Beethoven overture more vital. The music burst out, virile with rage and passion.

Liebermann closed his eyes and plunged into a sound-world of turmoil, torment — and incommunicable bliss.

30

THE LIVER PÂTÉ WAS studded with truffles and presented on a tray of ice crystals. Round loaves of brown bread were arranged in a rustic basket, and the pheasant — glazed with honey and fragrant with mixed herbs — sat in a large white dish, accompanied by green and yellow vegetables.

'You remember Cosima von Rath?'

Juno Hölderlin squinted at her husband.

How could I forget her, he thought.

'Herr Bruckmüller's fiancée', Juno continued. 'She came to some of Fräulein Löwenstein's meetings.'

'Yes,' said Hölderlin. 'A very striking woman, as I recall.'

Hölderlin untied his serviette, flapped it in the air, and placed it carefully on his lap.

'She telephoned today.'

'Really? What did she want?'

'She's arranging a circle.'

'My dear, another one?' Hölderlin's expression indicated extreme discomfort. 'Hasn't your appetite for the supernatural been tempered by recent events?'

'She wasn't suggesting we form a new circle to replace Fräulein Löwenstein's. No, Heinrich. She was suggesting an investigative sitting . . . a seance, the purpose of which would be to find out what really happened *that* night.'

'She means to contact Fräulein Löwenstein?'

Juno Hölderlin sliced the pâté and scraped a moist wedge onto the side of her plate.

'I imagine so. She also wishes to discover the whereabouts of Herr Braun.'

Juno's rate of blinking accelerated, until finally she squeezed her eyelids together in an effort to rid herself of the tic.

'Who else has she invited?'

'Herr Uberhorst, Fräulein Heck — all of them.'

'And they've agreed to attend?'

'As far as I know. Although Fräulein von Rath had still not been able to contact Count Záborszky when we spoke.'

'Do you . . . do you want to go?'

Juno looked down at her plate and was momentarily distracted by the beauty of the blue and gold surround. The china had been a wedding gift from Sielglinde.

'If it will help — then of course.'

Hölderlin sipped his wine.

'Very well,' he said. 'We shall go.'

31

'It wasn't a particularly warm day — quite cold, in fact — but Herr Schelling insisted that we should go. I asked Frau Schelling if she wanted her coat; however, she said that wouldn't be necessary — she wouldn't be joining us.'

Miss Lydgate's eyes shifted rapidly beneath closed lids and her words slurred under the influence of hypnotic sleep.

'Something passed between them,' she continued. 'Herr Schelling and Frau Schelling: a look, an odd look. Then Frau Schelling said: *I must go now — enjoy the woods, Miss Lydgate. They are very beautiful at this time of year.* And then she left the room. Very quickly, as though . . . as though she was running away.'

'From what?' asked Liebermann.

'I don't know.' Miss Lydgate coughed. 'The carriage took us through the city and out past Unterdöbling and Oberdöbling. Herr Schelling told me that Beethoven had once lived there — it was where he had written his third symphony. Beethoven had originally dedicated the work to Napoleon, but on receiving news that the First Consul had crowned himself Emperor the great composer became enraged and tore up the dedication. I knew this story already as my father had told me something very similar, but I thought it rude to interrupt. Herr Schelling asked me if I enjoyed music. I said that I did, but confessed to not being very knowledgeable. Herr Schelling then said that I must permit him to take me to a concert. I thanked him, feeling that I did not deserve such kindness. He said that it was his pleasure, and placed a hand on my arm . . .' Miss Lydgate's head rocked from side to side in its nest of flaming hair.

In the distance a church bell started to toll, slow and funereal.

'Herr Schelling did not remove his hand and moved a little closer. I didn't know what to do. It seemed improper. Yet Herr Schelling was not a stranger. He was a relative — my mother's cousin. Perhaps it was permissible for him to rest his hand on my arm. So I did nothing . . . and I fear . . . I fear I was mistaken. I fear that I may have been responsible for a misunderstanding.'

Liebermann studied his supine patient. She looked relatively calm. After a long pause, she spontaneously resumed her narrative.

'Even though the day was somewhat overcast, the woods were no less beautiful. I was fascinated by the flora — but Herr Schelling urged me not to stray from the path. *There are still bears in this wood*, he said. But I did not believe him. He was smiling, and showing no concern for his own safety. We climbed up a narrow, steep incline until we reached a viewing point. There we paused to admire the vista. Herr Schelling pointed out some villages on the lower slopes, and a vineyard. He was standing directly behind me. He traced an arc in the air with his forefinger — up and over the mountains. *They're the Alps*, he said. I took a step forward — and he followed. I could feel his body pressing up against me — and then — and then . . .'

Miss Lydgate's chest heaved and her breathing accelerated. Yet she continued to tell her story calmly and slowly.

'I felt his lips. They touched the back of my neck. I shivered with disgust and turned around. He was looking at me with a strange, fiery look in his eyes. He grabbed my arms and pulled me towards him. I thought he had gone mad. He said my name — twice — and buried his face in my shoulder. Again I felt his lips — moistness on the side of my neck. I wrested myself free of his embrace and took a few steps backwards. I was close to the edge of a precipice. The drop was sudden and for one terrible moment I thought Herr Schelling meant to push me over. But the fire in his eyes suddenly went out. He straightened his necktie and combed his hair back with his hands. He assumed a solicitous expression, *Whatever is the matter?* he said. I was angry and confused. *Herr Schelling, you must not do that again*, I said. *Do what again?* he replied. Such was his apparent sincerity that I began to question the evidence of my own senses. Had I misinterpreted his behaviour? He extended his hand. *Come, Amelia*, he said, *let us walk back to the carriage.* I didn't take his hand. Herr Schelling raised his eyebrows, and said, *Very well, if you feel that you can manage the downward path without my assistance.* He let his hand fall and he turned, at once setting off down the path. I paused for a moment and was not sure what to do. In the absence of any alternative, I reluctantly followed. We completed most of the return journey in silence. Occasionally he would urge me to watch my step where he thought the path might be dangerous — it was uneven in places and pitted with potholes. On the way down we passed some walkers coming up in the opposite direction. They greeted us, and Herr Schelling bid them a hearty good afternoon. It was all so . . . ordinary. I whispered good day, and straggled along behind Herr Schelling. I felt . . . I felt like a child in disgrace. As we descended, it seemed to me less and less likely that Herr Schelling had actually behaved improperly, and more and more likely that I had — I don't know.'

'More and more likely that you had what?' asked Liebermann.

'Overreacted. Behaved . . .' She paused before adding, 'Hysterically.'

Amelia Lydgate's body remained completely still, although her breathing was still slightly agitated.

'We managed a stilted conversation in the carriage back to Rennweg. But it felt deeply uncomfortable. We were greeted by Frau Schelling, who claimed that the walk had brought colour to my cheeks. I mumbled a polite answer, but said that I was in fact feeling unwell. *The air*, replied Frau Schelling. *Perhaps it was too damp. You may have caught a chill.* I ran upstairs to my room and sat at my dressing table. I looked at myself in the mirror and noticed that I was trembling. A few minutes later there was a knock on the door. It was Frau Schelling. She asked me if I wanted some tea. I said that I didn't want any. I said that I needed to rest for a while and that I was already feeling a little better. *Very well*, she said, and left me alone.

'Over the next few weeks, as I went about my daily business, I frequently discovered myself the object of Herr Schelling's unwelcome attention. I would catch him looking at me in *that* way. One evening, I was sitting with the Schellings in the sitting room, reading my book. Frau Schelling excused herself, and I became conscious of an oppressive atmosphere. It was as though the room had filled with a cloying, heavy scent — like that of some overripe fruit.' Miss Lydgate's shoulders shook as she coughed. 'I looked up to see Herr Schelling smiling at me. It was an extremely disagreeable smile. I felt like . . . I felt . . . it is difficult to express.' Suddenly, articulating her words with greater certainty, she said: 'I felt exposed.

'Herr Schelling made some trivial remarks, and then came and sat next to me on the settee. He sat very close. His leg was pressed against mine. I tried to move away, but I was trapped between Herr Schelling and the arm of the chair. He took my hand — I tried to pull it away but he squeezed it more tightly. *Amelia*, he said, *you know I am very fond of you.* Again, I didn't know what to do. I simply stared at him — aghast. His face came towards me and I got up. Twisting my hand from his grip, I rushed to the door. *Amelia?* he called. *Are you all right?* I opened the door and shut it firmly behind me. Looking up, I noticed that Frau Schelling was on the landing. I formed the impression that she had just been standing there since excusing herself. She looked down at me, saying nothing. I cannot describe the look in her eyes. But she seemed (is this possible?) triumphant. Eventually, she spoke: I am retiring for the evening. Good night, my dear. Then she turned and stepped into the shadows.

'I became very unhappy, even frightened. So much so that I contemplated returning to England — but then I baulked at the thought of what this would ultimately entail. What could I say to my parents? My mother had spoken so warmly of the Schellings. Indeed, she had corresponded with Herr Schelling since they were both children. He was a kind, generous man . . . I knew, I suppose, in my heart, that he had behaved improperly, but I still felt that I might be — in some way — mistaken. I still felt that if I accused him, or spoke to Frau Schelling, or to anyone, I would find myself looking foolish. It was unbelievable, that a man like Herr Schelling would find someone like me . . . would desire . . .' Her sentences fragmented and were finally smothered by a deep, melancholy sigh.

'Miss Lydgate,' said Liebermann, very softly. 'Can you remember the next time that Herr Schelling behaved improperly?'

The young woman's eyes trembled beneath their lids again and her head moved — ever so slightly — up and down: 'I had gone to bed quite early — where I read a little and completed some needlepoint. A design of my own, based on an illustration I had discovered in Rumphius's *Herbarium Amboinense*.' Liebermann assumed that the volume in question was some venerable work of botanical scholarship. 'I tried to get to sleep,' Miss Lydgate continued, 'but without success. A storm had started. The rain was incessant and the thunder very loud. So, I lay awake — thinking. It must have been in the early hours of the morning when I heard the sound of a cab stopping outside. It was Herr Schelling returning from a late sitting at the Reichsrat. Well, at least, that's where he'd said, during dinner, he was going.' As she said these words, Amelia Lydgate's brow tensed, as though merely questioning her employer's honesty was the cause of considerable discomfort.

'I heard him stumble in the hallway. Then there was some cursing. Then he started to climb the stairs: slow, heavy footsteps. I was expecting him to stop on the landing below but he continued his ascent. I felt sick, and was overcome with a terrible sense of foreboding. I could hear him approaching my room. As he came nearer, I was aware that he was trying to tread with greater care, but the floorboards were old and they creaked. There was a knock on the door. I did not answer. Then I heard the sound of the handle turning. I had, of course, locked the door. I had deposited the key safely in the lower drawer of my bedside cabinet. Herr Schelling persisted, turning the handle and then shaking it quite loudly. He called out my name. *Amelia, Amelia.* My heart was thumping in my ears and chest — I gripped the bed sheets and hoped that Frau Schelling would wake. *Amelia, Amelia. Let me in. I need to tell you something.* I wanted to shout out, *Go away, go away. Please leave me alone,* but I couldn't. The words caught in my throat. Instead, I just lay there in the darkness, consumed with terror. After some time — possibly only minutes, but it seemed like an eternity — Herr Schelling abandoned his efforts to gain entry into my room, and I heard him walk away. However, he did not go downstairs as I had assumed he would. He went up to the third floor.

'There was no point in trying to sleep — I was too distressed. I sat up, and stared at the window. The curtains were not fully drawn, and I was able to calm my mind by counting the seconds between lightning flashes. Eventually my nervous agitation subsided, and I was able to consider my predicament with greater self-possession. After much deliberation, I concluded that my position in the Schelling household was untenable. I decided that I would leave Vienna at the earliest opportunity.'

The trance state had rendered Amelia Lydgate's expression largely impassive — yet occasionally the ghost of an emotion would surface before evaporating. Now her features became troubled by a more tenacious melancholy.

'This realisation — that I must leave Vienna — filled me with a terrible sadness that was more like despair. I would have to relinquish all my dreams — of working with Doctor Landsteiner, of acquiring sufficient knowledge to edit my grandfather's journals. All my plans, all my aspirations would come to nothing. I wept bitterly. Although I was wholly absorbed in my own misery, the shock of hearing Herr Schelling descending the stairs again brought me quickly to my senses. He came directly to my room. There was no knocking, no calling. I heard the sound of a key in the lock and the bolt turning. The door quickly opened and closed — and he was in.

'I was stunned. I could barely believe what had happened. Yet I had to believe it for I could hear his breathing — a horrible, ragged sound. There was a flash of lightning, and the impression of his presence was confirmed. I saw him standing close, like some terrible visitation in a nightmare. The mattress tilted as he crawled onto the bed. *Amelia*, he whispered. *Amelia*. I was paralysed, unable to move. I felt the weight of his body on mine, and his lips on my face. His moustache was rough and scratched my cheeks. Then his lips pressed up against mine. I could not breathe . . . I could not breathe . . . I was choking, and started to—'

Miss Lydgate's chest heaved. She raised her left arm. It was a sluggish, lymphatic movement, like that of weeds caught in a languid stream. She stifled a cough — and tried to continue.

'It was . . .' She coughed again. 'It was . . .'

Suddenly her eyes flicked open — like those of a doll. They were unnaturally wide and staring. Her pewter irises moved from left to right, examining the ceiling, before dipping to examine what lay beyond her toes. Then, with unexpected fluidity, Amelia Lydgate slid her legs off the side of the bed and sat up — supporting herself with both arms. Liebermann noticed that the fingers of her right hand were gripping the bedstead as tightly as were those of her left. The hospital gown had slipped from her shoulder, revealing an area of pale flesh and the nascent curve of a small breast. There was something wholly different about her attitude — something casual, almost slovenly in her appearance. A curtain of hair fell across her face. She made no effort to brush it away. Yet Liebermann could still see Miss Lydgate's eyes, glowing behind the russet strands with a dull metallic light. She was staring at him — a fixed, forensic stare.

Liebermann had not instructed her to wake, and even if he had it was customary for hypnotic subjects simply to open their eyes and remain still. Amelia Lydgate had acted spontaneously, opening her eyes and sitting up in the absence of a command. Liebermann wasn't altogether sure what was happening. Before he could make a decision, she spoke: 'Who are you?'

Her voice was less hesitant than usual. Moreover, she had asked the question in English.

'I am your doctor,' he replied — in German.

Liebermann could see that she didn't understand him.

'I said — who are you?' She articulated each syllable with deliberate emphasis, as though talking to a stupid child.

Liebermann edged his seat back and responded again, this time in English.

'My name is Doctor Liebermann. Who are you?'

'Me?' Amelia Lydgate looked down at her feet and swung them backwards and forwards. Then, looking up, she brushed the hair from her face with her right hand, revealing a manic grin. 'My name is Katherine.'

32

THE OPEN-AIR CONCERT platform was situated near the Prohaska restaurant. Karl Uberhorst was seated a few rows from the front, enjoying a programme of popular pieces performed by the Ladies' String Orchestra of Vienna — a small ensemble of only nine players. Uberhorst was not a great music lover. He recognised the famous works by Strauss and Lanner but little else. He was not there for the music but for the leader of the orchestra, Fräulein Zöchling.

She was not as attractive as Fräulein Löwenstein, but nevertheless, there was something about her that Uberhorst found beguiling: her proud, almost defiant posturing — the way her torso swung backwards and forwards as she bounced the bow on the violin strings.

He had chanced upon the Ladies' String Orchestra while walking in the Prater a few days earlier and had felt compelled to return. It was like being granted a preview of heaven. The women, in high necked white dresses and gold sashes, looked like angels. At one point, Fräulein Zöchling had glanced directly into his eyes. The intensity of her gaze had been too much, and he had looked away — confused and ashamed.

The orchestra came to the end of *Fruhlingsstimmen* and the air crackled with applause. Fräulein Zöchling bowed and encouraged her colleagues to stand. Uberhorst noticed that all of the women wore their hair up, tied back with an identical yellow bow.

Their beauty tormented him — as *hers* had.

Why had Fräulein Löwenstein chosen to trust him with her secret?

Why not any of the others?

It was his duty to protect her honour — but at the same time, the information in his possession might be of considerable interest to the police. In addition, being truthful with them might free him from suspicion. Yet even contemplating this course of action felt like a terrible betrayal. Perhaps he would discover what to do at the seance? On the other hand, perhaps he should continue to experiment with the locks . . .

Fräulein Zöchling's orchestra sat down again as the applause gradually died away. Immediately, Fräulein Zöchling herself raised her violin, glanced at her fellow musicians and launched into a hectic polka.

Uberhorst found that he could no longer enjoy the concert. His lungs laboured to fill his ribcage and a patina of sweat coated his forehead. He felt dizzy with anxiety.

'Excuse me,' he whispered.

Fortunately he was only three seats from the end of the row and was able to leave without causing any disruption. He rushed away, gasping for air in the lilac-scented breeze.

When he was away from the crowds he stopped and looked back. The heavenly orchestra was still playing beneath the proscenium arch and, beyond, the Riesenrad was a black silhouette against the white sky.

33

THE FACTORY YARD was an expanse of damp gravel, strewn with empty crates and abandoned pushcarts. Above Haussmann and Rheinhardt's heads, the moribund sky, a canopy of charcoal and pepper clouds, was made even more oppressive by a plume of black smoke streaming from a tall chimney. The factory itself was long, low, and built of dirty yellow bricks. A single line of small, blind windows perforated an otherwise featureless block; however, at the nearest end of the building, two large wooden doors had been left open. Through them came the relentless clang and clatter of heavy machinery.

'There he is,' said Haussmann.

Leaning up against the wall and smoking a cigarette was a scrawny man in overalls. He was talking to two similarly dressed companions who — on seeing the two policemen — hurried into the building.

'How did we find him?' asked Rheinhardt.

'Through Tibor Király.'

'Who?'

'One of those magicians we consulted at the Volksprater.'

'The Great Magnifico?'

'No — that was Adolphus Farber. Király was Chan the Inscrutable.'

The scrawny man threw his cigarette on to the ground and stubbed it out with his boot. Then he wiped his hands on his overalls and stood up straight. There was something unexpected about his attitude — the way he pushed out his chest and straightened his back. Rheinhardt thought he looked rather haughty. This impression only strengthened as they drew closer.

'Good morning, Herr Roche,' said Haussmann.

'Good morning, my dear fellow,' said the man in a dry, refined accent.

'Detective Inspector Rheinhardt,' said Haussmann, gesturing deferentially towards his chief.

Rheinhardt bowed.

'Thank you so much for helping us, Herr Roche.'

Roche wiped his hands on his overalls again before giving them a cursory inspection.

'I am afraid that we shall have to forgo the usual courtesies,' said Roche, displaying his grubby palms.

'Is there perhaps somewhere we could sit, Herr Roche? It's rather loud here,' said Rheinhardt.

'It's a lot worse inside. I would recommend that we use some of those boxes over there.' Roche pointed across the yard. 'Not very comfortable, but they will serve our purpose.'

The three men walked over to a collection of crates by the main entrance, where they improvised some seating. Rheinhardt noticed that the ground was littered with spent rifle shells.

Before Rheinhardt could ask his first question, Roche said: 'You know, she had it coming to her. She deserved to die.'

Rheinhardt looked into Roche's eyes, and was shocked to see his crows-feet wrinkling with pleasure. Ignoring the man's curious opening gambit, Rheinhardt said, 'Herr Roche, could you explain how you came to know Fräulein Löwenstein?'

'She was my assistant,' replied Roche. Then, recognising that Rheinhardt was waiting for him to elaborate, he added: 'I didn't always work in that hell-hole, you know.' He thumbed over his shoulder in the direction of the factory. 'I used to be in the theatre. The Blue Danube — do you remember it?'

Rheinhardt shook his head.

'Small place on Dampfschiffstrasse?' Roche persisted hopefully.

'I'm sorry,' said Rheinhardt, shaking his head again.

'Well, I used to manage it,' Roche sighed. 'And I'd still be managing it today, if it wasn't for . . .' He paused for a moment before adding, '*That* woman' — each syllable was costive and contemptuous. 'Of course, she was never an official employee — there was no contract. Nevertheless, she performed all of the duties expected of an assistant manager.'

'Why wasn't her appointment official?'

'Unfortunately,' said Roche, 'I permitted her to become involved without notifying the proprietor.'

'Any reason?'

Roche took a small tin from his overalls and opened the lid. Inside, were three thinly rolled cigarettes. He half-heartedly offered them to Rheinhardt and Haussmann, but showed palpable signs of relief when they refused.

'Please, allow me.' Rheinhardt struck a match and lit Roche's cigarette.

'The proprietor would have objected,' said Roche. 'She had no experience of management — she was an actress.'

'Then why did you appoint her?'

'We were lovers,' said Roche, 'and I trusted her.' He drew on his cigarette and blew twin streams of smoke from his nostrils. 'In retrospect, I was foolish. But I really thought she could be trusted.'

'How did you meet?'

'She was with a provincial touring company — not a very good one, I might add — who had decided to try their luck in the capital. As you can imagine, the reviews were terrible, although Schnabel said some complimentary things about *her* in particular. Something like: *What she lacks in talent is amply compensated for by her stage presence and her beauty.* I forget exactly what now, but something to that effect. After the terrible reviews there was a lot of bad feeling — accusations and counter-accusations. The upshot of which was that the company finished their execrable run at The Danube and then immediately disbanded. She — Charlotte — came crying to my door and . . . Well, you know how it is, Inspector, you're a man of the world — things happen.'

Rheinhardt nodded sagely.

'She said that she didn't want my charity,' continued Roche. 'She was very insistent — said that she would rather leave Vienna than be a burden to me. So I gave her a few jobs — here and there — and it must have built up. She did more and more, and I suppose I got used to doing less and less. Then, one morning, she vanished. Just like that.' Roche clicked his fingers. 'All of her things were still in the apartment, but she was gone. When I got to my office, I discovered that the safe had been emptied. Worse still, it turned out that the accounts were completely inaccurate. The record of our box-office takings meant nothing. As you can imagine, the proprietor was not amused. I was blamed for everything.'

'Had you given her the combination of the safe?'

'No, but I'd opened it in her presence on many occasions. She was obviously far more observant than I'd thought.'

'Did you try to find her?'

'Yes, of course — but it was too late. She'd already left Vienna.'

'On her own?'

'No, I don't think so. Later I discovered that she'd been having an affair with a stage magician — right under my nose. Braun, I think his name was. He'd taken part in a few of The Danube's summer shows (never popular, everyone having gone off, of course). I imagine that they must have run away together.'

A few spots of rain speckled Roche's overalls and he looked up at the grim sky.

'You had no idea that Fräulein Löwenstein had returned to Vienna?' asked Rheinhardt.

Roche shook his head.

'No idea at all. Had I known, Inspector, you would undoubtedly have had the pleasure of charging me with her murder.'

34

Liebermann's mind raced as he tried to make sense of the curious transformation he had just observed. Miss Amelia Lydgate — in the person of Katherine — was still staring at him. She did not seem to present any immediate physical threat, but he knew well enough that the emergence of a secondary personality was a rare and unpredictable phenomenon: an occurrence that merited caution and a healthy respect for the complexities of human mental life.

Liebermann and 'Katherine' retained their respective positions for some time. The silence curdled, thickening slowly with disturbing possibilities. Still floundering a little, Liebermann began to rehearse some English in his head. The task steadied his nerves, providing him with a necessary focus.

'Where is Amelia?' he asked.

'She's asleep.' Even the timbre of Miss Lydgate's voice was strangely altered. She seemed to be speaking in a slightly higher register.

'Does she know that you are here?'

'No — she's asleep.'

It occurred to Liebermann that Amelia Lydgate's secondary personality might be that of a child.

'How old are you ?' he asked.

'Not as old as Amelia.'

'Yes — but how old are you?'

Katherine lifted her chin and said in a voice that was presumably supposed to create an impression of superiority: 'Doctor Liebermann, were you never told that it is impolite to ask a woman her age?' So saying, she pushed herself off the bed and landed squarely on the floor, her bare feet slapping against the tiles. Then she straightened her gown, pressing her palms against her waist and sliding them down over her hips. This stretched the cotton, emphasising the curves of her body. Though the movement might have been meant to be seductive, Liebermann recognised that there was still something very childish about the young woman's posturing. It reminded him of the half-innocent, half-knowing behaviour of girls on the cusp of pubescence: a natural, almost unconscious flirtation.

She took a step forward. Then, holding her gown at the hip, she raised it a little and stood on her toes. It was a curious, balletic movement — presumably meant to be some kind of parody of elegance.

'Do you think me pretty, Doctor Liebermann?'

Liebermann coughed uncomfortably, which reminded him that since Katherine's arrival, Miss Lydgate — or at least her dormant personality — had not coughed once.

Katherine tilted her head, clearly expecting an answer.

Liebermann swallowed before delivering his careful judgement: 'Yes.'

Satisfied but unsmiling, Katherine looked towards the door.

'Where is your friend?'

'I beg your pardon?'

'Yellow hair, blue eyes — and . . .'

'I think you mean Doctor Kanner.'

Katherine did not respond. Instead, she walked towards the sink where — on catching sight of herself in the mirror — she paused to arrange her hair. Piling it up with both hands, she turned her head this way and that to study the effect from several different angles. Dis-satisfied, she frowned and let it tumble down again, a cascade of burnished copper.

'I don't like him,' she said bluntly.

'Why not?'

'You are very inquisitive, Doctor Liebermann.'

Trailing her hand around the porcelain bowl, Katherine moved towards the table.

'What is this?'

'A battery.'

Katherine released the hasp and opened the box. After examining the contents, she closed the lid again.

'How is your arm?' Liebermann asked.

Katherine raised her right hand, causing the sleeve of her gown to fall and collect in folds around her shoulder. Then she examined her elbow and wrist.

'There is nothing wrong with my arm,' she replied. Then, turning, she walked back to the bed.

Pushing both palms on the mattress, Katherine lifted herself up. She manoeuvred herself into a sitting position and resumed swinging her legs. Suddenly her expression became quite vacant. It was as though, having performed a limited repertoire of actions, she was now in a state of suspension, waiting for the next cue or prompt.

Liebermann wondered whether Katherine would respond to a command. In all likelihood, 'Katherine' would not be a fully developed personality but merely a part of Miss Lydgate's mind that had become separated, achieving a degree of independence. Amelia Lydgate was still in a trance state. Therefore Liebermann deduced that Katherine might still be susceptible to hypnotic suggestion. Recovering some of his former authority, he said firmly: 'Lie down, Katherine.'

For a second or two, Katherine remained still. Then she swung her legs up and around before lying back. Liebermann sighed with relief.

'Amelia was telling me about what happened when Herr Schelling came into her room,' said Liebermann.

'Was she?'

'Yes. Were you there that night?'

'Of course I was.'

'Did you see Herr Schelling come into the room?'

'It was very dark.'

'What can you remember?'

Katherine's nose wrinkled and her mouth twisted.

'It was disgusting.'

'What was?'

'That horrible moustache — the scratching. His face was like a pumice stone. Amelia was terrified. She should have pushed him off, but she did nothing. Her heart was pounding so loud that I could hear it.' She tapped the bedstead, imitating the frantic, limping beat of a fearful heart. 'He was slavering like a dog — and grabbing, grabbing, grabbing . . .'

Katherine fell silent.

'What happened next?' asked Liebermann.

'There was a flash of lightning,' Katherine continued. 'I saw the embroidery basket and the scissors. He was so lost in his slavering and grabbing that it was easy to reach out. *Kill him*, I said. *Pick up the scissors and stab him in the back.* But Amelia did not move. I heard her say *No — I can't.* I urged her: *Come on, you must.* She said again, *I can't.* Her arm wouldn't move. So I said, *Very well, I'll do it if you won't.* I picked up the scissors, but Herr Schelling moved. Lightning, another flash. He was kneeling, looking down at me. Then darkness — but the picture stayed in my mind. A silhouette-head, shoulders — the curled ends of his moustache. I sat up, and thrust out with the scissors . . . I heard him gasp. I could feel some resistance and I pushed harder. He cursed — the mattress bounced as he changed position — and then he fell off the bed. There was a tremendous crash and more cursing. The door opened and then slammed shut and . . . and he was gone. I put the scissors back in the basket and pulled the blanket up to my neck. Outside the rain was falling. I could hear it drumming on the roof and splashing on the pavement below. Suddenly I felt weak. Tired and exhausted.' Katherine yawned and covered her mouth.

'Are you tired now?'

'A little . . .'

'Then sleep,' said Liebermann. 'You are safe here, Katherine. Let your eyes close, and you will fall asleep very soon.'

Katherine's eyelids trembled, and within moments her breathing became stertorous. Liebermann sat perfectly still, watching his slumbering patient.

'Doctor Liebermann?'

His shoulders jerked back with surprise.

Amelia Lydgate's eyes had opened again.

'Doctor Liebermann,' she continued. 'Could I have a glass of water, please? I am very thirsty.'

She was speaking in German.

35

THE THIRD RECEPTION room of the von Rath residence was supposed to be more intimate than the first and second, but it was still immense by ordinary standards. The ceiling was decorated with an awesome painting in the classical style, which showed pipe-playing rustics cavorting with nymphs below a powder-blue sky. At both ends of the room were fireplaces of red marble supporting high, gilded French mirrors, and the walls were hung with old Gobelin tapestries. By a long row of shuttered windows busts of ancient philosophers and gods, mounted on malachite plinths, stared at the company with opaque and sightless eyes.

Bruckmüller lit a tree of candles and placed the stand behind his fiancée. He then signalled to Hölderlin who extinguished the gaslights. The room instantly shrank, its centre becoming a sphere of hazy luminosity in a vast enveloping darkness.

When both men had returned to the table, Cosima von Rath examined her guests. It had been several months since she had last attended Fräulein Löwenstein's circle, but none of those present looked any different — except for the Count, perhaps, whose conspicuously swollen eye was studiously ignored by everyone.

To her immediate left sat Bruckmüller, then Uberhorst — nervously locking and unlocking his delicate little fingers — then the Count and, directly opposite, Natalie Heck — whose wide-open eyes had become as black as cinder pits. To Cosima's right sat the

Hölderlins: first Juno, blinking into the candlelight, and then Heinrich, his face set in an attitude of solemnity. Braun, the handsome young artist, was a notable absentee.

Cosima's ample figure cast a mountainous shadow across the polished surface of the round table. The letters of the alphabet and every number from zero to nine — all in Gothic script — were arranged in twin arcs on glazed tiles. Beneath these were four larger tiles on which could be read the words *Yes, No, Possibly* and *Goodbye*. In the centre of this arrangement was the planchette — a heart-shaped piece of wood mounted on three small castor wheels.

'Are we ready?'

The company whispered their assent.

'Then let us begin.'

Cosima rested a fat finger on the planchette, an action that was repeated by each of the company in turn.

'We are gathered here this evening to discover the fate of our friends Charlotte Löwenstein and Otto Braun. If there is a kindly spirit present who can assist us in our quest, please make yourself known.'

The planchette did not move.

Cosima's ample bosom rose and fell as she sighed. A precious stone flashed on her ankh.

'In the name of Isis and Osiris, Adonay, Eloim, Ariel, and Jehovam we humbly beg you, great spirits, who are in possession of the most priceless Treasure of the Light. Please assist us.'

A suffocating silence followed.

'None of us have the power,' said Záborszky, with characteristic bluntness.

'My dear Count,' said Cosima, turning her flat, round face towards the eccentric aristocrat, 'None of us have Fräulein Löwenstein's special gift. Yet—'

'We need a clairvoyant,' he cut in. 'A proper one.'

'If we are sincere in our wishes,' said Cosima, ignoring Záborszky's interruption, 'then the spirits will help us.' Looking around at the assembly she added: 'Please, we must all concentrate. Think of Fräulein Löwenstein, and open your hearts to the influence of the higher powers. Come, blessed spirits, come . . .' The pitch of her voice climbed and wobbled with an emotional vibrato. 'Come spirits, come . . .'

The planchette flinched, darting an inch or so from its central position.

Natalie Heck gasped and threw a sidelong glance in the direction of Count Záborszky.

'There, you see!' cried Cosima reproachfully. 'They are here . . . the spirits have arrived.'

The Count seemed indifferent.

'Who are you?' continued Cosima. 'Who are you, oh Spirit, who has answered our call?'

The planchette moved in small circles before flying towards the first arc of letters. The narrow end of the wooden heart, which served as a pointer, stopped abruptly below the letter F. After a brief pause, the planchette visited the letters L-O-R-E-S-T-A and finally N.

'Florestan,' said Cosima, beaming with satisfaction. 'Greetings, Florestan, you who are now in possession of the Treasure of the Light. What was your profession, Florestan, when you were incarnate?'

The planchette spelt out: KAPELLMEISTER.

'Where?'

SALZBURG.

'And when did you leave the realm of material things?'

1791.

'Will you help us, Florestan?'

YES.

'Blessed Spirit — it has been two weeks since our dear sister

Charlotte Löwenstein left this world. Does she wish to communicate with us?'

The planchette did not move.

'Does she have a message for us?'

Nothing.

'Can we speak to her?'

Still there was no movement.

Záborszky sniffed and said quietly: 'This Florestan is too feeble. We must summon a more potent spirit.'

'Dearest Count,' said Cosima, forcing a smile, 'we must show respect to all emissaries from the world of light.'

Frau Hölderlin, who was sitting next to Cosima, turned and whispered sharply: 'Ask again.'

'Florestan,' Cosima called, her voice still quivering, 'does Charlotte Löwenstein wish to communicate with us?'

Silence.

'Ask him what happened,' hissed Frau Hölderlin. 'Ask him what happened to her?'

'Was Charlotte Löwenstein taken by —' Cosima ventured tentatively '— a higher power?'

The planchette rolled around the table and halted close to where it had begun.

YES.

'Of the first altitude?'

NO.

'The second?'

NO.

'The third?' Incredulity had transformed Cosima von Rath's soprano into an unfeasibly high squeal.

The planchette rolled across the table to the adjacent tile.

YES.

The company began to whisper among themselves.

'But why?' Cosima wailed.

The whispering subsided and the planchette rolled towards the letters where it spelt out: SIN.

'Which sin?'

VANITY.

Cosima, her plump neck vibrating with excitement, asked: 'Did she attempt to make a higher power do her bidding?'

YES.

'For what purpose?'

The planchette failed to respond and a tidal silence washed back into the room.

'What was her purpose?' Cosima repeated.

The planchette remained resolutely still.

'Where is she?' Cosima continued. 'Where was she taken?'

Nothing.

'What about Otto?' said Natalie Heck. 'Ask what happened to Otto.'

Cosima acknowledged the request by inclining her head.

'Florestan — where is Herr Braun?'

Again, nothing.

'Was Herr Braun taken too?'

The planchette stirred and rolled gently towards an answer: NO.

'Is he still alive?'

The wooden heart rolled in several wide circles and ground to a halt on an empty patch of table, giving no discernible answer.

Uberhorst coughed to attract attention and said hesitantly: 'Please ... I would like to ask a question.'

'Of course,' Cosima replied.

'I want to know if ... if I should tell them?'

'Tell them? Tell who?'

'It is . . .' Uberhorst paused and then added: 'A private matter.'

'My dear fellow.' It was Bruckmüller, and his resonant voice seemed to shake the table. 'You are among friends!'

The little locksmith's pince-nez caught the light. His eyes were two ovals of flickering flame.

'It is a private matter, Herr Bruckmüller.'

The Count — who was seated next to Uberhorst — addressed him as though no one else was present. His tone was casual.

'She told you something? Fräulein Löwenstein?'

The locksmith searched the ring of faces for a sympathetic expression but was unable to find one.

'Herr Uberhorst,' said Cosima, 'if you want an answer to your question you must cooperate with the circle. We must assist the spirit Florestan with one will. This cannot be accomplished if you are guarding some secret.'

'Do you mean the police, Uberhorst?' said Hölderlin. 'Is that who you mean by *them*?'

Uberhorst took his hand off the planchette and began biting his nails.

'Please, all I want is . . .' The words were indistinct. 'All I want is a simple answer.' His panic was barely controlled. 'A *Yes* — or a *No*.'

The planchette moved, spiralling outwards and moving faster until it stopped abruptly among the letters.

TELL WHO?

'See,' said Bruckmüller, 'the spirit needs clarification, Uberhorst.'

'It is a matter of honour' Herr Bruckmüller, I cannot say any more.'

WHO? the planchette demanded.

'Herr Uberhorst,' said Cosima, 'Please do not deny the spirit emissary.'

Uberhorst shook his head.

'Very well, Herr Uberhorst,' Cosima continued. 'I will try on your behalf, but I do not believe that we shall meet with much success. Florestan, spirit, possessor of the Treasure of the Light: should Herr Uberhorst tell—' she paused, and raised her eyebrows. '*Them?*'

Uberhorst placed his finger back on the planchette.

The device remained perfectly still.

'There you are,' said Cosima. 'I thought as much.'

The company looked towards Uberhorst. He was staring at the planchette — his gaze transfixed on the wooden heart.

'This is not right,' he said softly.

'What do you mean?' asked Cosima. 'Not right?'

'I cannot believe . . .' Uberhorst's voice was torpid, as though he was talking through a dream. 'I cannot believe that Fräulein Löwenstein was taken — removed — by some demon. She was too good a person. Too kind.'

'To you, perhaps,' said Natalie under her breath. Uberhorst looked up. He could not see the seamstress's face very well, only the large glass earring dangling from her ear.

'Herr Uberhorst,' said Frau Hölderlin, 'the spirit says that Fräulein Löwenstein was guilty of the sin of vanity. And much as I admired her, much as I was impressed by her gift—'

'She was a very vain woman,' said Natalie, helping Frau Hölderlin's sentence to its inevitable conclusion.

'But undeniably very beautiful,' said Záborszky.

'Indeed,' said Hölderlin. 'However, we must remember that possession of physical beauty can easily weaken the moral faculty. Is it not generally the case that those whom we call beautiful are also peculiarly vulnerable to the sins of pride and vanity?'

'I'm surprised to hear you say that, Hölderlin,' said Záborszky.

'Why?' Hölderlin snapped back at him.

'You seemed to appreciate her beauty as much as the next man.'

'What on Earth do you mean by tha—'

'Gentlemen!' Cosima von Rath's voice was shrill and angry.

'Here, here,' barked Bruckmüller.

'Gentlemen, please!' Cosima blew out her cheeks and her retroussé nose, squeezed between bulging flesh, looked alarmingly like a snout. 'We must proceed.'

Frau Hölderlin squinted at her husband whose pate glittered with tiny beads of perspiration.

'Florestan,' Cosima cried. 'Florestan, is there anything we can do to help our departed sister Charlotte?'

The planchette rolled around the table top and stopped abruptly. NO.

'Shall we pray for her salvation?'

The planchette traced another circle.

NO.

'Then what shall we do?'

Rolling from side to side, the planchette hovered in the non-committal spaces of the table top before finally dropping and colliding with the largest of the tiles: GOODBYE.

'He has gone,' Cosima said, a note of melancholy lowering the volume of her voice.

Herr Uberhorst was the first to remove his finger from the planchette. His movement was swift and sudden, as though he had accidentally touched the hot plate of a stove. Frau Hölderlin, blinking frantically, was still staring at her husband.

Part Three

The Beethoven Frieze

36

THE CAB RATTLED off and was quickly absorbed into the steady flow of traffic: omnibuses, trams, and a veritable fleet of horse-drawn carts. The stalls of the Naschmarkt had spilled right up to the Secession building and the air was filled with noise: fishmongers, butchers and bakers — costermongers, barrow boys, and pedlars — all of their voices combining to create a disharmonious commercial chorus. Down the Linke Wienzelle, the most conspicuous building was the Theatre an der Wien, the venue where Beethoven's *Fidelio* had first been performed a hundred years earlier. It seemed fitting to Liebermann that the Secessionists should celebrate the great composer's genius only yards away from a site of almost spiritual significance.

'Well, then,' said Liebermann, straightening his necktie and adjusting his collar. 'Here we are.'

Clara and Hannah looked up towards the House of the Secession. Their gaze was naturally attracted to its most significant feature — a golden dome constructed from a delicate patchwork of gilded bronze leaves.

'You can see why they call it the golden cabbage,' said Hannah.

'Really, my dear, how can you say that? It's exquisite,' Liebermann retorted.

He offered his arms to Clara and Hannah and they walked in a line towards the building.

'To the Age its Art, to Art its Freedom,' said Hannah, reading the legend set in raised lettering beneath the dome.

'A sentiment that I hope you share.'

'And *Ver Sacrum*. What does that mean?'

'Sacred Stream — it's the title of their magazine.'

'But why? Why Sacred Stream?'

'It was a Roman ritual of concentration that was carried out in times of danger. The young were pledged to save the capital. The Secession, you see, have pledged to save Vienna from the forces of conservatism.'

'Do we really need to be saved?' asked Clara pointedly.

'Saved is probably too strong a word — relieved, I feel, would be more appropriate.'

Hurrying to avoid a convoy of timber-laden carts, they marched briskly across the street and ascended the stairs, watched from above by a trio of gorgons — their fossilised faces framed by more gilded foliage.

Once inside, Liebermann paid the entrance fee — one *krone* each — and took a catalogue. The cover showed a stylised angel holding a disc of light.

Excited, Clara and Hannah had rushed ahead.

'Wait a minute,' said Liebermann, opening the catalogue and flicking through the pages.

'Why?' asked Clara.

'I want to look at the orientation map.'

'Orientation map? Surely you don't think we're going to get lost, Max.'

Hannah giggled.

'No,' Liebermann replied, 'I don't think we're going to get lost, Clara, but I *do* want to know what I'm looking at.'

'The Klinger, surely,' said Clara. 'And the Klimt.'

'Indeed, but there are many more artists represented here.' He pointed to some names on the floor plan. 'See: Andri, Auchentaller, Moser — I don't know where to start. Let me see ...' He read for a few moments and added: 'They suggest the left aisle.'

Clara looked at Hannah and, and, assuming a mischievous expression, repeated, 'Left aisle.'

The two of them scurried off and Liebermann was forced to stop reading in order to keep up.

They entered a long room where several other people were already standing, looking upwards. Liebermann followed their gaze and felt his heart flutter with excitement. The upper sections of three of the four walls were decorated with an extraordinary fresco. Liebermann spoke softly to his companions: 'The Beethoven Frieze.'

Clara and Hannah glanced up, but had already been distracted by the centrepiece of the exhibition, Klinger's Beethoven sculpture, which could be seen through a large rectangular aperture in the wall. They both began to wander towards the brightly lit space.

'Hannah, Clara,' Liebermann hissed. 'The Klimt!'

Both turned, looking puzzled, frozen in a comical attitude with raised arms and limp, pointing fingers.

In response to their quizzical expressions Liebermann jerked his head up — their eyes followed the movement.

'Oh ...' said Clara, suddenly seeing the fresco truly for the first time.

Liebermann consulted his catalogue and beckoned, urging his sister and fiancée to come closer.

'The panels form a narrative,' he said, summarising the guide, 'based on Wagner's interpretation of Beethoven's Ninth Symphony. The first is called "Yearning for Happiness", the second "Hostile Powers", and the third "Longing for Happiness Fulfilled by Poetry". Together they are supposed to represent the triumph of art over adversity.'

The room was eerily quiet — like a crypt. The other occupants of the room were transfixed, staring up at Klimt's magical panorama as if it held a secret that would only be revealed to the most diligent observer.

Liebermann let his gaze roam from panel to panel and felt slightly giddy. The colours were so bold: the red of ox blood, then aquamarine, silver, rust, topaz, and, of course, acres of gold. It seemed to Liebermann that Klimt must use a palette of gemstones, iron ore, and precious metals.

As Liebermann's eyes became accustomed to Klimt's over-whelming carousel of colours, he was able to appreciate a cast of characters who gradually emerged as distinct individuals. Emaciated, naked figures appealed to a knight in armour; a monstrous winged ape squatted amid a crowd of disturbing death's heads and sirens: and a man and a woman — their bodies pressed together — kissed below a choir of angelic faces. Some parts of the fresco seemed cool and still, while others writhed with activity, every inch alive with movement: ripples, waves, swirls and eddies — vibrant detail, enlivened by the shimmer of appliqué mirrors.

A busty middle-aged woman had entered the room, accompanied by a younger man who seemed vaguely familiar to Liebermann. He thought, perhaps, that he might have seen him around Alsegrund and suspected that he too was a doctor, but could not be sure. The woman raised her lorgnette and peered at the frieze. Within moments she was tutting and grumbled something to her companion, raising her voice as she enunciated words such as 'obscenity' and 'sinful'.

The young man nodded his head and endorsed her condemnation: 'Images of madness . . . fixed ideas . . .' As he came closer Liebermann heard him more clearly: '. . . a shameless caricature of the noble human form. Only a certain *type* of intellectual would derive pleasure from contemplating such pathological scenes.'

Yes, thought Liebermann. *A doctor — and most probably an anti-Semite.*

He looked protectively at Clara and Hannah, and was satisfied that neither of them had understood the subtle slur.

The couple walked past, and as they did so the dowager aunt could not resist one more spiteful salvo: '. . . he has exceeded the boundaries of good taste — certainly not an exhibition that any self-respecting young lady would care to attend.'

Hannah suddenly looked worried, this time having caught the comment. Liebermann placed an arm around her shoulder.

'I think that was for my benefit Hannah — not yours.' His sister smiled nervously. 'I promise you, there's nothing wrong in coming to see great art. And this is great art — believe me.'

'Did you see the look she gave us?' said Clara indignantly. But then, returning her attention to the fresco, she added an equivocal: 'However . . .'

'However what?' asked Liebermann.

'She does have a point — of sorts . . .' Clara gestured at the centre wall and lifted her eyebrows. 'I mean to say, it's rather . . .' She paused, unable to find an appropriate word.

'Daring,' said Hannah.

'Yes,' said Clara. 'Daring.'

Klimt's nudes were sensuous and carnal. In the middle panel, a sublimely attractive woman sat with her cheek resting on her knee — a shock of luxurious hair falling between her open thighs. Her expression smouldered with wicked sexuality and her teeth were visible between parted lips.

'And what on Earth is that supposed to be?' continued Clara. 'That monster . . . thing.'

Liebermann consulted his catalogue again.

'The Giant Typhonoeus. Whom the gods themselves could not

destroy. He is accompanied by the figures of Sickness, Madness and Death.'

Clara looked towards Hannah. Something passed between them — a conspiratorial glance that brought them close to laughter.

The room had emptied and, taking advantage of the vacant floor, Liebermann stood for a while in several different positions, appreciating the work from a variety of perspectives. His eyes, however, were repeatedly drawn by the seated temptress. There was something about her face that reminded him of Katherine — the English governess's alter ego.

An image came to him, breaking the surface tension of his own consciousness. *Katherine — at the hospital — smoothing her gown. The tautness of the material as it clung to her hips and belly.*

Ashamed, Liebermann looked away.

Clara was whispering something in Hannah's ear. His sister smiled and placed a hand over her mouth — as though astonished. He felt an odd mixture of emotions: warmth and, surprisingly, disappointment. Clara was a woman — eight years older than Hannah. Yet she found it so easy to share girlish jokes with his sixteen-year-old sister. Of course, Clara's playfulness was part of her charm; but in this setting, in this great temple of art, her playfulness appeared less like high spirits and more like immaturity. Liebermann was discomfited by his own lack of charity and, reprimanding himself for being mean-spirited, walked back to join them.

'What's so funny now?'

'Nothing that would interest you,' said Clara archly. Liebermann shrugged. 'Shall we go through?' she added — and, taking Hannah's hand, she walked to the end of the room where some stairs led to the central aisle. Before leaving the Beethoven Frieze, Liebermann ran his fingers down the roughcast wall and pondered the significance of a marble head.

'Hurry up, Max, I want to see the Klinger,' said Clara. She made wide circles with her cupped hand, as though trying to create a draught that would move him forward. Hannah, impressed by Clara's impatience, joined in.

'Yes, Max. Hurry up.'

'But this is by Klinger too.'

'Yes, but it's not Klinger's Beethoven, is it?'

Liebermann smiled, enjoying the girls' frustration.

They emerged in a large austere space under a vaulted ceiling decorated with ceramic plaques and primitive sculptures. Liebermann was utterly enchanted. He felt like an archaeologist, exploring the miraculously preserved tomb of an ancient king.

'Isn't it wonderful?' he said.

'It is indeed,' said Clara. 'But if we continue at this rate, we'll never get to see the main exhibit.'

Ignoring Clara's remark, Liebermann continued: 'Curiously affecting, don't you think — the atmosphere they've created? You know, I was reading in the *Neue Press*, one of the critics, I forget which, but he wrote that by the time most people reach the central chamber they have already been lulled into a state close to hypnosis. I know exactly what he means, don't you?'

Stretching her hands out in front of her body, Clara closed her eyes and shuffled along like someone walking in their sleep. Unfortunately, at that moment a party of gentlemen appeared. One of them looked particularly flamboyant — a large, bearded man wearing a straw hat and a white piqué vest.

'Clara!' said Hannah.

Clara opened her eyes and, quickly appraising the situation, pretended to be reaching towards Liebermann in order to brush a hair from his jacket. After the men had passed, Clara and Hannah burst out laughing — chattering breathlessly about what had just happened.

'Ladies,' said Liebermann, wagging his finger. He walked on, aware that Clara and Hannah were following, feigning remorse but unable to stop giggling.

Klinger's Beethoven was situated in the middle of the central aisle, on a raised dais and surrounded by a low circular fence. Semi-nude and seated on a large throne, the great composer leaned forward with clenched fists, gazing into an infinite, visionary distance. He was entirely godlike — the familiar heavy, square head exuded gravitas, power and dignity.

Here, then, was the inner sanctum, the fulcrum of the entire exhibition, a sacred place where the votaries of art could worship and pray.

There was no sign of the frosty couple whom they had encountered earlier, but many other people were milling around the sculpture.

'Now, that is beautiful,' said Clara. 'He looks like . . . he looks like Zeus.'

'Yes,' said Liebermann, pleasantly surprised. 'I think that must have been the intention.'

'He looks thoroughly annoyed,' said Hannah.

'Well,' said Liebermann, 'Beethoven had a lot to be annoyed about. Did you know, Mahler conducted a chamber arrangement of the Ninth symphony here — on the opening night?'

'Did he?' said Hannah. 'Oh, that would have been wonderful.'

'And in the presence of the artist, I believe.'

'My dear,' said Clara, taking Hannah's arm confidentially, 'do you know the Molls? They live in a new semi-detached villa in Heiligenstadt — on Steinfeldgasse?'

Hannah shook her head.

'Well,' continued Clara, 'if you don't, your mother will. Frau Moll used to be married to Emile Schindler, the painter. He died a few years ago, and Frau Moll married one of his pupils. Anyway, the daughter, Alma Schindler —' Clara lowered her voice '— such a flirt, you wouldn't believe it. They say she's very good-looking but, to tell the truth, I can't see it. Well, she was married in February — to Director Mahler.'

'Oh,' said Hannah, 'how lovely for her.'

'Well,' continued Clara, 'perhaps not. I've heard it said that the wedding was rather hurried . . .'

Hannah looked puzzled, and Clara, bending close, whispered something into the young girl's ear. Liebermann watched his sister's expression change from amusement to disbelief.

'Clara,' said Liebermann. 'Must you fill Hannah's head with such idle gossip!'

'Maxim,' said Hannah, 'you sound just like father.'

Opening her fan, Clara peered over its quivering fringe like a coquette.

'Someone has to keep Hannah informed . . .'

Liebermann sighed and stared into Beethoven's eyes. Clara and Hannah continued to chatter — but they fell silent when two gaily dressed young men genuflected in front of Klinger's masterpiece.

37

'IT WAS VERY KIND of you to see me, Minister Schelling. I realise that you are a very busy man.'

Schelling's jowls wobbled when he rocked his head backwards and forwards as he ushered Liebermann into the drawing room.

'It is my earnest wish that Miss Lydgate should be returned to health as soon as possible — she seemed so distressed when she was living here. My schedule today is rather hectic but I am perfectly happy to place myself at your disposal for the next half-hour or so, if you feel that my layman's opinion will be of some value.'

Schelling was of medium build and wore a dark suit, wing collars and a black bow tie. A gold watch-chain hung from his waistcoat, the fabric of which bulged against the pressure of an incipient paunch. His formal dress suggested that he intended to leave for the parliament building as soon as the interview was finished.

'Thank you,' said Liebermann. 'I won't delay you any longer than is absolutely necessary.'

A woman appeared in the hallway and entered through the open double doors. Her face was rather careworn, and the style and cut of her floral dress gave her a somewhat matronly appearance.

'My wife,' said Schelling. 'Beatrice, this is Doctor Liebermann, Amelia's doctor.'

'Frau Schelling,' said Liebermann, bowing.

She stood on the threshold, seemingly unsure of whether to enter the room.

'Would you like some tea, Herr Doctor?' she asked.

'No, thank you,' Liebermann replied.

She glanced quickly and anxiously at her husband.

'In which case, you will excuse me.'

She stepped backwards and closed the doors.

'Forgive me, Minister,' said Liebermann, 'but I was hoping to speak with Frau Schelling.'

'I'm afraid that won't be possible,' said Schelling in a peremptory fashion. 'My wife has found this business most upsetting. I must insist that she be spared any further distress.'

'Of course,' said Liebermann.

'I knew that you would understand. Please, do sit down.'

The room was large and well furnished. In the centre was a circular table over which a tablecloth with tasselled edges had been draped. The impressive display of flowers that it supported consisted of blooms that were out of season and Liebermann suspected they were synthetic: probably expensive silk copies. On an ornate chest of drawers, a glass cabinet was crowded with a collection of objets d'art, and on either side of this stood two electric lamps with green shades. Numerous family photographs in silver frames had been arranged on a small corner table. Liebermann noticed that none of them showed Herr Schelling and his wife together.

'Minister,' Liebermann began. 'I understand that you are related to Miss Lydgate?'

'Indeed. Her mother is a distant cousin — our families have always corresponded. When Amelia completed the English equivalent of the *Gymnasium* she expressed a keen desire to study here in Vienna with Herr Doctor Landsteiner. I take it the girl has told you about her grandfather's journal?'

'Yes, she has.'

'I suggested to Greta — Amelia's mother — that Amelia should live here. It's a big house and I thought the children might benefit. I was happy to support Amelia if, in return, she was willing to provide Edvard and Adele with English lessons.'

'Were the children fond of their governess?'

'Yes, they were. It was a very satisfactory arrangement.'

Schelling leaned back in the well-upholstered chair and rested his hands on his stomach.

'When did you first realise that Miss Lydgate was unwell?'

'Doctor Liebermann,' said Schelling, creating a steeple with his fingers. 'May I be perfectly frank?'

'That would be most helpful.'

'I have always harboured doubts about the poor girl's mental health, right from the very beginning.'

'Oh?'

'She is of such an odd disposition. And her interests — blood, disease — is it not irregular for a woman, particularly a young woman, to be preoccupied with such morbid subjects? I am no psychologist, Herr Doctor, but I am inclined to believe that there is something in Miss Lydgate's character that can only be described as unnatural. She takes no pleasure in those activities that one ordinarily associates with her sex. She would rather attend a lecture at a museum than a ball — or search out a dusty volume in Wieblinger Strasse than go to Habig for a new hat. To tell the truth, within weeks of her arrival I had the most grave concerns.'

Liebermann noticed that, in spite of his age, Schelling's hair and moustache were totally black. He assumed that the man must use some kind of dying agent to achieve the effect.

'My wife reached the same conclusion,' Schelling continued. 'Beatrice — sweet soul that she is — encouraged Amelia to be more outgoing. She even tried to lift her spirits by introducing her to a circle of close friends — they meet here on Wednesday afternoons to play taroc. It was obvious that the girl did not enjoy participating, nor did she appear to derive any pleasure from the conversation of her female peers. Indeed, I gather that she persistently excused herself early, preferring the company of her books and her grandfather's journal to that of people. It cannot be right for a young woman to shut herself away in this manner. Although I am not qualified to comment on such matters, I would guess that too many hours spent in retreat from the world cannot be healthy. Is that not so, Doctor Liebermann?'

'I suppose that rather depends on the individual.'

'Perhaps, but it is my opinion — for what it may be worth — that the isolated mind loses its purchase on reality all too easily and becomes prone to fantasy.'

Schelling looked directly into Liebermann's eyes and held his gaze. He seemed to be expecting the young doctor to say something. Liebermann remained silent and did nothing, apart from noticing the appearance of a pulse at Schelling's temple.

'Is that not so, Herr Doctor?' Schelling insisted. On the mantel-piece the mechanism of a carriage clock whirred and a delicate chime sounded the hour. Schelling turned to look at the clock face and Liebermann noticed that he moved his whole body. The wicker of his chair creaked as he shifted position.

'When did Miss Lydgate's symptoms develop?' asked Liebermann.

Schelling considered the question before answering.

'My wife noticed that she had lost her appetite some time ago. The cough, and that business with her arm . . .'

'The paralysis.'

'Yes, the cough and paralysis came on suddenly. About three weeks ago now.'

'Did anything significant occur,' asked Liebermann, 'around the time when the paralysis first appeared? Let us say, the night before?'

'Significant? What do you mean, significant?'

'Well, did anything happen that might have caused Miss Lydgate distress?'

'Not that I know of.'

'Can you tell me what happened? How you learned of the paralysis?'

'There isn't a great deal to tell. Amelia didn't rise at her usual time and said that she was feeling sick. This in itself wasn't unusual: she often complained of sickness. Weak constitution. She wouldn't open the door, and Beatrice became quite desperate. Eventually, Beatrice demanded that Amelia open the door and was shocked when she entered. The room was in disarray, and the girl was in a dreadful state. Dishevelled, tearful — and coughing. Beatrice suspected that Amelia might have tried to harm herself — there was blood on her scissors.'

'You weren't present?'

'No, I had already left the house. The family doctor was called and he advised that Amelia should be attended by a specialist. Beatrice thought that it would be better for all concerned if Miss Lydgate was treated in hospital. She found Miss Lydgate's appearance very distressing, and she was also worried about the children. She did not want them to see her looking so . . . unwell.'

'Have Miss Lydgate's parents been informed?'

'Of course — I sent a telegram immediately. They asked me whether they should come, and I assured them that this would not be necessary. I explained that, with respect to hysteria, we in Vienna boast the best specialists in the world. Isn't that so, Herr Doctor?'

Liebermann acknowledged the disingenuous compliment with a forced smile. Looking over Schelling's shoulder he pointed to a dull landscape on the wall.

'Is that a Friml, Minister?'

Schelling turned, again moving his whole torso.

'Friml? No, it's a German artist. Frauscher. I have several.'

Feigning interest, Liebermann rose and as he did so he stole a glance down at Schelling's shirt collar, where he glimpsed the edge of what appeared to be a bandage dressing.

'Do you collect, Doctor Liebermann?'

'A little,' Liebermann replied. 'Minor Secessionists, mostly.'

'Really?' said Schelling. 'I'm afraid I cannot claim to be an admirer of their work.'

'Well,' said Liebermann, 'they are an acquired taste. Thank you for your time, Minister.'

'Is that all?' said Schelling, somewhat surprised. He stood. 'I doubt this interview has helped you very much.'

'Not at all,' said Liebermann. 'I've learned a great deal.'

The two men shook hands and Schelling escorted Liebermann to the door.

As he left the house, Liebermann was eager to get back to the Hospital. He needed to talk to Stefan Kanner. Kanner and Schelling were very different men but they shared one thing in common. It was a trivial observation, but potentially very significant. In order to test how significant, Liebermann would need Kanner's cooperation with an experiment.

38

Liebermann and Rheinhardt had finished their musical evening with a near-faultless performance of Schumann's *Dichterliebe*. After the brandy had been decanted and the freshly cut cigars lit, the two men spoke little and, as was frequently the case, stared silently into the fire. The jaunty melody of the third song in Schumann's cycle lingered in Liebermann's imagination — and particularly the words *Ich liebe alleine* . . .

I love only her — she who is small, exquisite, chaste, unique.

Why had that phrase stuck in his mind?

It was, in effect, a description of Clara. Yet there was something unsettling about its persistence.

I love only her.

The music continued to resonate in Liebermann's head, acquiring with each repetition an ironic quality. Gradually the ghostly concert faded beneath the crackle of burning logs and the sound of his man-servant Ernst tidying up song books and closing the piano stool.

'Oskar?'

Rheinhardt turned to look at his friend. Unusually, the young doctor was looking somewhat perplexed.

'Oskar, I would like to ask you a personal question, if I may?'

'Of course.'

'I was wondering . . . have you ever . . .' Liebermann paused and winced. 'What I mean to ask is . . . after announcing your engagement, were you entirely sure that you were doing the right thing? In getting married, that is.'

Rheinhardt's expression immediately softened. 'My dear fellow, of course I had doubts. Everyone does.'

Liebermann blew out a cloud of smoke and the tension eased from his shoulders.

'How many weeks has it been now?' Rheinhardt continued. 'Since your proposal?'

'About three weeks. Although it feels much longer.'

'Well, now that the initial excitement has passed it's inevitable that the happier emotions should give way to a more thoughtful frame of mind. Doubts creep in — and rightly so. After all, a man who did not give proper consideration to such a momentous decision would be correctly identified as a fool, wouldn't he?'

'Yes,' said Liebermann, 'I suppose he would.'

'I cannot give you any advice, Max,' Rheinhardt continued, 'because every man must make his own way in life. But I can tell you a little of my experience — which may or may not be helpful.' The Inspector's tired eyes became oddly bright. 'Had I taken heed of those doubts, I don't know what would have become of me! What a sorry existence I would have led. Gentlemen's clubs, trips to Baden, a little shooting, perhaps, and the occasional company of a shop girl . . . I tell you, Max, there isn't a single day that passes when I am not forced to count myself among the most fortunate of men. My life would have been empty and cheerless without the love of my dear Else and the endless diversion and amusement afforded me by my beautiful daughters.'

Liebermann found his friend's words deeply reassuring.

Rheinhardt continued to talk in glowing terms about his wife and family, and Liebermann reciprocated, describing Clara and something of her background. He felt slightly uncomfortable: it seemed as though he was aping his father, talking of the long association between the Liebermann and Weiss families. However, he also felt curiously relieved, as though he had embarked on a process of bridge-building, linking the various parts of his life together — making the entirety more coherent and secure.

In due course the subject of their conversation changed, and by degrees they returned reluctantly to the dreadful experience that they had shared at the Institute.

'You know,' said Rheinhardt, 'I haven't been able to clear my mind of it. The mental picture of those poor . . .' He paused before adding: 'Babies.'

'Indeed,' Liebermann replied. 'It was a pathetic sight.' He lit another cigar and added: 'It hasn't been reported in the newspapers?'

'No.'

'Because of Commissioner Brügel?'

'Of course.' Rheinhardt frowned at the mention of his superior. 'He says that such a discovery will only make matters worse — make the murder appear even more sensational.'

'Have there been any more developments?'

Rheinhardt began describing the interview that he had conducted with Roche. Occasionally Liebermann asked him to elaborate some detail, but on the whole the young doctor was content to listen. The cigar in his hand burned slowly — turning inch by inch into a length of wilting ash.

'I'd put that cigar out if I were you,' said Rheinhardt.

Liebermann turned lazily and flicked his thumb. The ash fell into the tray producing a small, dusty cloud.

'What's his first name, this Roche character?' asked Liebermann.

'Theodore.'

Liebermann thought for a few moments, stubbing out his cigar before saying: 'They were aware he might seek revenge.'

'Who, Fräulein Löwenstein and Braun?'

'Yes.'

'Why do you say that?'

'When I hypnotised Rosa Sucher and she spoke in Löwenstein's voice, the name Theo was mentioned.'

'I don't remember that.'

'Yes, right at the every end. It was when her speech had become quite incoherent . . . she was saying things like, *Never, I swear*, and *God help me* . . . Among all that was the name Theo.'

'How interesting.'

'A large city must offer those who live by fraud endless possibilities for deception. Where else could one find so many willing dupes? Once Fräulein Löwenstein and Braun had squandered their ill-gotten gains, returning to Vienna might have been something of a necessity; however, by doing so they were taking a considerable risk. They had ruined Roche — and, as we all know, desperate men are dangerous. It doesn't surprise me in the least that his name should have arisen during their argument.'

Rheinhardt shook his head.

'I don't know, Max. Just because they mentioned his name . . . it doesn't mean that they were worried about him, does it? We don't even know if they were talking about the same Theo.'

'True, but it is a reasonable hypothesis. Did he strike you as a man capable of murder?'

'I fear that all men, once betrayed — particularly by a lover — are capable of murder.'

'And then there is also the tantalising issue of his current occupation: working in an armaments factory. Is it possible that he might have in his possession the means to construct a bullet with unusual, seemingly magical, properties?'

'I really don't see why a former theatre manager, simply by

working in an armaments factory, should acquire more knowledge about ballistics than our police experts possess. That seems implausible to me. Also, would a guilty man really make such an admission?'

'How do you mean?'

'He said that he would have killed Charlotte Löwenstein — if only he'd had the opportunity.'

'Perhaps that was his intention, Oskar, to mislead by simulating honesty.'

'No, I don't think so. Besides, the more we find out about Braun, the more likely it seems that he is the perpetrator. Wouldn't you agree?'

Liebermann did not respond.

'It is clear that he was Fräulein Löwenstein's lover and accomplice,' continued Rheinhardt. 'And, being a stage magician, he might have had the ability to work the illusion of the murder scene — you yourself have insisted that it was an illusion.'

Still Liebermann did not respond.

'Clearly, the man has no principles.' Rheinhardt's invective became more impassioned. 'Think, for example, of how he was taking advantage of the little seamstress. It's unconscionable. He's hotheaded, and what's more, he hasn't been seen since the night Fräulein Löwenstein was murdered.'

Liebermann pinched his lower lip and grunted, without committing himself.

'What?' asked Rheinhardt, slightly annoyed at his friend's reticence.

'It still doesn't make much sense to me.'

Rheinhardt gestured, urging Liebermann to elaborate.

'We must ask ourselves what motivated Braun,' Liebermann murmured. 'What did he have to gain?'

'Money. He was happy to ruin Roche for money.'

'That's not quite the same as murder. Besides, Fräulein Löwenstein was hardly wealthy.'

'Perhaps it was something to do with the pregnancy — the children.'

'Unscrupulous individuals rarely expend energy worrying about their illegitimate offspring.'

'Perhaps he killed her on the spur of the moment — during one of their arguments?'

'Impossible. An illusion requires planning.'

'Then the motive is as yet unknown — and we'll find out when we catch him.'

'With respect, Oskar, that is no way to proceed.' After a brief pause Liebermann added: 'It lacks elegance. Wishful thinking should play no part in the process that leads to a satisfying solution.'

Rheinhardt suppressed a smile but could not refrain from raising his eyebrows. Liebermann picked up his glass and, disturbing the brandy with a swirl, inhaled the rich, full-bodied fragrance.

'And there's another thing,' he continued. 'Having gone to the trouble of devising such a brilliant illusion, why would Braun then choose to run away like a common street thief? What purpose could that serve, save to draw attention and create suspicion?'

'He had second thoughts — lost confidence in his illusion, decided that it wouldn't fool anyone after all.'

'Surely not.'

'People behave inconsistently,' said Rheinhardt. 'You of all people should appreciate that. We can't always expect to find elegant solutions.'

'Indeed,' replied Liebermann, 'but I have a firm conviction that the most elegant solutions are also the right ones. Why don't you have another cigar, Oskar?'

Before taking one from the box, Rheinhardt produced from his pocket a photograph, which he handed to Liebermann. 'Take a look at this.'

It was an image of a handsome clean-shaven man in his late twenties.

'Otto Braun?'

Rheinhardt lit his cigar, expelling several clouds of blue smoke as the tobacco kindled.

'We acquired it from a theatrical agent, the man who represented the scoundrel when he was doing his magic shows at The Danube. It's an old photograph but apparently a good likeness. I've had it reproduced and distributed to police departments all over the country.'

Liebermann examined the portrait, tilting it in the firelight.

'So, what do you make of that face, Herr Doctor? Do you see anything of interest?'

'Oskar,' said Liebermann, adopting a pained expression, 'you are asking me to engage in pseudo-science, a form of divination no better than palm-reading.'

'I thought you doctors accepted physiognomy?'

'There are many who subscribe to Lombroso's doctrine that it is possible to identify a criminal by the location of his ears or the size of his jaw; however, I have very little sympathy with that school of thought.' Liebermann turned the photograph towards Rheinhardt. 'Look at him. Can you see the stamp of our animal ancestry in his face? Atavisms? I certainly can't. In fact, I would go so far as to say that his appearance suggests the very opposite. There is something rather noble about the configuration of his lineaments. He looks more like a romantic poet — a young Schiller, perhaps — than a cheat. No, Lombroso is wrong. A criminal cannot be identified by the cast of his nose and mouth. Only the nature of his mind has any significance.'

Liebermann handed the photograph back to Rheinhardt, who glanced at it once more before shrugging and slipping it into his pocket.

'And what about the other members of the Löwenstein circle?'
asked Liebermann. 'Have you found out any more about them?'

'Yes, I have,' said Rheinhardt. 'I started taking an interest in
Bruckmüller after we saw him with the Mayor at the Philharmonic
concert.'

'Oh?'

'I thought it rather odd, that a man who mixed with the Mayor
and his friends — men concerned with the commerce and traffic of the
real world — should also attend seances in Leopoldstadt.'

Liebermann turned the brandy glass in his hand and observed how
the refracted light splintered into a kaleidoscope of jagged rainbows.

'There are many superstitious people in the world, Oskar.'

'True. But I can remember, even as I was interviewing him,
thinking *This man isn't the right type.* The locksmith, yes. Or Záborszky
— the mad Count. But Bruckmüller? No.'

'You also felt the same way about Hölderlin — the banker.'

Rheinhardt started: 'Yes, I did. However did you know that?'

'Never mind,' said Liebermann, waving his hand. 'I'm sorry, do
carry on.'

'I decided to make some inquiries,' continued Rheinhardt, looking
at his friend suspiciously. 'The first thing I learned was that
Bruckmüller is an active member of the Christian Social Party — so,
there's the Lueger connection. And the next thing I learned was that
he's betrothed to Cosima von Rath.'

'The heiress?'

'Indeed. Do you know much about her?'

'Only that she is very rich and very large.'

'She is also very strange.'

'Why do you say that?'

'She is greatly interested in the occult, and believes herself to be the
reincarnation of an Egyptian princess. It's no secret. In fact, her arrival

at certain society functions has become something of a spectacle. One wit, I think it was Krauss, said that her entrance at a society gathering is more impressive than a production of *Aida*.'

Liebermann laughed.

'I should get *Die Fackel* more often. He's a great wit, Krauss, but he's so conservative when it comes to art . . .'

'This von Rath woman,' continued Rheinhardt, 'is a great patron of spiritualist organisations. Apparently it was von Rath who discovered Fräulein Löwenstein, introducing her fiancé at a later stage. Bruckmüller remained loyal to Fräulein Löwenstein's group, while von Rath continued her spiritual quest elsewhere, sampling numerous other circles and psychics — as was, and still is, her wont.'

'How do you know all this?'

'Bruckmüller told me, when I interviewed him. But, at the time, I had no idea that Cosima von Rath was his fiancée.'

Liebermann placed his glass on the table and turned to look at his friend.

'I wonder if she is a devotee of Seth?'

Rheinhardt nodded, silently savouring the implications and possibilities of such a connection.

'Anyway,' Rheinhardt continued, 'there's more to tell. Yesterday I received a note from Cosima von Rath, urging me to abandon my futile investigation. Apparently she has been in receipt of a communication from the spirit world confirming that Fräulein Löwenstein's demise was a supernatural event.'

'How very good of her to keep you informed. What else do you know about Bruckmüller?'

'Not a great deal. He's very much a self-made man — and highly ambitious. He was born the son of a provincial butcher, inherited the family business, and through hard work and some very shrewd investments managed to better himself. As you know, he is the proprietor of

Bruckmüller & Co, the surgical instrument suppliers, and I believe he owns two factories.'

'And now he's marrying into one of the wealthiest families in Vienna.'

'Which, as you can imagine, has been the subject of much gossip. When old Ferdinand dies and Cosima inherits her fortune, Bruckmüller will be in a position to wield considerable political influence.'

Both men fell silent.

'You mentioned the locksmith . . .' said Liebermann. 'Have you learned any more of his history?'

'Yes, although it's all fairly inconsequential. He's a peculiar fellow, and the nature of his work inevitably arouses suspicions. But . . .'

'You still don't think he did it.'

Rheinhardt shook his head.

There was a soft knock. The double doors swung open, and Ernst stepped into the room.

'I'm sorry to trouble you, sir, but Inspector Rheinhardt's assistant is outside. He says it is a matter of some urgency.'

'You had better show him in,' said Liebermann, rising from his seat.

'Always something!' said Rheinhardt. 'I should never let them know where I'm going to be.' He stood up and walked to the fireplace where he rested an elbow on the mantelpiece. A few moments later Ernst reappeared, accompanied by Haussmann.

'Herr Doctor, Inspector Rheinhardt.' The young man bowed.

The servant discreetly excused himself and the doors closed.

'Haussmann, what is it now?' Rheinhardt was unable to conceal his irritation.

'My apologies for disturbing you sir, and the good doctor, but something's just happened that I thought you'd want to know about.'

'Well, man, what is it?'

'Otto Braun, sir. He's just presented himself at the Grosse Sperlgasse station. Gave himself up — said he'd like to help us solve the mystery.'

Rheinhardt said nothing. He drew on his cigar and threw what remained of it into the fire. Haussmann shifted uncomfortably.

'I had to act on my own discretion, sir. I couldn't find a senior officer. I hope—' Liebermann raised his hand, indicating that he didn't need to justify himself.

'Well . . .' said Rheinhardt, puffing out his cheeks, hopelessly searching for words that might express his surprise.

39

'Excuse me, Stefan,' said Liebermann, leaning forward and sniffing around the lapels of Kanner's jacket. Kanner's posture stiffened with embarrassment and discomfort.

'Well?' said Kanner.

'Not a trace.'

'Nor should there be. This suit was collected from the cleaner's this morning and I took my shirt straight out of the airing cupboard — it hasn't been anywhere near my wardrobe.'

'Excellent. Are you ready?'

'Yes,' said Kanner, although the tone of his voice suggested quite the opposite.

Liebermann slapped his hands on Kanner's shoulders and gave him a good-humoured shake.

'You'll be fine. Trust me.'

He opened the door for Kanner who reluctantly stepped out into the corridor. They walked its length and began to climb the austere stone staircase.

'I asked Nurse Rupius to meet us at nine-thirty.'

'Max, if your experiment makes me look foolish in any way — I will expect to be compensated.'

'Dinner at the Bristol?'

'Done.'

'But you won't look foolish.'

When they reached the second floor, the two men turned along a narrow passage, on either side of which were examination rooms. 'This is the one,' said Liebermann. Pausing for a moment, he looked at his wristwatch. 'We're late.' He turned the door handle and pushed the door wide open.

Inside, Nurse Rupius and Miss Lydgate were sitting next to each other.

The nurse stood up: 'Doctor Liebermann, Doctor Kanner.'

Her cheeks flushed a little.

'Good morning, Nurse Rupius,' said Liebermann. 'And Miss Lydgate — good morning.' Turning, and gesturing towards his friend, Liebermann said, 'Miss Lydgate, you will no doubt remember my colleague, Doctor Stefan Kanner.'

The English woman looked at Kanner, her gaze limpid.

'I do not recollect being formally introduced.'

Kanner executed a small bow and advanced with caution, keeping his gaze trained on the patient.

'Doctor Kanner is here today to examine your throat,' said Liebermann. 'He has much experience of treating nervous coughs and bronchial disorders, and I would very much value his opinion.'

Liebermann took a step backwards, leaving Kanner standing on his own.

'How are you feeling today, Miss Lydgate?' asked Kanner, very tentatively.

Looking up, Amelia Lydgate stared into Kanner's bright blue eyes.

'I do not believe, Doctor Kanner, that there has been any change in my condition.'

'I see,' said Kanner, moving forward warily. As he did so, Miss Lydgate's left hand flew up and Kanner stopped dead in his tracks. The patient covered her mouth and began to cough. Kanner looked back at Liebermann who gave a single curt nod, urging his friend to proceed. Kanner took a deep breath and drew up a wooden chair.

Sitting directly in front of his patient, Kanner smiled, and said: 'Would you open your mouth, Miss Lydgate? As wide as you can, please.'

Lydgate opened her mouth and Kanner peered down her throat.

'Now, if you would just turn towards the window and tilt your head back a little ... Good. Now say *Ahhh.*'

Amelia Lydgate did as she was told.

Kanner moved his chair forward, nervously glancing down at Miss Lydgate's unpredictable right hand. He opened his medical bag and took out a small spatula.

'This may feel a little uncomfortable.' He placed the spatula on her tongue and pressed down.

'Would you cough, please?'

She coughed.

'And again — a little louder. Thank you.'

He removed the spatula and handed it to Nurse Rupius. Reaching into his bag, he picked up a stethoscope.

'Please lean forward.'

Standing up, Kanner placed the chest-piece at several points on her back and asked Miss Lydgate to either cough or breathe in deeply.

'Very good,' he said finally, removing the stethoscope. As he did so, Nurse Rupius handed him the spatula, which she had disinfected and dried by the sink. He dropped the stethoscope and spatula back into his bag and closed the hasp.

'Thank you,' he said. Then, turning to Liebermann and picking up his bag, he added: 'The examination is complete.' He was grinning with relief.

'Nurse Rupius,' said Liebermann, 'would you take Miss Lydgate back to the ward?'

The nurse smiled, and pushed Miss Lydgate's wheelchair forward.

As Liebermann opened the door, he addressed his patient: 'I'll be along in a few minutes, Miss Lydgate, after I've spoken to Doctor Kanner.'

He closed the door.

'Well,' said Kanner. 'Quite extraordinary. Remarkable, in fact.'

'See? I told you it would be all right.'

Kanner shook his head. 'So it was all because of my cologne.'

'That's right. Minister Schelling wears the same one.'

'Minister Schelling?'

'Yes, Stefan — the man who tried to rape her.'

40

Cosima von Rath was struck by the change in Frau Hölderlin's appearance. She looked much younger. Her hair had been dyed red, piled up in plaits and was held in place by a large tortoiseshell comb. She was wearing an exquisitely cut dress of scarlet tulle, with light brown doeskin shoes that matched her stockings precisely. The overall effect of the transformation was marred, however, by the persistence of her nervous blinking.

'He is a strange man,' said Cosima, 'without a doubt. However, I fear that he is also a *bad* man.'

Frau Hölderlin offered the heiress some more tea and *guglhupf* — which she politely declined.

'It was delicious, Dorothea — but I cannot eat another crumb.'

She appealed to her host by resting a hand on her bulging stomach.

Frau Hölderlin nodded. 'I must say,' she continued, 'I've never felt entirely comfortable in the Count's company.'

'Do you know the story?' said Cosima, nonchalantly stroking the flowered chintz of the arm of the sofa on which she sat.

Frau Hölderlin leaned forward. 'I've heard rumours, of course. Nonsense, I'm sure. That he—' She blinked twice. 'That he killed his father to inherit the estate, and then squandered the family fortune.'

Cosima laughed.

'He *is* a bad man, but I do not think that he would have killed his own father. The old Count died of tuberculosis — he wasn't murdered.'

'But how do you know that?'

'My father has business interests in Hungary — some farms and a factory — and some property in the capital. He is a good friend of Count Cserteg, whose family come from the same area.'

Cosima paused.

'And . . .?' said Frau Hölderlin, indicating that she was anxious for her guest to continue.

'The rumours,' said Cosima, 'contain a kernel of truth. It is almost certainly the case that Count Záborszky lived a dissolute life. Apparently, he spent little time on the estate and showed no interest in its management. He was always in Pest, enjoying the company of singers and other ne'er-do-wells. He was very fond of the theatre, so they say, though in truth it is more probable that he was only fond of actresses . . .'

Frau Hölderlin remembered how the Count would raise Fräulein Löwenstein's hand to his lips and let his mouth linger on her thin, pale fingers.

'Or perhaps I am doing him an injustice,' Cosima continued. 'He was sufficiently fond of the theatre to waste a good deal of his money subsidising a number of third-rate establishments which failed miserably. So I suppose it wasn't just the actresses — whose acquaintance he could have made, presumably, without making such a large investment.'

'Men can be such fools,' said Frau Hölderlin.

'Indeed,' said Cosima. 'Whatever his intention, as a result of his activities he incurred some very serious debts, which he then tried to reduce by gambling — with predictable results. When the old Count Záborszky fell ill his son appeared to take a more active role in the management of the estate. But in reality he was simply exploiting his father's weakness. By the time the old Count died there was virtually nothing left — a meagre inheritance that was subsequently deposited in a Viennese bank account. His mother and sisters were left to fend for themselves. If it hadn't been for the assistance of some of the local gentry, Count Cserteg among them, the women would have been destitute. Needless to say, the family seat and land had to be sold, the proceeds of which were absorbed almost entirely by the young Count's outstanding debts.'

'Scandalous,' said Frau Hölderlin. 'I knew it. I rarely take a dislike to someone without good cause. I do not have the gift, but I have always trusted my intuition.'

Detecting a cake crumb nestling in a fold of her scarlet dress, Frau Hölderlin removed the offending particle and discreetly returned it to her plate.

41

OTTO BRAUN HAD not expected to find himself lying on a divan in a featureless hospital room. Nor had he bargained for the doctor, whose watchful presence he could sense behind him.

'We were staying at The Grand, in Baden. There were a lot of wealthy people there, as you'd expect — it's a splendid hotel. One of the guests was a medium, a woman called Frau Henneberg. She was attracting a lot of attention, particularly from those patrons who were visiting the spa because of ill health. She agreed to hold a series of evening seances, and I attended one — just out of interest. It was a show, of course, nothing more, and I could see how the illusions were achieved: the rapping, the apparitions, the appearance of objects. One of the gentlemen present was undoubtedly an accomplice — I had no trouble identifying him. At the end of the seance, Frau Henneberg invited all those present to make a voluntary donation. I swear she must have made ninety florins. It was all so easy.' Braun stopped and slid both hands through his hair. 'How long do I have to stay like this?'

'Until the interview is finished.'

Resigning himself to the peculiarity of his circumstances, the young man sighed, releasing the tension in his shoulders.

'That's better' said Liebermann. 'I want you to feel comfortable — close your eyes if it helps.'

Braun did as he was instructed and crossed his arms over his chest. Liebermann was reminded of a corpse, and wondered whether the gesture represented some subtle communication from Braun's unconscious. Was he already unintentionally confessing to having committed murder?

'When you arrived at Fräulein Löwenstein's apartment,' asked Liebermann, 'why did you choose to run away?'

'There were police officers outside — they'd stopped Hölderlin and his wife. I thought they'd finally caught up with us. There was that business at The Danube . . . and some other business.'

'What other business?'

Braun frowned: 'It was my understanding, Herr Doctor, that I was brought here to discuss Fräulein Löwenstein's murder.'

'Indeed, Herr Braun, and it was *my* understanding that you wished to help the police with their inquiries.'

'All right,' said Braun, curling his upper lip. 'We met an old woman in Baden — a widow. She had some valuable jewellery, a diamond bracelet, a sapphire pendant . . .' He waved his hand in the air, suggesting that further itemisation was unnecessary. 'When the opportunity presented itself, Lotte took the lot.'

'Were you party to this theft? Did you assist Fräulein Löwenstein?'

Braun opened his eyes, his mouth twisting to form a sardonic smile.

'No,' he said. His eyelids came down slowly, like those of a sated cat. 'Lotte was always taking things.'

Liebermann noticed that Braun's hands were trembling a little. Yet the young man did not seem particularly anxious.

'You ran. But where to?'

'A public house.'

'Which one?'

'I don't know — a small one. It's out in Meidling . . . The landlord's a big Ruthenian fellow. I think his name's Gergo. I met a woman there. I was able to stay with her for a while.'

'What's her name?'

'Lili.'

'Was she a prostitute?'

'As good as . . .'

'So you never left Vienna. You've been here all the time?'

'Yes. The day before yesterday, I wandered into a coffee house and picked up an old copy of the *Wiener Zeitung*. It was in the evening, about eight o'clock. I found the article — you know, the one about Lotte's murder — and immediately realised that I'd made a big mistake. I went straight to the police station.'

Braun swallowed. His skin looked clammy.

'How would you describe your relationship with Fräulein Löwenstein?'

'I'm not sure what you mean.'

'Were you happy together?'

'Were we happy?' Braun repeated the question. 'Yes, I suppose we were, particularly at the beginning. We seemed to have, how can I put this, a similar approach to life, a similar way of seeing things — and she was very beautiful, of course. Very beautiful. But it didn't last. Things weren't so good once we were back in Vienna. We argued and argued — and Lotte, who had been such a carefree woman, so unconventional, became preoccupied. Things that had never bothered her before acquired greater significance — she started worrying about the future . . . our security. And she became quite irritable. Sometimes, weeks would pass without either of us saying a single civil word to the other.'

'What did you argue about?'

'Money, usually. Somehow, there was never enough. She said that I drank too much. *You disgust me* — that's what she used to shout. *You disgust me* . . . You know, it's ironic that I'm here now, suspected of killing her. It could so easily have been the other way around. She tried to stab me once — and she almost succeeded. I'd been drinking and was in no mood for her nonsense. I can remember thinking, if she says *You disgust me* once more I'll . . . I'll . . .'

Braun fell silent.

'Did you strike her?' asked Liebermann.

Braun lowered his chin, a movement so subtle as to almost escape detection.

'Lotte left the room and came back with a kitchen knife in her hand.' Braun's eyelids tightened, creating a delta of creases that spread across his temples. Lowering his voice, suddenly absorbed by his own narrative, he murmured: 'I can see her now, standing there in the doorway, brandishing that great knife — out of breath — panting like an animal. She looked at me for a few moments, and then came rushing in. All that I can remember are those eyes and thinking *How beautiful — and how terrible* . . . I didn't try to defend myself, I felt curiously detached. She would have killed me, I'm certain. But something happened. There was an accident — an act of God, you might say — and I was saved. She tripped over the rug, and fell. She ended up sprawled out at my feet, and the knife went skittering across the floor — it went under the chaise longue. I suddenly came to my senses. Before she could get up again I threw myself on top of her. Of course, she struggled — kicked and shouted. But I managed to hold her down. Eventually she gave up, just went limp and started crying . . . It was a close thing — she could have killed me.' Braun shook his head and mumbled: 'It was difficult to loathe — I'm sorry — love her, after that.'

Liebermann immediately seized on the implications of Braun's verbal slip. It suggested to him that, although Braun might claim otherwise, he still harboured feelings of affection for his beautiful and volatile paramour.

'What do you know about her past? Her childhood?'

'We didn't talk about such things.'

'Why not?'

'I don't know, we just didn't — although I think Lotte had an unhappy childhood. Her parents died when she was quite young, and she had to fend for herself — but I don't know a lot more than that.'

'Were you not interested?'

'She didn't want to talk — and I didn't want to press the matter. Besides, the past is the past, Doctor. What's done is done, eh?'

'Herr Braun,' asked Liebermann, 'who do *you* think killed Fräulein Löwenstein?'

'At first I thought it might have been Theodore Roche — but I'm not so sure now. He was a proud man, just the sort to seek revenge. But he had no imagination. That business with the bullet and the locked door . . . the figurine in the box . . . extraordinary. I have no idea how it was done.' Braun's lips curved to form a faint, cynical smile. 'So maybe it was a devil. Maybe they do exist, after all.'

The young man opened his eyes and looked up, straining to see Liebermann.

'I don't suppose, Herr Doctor, that you have a bottle of something or other hidden away in here?'

'No,' said Liebermann. 'I don't.'

'I find that difficult to believe. I know how much you medical men appreciate a tipple.'

Liebermann did not respond, and Braun let his head fall back into its original position.

'I understand that Fräulein Löwenstein met privately with Herr Uberhorst. Do you know anything about that?'

'Yes, that's right. He was always dropping in to see her — for extra consultations. To tell the truth, I think she had a bit of a soft spot for him — poor Karl.'

'Why do you say "poor Karl"?'

'Have you met him?'

'No.'

'Well, if you had, you'd understand. Pathetic man. Lonely. Suffers from nerves, if you ask me.' Braun turned his head and said quickly, 'Only a layman's opinion, of course, but I'm sure you'd agree.'

'Fräulein Löwenstein felt sorry for him?'

'Yes, certainly. She could have fleeced him — relieved him of everything, down to his last heller. But do you know what? She was satisfied to accept two krone for an hour of her time.'

'Did she entertain any of the other men privately?'

'From the circle?'

'Yes.'

'None that I know of — only Karl. I used to say to her, "What on Earth do you think you're doing, running a charity?"'

'And what did she reply?'

'She said that he was a sad man and needed help. It was a side of her character that she rarely exhibited. He's a small chap . . . I think he brought out her maternal instinct.'

'Herr Braun, what did you intend to do — after the child was born?'

'What child?'

'The autopsy showed that Fräulein Löwenstein was three months pregnant. She would have had twins.'

'You must be mistaken, Herr Doctor. Lotte and I . . . we had stopped having relations of any kind. We had not made love for many, many months.'

'I can assure you, Herr Braun, that at the time of her death Lotte Lowenstein was pregnant.'

Braun sat up and, turning, let his legs slide over the side of the divan. His eyes flashed with anger.

'Don't try to trick me, Herr Doctor. There's only one magician in this room — and it isn't you.'

42

THE DOORMAN BOWED and clicked his heels as the couple left the Hotel Bristol. Rheinhardt rewarded the man with a generous tip, given so discreetly that his wife — even though her arm was linked with his — did not notice. If their progress was more ponderous than usual, it was on account of the meal that they had just enjoyed. It had stretched to accommodate some five courses, the last of which was (to Rheinhardt's satisfaction) a particularly sweet Marillenknödel — apricots in curd cheese dumplings, sprinkled with breadcrumbs and roasted in butter.

A cab was already waiting outside, the driver patiently stroking the horse with the handle of his whip. Rheinhardt opened the door for his wife and, holding her hand, guided Else up onto the footplate. A strand of mousy brown hair had fallen from beneath her hat. Although her face had become more round with age, it retained a certain girlish quality and her full figure had not exceeded the limits of Rubenesque beauty. As Else stepped into the cab, Rheinhardt took the liberty of raising her skirt, just a little, to ensure that she would not stumble. This small service was administered so tactfully that, like his tipping, it escaped Else's attention completely.

The cab rolled down the Ringstrasse, past the art and natural history museums and west into Josefstadt. As Rheinhardt looked out of the window, Else, replete with the evening's indulgences, rested her cheek on his shoulder. The cab rumbled along, bouncing on the cobbles, rocking her head from side to side. The interior became warm and slightly stuffy. Rheinhardt's thoughts, like detritus in a whirlpool, were drawn in ever-decreasing circles towards a single point of contemplation: Otto Braun.

Rheinhardt had assumed that Else had fallen asleep and was therefore surprised when his cogitations were disturbed by a question: 'What are you thinking?'

Rheinhardt gave himself a moment to compose an anodyne response and replied: 'I am thinking how beautiful you look in your new dress.'

'Oskar,' said Else, a certain drowsiness thickening her voice, 'you should know by now that I am not one to be bamboozled with flattery.'

The Inspector chuckled, and turned to kiss the ribbon on his wife's hat.

'All right, I confess,' said Rheinhardt. 'I am a little preoccupied. But I have no wish to spoil our anniversary by discussing a murder inquiry.'

'Nothing could spoil our anniversary,' said Else. 'It has been a wonderful evening, and I am very, very happy.' Saying this, she heaved herself up and nuzzled more deeply into his shoulder.

'And you like your dress?'

'I love it.'

As they progressed past the regularly spaced lamp-posts, the cab was softly illuminated with pulses of amber. The black leather of the upholstery creaked as Rheinhardt made himself more comfortable, leaning more heavily against the woodwork.

'Well?' asked Else.

'Well, what?'

The regular rhythm of the lamplight was strangely calming.

'What are you thinking?'

Rheinhardt hesitated and Else continued: 'It's the Leopoldstadt murder. You're thinking about that, aren't you?'

'Yes,' said Rheinhardt, sighing. 'Max interviewed the principal suspect today — a man called Otto Braun. He was a member of Fräulein Löwenstein's spiritualist circle and he hadn't been seen since the night of the murder. He's a stage magician — a fact that we considered highly relevant, given the circumstances of the crime.'

'And . . .?' said Else, with gentle persistence.

'I was hoping that he would confess. But he did nothing of the sort. And the Commissioner is growing increasingly impatient.'

'Will you let Braun go?'

'We'll have to.'

'And what will you do then?'

'I really don't know . . .'

The cab slowed, before picking up speed again, to let an omnibus pass at the crossroads.

'You know,' said Else, yawning, 'I was reading a very interesting article in my *Ladies' Journal* the other day.'

'Oh?'

'About a woman called Madame de Rougemont — she lives in Paris. She has helped the French police solve many crimes.'

'How does she do it?'

'She's a medium, like Fräulein Löwenstein.'

'Are you suggesting that I—'

'The *Sûreté* are not too proud to use her,' Else cut in.

'The *Sûreté* are . . . well, French. We have very different ways of doing things here in Vienna. Besides, I dread to think what Max would say if I suggested such a thing.'

'Doctor Liebermann does not know everything,' said Else bluntly.

43

LIEBERMANN TURNED A corner and came face to face with Professor Wolfgang Gruner. The two men started — and even recoiled a little — as though they had both walked into an invisible wall.

'Ah, Doctor Liebermann,' said Gruner, collecting himself. 'If you have a moment, I would like to see you in my office.'

'Now?' asked Liebermann tentatively.

'Yes, now,' said Gruner.

Liebermann looked at his wristwatch.

'My next patient is at three.'

'What I have to say will not take long.'

The two men marched down the corridor in silence, sustaining a synchronised, almost military step. However they maintained a conspicuous distance from each other, as though each possessed the polar properties of magnets and were driven apart by mutually repellent fields of force. In due course, the absence of polite pleasantries and their palpable antipathy became embarrassing and uncomfortable in equal measure. Liebermann was greatly relieved when they finally reached the door of Gruner's office.

Inside, the room was gloomy and seemed curiously subaquatic. Weak spears of watery light angled through the mossy curtains, illuminating motes that glided through the air with the lymphatic grace of protozoa. Scattered around the floor were numerous battery boxes — like ancient treasure chests long since forgotten on the seabed of the Spanish Main.

A tall glass cabinet displayed several rows of specimen jars in which spongy brain parts trailing threads of nervous tissue floated in a suspension of yellowing formaldehyde. The cabinet looked like a gruesome aquarium and one vessel — slightly larger than the rest — contained an object that made Liebermann shudder: a decomposing abortus with two heads. Flakes of white flesh had collected at the bottom of the jar, indicating that the specimen was of considerable age. This medical oddity — of unknown provenance — was the centre-piece of Gruner's macabre collection.

'Please sit,' Gruner commanded.

'Thank you,' replied Liebermann, drawing a heavy wooden chair closer to Gruner's imposing desk.

'Doctor Liebermann,' Gruner began, 'I understand that you have been treating the English governess, Miss Amelia Lydgate. She was expecting to receive electrotherapy for a persistent hysterical cough and associated paralysis. How many sessions of electrotherapy have you administered, Doctor Liebermann?'

'None, sir.'

'Could you explain why?'

'Her symptoms are not the result of a weakened nervous system. They are the logical consequence of several traumatic experiences. As such, they have meaning. Consequently I am of the opinion that electrotherapy is not the treatment of choice, sir.'

Gruner sat back in his chair like Neptune on his throne. The desk had been placed in front of the window and Liebermann could not see Gruner's face against the glare. All that he could make out was the silhouette of the professor's head and a glowing aureole of frizzled hair.

'So,' said Gruner. 'Miss Lydgate's symptoms have meaning. Would you care to elaborate?'

'Since taking up her position as governess,' Liebermann began, 'Miss Lydgate has been repeatedly importuned by her employer.

Eventually the man lost control of himself and assaulted her. He succeeded in kissing Miss Lydgate — which she experienced as a feeling of suffocation. Her cough, therefore, is the result of a repressed traumatic memory.' Liebermann noticed that Gruner was already drumming his fingers on the desk impatiently. 'Miss Lydgate's paralysis,' Liebermann continued, 'arose at the same time as her employer — frustrated and probably drunk — attempted to penetrate her. His abominable behaviour produced in Miss Lydgate a powerful but to her unacceptable wish to kill him. A pair of scissors lay within reach. Torn between the need to protect herself and the unacceptability of committing a murder, she became paralysed. Her murderous impulse was repressed and around it the contents of her own unconscious became organised in the form of a secondary, more primitive personality, which calls itself Katherine. It is this secondary personality, that now controls Miss Lydgate's right arm. In my opinion, when this psychic breach is repaired, when the division between Katherine and Miss Lydgate is healed, Miss Lydgate's paralysis will disappear. I believe that this can only be achieved through psychotherapy.'

Gruner stopped drumming his fingers and leaned forward.

'And what evidence do you have for this extraordinary formulation?'

'The secondary personality surfaces when Miss Lydgate is reminded of the sexual assault. At such times she experiences a seizure, during which she behaves aggressively and recovers the use of her right arm. These seizures are reliably induced by an olfactory stimulus — namely, the cologne used by her employer. It should also be noted that this cologne may have played some part in provoking Miss Lydgate's cough — it is of a heavy and cloying variety.'

'Herr Doctor,' Gruner responded, 'I am appalled at your naivety.'

Gruner paused, allowing a lengthy and profoundly unsettling

hiatus to ripen. Liebermann squinted into the glare that was blazing in through the window, trying to read Gruner's expression — but it was impossible. Eager to end the excruciating deadlock, Liebermann responded, finding words that were honest rather than diplomatic.

'I'm afraid that I must disagree, sir.'

'Doctor Liebermann,' Gruner began again, this time without any pause, 'I find it difficult to believe that a young man educated in one of the finest medical institutions in the world should be duped quite so easily. As we all know, the female hysteric is cunning, malicious and histrionic. She is a consummate seductress. The credulous physician is easy prey, lured by her confessions into her world of sordid fantasy. By taking her ridiculous flights of fancy seriously, you engage in an act of collusion that legitimises her psychopathology. Only a fool would attempt to interpret hysterical symptoms — as only a fool would attempt to interpret dreams.'

Liebermann resisted the urge to respond to Gruner's pointed dig at Professor Freud.

'Have you taken the trouble, Doctor Liebermann,' Gruner's voice was becoming louder, 'to discover the identity of Miss Lydgate's employer?'

'Yes,' Liebermann replied. 'I have. His name is Schelling.'

'That is correct,' said Gruner. 'Minister Schelling. He is greatly admired by his colleagues and possesses a deserved reputation for upholding the highest standards of moral rectitude. It has been my great privilege to sit with Minister Schelling, in my capacity as a trustee, on several committees for the promotion of charitable causes. To suggest that he would have repeatedly molested a young governess is utterly absurd. The girl is clearly disturbed. I would strongly suggest that when you next see Miss Lydgate, you administer the appropriate treatment immediately. I would recommend the Faradic moxa, an electrical brush passed through the throat cavity that will deal with her cough in one session. You will find the procedure detailed in Erb's *Handbook*. The paralysis may take a little longer, but will probably remit within seven days. Good afternoon.'

Liebermann remained seated.

'I said "Good afternoon", Herr Doctor.'

Liebermann swallowed.

'With respect, Herr Professor, I do not think that I am prepared to follow your instructions.'

'Are you refusing to treat the patient?'

'No . . .'

'Then what are you saying?'

'In my opinion, the patient's account of her traumatic experiences is accurate. Therefore I should continue to treat her psychologically.'

Gruner slammed his hand down on the desk. The dull thud was followed by the ethereal thrum of vibrating glassware — the ghostly, high-pitched song of things unspeakable floating in their dusky preservative media.

'Doctor Liebermann,' the professor growled, 'a refusal to administer the appropriate treatment is tantamount to negligence. I regret to say that I will be obliged to request your immediate dismissal.'

Liebermann had known that a confrontation with Professor Gruner was inevitable at some point; however, now that the long-awaited ultimatum had actually been delivered he felt unprepared.

'Well?' asked Gruner.

Liebermann began to compose a reply in his head. His heart was beating wildly.

Professor Gruner, much as I would like to retain my position at this hospital, I cannot act against my conscience . . .

Liebermann took a deep breath and.began to speak:

'Professor Gruner, much as I—'

There was a loud knock on the door and Liebermann stopped as

Gruner shouted, 'Enter.'

The door opened and Nurse Rupius appeared.

Gruner shook his head violently.

'Not now, Nurse Rupius, not now! I am engaged in discussion with Doctor Liebermann.'

The nurse hesitated and was about to close the door when she seemed to change her mind. Two orderlies ran past in the corridor outside.

'Professor Gruner,' said Nurse Rupius. 'One of your patients — Signora Locatelli — she's dead.'

'Dead!' Gruner rose from his chair. 'What do you mean, dead?'

The nurse stepped into the room.

'It appears that she tied her bed sheets around a water pipe in the washroom and hung herself. We don't know how long she's been there.'

44

Heinrich Hölderlin was walking briskly down a narrow street. He entered a cobbled square at the centre of which stood a large statue of Moses. As he passed the monumental bronze a resonant voice filled the enclosed space: 'Herr Hölderlin.'

The banker was startled: it was as though he had just been addressed by the lawgiver.

'Herr Hölderlin — over here!' the voice boomed.

Peering around the statue, Heinrich Hölderlin caught sight of Hans Bruckmüller, seated by himself at a single table outside a tiny coffee house aptly named the Kleines Café. It had no front windows and the entrance was a very modest double door, one half of which had been propped open with an iron doorstop. A bicycle was leaning against the wall next to Bruckmüller's table. Hölderlin assumed that it did not belong to the big man. It was impossible to imagine him perched on such a spindly frame.

'Good afternoon, Herr Bruckmüller.'

'Good afternoon, Hölderlin. Coffee?'

Hölderlin made a show of examining his pocket watch and then, after feigning some mental calculations, replied, 'Yes, why not?'

Bruckmüller leaned back in his chair and bellowed into the gloomy interior of the tiny coffee house.

'Egon!'

Immediately a rangy young man with a downy moustache and sparse side-whiskers appeared. He was little more than a boy.

'Another *fiacre* for me. And you, Hölderlin?'

'A *melange*.'

The boy bowed and loped into the darkness.

Hölderlin sat at the table, removed his hat, and wiped a flat hand over his bald head.

'You are a frequent patron, Bruckmüller?'

'Yes, I am. It's a little haven, a splendid place for quiet contemplation.'

'Then perhaps I have disturbed you?'

'Not at all,' said Bruckmüller, smiling. But the smile was too hasty and lingered for longer than was strictly necessary.

Hölderlin placed the volume he was carrying on the table and Bruckmüller lowered his head to read the spine.

'*Isis Unveiled.*'

'By Madame Blavatsky.'

'Interesting?'

'I don't know. To be honest, I haven't read it — it belongs to my wife. I've just been to collect it from Herr Überhorst. Juno lent him this book over a month ago.'

'And he didn't return it?' said Bruckmüller, surprised.

'No,' said Hölderlin. 'Although such an oversight can be forgiven.'

'Yes,' said Bruckmüller, relenting. 'Under the circumstances . . .'

The waiter returned with a silver tray and slid it onto the table. Bruckmüller's *fiacre* exuded a strong smell of rum and was topped with a spiral shell of whipped cream. The frothed milk in Hölderlin's *melange* seemed animate and bubbly, like frog's spawn, and was creeping over the lip of his coffee cup. He interrupted its journey with a teaspoon and scooped the foam into his mouth.

'His behaviour — at the seance . . .' Bruckmüller looked across the square at the Renaissance façade of the Franziskankirche. The church's high, involute gable was adorned with saints and Egyptian obelisks. 'What did you make of it?'

'Difficult to say . . .'

'He wanted to know whether he should tell *them*. You thought he meant the police, didn't you?' The banker looked distinctly uncomfortable. 'And a matter of honour? What on earth did he mean by that?'

Hölderlin took a handkerchief from his pocket and mopped the beads of perspiration from his crown.

'It's a long walk from Herr Uberhorst's,' he said apologetically.

'I've never had the pleasure.'

'He has a small workshop in Leopoldstadt.'

'Then you should have hailed a cab!'

Hölderlin applied the handkerchief to his forehead.

'The weather is improving — I thought it would be pleasant to walk.'

'The taking of regular constitutionals is undoubtedly a good habit and it aids digestion, so I'm told.' Bruckmüller lifted his glass and took a sip of his *fiacre*. 'Are you all right, Hölderlin? You seem a little—'

'Hot, that's all.' Hölderlin interrupted. 'I think I overdid it.'

Bruckmüller nodded and gestured towards the Blavatsky.

'May I?'

'Of course.'

Bruckmüller picked up the volume and let the pages fan beneath his thumb, stopping occasionally. When he had completed this cursory examination he lifted his head and looked at his companion.

'Was it some demon, do you think?' Bruckmüller's voice was a confidential rumble.

'The spirit said so.'

'Yes . . . but I'm asking what *you* think, Hölderlin. I know what the spirit said, but what's your opinion?'

Hölderlin looked around the square uneasily, as if trying to locate any eavesdroppers. The area was empty.

'I think such things are possible. However—' He paused and toyed with his teaspoon. 'I suspect that Herr Uberhorst would no longer subscribe to such a view.'

'He cannot accept that Fräulein Löwenstein dabbled in the black arts,' said Bruckmüller sagely. 'How naive.'

'Indeed. But there's more to it than that, I feel.'

'Oh?'

'In his workshop I noticed numerous lock mechanisms. In vices and on the table. He had been dismantling them . . . and there were instruments everywhere.'

'The man's a locksmith, Hölderlin! What did you expect?'

'Tweezers? Knitting needles? Magnets? There was even a hospital syringe. It was like a laboratory.'

Bruckmüller shook his head: 'I don't understand . . .'

'I think,' said Hölderlin, 'that Herr Uberhorst is trying to work out how it was done. I think he's trying to solve the mystery of the locked door.'

45

ELSE RHEINHARDT HAD been shopping in Leopoldstadt, where everything was so much cheaper. She had ordered a roll of fabric from a draper in Zirkugasse that was at least half the price she would have paid on Karntner Strasse. Her expedition had taken her as far east as the Prater, and she decided to reward herself with lunch at the Café Eisvogel. She had a particular weakness for their honey-and-almond tart.

Else lingered for a while, watching the people come and go, observing the little dramas that constituted the affairs of the world: a couple in the corner were clearly enjoying an assignation; a group of gentlemen at the next table looked like conspirators; and a solitary young man by the window was writing what she imagined to be a poem on his napkin. In Vienna, the cafe had replaced the theatre. One could learn as much about human nature in the Eisvogel as one could by reading all the plays of Goethe, Molière or Shakespeare.

Else noticed the time and felt her conscience nettle. She had to return home. She had only accomplished the first three items on the crumpled list that occupied one of the pockets in her purse.

The sun was burning in a cloudless sky, and Else opened her parasol. She walked across a wide, open concourse in the direction of the Riesenrad. The giant wheel dwarfed the other buildings, even the four towers of the water chute. As she approached the Prohaska restaurant, Else was surprised to see her husband sitting at one of the many outside tables. Her instinct was to call out and run over. Her step had already quickened when the automatic smile on her face froze and disintegrated.

There was a woman sitting next to him — and they were both laughing.

Else did not recognise her, and judged her, even at a distance, to be quite attractive. She and Oskar seemed perfectly at ease together. Rheinhardt was smoking a cigar, and the woman seemed to be entertaining him with an amusing story.

It did not look like a police interview — or any other kind of professional engagement.

The woman leaned forward and, reaching over the table, rested a flirtatious hand on the sleeve of Rheinhardt's jacket. The gesture was confident enough to suggest an atmosphere of relaxed intimacy — and enough to shake the ground beneath Else's feet.

Else turned abruptly and walked back in the direction of the Café Eisvogel. She was utterly confused and proceeded in a daze. The Riesenrad, like the great wheel of fortune itself, turned slowly and impartially as the first angry tear rolled down Else's cheek.

46

KARL UBERHORST HAD got as far as the police station on Grosse Sperlgasse. He had stood outside the modest building for almost an hour, pacing, deliberating, doubting, questioning, before finally heading off towards the centre of town.

Since the ill-fated seance he had experienced considerable difficulty sleeping — and even when he did sleep there were the nightmares to contend with. The visitations from a now familiar company of vengeful demons and repulsive succubi; the shocked awakening followed by an icy trickle of sweat; the lingering terror that paralysed his body; and the hypnompic presences that melted into darkness. As a result Uberhorst preferred to eschew sleep and spend the small hours wandering the streets of the Inner Stadt. The comforting monotony of his night-time tread on the cobbles helped to calm his troubled mind.

It was approaching midnight when Karl Uberhorst found himself walking across the Graben. He slowed as he approached the plague monument — a mountain of writhing, tumbling bodies. There was something orgiastic in its excess, its unfettered, hysterical mass of swirling cloud, saints and putti. Indeed, it was as though the monument itself was diseased and had started to become excrescent, an amorphous mass of weeping chancres and swollen nodules. Climbing a few steps, he rested his hands on the balustrade and contemplated Faith and a winged cherub gleefully impaling the old hag Plague.

'Good evening, sir.'

She was suddenly standing next to him — a woman wearing a long flared coat and a veiled hat. He had not seen her standing behind the monument on his approach, and was startled by her appearance.

'Good evening,' he replied, stepping down.

'Lonely, are you?' Her voice was coarse and accented but her question was curiously penetrating.

Uberhorst wanted to answer: *Yes, I am lonely.* He missed their little conversations, the smell of her golden hair as she examined the lines on his palm.

'I'm sure a man like you has a few krone to spare.' He couldn't place her accent — was she a Ruthene or a Pole? 'Why don't you walk me to my room, over in Spittleberg? It's a long walk, but by the time we get there we'll have got to know each other really well. How about it?'

As he looked at her, the woman's face blurred. Her eyes became enlarged and her lips more full: Fräulein Löwenstein's smile shimmered across the whore's broad features.

Perhaps he could ask this woman to sit with him, to hold his hand, like *she* had?

The whore laughed and came closer, reaching out and rubbing the collar of Uberhorst's coat between her thumb and forefinger, like a tailor establishing the quality of the cloth. She was taller than him and he found himself staring into her bosom.

He looked away, embarrassed.

'Don't be shy . . .'

Again he was forced to contemplate the old hag, and was reminded that Vienna was in the grip of another plague. If he allowed himself to be seduced, not only was there the risk of infection to consider but also the indignity of subsequent treatment. Weeks spent lying in a hospital

bed, having mercury rubbed into his body, until his teeth fell out —
one by one.

'No, thank you, Fräulein,' he said curtly, touching his hat. 'Good
evening.'

Uberhorst pulled away and walked off at a brisk pace.

'You'll regret it later,' the prostitute called out.

He lengthened his stride, eventually breaking into a graceless
canter.

The shadow-memory of Fräulein Löwenstein's face had played on
the whore's lineaments like bright sunlight on murky water.
Uberhorst was still obsessed with the dead medium.

He must tell the police.

He must tell them what he knew.

He must tell them what he suspected . . .

Looking up, he caught sight of the cathedral spire tapering off into
ghostly invisibility as it climbed beyond the luminescent haze of the
street lights.

Uberhorst felt like a haunted man. How could he be sure
that Charlotte Löwenstein was not with him even now? Her spectral
step shadowing his, her cold ectoplasmic arm linked with his.
Would she chastise him from beyond the grave for not keeping her
secret?

I'm pregnant, she had said.

Her head had touched his shoulders. Her golden curls had touched
his mouth.

What am I to do? she had asked.

He had not known — and they had sat in impotent silence as the
minutes of the afternoon had ebbed away.

Now he was prompted to ask himself the same question.

What am I to do?

The door of the cathedral was open, and Uberhorst crept into the cold, redemptive world of St Stephen's. As he did so, he felt something close to relief. He had been yearning for the security and certainty of his former faith: the stolid predictability of stations and ritual, the spiritual epicentre of Rome.

The vastness of the cathedral was suffused with a Stygian gloom. A seemingly boundless obscurity concealed a lofty vaulting that could be sensed — as a continent of stone pressing down from above — but not seen. Uberhorst made a sign of the cross and walked past the flickering remnants of votive candles down the central nave.

The sepulchral silence was disturbed by a curious squeaking, which heralded the appearance of a moving light in the distance: an ignis fatuus, blinking in and out of existence as it floated behind the colossal Gothic columns. It was the sacristan lighting the lamps.

Uberhorst felt trepidation as he approached the high altar where a baroque panel showed St Stephen being stoned to death in front of the walls of Jerusalem. Above him the heavens had been rent apart, revealing Christ at the right hand of God.

Uberhorst genuflected and slipped into a pew. Kneeling, he touched his forehead against hands joined together in prayer.

Somewhere a door opened and closed.

'Father, forgive me,' he whispered.

His sibilant prayer of atonement bounced between columns of black marble, heeded only by the mute statues of clerics, madonnas and angels.

'What shall I do?'

The ensuing silence was not disturbed by divine intervention but by a dull, echoing thud from the back of the nave. It sounded as though a prayer book had been knocked or dropped to the floor.

Uberhorst raised his head and looked back over his shoulder, squinting into the shadowy vastness. There was no longer any squeaking — and no floating light. The sacristan had gone.

Uberhorst placed his hands together again and continued his prayer, only to be disturbed by another sound: a single footstep.

He was not alone.

47

THE DOOR FLEW open and a hatchet-faced man, pursued by a porter, came marching into Professsor Gruner's room.

'I'm sorry, sir,' said the porter. 'I couldn't stop him.'

The man brushed the porter aside and strode up to Gruner's desk.

'What is the meaning of this!' Gruner demanded, rising from his chair.

The man's eyes were hollow and a thin moustache hugged his upper lip. His hair was black and oily, combed back from his forehead and over the crown in a single wave.

'Aah...' said Gruner, his voice softening with recognition. 'Signor Locatelli. Please sit down, I am so very sorry—'

'Where is she?' The Italian diplomat's voice was hoarse.

'Please, I understand how distressing this must be for you.'

'Where is she?' the diplomat repeated.

'Sir?' The porter looked towards Gruner.

'Wait outside,' replied Gruner. 'I know this gentleman.' The porter looked at Gruner in disbelief. Gruner nodded once and the porter reluctantly left the room.

The diplomat leaned across Gruner's desk.

'I want to see my wife.' His voice was more resonant, and for the first time Gruner detected an accent.

'If you wish to visit the mortuary,' Gruner replied, 'then of course this can be arranged. However, might I suggest that first you sit and compose yourself.' The Italian turned and looked at the empty chair, a single finger lingering on the desktop as he withdrew. Gruner walked to the window.

'Please accept my condolences. I had hoped to inform you of this tragedy in person. You must have been travelling all night.'

'I left Venice as soon as I received your telegram,' said the diplomat, sitting down. 'The train didn't get into Westbahnhof until seven.'

Gruner placed his hands behind his back and stepped forward a pace.

'Signor Locatelli, I would like you to know that we did everything in our power to help your wife. She received the very best treatment, I can assure you. There are few hospitals in Europe better equipped to treat hysteria.' He paused and gestured towards a tower of battery cases. 'Indeed, some would argue that we occupy the pre-eminent position. Be that as it may, some patients, inevitably, are beyond help. By the time they come to our attention their nervous systems have been so weakened that they cannot benefit from our ministrations. This, sadly, was the fate of your wife. She was suffering from a progressive loss of nerve strength that could be neither arrested nor repaired through the administration of electrotherapy. Although her hysterical paralysis had begun to respond — as I predicted — any such therapeutic gains were nullified by deteriorating levels of mood disturbance. In the end, her melancholia was so severe that her faculty of reason was compromised and she became the architect of her own demise.'

Locatelli had been staring blankly at Gruner. When the professor had finished speaking, Locatelli seemed to become more aware of his surroundings, and his attention was captured by the gruesome contents of Gruner's specimen jars. His face creased in disgust.

Without turning to look at Gruner, he said quietly and clearly: 'You murdered her.'

Gruner cleared his throat.

'I beg your pardon?'

'I said, Professor: you murdered her.'

The Italian fixed Gruner with a cold accusatory stare.

'Signor Locatelli,' said Gruner, spreading his hands in a placatory gesture. 'You are clearly in a state of shock. Please permit me to prescribe a sedative. I will arrange for you to be accompanied home by a junior doctor who will make sure that you take the correct dosage. Tomorrow, when you are properly rested, you will feel better and we can continue our conversation.'

Ignoring Gruner, the Italian reached into his pocket and produced a sheet of paper. It was covered on both sides in an inky scrawl.

'This letter was the last I received from Julietta, my wife. Let me translate it for you: *The professor does not listen to a word I say — he is only interested in his infernal machines. I have asked him about alternative treatments but he refuses to discuss the matter. I have heard that there is a new talking cure but he says that no such cure exists. I know that this is not true. The electrotherapy is unbearable — I feel like I am being punished. I cannot go on like this. Please come back soon. I am so unhappy.*'

Locatelli folded the sheet and placed it back in his pocket.

'There is much more, Professor.'

'I'm sure there is,' said Gruner, suddenly showing signs of irritation. 'But your wife was ill — very ill. That is why you admitted her. If you are trying to suggest that your wife was mistreated while she was in my care, then you are very much mistaken. She was in the throes of a suicidal melancholia: that she should have taken a dim view of her treatment is hardly surprising, Signor.'

During the ensuing pause each torturous second registered like the creaking turn of a rack. Finally the Italian diplomat stood up.

'Concerning the propriety of her treatment, this is a matter that I will be raising, in due course, with your minister responsible for hospitals and health. Now, Professor, if you would kindly ask the porter to come back in, I wish to be escorted to the mortuary.'

48

'Stefan, would you cover for me? Just this morning?'

'Aren't you in enough trouble already, Max? If Gruner finds out—'

'He won't. Today's demonstration has been cancelled.'

'Really? That's unusual. Even so, why tempt fate, Max?'

'It's an emergency, I think.'

'You think?'

'Yes, I've just received this note — it's from Rheinhardt, my friend the police Inspector.' He handed it to Kanner.

'*Dear Max,*' Kanner read aloud, '*please come to the following address in Leopoldstadt. It is a matter of some urgency.*'

'Will you cover for me? Please?' said Liebermann.

'Of course. But you must return by midday.'

Liebermann rushed out of the hospital and ran to the main road where he found a cab waiting on the corner.

'Leopoldgasse,' he called to the driver as he opened the door. 'And I'd appreciate it if you could get me there fast.' The cab driver touched his hat and whipped the horse. The carriage jolted forward and Liebermann fell back onto the black leather seat. Dodging two tram cars the driver crossed Wahringerstrasse and headed down Bergasse towards the Danube. They were over the canal in minutes and rattling down a small road that took Liebermann to his destination.

When he got out of the cab Liebermann found himself standing in front of a small row of shops. The entrance to one of them, painted in dull green paint, was made conspicuous by the two police constables standing outside. He introduced himself and they allowed him to pass. It wasn't until he stepped inside that Liebermann realised the shop belonged to a locksmith.

A worn brown curtain separated the vestibule from the workshop. Liebermann could hear Rheinhardt's voice. As Liebermann was deciding whether or not to proceed, Haussmann followed him through the front door, his notebook and pencil in his hand.

'Inspector Rheinhardt is interviewing one of the neighbours,' he whispered. 'Would you be kind enough to wait in here, Herr Doctor?' Haussmann offered Liebermann a chair.

'What has happened?'

'Murdered in his sleep.'

'Who?'

'Herr Uberhorst — one of the medium's circle. An ugly business.'

Haussmann walked towards the curtain, shaking his head and looking rather pale. The brown material billowed in his wake.

Liebermann took the seat and waited. He strained to hear Rheinhardt's interview but Herr Uberhorst's neighbour was too softly spoken. He could hear questions, but no answers.

Eventually, Rheinhardt raised his voice: 'Thank you for your assistance, Herr Kaip. I am much obliged.'

'Not at all, Inspector. I only wish I could have been more helpful.'

The curtain parted and Rheinhardt ushered a bearded man in a kaftan to the door.

'Goodbye, Herr Kaip.'

'Inspector.'

Liebermann rose from his seat.

'Max,' said Rheinhardt, 'I'm so glad you could come.'

'I persuaded a colleague to do my ward round — I can only spare an hour.'

'That will be quite enough. Did Haussmann tell you what happened?' Liebermann nodded. 'Let me warn you, it's not a pleasant sight.'

Rheinhardt led Liebermann through the cluttered workshop to a staircase that spiralled up to the first floor. The landing had only two doors, one of which was ajar. As Liebermann crossed the threshold he knew that something dreadful had happened. The air was tainted with an ominous metallic fragrance.

The room itself was small and bright. Shafts of sunlight slanted through the angled slats of a battered jalousie; the blind swung backwards and forwards, rocked by a gentle breeze, sounding an irregular tattoo against the window frame. A crude rustic table stood against the wall. On it rested a large washbowl, a jug, a hand mirror and a pair of pince-nez. The room was dominated by a large four-poster bed veiled with white muslin drapes. From Liebermann's position he could see that the two visible drapes were dappled and striped with blood.

'How was he killed?' Liebermann asked.

'Bludgeoned to death, we think.'

Liebermann approached the bed and gently pulled the nearest piece of muslin aside. What he saw filled him with a deep sense of revulsion. His stomach heaved and for a moment he thought that he might be sick.

The drapes made a luminous white box, the sides and top of which were splattered with congealed blood and globs of fibrous tissue. Herr Uberhorst (or at least the person whom Liebermann presumed had been Herr Uberhorst) was still lying beneath the bed sheets, but half his face had been destroyed. His left cheek had been stoved in and the maxilla had been smashed. Liebermann could see directly into the corpse's mouth, as far back as the soft palate. Several teeth were scattered around the dead man's shoulders and some had got caught in his hair, which was matted with yet more blood and a dried crust of cerebrospinal fluid. Worse still, the upper cranium had been perforated, revealing the wrinkled grey-pink matter of his brain: it glistened wetly, a strange fruit surrounded by petals of shattered bone.

Liebermann swallowed. He let the drape fall back.

'He was discovered,' said Rheinhardt, 'at seven o'clock this morning by the maid. She'd come to change his bedding.'

'Poor girl.'

'Yes, she's speechless. The lock on the front door is intact, and there's nothing here to suggest a forced entry. Herr Kaip — the neighbour — didn't hear anything in the night. He and his family weren't disturbed.'

'There's no sign of a struggle.'

'And the bed sheets are still quite tight.'

'Indeed. So he must have killed Herr Uberhorst while he slept.'

'Why do you say "he"?'

'Oskar, a woman — even one with a heavy club — could not inflict such wounds. Look at how deep they are. This is a man's work.'

'Alternatively,' said Rheinhardt, 'he could have been killed quite suddenly. In which case, the man's presence in the bedroom did not alarm him.'

Liebermann looked at his friend quizzically.

'What I mean,' Rheinhardt continued, 'is that he may have known the assailant.'

'He was killed by a friend?'

'Perhaps.'

'Was Herr Uberhorst a homosexual?'

Rheinhardt shrugged. 'He was a sensitive man, certainly. But whether or not he was a homosexual, I have no idea.' He paused for a moment and then added: 'However, I do not think so.'

'Why?'

'The way he talked about Fräulein Löwenstein. It's unlikely.'

Liebermann looked over at the jalousie, which continued to knock loudly against the woodwork.

At that moment Haussmann entered the room. He still looked very pale.

'Sir, Herr Kaip has come back again. He says that his wife has just told him something that he thinks might be important.'

'Excuse me, Max.'

In spite of the revulsion that he had felt earlier, Liebermann felt compelled to examine the corpse again. He pulled the drape aside.

Death was revelatory. It exposed the fundamental physical nature of the human condition. He looked from the pulpy mass of Herr Uberhorst's face to the abandoned pince-nez and back again. Some obscure connection made him feel inexpressibly sad.

This is what we are, he thought. *Meat and bone. Cartilage and viscera.*

'Max.' Rheinhardt appeared again at the door. 'Frau Kaip — she said that Herr Uberhorst had a visitor early yesterday evening. An odd-looking man with a drooping moustache who carried a cane.'

49

'Yes,' said Professor Spiegler. 'A definite improvement. The catch is so much easier to operate.'

'Thank you, sir,' said Bruckmüller, assuming an ingratiating and somewhat insincere smile.

The professor of surgery placed the clamp on the table and then picked up a curette whose weight he gauged in his expert hand.

'This is very light.'

'A new amalgam,' Bruckmüller replied. 'The scoop is made from the same alloy.'

Spiegler exchanged the curette for the scoop, and then compared the weight of each against an equivalent instrument of the same size.

'Have you sold many?' Spiegler asked.

'Yes,' said Bruckmüller. 'We recently had a large order from Salzburg.'

'Professor Vondenhoff?'

'I think it was, sir. And we also sold several of the large curettes to Professor Surány.'

'In Pest?'

'Profesor Surány is a frequent visitor.'

'Indeed,' said Spiegler, clearly satisfied with the intelligence that he had gathered concerning the acquisitions of his academic peers.

Bruckmüller turned to the junior sales assistant.

'Eusebius, fetch the specula, there's a good chap.'

The young sales man crossed the room and began to remove a wide drawer from a large cabinet.

'No, no,' Bruckmüller called. 'Those are the hook scissors!'

'Sorry, Herr Bruckmüller,' said the assistant.

'Next cabinet along — third drawer from the top.'

'Very good, Herr Bruckmüller.'

Bruckmüller smiled at the professor and rolled his eyes.

'Just started,' he whispered.

The young man pulled the correct drawer from the adjacent cabinet and struggled back to the table. The drawer contained several rows of silver instruments with wooden handles.

Bruckmüller picked out the largest and offered it to the professor, whose face beamed with pleasure.

'Excellent. You made it!'

'Exactly to your specifications. See how much larger the bills are. We will describe it in our catalogue — with your permission — as *The Spiegler*.'

'Well, I'm honoured, Bruckmüller.' The professor squeezed the handles together and watched the flat metal bills open. 'It's a beauty.'

'To lock the bills, the long handle slides up and the short handle slides down,' said Bruckmüller.

The professor followed Bruckmüller's instructions and the various parts of the speculum moved, snapping into place.

'Do you know what this is for, young man?' said Spiegler to the junior assistant.

Eusebius looked towards Bruckmüller.

'It's all right, Eusebius — you can answer.'

'No, sir. I only know that it is a speculum.'

The professor laughed.

'Make a little circle with your thumb and forefinger — like so.' The professor demonstrated and the young man followed suit.

'When I wish to examine a growth in a patient's rectum, I slide this instrument into the anus.' Spiegler pushed the closed bills through the small hole created by the assistant's thumb and forefinger. 'And I prise it open.' He squeezed the handles and the metal bills drew apart, widening the simulated sphincter.

The assistant swallowed.

'Does it hurt, sir?'

'Of course it hurts!' said the professor, laughing amiably.

Bruckmüller joined in with a hearty guffaw and slapped the junior assistant hard on the shoulder. But his good humour was immediately moderated by the sudden appearance of a policeman looking through the shop's front window. Bruckmüller recognised him immediately. The young man had been at Fräulein Löwenstein's apartment.

'Excuse me, Herr Professor,' said Bruckmüller. He marched across the shop floor and opened the door. There was a blast of noise. The street outside was full of afternoon traffic. A tram rolled by, its bell clanging loudly.

'Yes?' Bruckmüller was almost shouting.

'Herr Bruckmüller,' replied Haussmann. 'I wonder if you could spare a few minutes?'

'Again?'

50

Count Záborszky pressed the needle through the parchment-like skin of his arm and depressed the plunger of the syringe. He closed his eyes and waited for the morphine to take effect.

The police had found him taking his lunch at the Csarda restaurant. They had insisted that he accompany them to the Schottenring station where he had been questioned all afternoon. During one of the rest periods he had been allowed outside to smoke a cigarette. He had strolled towards the Danube canal. On his return, he had seen a carriage pull up outside the station. A young man had been frogmarched into the building. It looked like Otto Braun.

The police had wanted to know why he had been to see Herr Uberhorst the previous evening.

'I have enemies,' he had said, pointing at his bruised eye. 'I wanted to consult Herr Uberhorst on a matter of security.'

'You wanted him to supply a lock?'

'Yes. A good one for my front door.' The Inspector had looked at him sceptically. 'I lost some money at cards . . . to a gentleman. It is my understanding that he is anxious to get it back.'

'Why did you not come to the police for protection?'

'The gentleman in question is from my homeland. We have our own way of doing things.'

And so the questions had continued — a relentless inquisition.

That irritating, fat Inspector!

As the morphine took effect a gentle warmth spread through Záborszky's body. His eyelids became heavy and a blurred impression of the world flickered for a few moments before giving way to shadow. The day faded and magical colours began to coalesce out of the infinite darkness. He saw a great house sitting on a wall of rock and heard the sound of a foaming river, rushing through a deep valley.

'Zoltan.' The voice was female and sounded distant. 'Zoltan?'

Was it his mother? One of his sisters?

He tried to open his eyes but found it difficult to do so.

'Here, let me take that.'

Slowly, his lids lifted and he saw the vague shape of a woman kneeling beside him.

His hand was still holding the depressed syringe and the needle was still in his arm. She carefully placed her thumb and forefinger on the glass body of the syringe and tugged it from his weak grip. Záborszky watched a bead of blood well up from the dermal puncture. It grew, and finally trickled along the crease of his elbow joint. He was fascinated by its brilliance — a bright scarlet.

The woman's feet appeared in his field of vision.

She was wearing a pair of small leather boots with high heels — the laces crossing between two columns of silver-edged holes. He could not see the hem of a dress or any evidence of an undergarment. She was wearing black cotton stockings, and as he raised his eyes he noticed that her legs were slim and shapely.

It wasn't his mother.

The woman's stocking tops were heavily embroidered with a complicated floral pattern, and were supported by green garters that bit into thighs of luminous white flesh.

In order to continue his examination Záborszky had to raise his head — a task that seemed to require an extraordinary amount of effort.

Struts of whalebone fanned out from a tiny waist, supporting sails of shiny red silk. Záborszky became engrossed by every detail — the dangling ribbons, the threads of green and gold, the hook-and-eye arrangement that kept the corset tightly closed. The woman's statuesque breasts were pressed together, and were powdered. For the first time Záborszky became aware of her perfume — which reminded him of night-scented stock.

With one final Herculean effort, Záborszky tilted his head back and looked up at her face.

'Well.' Her lips were moving, but there seemed to be no correspondence between the motions of her mouth and the sounds that she produced. 'Do you want some *kätzchen?*'

She opened her legs and sat on his lap — straddling him as though he was a horse. She pulled his face on to her breasts, and without thought he began to kiss them. The flesh was firm and remarkably cool.

Her hands were in Záborszky's hair. She pulled her fingers together and jerked his head back.

There was something about her face that made him feel uneasy. She was curiously familiar.

'What's the matter?' Her words had a shifting, liquid quality. 'You look scared.'

Those blue eyes . . . those spirals of blonde hair.

'You mustn't be scared.'

How could this be?

'I've got something for you.'

'Lotte,' he whispered. 'Lotte?'

Szépasszony. Fair one. Demonic seductresss.

His hands slid up the woman's bare arms, over her smooth shoulders and settled in the hollows beneath her lower jaw.

The witch had said: *She will get you.*

'What are you doing?'

Záborszky's fingers closed around the woman's neck.

Those blue eyes. Storms and showers of hail.

The woman tried to move but discovered that the Count's grip was resolute. His expression betrayed the kindling of a strange passion.

'Please . . . let me go,' she said.

Squeezed through the passage of a constricted windpipe, her voice was suddenly very thin.

51

CosIMA VON RATH seemed entirely out of place in Rheinhardt's office: too large and too colourful for such a functional space. She shifted her weight on the hard wooden chair, her capacious haunches spreading and bulging over its edges. Rheinhardt would have found her presence less disconcerting had she been held aloft in a palanquin, supported on the shoulders of eight Nubian slaves.

Waving a fan in front of her round face, she continued her account: 'Herr Uberhorst did behave strangely. He wanted to ask the spirit a question, and he was quite adamant that he should receive a definitive answer — a yes or a no: I recall that quite clearly.'

Rheinhardt twisted the tip of his moustache between thumb and forefinger: 'And the question he wanted to ask was?'

'Should I tell . . . *them*.'

'"Them" being who?'

'I have no idea, Inspector — he wouldn't say. We assured him that he was among friends and had nothing to fear, but nothing would induce Herr Uberhorst to provide us with an explanation. He said that it was a private matter.'

'Did he say anything else?'

'No.'

'Please, Fräulein, think harder — it might be important.'

Cosima stopped fanning herself and paused. Rheinhardt could see that his request had been taken seriously. Her brow became corrugated with deep lines as her lips puckered.

'Well,' she said finally. 'He said it was a private matter . . . but he also mentioned honour. Yes, that's right — he couldn't explain himself because it was a matter of honour.'

'And what do you make of that?'

Cosima closed her fan and tapped it against her protrusive lips.

'I imagine he supposed that if we learned who he intended to communicate with then it would reflect badly on Fräulein Löwenstein. I suppose he was trying to protect her reputation. Which suggests that he was in some way implicated in her scheme.'

'Scheme?'

'To subjugate a higher power. Given Herr Uberhorst's fate, I am now even more convinced that this was the case.'

'So, you think that Herr Uberhorst too was killed by a supernatural entity?'

Cosima dropped her fan and clutched the ankh that hang around her neck.

'Yes, I do.'

'Would that be Seth — again?'

Cosima's eyes widened and her knuckles paled as she clutched the talisman.

'He is a great god, and a mischievous god . . . Yes, it is possible.'

Rheinhardt made some notes. As his pen scratched across the paper he said: 'I owe you an apology, Fräulein von Rath. I am sorry I did not respond more promptly to your letter. Unfortunately, I have been rather busy.'

'I feared that you would dismiss my discovery,' said Cosima.

'No, not at all,' said Rheinhardt. 'In actual fact, I was in the process of planning a similar investigation myself.'

Cosima opened her fan again and fluttered it close to her neck.

'A seance?'

Rheinhardt placed his pen on the table.

'Fräulein, have you heard of Madame de Rougemont?'

'No,' said Cosima, her voice dropping in pitch. 'I don't think I have.'

'She is a French medium employed by the *Sûreté* in Paris. She is reputed to possess an extraordinary gift. It is my understanding that she has solved numerous crimes and mysteries.'

'Really?' Cosima's eyes glinted with interest. 'I've never heard of her.'

'Few people know of Madame de Rougemont's existence,' said Rheinhardt. 'The *Sûreté* guard her jealously.'

'Fascinating,' said Cosima, shifting her bulk forward.

'I had already telegraphed Inspector Laurent in Paris, requesting Madame de Rougemont's assistance, when I received your letter.'

'And?'

'The request was granted.'

'She has agreed to visit Vienna?'

'Madame de Rougemont will be here on Wednesday.'

Cosima seemed agitated with excitement, her wide mealy face becoming speckled with little red blotches.

'It may be that Madame de Rougemont will confirm your findings,' continued Rheinhardt. 'She may also help us to solve the mystery of Herr Uberhorst's tragic demise. To this end, she has proposed that we arrange another seance — to be attended by all the members of Fräulein Löwenstein's circle. I was wondering, would you be willing to assist with the arrangements?'

'Of course . . .' Cosima looked flushed and breathless.

Rheinhardt scribbled something in his notebook.

'Madame de Rougemont will be staying at this address,' he tore the sheet out. 'It's near the Peterskirche. I would like everyone to be there at eight o'clock on Thursday.'

Cosima took the sheet of paper. Her hand was shaking with excitement.

'I will send invitations immediately — to everyone — except for Herr Braun, of course.'

'No, include Herr Braun too.'

'You've found him?'

'He returned to Vienna last week. He had been called to the bedside of an ailing aunt in Salzburg — apparently.'

Rheinhardt's delivery was as dry as tinder.

52

'Apparently, when Signor Locatelli was taken to the mortuary he was horrified to discover that his wife's legs had been badly burned. This of course confirmed what she had already written — that Professor Gruner had been subjecting her to an over-zealous regimen of electrotherapy. Locatelli spoke to some of his friends in the parliament building and a few days later a government inspector arrived. There's obviously some sort of inquiry under way — we're all going to be interviewed.'

'And what of Gruner?' asked Professor Freud.

'I don't know,' said Liebermann. 'I haven't seen him since he threatened to dismiss me.'

'It would seem, then, that you have been favoured by the god of healing.' Freud tapped the head of a small bronze figure seated on a primitive square throne. 'You will be able to continue your work with the English governess after all.'

'Well, for a few more weeks, perhaps. Until Gruner returns.'

'*If* he returns,' said Freud, exhaling a voluminous cloud of cigar smoke and smiling wickedly.

'I'm sure Professor Gruner has some very influential friends too,' said Liebermann.

Freud shrugged his shoulders and continued to toy with the bronze figure on his desk. It was a new acquisition and, typically, he seemed unable to leave it alone.

'Imhotep,' said Freud, suddenly aware of Liebermann observing him.

Liebermann's blank expression invited an explanation.

'He was identified during classical times with the Greek god of healing — Asklepios.'

'Ahh,' said Liebermann.

Freud pushed the bronze figure back into its space among the ancient statuettes and suddenly picked up the thread of their original conversation.

'The case you describe is extremely interesting, Max. But I have some reservations concerning your technique and interpretation.'

Liebermann raised his eyebrows.

'As you know,' continued Freud, 'I have abandoned hypnosis in favour of free association — encouraging the patient to say whatever comes to mind, without censorship. The analyst listens, and learns not only from what is said but also from its character and form: the silences, the hesitations, the changes of volume and direction. Hypnosis is fraught with problems . . . for example, not all patients are susceptible to the trance state. I remember, when I visited Nancy a few years ago, that Liébeault was perfectly happy to acknowledge this. Bernheim had greater success but, from my experience, true somnambulism is achievable in far fewer cases than Bernheim's reports would lead us to expect. Be that as it may, in my estimation the most significant problem associated with hypnosis is that one can never be entirely sure whether or not the phenomena under observation are genuine. The hypnotic trance renders the patient uniquely suggestible . . . I think it no coincidence that conditions such as multiple personality emerge more frequently in those clinics where hypnosis is practised.' Liebermann's disappointment was clearly evident, and the older man was moved to soften the blow of his critique with a modest qualification. 'Naturally, I cannot comment

on the clinical authenticity of your governess — but it is something
to bear in mind, Max.'

'Of course,' said Liebermann respectfully. Then, steeling himself
for more disapprobation, he added tentatively, 'And you also had some
reservations about my . . . interpretation?'

Freud stubbed out his cigar and leaned forward, resting his elbows
on his desk and linking his hands.

'You assume that your governess's symptoms are the direct result
of traumata — the ostensibly offensive sexual overtures of her relative.
But what if . . . what if your governess is ambivalent? What if she is
attracted, albeit unconsciously, to this man? Perhaps her symptoms are
not a defence as such against him, but a defence against her own
powerful desire to reciprocate.'

Liebermann's brow was creased by a pronounced frown line.

'Ahh . . .' said Freud. 'I can see that you do not find such an
explanation plausible — but you should not underestimate the
significance of erotic life in the etiology of hysterical symptoms. I had
a similar case a few years ago — an eighteen-year-old woman with
tussis nervosa and aphonia. She too had been importuned by a family
friend; however, it transpired that her symptoms were the result not of
his transgressions but rather of the repression of her own libido. The
entire case history is somewhat complicated and the conclusion
unsatisfactory. But I wrote up my notes last year and the article was
accepted for publication in the *Monatsschrift für Psychiatrie und Neurologie*
by one of the editors — a chap called Ziehen.'

'Well, I look forward to reading it,' said Liebermann. Nonetheless,
he was a little troubled by the professor's customary insistence on the
importance of repressed sexual desire. Freud had a reputation for being
dogmatic in this respect, and Liebermann could not believe that
Amelia Lydgate harboured a secret wish to be intimate with a man like
Herr Schelling.

Freud offered Liebermann another cigar.

Liebermann hesitated.

'Go on,' said Freud. 'These are far too good to pass over.'

As Liebermann took a cigar from the box, Freud asked: 'Do you know Stekel?'

'Wilhelm Stekel?'

'Yes.'

'Not personally.'

'He's a general practitioner, but he's extremely interested in my work. He wrote a very enthusiastic review of my dream book for the *Neues Wiener Tagblatt*.'

'Yes, I remember reading it.'

'Well, we met in The Imperial a few days ago, and he made a splendid suggestion. He proposed that we should hold a meeting — about once a week — to discuss cases and ideas. Perhaps we could start in the autumn. There are a few other people interested: Kahane, Reitler, and you must know Adler. How would Wednesday evenings suit you?'

'Wednesday . . .' Although Liebermann greatly respected Freud, the younger man was not sure whether he was ready to become a fully fledged disciple.

'Is there a problem?'

'I currently have a fencing lesson on Wednesdays — with Signor Barbasetti — but . . .' Liebermann decided that it would be ungraceful not to accept Freud's invitation. 'I'm sure I can change that.'

'Good,' said Freud. 'I'll keep you informed.'

The two men lit their cigars, and wreaths of blue smoke thickened the already dense atmosphere.

'How is your book on jokes progressing, Herr Professor?' asked Liebermann — struggling to get an even burn on his cigar's tip.

Freud sat back in his chair, taking Liebermann's enquiry as an opportunity to perform: 'The matchmaker goes to discuss the bride, and he's brought his assistant to support his suit. She's built like a fir tree, says the matchmaker. *Like a fir tree*, the assistant repeats. And what eyes she has — you've got to see them! *Oh and what eyes*, says the assistant. *Beautiful*. And as for education, there's no one like her. *No one like her!* comes the echo. But there is *one* thing, the matchmaker concedes: she does have a hump. *But such a hump!*'

Against his better judgement, Liebermann found himself laughing.

Part Four

The Last Seance

53

'So, WHAT DO YOU think Uberhorst meant?' asked Rheinhardt.

A street-cleaning wagon with a man on top swinging a hose indiscriminately came towards the two men. They both had to step back to avoid the splashes.

'He meant to inform the police that Fräulein Löwenstein was pregnant,' Liebermann replied.

'Yes — that's what I thought, too. Fräulein von Rath had a very different opinion, of course.'

'Oh?'

'She believed that Uberhorst was aiding Fräulein Löwenstein in her ambition to enslave a demonic power — and that he had wanted to know whether he should seek guidance from a cabal of black magicians.'

Liebermann shook his head: 'You are still quite certain that Uberhorst could not have been Charlotte Löwenstein's lover?'

'Absolutely.'

'In which case Fräulein Löwenstein simply confided in him — I wonder why?'

'Well, given her predicament, she could hardly expect sympathy from Braun.'

A lacquered black carriage, its curtains drawn, sped past.

'The pregnancy has still not been reported in the newspapers.'

'No — and as far as we know Braun hasn't spoken to any journalists.'

'So, none of the others are aware that she was pregnant.'

'That's correct. Only Braun.'

Two Ursuline nuns, with heads bowed, crossed their path.

'Did you notice the odd collection of equipment in Uberhorst's workshop?' said Liebermann. 'The syringe, the magnets . . . I strongly suspect that he was trying to work out how the illusion of the locked door was accomplished. He was an obsessional and I imagine that he would have succeeded, given time. Who else, apart from Záborszky, had visited Uberhorst's shop?'

'Herr Hölderlin had been there to collect a book on Friday afternoon.'

'What kind of book?'

'Something by Madame Blavatsky. Fräu Hölderlin had lent it to the locksmith several weeks earlier.'

'So both Hölderlin and Záborszky might have reached a similar conclusion. What about Braun?'

'He says that he's never been to Uberhorst's shop.'

'Where was he on Friday night?'

'He says he was alone in his room — having drunk too much.'

Three cavalry officers turned along the road ahead of them. Their spurs jangled like the strumming of a distant guitar.

'How can you be sure that Braun will be there this evening?' asked Liebermann.

'Haussmann has been with him all day,' said Rheinhardt, 'and will escort Herr Braun to Madame de Rougemont's should he demur.'

'That was a very sensible precaution, Oskar.'

'Indeed. He didn't want to come tonight. He didn't want to see any of them again. Not because he was feeling any remorse but because he thought we might have told them about his trickery — he was worried about them confronting him and asking him for their money back.'

'Did you tell Cosima von Rath that they'd all been duped?' asked Liebermann.

'No.'

'What does she know about Braun's suspicious disappearance?'

'I told Fräulein von Rath that he had been called to Salzburg in order to attend an ailing aunt. Braun knows what to say, should anyone ask any difficult questions. I dare say they'll learn the truth in due course.'

The two men followed the fenestrated cliff face of the Hoffburg Palace towards Josefplatz. As the light failed, a lamplighter went about his business on the other side of the road.

'You know, Max, I was quite surprised that you agreed to accompany me this evening.'

'Why?'

'Because you think seances are ridiculous.'

'They are.'

'Then why were you so eager to attend this one?'

'Isn't it obvious?'

'Not really.'

'This will probably be the last time Fräulein Löwenstein's circle meet. I'll never get another opportunity like this — it'll be extremely interesting to see them all together.'

They walked past an equestrian statue of the second Emperor Josef, set in the middle of an imposing square of white baroque façades.

'Aren't you even a little curious about Madame de Rougemont?' asked Rheinhardt, a note of desperation creeping into his voice.

'No.'

'She's supposed to be genuine.'

'Oskar, there's no such thing as a genuine medium.'

'She's helped the Sûreté on many occasions.'

'Who told you that?'

'Inspector Laurent — he sent me a complete record of her accomplishments.'

'Well — the man must be . . .'

'What?'

'Credulous.'

Liebermann examined his friend. He was wearing a hard bowler hat, a fine English suit, and the ends of his moustache had been waxed and precisely tapered. He looked curiously stiff and uncomfortable.

'Max — I admit that my decision to seek Madame de Rougemont's assistance in this matter is indeed irregular. However, on Monday morning I had to face Commissioner Brügel again. Needless to say, the discovery of Herr Uberhorst's corpse has made him no less impatient.'

They entered a long tunnel-like archway that spanned the road.

'But to consult a medium, Oskar?' Liebermann's voice sounded glum.

'Are you familiar with Shakespeare, Max?'

'Reasonably.'

'Then you will recall Hamlet: "There are more things in heaven and earth, Horatio—" '

' "Than are dreamt of in your philosophy",' Liebermann cut in. 'Well, Oskar, I will endeavour to keep an open mind — but I very much doubt that I shall be converted to spiritualism by this evening's—' He paused before adding, 'Entertainment.'

Exiting the tunnel, they veered off in a north-easterly direction, eventually crossing the Graben and entering a narrower street leading to the Peterskirche. Its large green dome and two towers dominated the view. Outside the church several fiacres were parked, waiting for fares. Beyond the Peterskirche they found Madame de Rougemont's address — a ground-floor apartment in a well-maintained block.

They were received by a male servant who took their coats and led them to a large reception room. Most of Charlotte Löwenstein's circle were already present: Záborszky, the Hölderlins, Heck and, most notably, Braun. Seated next to Záborszky was a small woman dressed in black satin. She stood and offered her hand.

'Gentlemen,' said the Count. 'Madame Yvette de Rougemont.'

Rheinhardt took Yvette de Rougemont's hand, which was covered in a fingerless glove of black lace, bowed, and raised it to his lips.

'Detective Inspector Rheinhardt,' said the Count to Madame de Rougemont. Záborszky seemed to have taken it upon himself to chaperone the medium; however, the eager light in his eyes suggested rather more than mere innocent gallantry.

'I am honoured,' said Rheinhardt, straightening up and gesturing towards his friend. 'And may I introduce my colleague, Doctor Max Liebermann.'

The medium turned to face Liebermann, obliging the young doctor to repeat Rheinhardt's formal greeting.

'Inspector,' said Madame de Rougemont, her German softened by a sweet French accent. 'It has been my privilege to place my gift at the disposal of the police on many occasions. I sincerely hope that I will not disappoint you.'

'We would be most grateful for any assistance,' said Rheinhardt.

'Of course,' continued the Frenchwoman, allowing a cautionary tone to enter her voice, 'I can promise nothing. I am merely a servant — a vessel. Perhaps the higher powers will allow us to make some discoveries this evening — or perhaps they will deny us. Who can say? All that I can do is humbly beseech them to be merciful, and pray that they will judge us kindly.'

She spoke with a certain breathless urgency, gesticulating and punctuating her speech with exaggerated facial expressions.

Liebermann was about to deliver a sceptical response when the double doors swung open to reveal Hans Bruckmüller and Cosima von Rath.

'Excuse me, gentlemen,' said Madame de Rougemont. She offered Záborszky her arm and they glided across the floor to greet the new arrivals. The smaller woman almost disappeared in the larger one's ample embrace.

Liebermann had expected Cosima von Rath's entrance to be a colourful affair, but he was still taken aback by her appearance. She was wearing a hat, the design of which was clearly inspired by the headdress of some Egyptian deity, and a loose, billowy blue gown made from material that shimmered and glittered as she moved. A thick yellow cord followed the equator of her stomach, and a large golden ankh dangled over the precipice of an overwhelming bosom. Cosima von Rath's neck was concealed by several folds of puffy pink flesh that hung from a receding chin and her eyes were like raisins pressed into marzipan. The effect was almost hallucinatory. She looked like a prize pig that had been bedecked for some obscure rustic festival.

For a moment, Cosima von Rath commanded everyone's attention. The other members of Löwenstein's circle, who had been quietly talking amongst themselves, fell silent. Braun, however, seemed less overwhelmed than the others, and even winked at the seamstress — whose fan immediately rose up to hide a collusive smile.

Conversation in the room began again, slowly regaining its former volume.

'Well, Herr Doctor,' whispered Rheinhardt, 'you might consider closing your mouth now.'

54

THE COMPANY ASSEMBLED around a large circular table, their faces lit by a solitary fitful candle. Its uncertain light made shadows leap from wall to wall — a flapping cloak of darkness.

Madame de Rougemont had asked them all to join hands for the duration of a lengthy invocation, which took the form of an appeal to the higher spiritual powers. Her antiquated style of delivery suggested a medieval source — some ancient rite of ceremonial magic.

'I invoke and conjure thee, O Spirit Morax, and fortified with the power of the Supreme Majesty I strongly command thee by Baralamensis, Baldachiensis, Paumachie, Apoloresedes and the most potent princes, Genio, Liachide, Ministers of the Tartarean Seat, chief princes of the seat of Apologia in the ninth region; I exorcise and command thee, O Spirit Morax, by him who spake and it was done, by the most glorious names Adonai, El, Elohim, Elohe, Zeboath, Elion, Escherce, Jah, Tetragrammaton, Sadai . . .'

While Yvette de Rougemont droned on, Liebermann studied his companions: the languid Count, the ludicrous heiress, and the businessman. He turned to examine the remainder: the stolid bank manager and his wife, the conman, and the seamstress. What a motley collection of people! How strange that their different paths had crossed in Charlotte Löwenstein's apartment. One of them — in all probability — was guilty of murder. But which? Looking at their ill-assorted, perplexed faces, he could detect no obvious clue.

The room had filled with a rich redolence, like the heady fumes of a church censer. But these fragrant emanations had no visible source — no dragging cassock or swinging chain emerged from the room's obscure recesses. Liebermann looked over at Rheinhardt, who returned a puzzled stare.

Although Rheinhardt did not say a word, his expression clearly assked: *Where's it coming from?*

Liebermann shook his head.

'Do thou forthwith appear and show thyself unto me,' the Frenchwoman continued her invocation, 'here before this circle, in a fair and human shape, without any deformity or horror; do thou come forthwith, from whatever part of the world, and make rational answers to my questions; come presently, come visit, come affably, manifest that which I desire, being conjured by the Name of the Eternal, Living and True God, Heliorum.'

Madame de Rougemont paused, and the ensuing silence was broken by the unmistakable sound of a coin falling to the floor and spiralling around to a tremulous halt.

'An apport,' said Cosima von Rath.

Frau Hölderlin nodded vigorously in agreement.

'I conjure thee,' Yvette de Rougemont continued, 'also by the particular and true Name of thy God to whom thou owest thine obedience; by the name of the King who rules over thee, do thou come without tarrying; come, fulfil my desires; persist unto the end, according to mine intentions.'

There was a strange skittering. Something like tiny claws on hardwood. Only Liebermann and Rheinhardt turned, peering into the blackest and furthest corner of the room. Frau Hölderlin leaned a little closer to Liebermann and whispered a curt admonishment: 'No, Herr Doctor. Do not look into the darkness.'

Liebermann wanted to ask *Why not?* But recognising his anomalous position as an interloper, he smiled politely instead and returned his attention to Madame de Rougemont. In the poor light the medium's black satin dress was almost invisible, making her head look unattached to her body. Her serene face floated in space like a bubble of ectoplasm.

'I conjure thee by Him to Whom all creatures are obedient, by this ineffable Name, Tetragrammaton Jehovah, by which the elements are overthrown, the air is shaken, the sea turns back, fire is generated.' The candle suddenly sputtered and Liebermann felt Natalie Heck grip his hand more tightly. 'The Earth moves and all the hosts of things celestial, of things terrestrial, of things infernal, do tremble and are confounded together; speak unto me!'

Yvette de Rougemont's injunction was swallowed by a hungry silence. A chair creaked, and Liebermann detected a slight asthmatic whistle in Frau Hölderlin's lungs.

The moment of anticipation unfurled like a roll of cloth, and with each revolution the suspense intensified. Finally, a beneficent smile lifted Madame de Rougemont's anxious features.

'I see him . . .' she murmured, her voice shaking with suppressed excitement. 'He is here. Oh welcome, Spirit. Welcome, Morax.'

Liebermann felt a movement of air, the slightest draught, as though a door had been slammed in another, distant room. The candle flame twisted and flared — a wisp of blue smoke ascended. Madame de Rougemont's spirit guide had apparently arrived.

'Welcome,' whispered the others. Frau Hölderlin and Natalie Heck released Liebermann's hands.

'Morax,' began the Frenchwoman, 'we — who live in ignorance — beg you to help us. We wish to contact our sister Charlotte who recently passed from this world to the next, from darkness to light.'

In the agitated lambency of the flickering candle, Yvette de

Rougemont's face suddenly took on a different cast: her brow furrowed and her jaw projected forward. Her eyelids fluttered and opened, revealing nothing but the glistening whites of her eyes. Speaking in a convincing masculine voice that was completely free of any Gallic inflections, she said: 'She is here, Madame.' Several among the company gasped, and Liebermann noticed that the Count had placed a hand over his heart. 'I see a young woman, with golden hair and a smile of such radiance . . . but she cannot rest. Her soul is deeply troubled. What ails thee, maid? Why can you not avail yourself of eternal peace? Ahh . . . I was murdered, says she, and I cannot rest until this wicked creature is brought to book . . .' The medium's voice reverted back to its usual soprano register and her eyelids closed. 'Then her soul was not taken by a demon?' 'No, Madame,' came her own tenor reply — the whites of her eyes showing again. 'She was killed by a mortal, with nothing more than mortal means . . . and this wicked creature sits among you — this very night.'

Natalie Heck let out a small cry, which was followed by an outburst of prayers and protests. Frau Hölderlin crossed herself, and Cosima von Rath produced a large handkerchief which she dabbed against her forehead. 'Oh Madame,' she whispered, 'oh Madame . . .' Záborszky muttered, 'Jesu, Jesu.' Bruckmüller stared impassively at the candle, and Hölderlin placed an arm around his wife's shoulders. Liebermann caught Braun's eye. The young man smiled cynically, shrugged his shoulders and looked away.

'Is there one among you whose name is Natalie?' asked Madame de Rougemont in the ponderous voice of Morax.

Even in the half-light it was possible to see that the seamstress had gone quite pale. She shook her head violently. 'No,' she whispered, 'it wasn't me, I swear.'

'Natalie,' Morax declaimed. 'The maiden has a message for you.'

The general agitation subsided — and the room became utterly silent. The candle spat, and a droplet of hot wax fell like a plumb line, leaving a sinewy thread in its wake.

'Natalie?'

Liebermann felt the little seamstress sitting beside him flinch.

'Yes,' she said warily. 'I am here'

'How you loved my butterfly brooch.'

'I did, I did . . .'

'I want you to have it. How pretty you will look, with my brooch pinned to your white summer dress.'

Natalie Heck clapped a hand to her mouth, then looking around at the others cried: 'I *did* love that brooch, I *do* have a white summer dress.' Then, suddenly becoming subdued, she whispered: 'It *is* her . . .'

Morax continued: 'Is there one among you called Otto?'

'Yes,' said Braun, sitting up straight. 'My name is Otto.'

The medium tilted her head to one side as though listening carefully. Then, still in the person of her spirit guide, she said: 'Otto, how foolish you have been. You have chosen a headlong path that will end in despair. What is meat to the body is sometimes poison to the soul.' The young man seemed mildly perplexed, but nothing more. Then, after a slight pause, Yvette de Rougemont added: 'Remember the Danube. Remember Baden . . . and the poor widow. There is no sin so small that it can escape the notice of the divine auditor — no punishment is overlooked. Repent!' The voice of Morax became louder. 'Behold, ye have sinned against the Lord: and be sure your sin will find you out.'

Braun's expression changed. He was no longer superior, indifferent and contemptuous. Now he looked confused. Heck threw him a sharp glance.

'But how . . .' He looked anxiously at Madame de Rougemont. She did not respond but sat perfectly still, the candlelight glittering in the nacreous sockets of her skull.

'Count Zoltán Záborszky,' Morax proclaimed. 'How sad you are. I feel your sadness. It is like a canker, eating away at your heart. I see a great and noble house betrayed. A family in despair.'

The Count crossed himself, bowed his head, and pressed his jewel-encrusted fingers together in the attitude of prayer.

'Heinrich? Is there one present called Heinrich?'

Liebermann was sitting directly opposite Hölderlin. He could see the sheen of perspiration on the man's forehead.

'Heinrich,' Morax proclaimed. 'I have something important to tell you . . .'

Frau Hölderlin looked at her husband — her face showed suspicion and concern.

'No!' cried Hölderlin. He stood up abruptly and banged his fist on the table. The candle jumped and the shadows chased each other out of corners and across the ceiling. 'No, this cannot go on. It is unnatural — I am sorry, but I must insist that we bring this meeting to an end.'

'Morax?' Yvette de Rougemont's voice had returned to normal, and her eyelids had closed; however, her intonation was now weak and dreamy. 'Morax — where are you?'

'Herr Hölderlin, you must sit down!' shouted Záborszky. 'Madame de Rougemont is still in contact with the spirit world! You are placing her in great danger.'

'No, I will *not* sit down!' shouted Hölderlin. 'We have no right to be doing this. It is sacrilege. Blasphemy. Fräulein Löwenstein meddled with things beyond her understanding — and look what happened! Enough is enough! I will not be party to this any more!'

Without warning, Yvette de Rougemont's eyes suddenly opened. For a few moments, her expression was vacant. Then the contours of her face shifted to produce a fixed mask of fear. Her lips began to tremble. Opening her mouth wide, she released a chilling, sustained wail. Its rapid rise in pitch and volume was followed by a prolonged and steady descent — which left her clutching at her throat. Choking sounds were followed by a liquid rattle. Then she slumped forwards onto the table, flinging her arms out, knocking over the candle — and plunging the room into total darkness.

55

LIEBERMANN AND RHEINHARDT entered the dim ante-room of the Café
Central and passed through a narrow corridor smelling of coffee —
and of ammonia from the urinals. Climbing a small flight of stairs they
entered the arcade court: a pillared vaultlike arena that hummed with
conversation and clicked with the brittle collision of billiard balls. A
thick cloud of cigarette smoke provided a low canopy beneath which
a milling crowd seemed to have gathered. The tables were well spaced,
but most were surrounded by audiences of onlookers, openly
criticising the moves in a chess game or praising a taroc player for
increasing his stake.

The two men squeezed past the press of bodies and found
somewhere to sit at the back.

Rheinhardt touched the arm of a passing waiter.

'A *türkische* for me and a *schwarzer* for my friend.'

The waiter bowed.

'Oh — and some *Dobostorte*. Max?'

'Nothing for me, thank you.'

The waiter vanished behind the nearest pillar.

'Well,' said Rheinhardt, puffing out his cheeks. 'Quite
extraordinary, don't you think?'

'She is a fraud.'

'Come now, Max, you're being churlish. I thought you said you'd
be coming with an open mind.'

'I did — and she's a fraud. That absurd fainting fit at the end — I've seen more convincing swoons at the opera. Her pulse was perfectly normal.'

'If you say so . . .' said Rheinhardt. 'But I can't help feeling that there was something more to those messages. More than trickery, I mean. Did you see Braun's face? He looked utterly flabbergasted when she mentioned the Danube, Baden, and the widow. He clearly wasn't expecting that . . . And what about Fräulein Heck? How on Earth did Madame de Rougemont know about a specific brooch that Heck coveted? And Heck's white summer dress! How could she know?'

'Every woman I've ever known owns a white summer dress, Oskar.'

'All right, but what about the brooch?'

Liebermann sighed.

'I don't know — I don't know how she managed to get *that* right. But I imagine she found out all she needed to know by talking to the members of Löwenstein's circle before our arrival. She is clearly a very skilled observer, able to read even the most minute reactions. In fact, she must possess skills very similar to those of a psychoanalyst. Professor Freud says that human beings are incapable of keeping secrets — we are always confessing something or other with fidgeting fingers and slips of the tongue. He once told me that betrayal forces itself through every pore. Madame de Rougemont is simply a consummate observer of human behaviour.'

Rheinhardt still looked troubled.

'That voice, though — Morax. It was unnerving.'

'Oskar, I've seen similar phenomena in the clinic. Morax was a kind of sub-personality, something created and cultivated by repeated use of self-hypnosis.'

The waiter arrived with the coffee and Rheinhardt's cake.

'Are you sure you don't want anything to eat?' asked Rheinhardt.

'Quite sure.'

Liebermann scooped the froth off his coffee with a teaspoon, while Rheinhardt plunged his fork through several layers of sponge and chocolate cream.

'Mmm . . .' Rheinhardt closed his eyes. 'Delicious.'

Liebermann reached into his pocket and took out a crumpled letter and a pen.

'Here . . .' he said.

'What? You want me to read it?'

'No, I want you to draw something on it. Something simple. But don't let me see.'

Liebermann looked away, while Rheinhardt, puzzled, produced a small sketch.

'Have you finished?'

'Yes.'

'Turn the paper over so that your drawing is underneath.'

'I've done that.'

'Good.'

Liebermann then turned around and said: 'Hand me the letter.'

Rheinhardt handed the letter back to his friend, who promptly popped it into his pocket without attempting to look at the underside.

'You drew the Habsburg coat of arms — the double-headed eagle,' said Liebermann.

'God in heaven!' exclaimed Rheinhardt. 'How on Earth did you do that?'

'I read your mind, of course,' said Liebermann coldly.

Rheinhardt burst out laughing.

'All right, all right . . . you've made your point. Now tell me how you did it.'

'I glanced into my coffee cup as I took the letter. I could see your drawing reflected on the surface of my *schwarzer*.'

'Very good,' said Rheinhardt, impressed. 'I'll try that one on Else — she'll be mystified.' He picked up his fork again and continued to attack the *Dobostorte.* 'So what did you make of Hölderlin's outburst?'

'He was clearly very uncomfortable—'

Rheinhardt leaned forward, raising a hand to his ear.

'Speak up, Max, I can't hear you.'

The clattering cups, the babble of conversation and the sound of laughter had combined to create a sudden swell of sound.

'He was clearly very uncomfortable,' Liebermann repeated, 'and wanted to bring the seance to a swift end. He was obviously concerned — worried that something incriminating was about to be revealed. And did you notice how he looked at his wife?'

'No.'

'He seemed excessively attentive.'

'Which makes you think what?'

Liebermann gazed into his coffee: 'Löwenstein was pregnant. And I must admit, I'm inclined to believe Braun when he says he wasn't the father.'

'But Hölderlin! Really, Max . . .'

'He's middle-aged, respectable, a man with responsibilities. Trusted. Just the kind of man I'd expect to become embroiled with a young woman.' Rheinhardt shook his head and laughed. 'His sanctimonious speech had precious little to do with genuine spiritual conviction. I found it very unconvincing.'

'And what about that . . . that woman!' said Rheinhardt. 'What a character! It is not for me to speculate on medical matters, Herr Doctor, but surely . . .' Rheinhardt rotated a finger close to his temple.

'Indeed,' said Liebermann, picking up his coffee and taking a small sip. 'The rumours about Bruckmüller's political ambitions must be true: why else would he want to marry Cosima von Rath? And there was something about his behaviour, too . . .' Liebermann sank into a silent reverie.

'What?'

'He was so controlled. He didn't startle or jump at any point — just stared at the candle. He was overcompensating. People who have something to hide often present a conspicuously opaque exterior to the world.'

'Could he have done it, do you think?'

'The murder?' Liebermann shrugged.

Through wreaths of cigarette smoke they both watched a man removing the piano cover and propping up its lid.

'You've never identified the Count as a suspect,' said Liebermann bluntly. 'Why's that?'

'Well,' Rheinhardt replied, 'on the night of Charlotte Löwenstein's murder he was playing backgammon in his club. He stayed there until morning.'

'And you have witnesses?'

'Yes.'

'Reliable witnesses?'

'I think so,' said Rheinhardt, heaping sugar into his *türkische* coffee.

'Could he have bribed them?'

'Some of them, I suppose, but not all. There were simply too many people there.'

'As far as you know . . .'

The man at the piano sat down in readiness to play. But before he could begin, another man leaped up from a nearby card table and engaged him in conversation. A few people started to cheer and clap.

The pianist stood and took a volume of music out of the piano stool. One of the card-players brought a chair over to the piano, and the two men — evidently both musicians — sat down and cracked their knuckles.

'I think that's Epstein, the concert pianist,' said Liebermann.

A moment later the air was alive with sound — a musical detonation like the starburst of a firework. The hubbub subsided as the pianists ripped through a very fast four-hand arrangement of a gypsy dance tune.

'That's rather wonderful,' said Rheinhardt, leaning towards his friend and raising his voice. 'What is it?'

A ravishing melody in the lower register was immediately answered by a shower of descending notes — a crystalline flurry.

'Brahms,' replied Liebermann. 'One of his Hungarian dances.'

Before long Liebermann was leaning forward, on the edge of his seat, totally absorbed by Epstein's virtuosity. When the first piece ended and the applause began, he turned to face Rheinhardt. He could barely believe what he saw — and jumped as though in the presence of an apparition. There, standing next to his friend, was Madame de Rougemont.

'Max,' said Rheinhardt, grinning broadly. 'May I introduce Isolde Sedlmair? A very talented actress, I'm sure you'll agree.'

'I can see you are a great admirer of Brahms, Doctor Liebermann,' said the woman in black, her German completely free of any Gallic inflection.

56

HEINRICH HÖLDERLIN, wrapped in a large Turkish dressing gown, had been sitting in his study, smoking, for the entire evening. It was a medium-sized room, soberly decorated and illuminated by two electric lamps. On his desk a pile of papers, letters and forms awaited his attention.

Hölderlin stubbed out his fourth cigar and stared vacantly at the green-striped wallpaper. Resting his elbows on the ink blotter, he supported his chin on clenched fists.

What a fool!

The self-accusation reverberated in his head like a Russian bell. Its relentless tolling had given him a pulsing headache.

Hölderlin picked up a bundle of correspondence. He should have replied earlier in the day, while at work, but he had been unable to concentrate.

Dear Herr Hölderlin — further to my recent enquiry . . .

The first few lines made sense, but then each sentence became increasingly incomprehensible, eventually fragmenting into a string of meaningless words and phrases.

She was genuine, Madame de Rougemont. Her spirit guide was undoubtedly conversing with Charlotte Löwenstein. Those messages — particularly the one given to the seamstress . . .

Hölderlin tried to focus his attention on the letter.

... Business account ... intend to arrive in Pest next week ... securing interests ... Herr Balázs ... at your earliest convenience.

Hölderlin groaned, pushed the letter away, and rubbed his chin. It was rough with stubble. He usually shaved before the evening meal, but as he'd had no intention of joining his wife for dinner his toilette had been neglected.

What else could I have done? She had to be stopped ... there was no other way — the risk was too great ...

A faint knock roused him from his malaise. A timid, muted double heartbeat.

Hölderlin did not respond.

'Heinrich?'

It was his wife.

'Heinrich?'

The door opened, and she entered.

'Why didn't you answer? What are you doing, Heinrich?'

'My correspondence.'

He could see that his wife was not fooled.

'Heinrich, I want to talk to you about what happened last night.'

'I have nothing more to say, Juno.'

'But ...' She closed the door and walked up to the desk. 'I still don't understand why.'

'Juno,' Hölderlin cut in. 'I acted on principle.'

'I'm sure you did, dear. But what principle?'

'That is quite enough. Please leave ... there is much to do here.' He gestured towards his pile of papers.

Juno did not move. Although small-boned, her intransigence endowed her with a certain resolute quality. Her husband noticed that she was no longer squinting.

'Surely, Heinrich, you must appreciate how your behaviour appeared to everybody else?'

'Juno, I do not care what the others thought. I acted in good faith — according to principle. Now, if you would be so kind as to let me attend to these pressing—'

'Heinrich!' Juno's voice was shockingly shrill and loud, lifting Hölderlin's headache to a much higher register of throbbing pain. It was the first time that he had heard his wife raise her voice in nearly thirty years.

'You may not care what the others thought — but I do. I care very much indeed. And I am particularly mindful of what that police inspector thought. Dear God, I have been expecting him to arrive at the door with a squad of constables all day!'

'Dearest, please.' Hölderlin raised a finger to his lips. 'The neighbours, the servants . . .'

Juno Hölderlin became even more incensed.

'Why did you do it, Heinrich? Do you think I am an idiot?'

Hölderlin looked down at his papers.

'I . . .' He lifted the pen out of the inkwell. 'I *must* attend to my correspondence.'

He did not look up again. But when he did his wife had gone — and the sound of the slammed door was still inflaming his raw nerves.

57

LIEBERMANN'S FINGERS HESITATED over the keys. Instead of playing the opening bars of Brahms's *Nachtigal*, he closed the lid of the Bösendorfer and looked up at his friend.

'You know, I still can't believe that you didn't tell me.'

'How could I, Max? It would have biased your perception of the evening. I wanted an objective opinion.'

Liebermann picked some lint from his sleeve.

'How did you know I would accompany you?'

'I didn't. But I knew that, as a student of human nature, you would be curious to observe the suspects on such an occasion.'

'Ha!' said Liebermann, opening the piano lid again. He played a four-octave ascending scale of C sharp minor.

'Perhaps I am mistaken,' said Rheinhardt tentatively. 'But it is my feeling that the happiness you felt on discovering that your old comrade hadn't succumbed to superstition exceeded the irritation you felt at being duped!'

Liebermann smiled: 'Yes — that is true. Insofar as you did not sink so low as to employ the real Madame de Rougemont, you have retained my respect and high esteem . . .' Liebermann's intonation suggested an interrupted train of speech.

'But?'

'I still cannot believe that you didn't tell me!'

Rheinhardt shook his head.

'Come now, Max, shall we see if we can do some justice to this Brahms song?' The Inspector tapped the score like a music master.

Liebermann let his fingers find the mysterious opening notes, but before he had completed the introduction he stopped abruptly.

'Though I have to admit, Oskar — it was a magnificent idea.' Liebermann began to laugh softly and, still chuckling, started *Nachtigal* for the second time.

Rheinhardt, delighted that his friend had finally forgiven him, rested a companionable hand on the young doctor's shoulder and filled the room with his mellifluous baritone.

58

'There was a flash of lightning, and the impression of his presence was confirmed. I saw him standing close — very close.'

In her hypnotised sleep, the English governess was reliving her trauma.

'The mattress tilted as he crawled onto the bed. *Amelia, Amelia.* I was unable to move. I felt the weight of his body on mine, and his lips on my face. I could not breathe — I could not breathe . . . I was choking, and started to—'

As she began to cough, Liebermann cried, 'Stop, don't go on.' Then, more gently, he whispered: 'I want you to hold that moment in your memory.'

Miss Lydgate nodded.

'Tell me, how do you feel?'

'Distressed.'

'Do you not feel any anger?'

Amelia Lydgate's face was expressionless, but the forefinger of her right hand began to twitch — signalling the approach of Katherine.

'I feel distressed,' said Miss Lydgate again — denying the more primitive emotional forces in her psyche.

Liebermann wanted the traumatic narrative to move forward, like frames of film being passed slowly through a cinematic projector.

'Herr Schelling's face is rough,' he said, confining the young woman's awareness to the focal point of a single sensory memory.

'Yes — it hurts.'

'His moustache scratches,' Liebermann continued.

'Yes . . . it does.'

Amelia Lydgate's anger was rising and simultaneously displacing into the surfacing sub-personality. Liebermann imagined it, rising from the unconscious, becoming more powerful, gradually taking control of her right arm — gradually flexing its fingers into the corporeal glove of Miss Lydgate's hand. Taking over.

'Amelia . . .' whispered Liebermann. 'Look into yourself. What do you see?'

'Nothing . . .'

'There is someone coming out of the darkness.'

Miss Lydgate's eyelids tightened.

'What do you see, Amelia?'

'A young girl.'

'What does she look like?'

'She has long red hair — like mine . . . and a white dress — like a nightgown.'

'Do you know who she is?'

'Her name is . . . I think her name is Katherine.'

'How do you know her name?'

'I read about her in a story book — when I was very young. It was a book about a naughty girl with red hair. The picture in the book looked just like me. She did things that I would never do — she was disobedient, and had tantrums.'

'She spoke to you, that night . . . when Herr Schelling came into your room. Do you remember?'

'No — I can't remember hearing anything.'

Liebermann rested his fingers on Amelia Lydgate's temples and began to press.

'Feel the pressure. Feel it increasing — as the pressure increases, your recollection becomes clearer . . .'

'I can't remember.'

'Katherine's voice — in your head. What did she say?'

Suddenly Miss Lydgate gasped, as though experiencing a sharp pain.

'Kill him — that's what she said. She wanted me to kill him. It was a terrible thing to suggest.'

Liebermann released the pressure.

'And what did Katherine do?'

'She picked up the scissors — she picked up the scissors and stabbed him.'

'And if Katherine had not done this, what would Herr Schelling have done to you?'

'He would have — he would have . . .' The young governess's head rocked from side to side. 'I don't know.'

'But you do, Amelia. What would Herr Schelling have done to you?'

Miss Lydgate's breathing began to quicken.

'He would have overpowered me — he would have —' her voice rose '— violated me.'

'An unconscionable, heinous crime.'

'He betrayed me.'

'And the trust of your mother and father. What do you feel towards Herr Schelling — at this moment?'

'Anger.'

'Yes, Amelia — *your* anger. Not Katherine's anger. *Your* anger.'

A tear escaped from the corner of her eye and her chest heaved as she began to sob.

'It is wrong — to want to kill someone. Barbaric.'

'But you were being abused. His hands were on your body — you could smell his cologne. Remember the roughness of his face — the grabbing, grabbing, grabbing . . .'

Miss Lydgate's face became contorted and a pulse appeared on the side of her neck.

'I hate him, hate him.'

'The roughness, like pumice stone.'

'Hate him.'

'The grabbing.'

The young woman's right arm suddenly reached for the invisible scissors. Fully aware now of her murderous wishes, she screamed and lunged forward. When the movement was complete, she remained perfectly still. She seemed frozen in time, her arm fully extended. The room was silent but for her rasping breath.

Amelia Lydgate's eyes opened — and blinked.

She turned to look at Liebermann.

'It's all right, Miss Lydgate,' he said softly. 'It's over now.'

She lowered her right arm, and a ripple of movement animated each finger in turn. The faintest of smiles crept across her hitherto tearful face.

59

COMMISSIONER BRÜGEL SAT behind his desk, looking through the notes and papers that had spilled out of four stationery boxes

'It seems to me that you haven't got very far, Rheinhardt.'

His voice was grave.

Rheinhardt began what promised to be a weaselly sentence: 'Well...'

'And you've neglected some of the paperwork,' the Commissioner butted in.

'Have I?'

'You know you have, Rheinhardt.'

'So many forms...'

'All essential, I think you'll find.'

'Of course, sir.'

Inwardly, Rheinhardt groaned at the prospect of wading through more red tape. He was a policeman, not an auditor.

'This won't do, Rheinhardt,' said Brügel sternly. 'This won't do at all.'

Rheinhardt was about to say something in his defence but Brügel's hand came down heavily on the desktop. It was not a loud report, but it constituted sufficient warning to silence the beleaguered Inspector.

'From the outset of this investigation, I made it plain to you that I considered the resolution of this case to be a matter of utmost importance.'

'Yes, sir.'

'I trusted you.'

'Yes, sir.'

'But the longer this investigation goes on, the more I fear that my trust was misplaced.'

Brügel thrust his head out from his collar and allowed a cruel silence to play on Rheinhardt's nerves. Then he spoke once more: 'There's a lot at stake here, Rheinhardt — more than you realise.' The Commissioner grunted and shook his head. He looked like an ox worried by flies. 'Very unsatisfactory,' he muttered under his breath. 'Very unsatisfactory indeed.'

Rheinhardt was puzzled. He wanted to ask the Commissioner what he meant exactly? However, Rheinhardt recognised that it would be in his interests to hold his tongue. Brügel had always been an impatient man but on this occasion he seemed particularly irascible.

'Fräulein Löwenstein.' The Commissioner barked the name like a challenge. 'The door, the bullet — any progress?'

'I'm afraid not, sir,' said Rheinhardt meekly.

'But you still think we're dealing with an illusionist — I hope. Hence your initial interest in Roche and Braun.'

'That's correct, sir. Although they're not the only ones with a theatrical background. The count — Záborszky — he's been involved with theatre people too, although only as an investor. We received an anonymous note detailing his dubious history.'

Rheinhardt leaned forward and scanned the desktop anxiously.

'It should be there, sir.'

Brügel rifled through a pile of disordered papers but was unable to find the note.

'What did it say?'

'It contained some fairly wild accusations, about Záborszky emptying the family coffers — leaving his mother and sisters destitute in Hungary. I used the information to unsettle him in the sham seance.'

'Do you have any idea who sent it?'

'No — but Záborszky has many enemies.'

'I understand the Count had an alibi for the night when Charlotte Löwenstein was murdered?'

'That's correct, sir.'

'But he was seen leaving Uberhorst's shop the night before the locksmith's body was discovered?'

'Yes, sir. Záborszky said he had been to see Herr Uberhorst to discuss purchasing a lock for his front door — which is not, on reflection, implausible. The Count was recently assaulted.'

'Who by?'

'One of his gambling associates. The Count has significant debts.'

'How did he react when you told him that Uberhorst had been killed?'

'I wasn't present when the Count was found on the Prater. But I'm told that he insisted that he be permitted to finish his lunch.'

'I see,' said the Commissioner.

'Sir, Herr Hölderlin — the banker — he too had visited Herr Uberhorst on the same day.'

'The fellow who disrupted your sham seance?'

'That's right. He had been to collect a book and might also have observed Herr Uberhorst's experiments.'

'What experiments?'

'We believe that he might have been trying to discover how the illusion of the locked door was achieved. If Fräulein Löwenstein's murderer knew about his efforts . . .'

Brügel drummed his fingers, a five-beat roll that he repeated between lengthy pauses. It sounded to Rheinhardt like a funeral march. Finally, abandoning percussion in favour of speech, Brügel said: 'How do you know the two murders are connected?'

'I don't.'

'The methods employed were so very different that one can scarcely believe they share a common perpetrator.'

'Yes, sir. It is possible that we are looking for two murderers rather than one. But . . .'

'Yes, spit it out, man.'

'I think it improbable.'

Brügel flicked through some more papers and began reading. After a few moments he said: 'Having spent quite some time with that medical fellow establishing that Charlotte Löwenstein was pregnant . . .'

'Doctor Liebermann.'

'Yes, Liebermann: how has this information furthered your understanding of the case?'

Rheinhardt realised that it was probably better to accept defeat.

'It hasn't been *very* helpful, sir.'

'No,' said the Commissioner, scratching his chin between the silver-grey strands of his whiskers. 'It hasn't been very helpful — especially now that this same information has found its way into the newspapers.'

'That must have been Braun, sir. I expect he sold the story to a journalist at the *Zeitung* for the price of a bottle of vodka.'

'Which is splendid for Braun, but very inconvenient for us. Very, very, very inconvenient.'

Rheinhardt thought it politic to remain silent.

'Rheinhardt,' the Commissioner continued, 'there's something you should know.' The sentence sounded ominous. 'A Commissioner's duties are many and varied and I am often obliged to attend social functions, with other dignitaries — from parliament, the town hall, the Hoffburg — and one hears things. Gossip, for the most part — but not always. Now, as luck would have it, I chanced upon a rumour, a rumour that I cannot afford to ignore. It was suggested to me that a very high-ranking member of the royal family took an interest in the Löwenstein case when it was first reported in the newspapers. This elevated person was assured by a senior civil servant that the mystery would be solved by the security office soon enough. Fortunately, the said royal forgot about the case — presumably distracted by other more pressing matters of state and court. The recent article announcing that Fräulein Löwenstein was pregnant at the time of her murder is very embarrassing because it has once again brought the case to the aforesaid gentleman's attention.'

Commissioner Brügel paused and let his eyes roll upwards. Rheinhardt followed the movement, raising his head until the massive portrait of the Emperor completely filled his vision.

'Surely not,' said Rheinhardt.

'I'm afraid so,' said the Commissioner. 'And my source is very reliable.'

Rheinhardt took a deep breath, and hissed it out slowly between his teeth.

Brügel nodded and tidied some of the papers on his desk.

Now, at last, Rheinhardt understood why his superior was so agitated.

'I must be blunt, Rheinhardt,' said the Commissioner. 'Given the circumstances, it is essential that this case be solved as soon as possible. To that end, I think we need some new blood, someone to take a fresh look at all this.' He swept his hand over the papers. Brügel observed the flicker of disappointment that crossed the Inspector's face. 'Look,' he continued, his tone warming slightly. 'I'm not going to take you off the case, Rheinhardt, but I think you could do with some help.'

'Help, sir?'

'Yes. I've invited Detective Inspector von Bulow to examine the evidence.'

'Very good, sir,' said Rheinhardt. He had managed to preserve a façade of calm, professional resignation, but the mere mention of von Bulow's name had already induced a feeling like that of nausea.

'As you know, he's studying with Professor Gross at the moment in Czernowitz, but he has kindly agreed to return to Vienna for about a month. You've worked with von Bulow before, haven't you, Rheinhardt?'

'Yes, sir,' Rheinhardt replied. 'A very talented policeman.'

'My sentiment exactly,' said Brügel. 'I'm glad you appreciate my thinking.'

60

A WOMAN WEARING a large feathered hat was complaining about the quality of her *Esterházytorte*, and threatening to change her allegiance from The Imperial to the Hotel Sacher or The Bristol. She had attracted the attention of the head waiter and a flock of concerned inferiors who were mobbing her table like crows. Their avian appearance was emphasised by frequent bowing, which made them look as though they were pecking the air. Nearby, a large party, clearly from the Court Opera, was generating an extraordinary amount of noise, laughing loudly and toasting the ceiling with raised champagne flutes. Meanwhile, the pianist was pounding out Chopin's *Grande Valse* at almost twice the usual speed, showing remarkable dexterity by executing faultlessly the repeated notes of the melody. Liebermann was very impressed.

'Things still aren't right yet with the Bohemian factories,' Mendel grumbled on. 'There's still a lot of bad feeling — these Czech and German nationalists! They've made it impossible to run a business there. I don't think things will pick up for another few years at least. Profits and investments have virtually collapsed. I don't suppose you know the Bauers . . . Well, the problems they've had. When Badeni resigned he left a complete mess. Are you listening, Max?'

'Yes — you were saying that after Badeni resigned . . .'

Mendel looked at him suspiciously.

'And as for our kind.' Mendel raised his hands and shook his head. 'What a situation!'

Our kind?

Liebermann felt distinctly uncomfortable with his father's over-inclusive vocabulary.

'We were never welcomed by the Germans in the north-west, and yet the Czechs treat us as allies of the Germans. How can you win?'

Mendel paused and stirred his *Pharisäer*.

'An old friend from the lodge — Rubenstein — he died last month: weak heart.' Mendel patted his own chest. 'Lost most of his assets there — what with the riots and the political uncertainty. He didn't have any children, which was probably just as well. His wife has a small income from investments, but not a lot. Which reminds me, I must visit her with your mother . . . it must be difficult, all alone in that big house — all those memories.'

A party by the door got up to leave, just as another arrived. Waiters swooped to clear the empty table and the humming, bustling confusion became louder and more intense.

'Where is it?'

'The house?'

'Yes.'

'Alsegrund.'

'And what's she like, Frau Rubenstein?'

Mendel was surprised by his son's sudden interest.

'You want to know what Mimi Rubenstein is like?'

'Yes — is she a pleasant woman?'

'Pleasant enough, but shy — and bookish. I always found her a little difficult to talk to . . . I'm not a great reader, as you know. Why on Earth are you so interested in Mimi Rubenstein?'

'Does she have a female companion?'

'I don't know.'

'Would she like one?'

Mendel tasted his *Esterházytorte* and gave an approving nod. 'Tastes all right to me.' Then, with his mouth still full, he asked: 'Why? Do you have someone in mind?'

'Yes,' Liebermann replied. 'An English governess who's looking for a new position — she'd be very suitable, I think. I wonder whether Frau Rubenstein would like to meet her?'

'I could always ask. Where did you meet her, this governess?'

Liebermann took a deep breath and began a lengthy but carefully doctored explanation.

61

Rʜᴇɪɴʜᴀʀᴅᴛ ᴡᴀs sɪᴛᴛɪɴɢ in an armchair and had not heard his wife's quiet approach. Looking up, he smiled and touched her hand. She did not respond and withdrew a little.

'Are the girls asleep?'

'Yes.'

'I was impatient with Mitzi earlier — I'm sorry.'

'It was nothing,' said Else, moving away and pulling a chair from beneath the parlour table. 'She was being difficult.'

Rheinhardt sighed and closed the police journal that he had been attempting, somewhat unsuccessfully, to read.

'What's the matter?' Else asked. 'I know that something's on your mind — you've been on the same page all evening.'

'You're an uncommonly observant woman, Else,' said Rheinhardt. 'Sometimes I think you'd make a much better Detective Inspector than me.'

He leaned back in his chair.

'Well?' said Else. 'What is it?'

Rheinhardt did not want to burden his wife with his troubles; however, he recognised that if he chose to be evasive she would become inexhaustibly inquisitive.

'I was summoned to the Commissioner's office today. He doesn't think we've made sufficient progress with the Löwenstein case.'

'Herr Brügel is never satisfied.'

'Indeed. However, this time he does have a point — and he's invited a colleague to assist with the investigation, a man called von Bulow.' He paused before adding, 'And if there's one man I detest above all others, it's von Bulow.'

Else sat down.

'He is insufferably arrogant,' continued Rheinhardt. 'Something to do with his background, I believe. He considers himself a cut above the rest of us, superior by virtue of his birth. His family were ennobled because an ancestor — God knows how many generations back — distinguished himself in a military campaign.'

'But is he a good policeman?'

'He's clever, certainly. Sharp. But rather too fond of protocol and procedure for my liking. Needless to say, he's a great favourite of the Commissioner.'

Else left the table and returned a few moments later with a glass of brandy.

Rheinhardt kissed her hand and held it against his cheek.

'Thank you.'

Again, she pulled away. Had he not been so preoccupied, her coolness would almost certainly have aroused his suspicion.

Rheinhardt sipped the lucent, warming liquid and his spirits rallied a little — partly because of the alcohol and partly because of the presence of his wife.

'Oskar?' Else's voice was quiet but determined.

'Yes, my darling?'

'It isn't work that's been on your mind, is it?'

Rheinhardt looked at his wife. Outwardly she seemed composed, but there was something about her manner that suggested tension. Her lips were pressed together, forming a severe line.

'Whatever do you mean?' Rheinhardt asked.

'You're unhappy — aren't you?'

'Else?'

'With our marriage.' The words were so unexpected that Rheinhardt coughed on his brandy.

'My darling — what . . . what in God's name are you talking about? Whatever has possessed you to suggest such a thing?'

Else straightened her back and said: 'I saw you on the Prater — dining with a woman.' The accusation tumbled out, brittle and pointed.

Rheinhardt's mouth fell open.

'She was being very . . . familiar,' Else added.

For a moment, Rheinhardt appeared to be completely dumbfounded. Then, slowly, a flame of recognition ignited behind his eyes. His large chest heaved and he released a storm of laughter.

'My darling, my darling . . . my dear wife, do come here.'

Else hesitated before going to her husband. When she was close enough, Rheinhardt pulled her down onto his lap. She looked into his eyes, still uncertain.

'Please,' said Else. 'Do not try to persuade me that you were engaged in police work.'

Rheinhardt kissed her fingers.

'Ahh . . . but it *was* police work, my dear! Her name is Isolde Sedlmair — and she's an actress!' Else's eyes narrowed. 'No,' added Rheinhardt. 'That didn't sound quite as I had intended.'

Rheinhardt pulled Else closer and pressed his face against her dress. He could feel the stiff struts of her corset underneath.

'I can explain everything,' he said. 'And after, when you are fully satisfied, I propose that we should retire early.'

Von Bulow was no longer on his mind.

62

LIEBERMANN WAS WAITING in the drawing room of Frau Rubenstein's house. He had decided that it would probably be best if the widow interviewed Miss Lydgate alone; however, he had excused himself over an hour before, and was becoming slightly concerned. He could not hear their voices.

She's not mad, is she?

Mendel had taken some persuading, and perhaps Liebermann had underplayed the severity of Miss Lydgate's symptoms. Now, left to reflect on the propriety of his behaviour, he began to experience a creeping sense of self-doubt.

No, of course she's not mad, father.

Had he been right to make such an assertion?

If he had told Mendel about 'Katherine', then the old man would never have agreed. A whole treatise on the subtleties of psychiatric diagnosis would have failed to persuade Mendel that a woman who had once exhibited two personalities could ever be considered sane. He had furnished his father with a thoroughly sanitised account of Miss Lydgate's hysteria and treatment. Moreover, he had been particularly manipulative by appealing to Mendel's charitable instincts, portraying the governess as a poor, vulnerable stranger. Liebermann knew that his father was generally sympathetic to the dispossessed — a class of individual likely to evoke memories of his own father.

Liebermann examined the face of his wristwatch.

One hour and twelve minutes.

He got up from his seat and walked to the door. Opening it a little, he tilted his head to one side and listened.

Nothing.

Stepping into the long, dimly lit hall, he resolved to find out what was going on. However, just as he had reached this decision, the door of the sitting room opened, and Miss Lydgate appeared. She was obviously surprised to see him there — but she did not flinch.

'Oh — Doctor Liebermann.'

'Miss Lydgate.' Now that he saw her again — looking sober-minded and composed — he felt rather foolish. His worries vanished. 'I was just coming to find out . . .' Liebermann was unable to finish his sentence. The redundancy of his anxiety was self-evident and he smiled with relief.

'Frau Rubenstein would like to see you.'

As Amelia Lydgate held the door open for him, he could not tell whether the interview had been successful — the young woman's features showed no emotion. Liebermann executed a modest bow before entering the large, musty sitting room.

Frau Rubenstein, dressed entirely in black, was seated in an arm-chair by the large bay window. She was a small woman, shrunk, perhaps, not only by age but by recent grief. Yet, when she looked up, her expression was bright, and her eyes sparkled. At her feet were several books that had not been there when Liebermann had left the room. Clearly, the two women had been discussing or reading them.

'Herr Doctor,' said the widow in a soft but clear voice, 'I am so sorry to have kept you waiting. I was showing Amelia these volumes from my collection — and I quite forgot you were there.'

Liebermann stood in the centre of the room, uncertain of how to respond. He glanced at Miss Lydgate who for the first time produced a fleeting smile.

'Amelia and I have come to an arrangement concerning her position,' continued Frau Rubenstein. 'Would you be so kind, Herr Doctor, as to show her the rooms situated on the top floor? It is a steep climb, and my legs are not as strong as they once were.'

'Of course,' said Liebermann.

Amelia Lydgate, usually reserved, rushed across the room and took Frau Rubenstein's hand.

'Thank you,' she whispered.

The old woman shook her head and said: 'I hope you will be happy here.'

Liebermann and Miss Lydgate left the room and began to ascend the first of several wide staircases.

'Frau Rubenstein is delightful,' said Miss Lydgate, lifting her dress a little and carefully stepping over a loose carpet rail. 'And she is so interested in matters of literature and science.'

'I knew that she was well read,' said Liebermann. 'But I had no idea that she was such an enthusiast.'

'She was even interested in my grandfather's journal.'

'Was she?'

'Yes — when Frau Rubenstein was a little girl she lived in the country, and her grandmother taught her much about the use of medicinal herbs. She is extremely knowledgeable.'

'Well, you will make an ideal companion.'

'I will do my best, Doctor Liebermann.'

They were both a little breathless when they reached the top floor. The rooms, of which there were several, had formerly been occupied by servants; now, though, the fusty atmosphere suggested that they had been vacant for some time. Perhaps Herr Rubenstein's financial problems had had a much longer history than Mendel had realised.

Amelia Lydgate systematically examined each room, her face flushed with excitement; Liebermann, however, was somewhat disappointed. The rooms were small and gloomy in the fading light. He ran a finger across a table top and examined the dust on his fingertip.

'Of course, it will need a thorough clean,' he said.

Miss Lydgate did not respond. Instead, she rushed between rooms, finally stopping on the landing.

'It's wonderful,' she said.

'Is it?'

'Oh yes.' She turned and pointed at the various doors. 'This will be my bedroom, this my library — and the smaller room at the back will be my laboratory.'

Liebermann watched her — and became acutely aware of her appearance. He had become accustomed to seeing Amelia Lydgate in a plain, shapeless, hospital gown. Now she was transformed. Although she was only wearing a simple green dress with a high collar, the effect was striking. Her bosom and the pleasing symmetry of her hips had become conspicuous. Her hair seemed like fire: a deep, burning red. She looked elegant, sophisticated.

'I will inform Doctor Landsteiner immediately,' said Miss Lydgate.

Their gaze met, and Liebermann looked away.

'Yes,' he said, loosening his necktie a little. 'Yes, you must resume your work as soon as possible.' Then, after a short pause, he added: 'Miss Lydgate, could we sit down for a few moments? There are some practical matters that I wish to discuss.'

They entered the rear room where they found a folded gateleg table and two hard chairs.

'Miss Lydgate, what are your immediate plans?'

'Is it possible to stay here — this evening?'

'Yes, of course. I can write your discharge summary when I return to the hospital.'

'I have a trunk . . .'

'Which you can collect when you are ready. Or I can arrange to have it sent on.'

Amelia Lydgate looked down at her hands and slowly locked her fingers together.

'I shall write to Herr Schelling. He will receive my letter of resignation tomorrow.'

'And your parents?'

'Yes, I will write to them too. But I will spare them such detail that is likely to cause them distress. They do not need to know everything.'

Miss Lydgate looked up, and her cool, metallic eyes caught the light.

'Well,' said Liebermann, 'I suppose I should say goodbye to Frau Rubenstein, and allow you to settle into your new home.'

They both stood — but did not move. The moment became oddly uncomfortable.

'Doctor Liebermann . . .' said Amelia Lydgate, her customary restraint perturbed by a trace of agitation. 'I cannot thank you enough.'

'Not at all,' said Liebermann, shaking his head. 'I am sure that Frau Rubenstein will thoroughly enjoy your company.'

'No, not just for this.' She swept her hand around the room. 'Frau Rubenstein . . .' She paused before adding: 'I mean, thank you for everything.'

Liebermann smiled but — as usual — the smile was not returned. The young woman's expression remained intense.

'I will of course . . .' His words petered out.

'Visit?' There was the slightest inflexion of hope in her voice.

'Yes, visit,' said Liebermann decisively. 'To see how you are.'

'I would like that very much,' came Miss Lydgate's half-whispered response.

63

VICTOR VON BULOW RAN his hands over the silver stubble on his head. It made a rough, abrasive sound. Unlike most of his contemporaries, his face was hairless but for a trim rectangle of bristle on his chin. His features were sharp. An aquiline nose separated two widely spaced eyes and his ears tapered to become slightly pointed. However, there was nothing comic about his looks. Indeed, the severity of his lineaments conveyed an impression of quick intelligence. It was in many ways a handsome face: unconventional, arresting and singular.

Rheinhardt noticed the stylish cut of von Bulow's suit, the glint and glimmer of diamond cuff links.

He looks like a court official, thought Rheinhardt. He imagined him in a remote chamber of the Hoffburg Palace, lecturing his acolytes on the arcane and Byzantine complexities of royal protocol. Imperial Vienna was a pedant's heaven — a place where the importance of a visitor could be determined by observing the angle of a coachman's whip.

Von Bulow made Rheinhardt feel shabbily dressed and overly conscious of his own modest origins. Rheinhardt pulled in his paunch and straightened his back.

'Well, Rheinhardt,' said von Bulow. 'I've looked through the files and I haven't found them very illuminating.' As he said these words he glanced up at the Commissioner. Brügel, sitting under his portrait of Emperor Franz Josef, nodded in tacit agreement. 'I couldn't find the floor plan,' he continued. 'I take it a floor plan was drawn up?'

Von Bulow's eyes were of the palest watery grey — almost entirely bleached of colour.

'Yes,' said Rheinhardt. 'My assistant Haussman would have done it.'

'Then where is it?'

'It isn't with the principal summary?'

'No.'

'Then it must . . . it must have been . . . mislaid.'

Von Bulow shook his head: 'Or he forgot.'

Rheinhardt realised that any further attempt to protect his assistant would be futile.

'If Haussmann neglected the sketches — then that was only because he was otherwise engaged. We had an unusual number of witnesses to interview.'

'Assistants learn by example, Rheinhardt,' said von Bulow.

'Indeed, and it is my judgement that people matter more than the position of objects.'

'Well, you are entitled to that view — but it is one that goes against the climate of expert opinion.' Again, von Bulow glanced at Brügel before continuing. 'And while we are on the subject of correct procedure — I was surprised to come across the original of Fräulein Löwenstein's note . . . in an envelope.'

'Is that a problem?' asked Rheinhardt.

'Given that such a note is liable to become damaged with handling, a photographic reproduction should have been made. This could then be handled at will.'

'Had I done that,' interrupted Rheinhardt, 'Herr Doctor Liebermann would never have been able to make his interpretation of Fräulein Löwenstein's error. A photographic reproduction wouldn't—'

Von Bulow raised his hand.

'If you would kindly allow me to finish. After photographic reproductions had been made, the original should have been enclosed between two sheets of glass bound with gummed paper round the edges. It allows both sides of the document to be seen and makes it easy to examine against the light.'

'That's all very well, von Bulow, but—'

'Inspector!' Brügel silenced Rheinhardt with a minatory stare.

'I'm afraid I am completely unable to form a mental picture of Fräulein Löwenstein's apartment,' continued von Bulow.

'Aren't the photographs satisfactory?' asked Rheinhardt.

'Not without a floor plan indicating dimensions and distances.' Looking at Brügel, he continued: 'I'm afraid I'll have to visit the apartment.'

'Of course,' Brügel replied. 'Rheinhardt, perhaps you could escort Inspector von Bulow tomorrow?'

'It would be an honour,' said Rheinhardt.

Von Bulow's eyes flicked upward. He stared at Rheinhardt, attempting to decipher the other man's expression. Rheinhardt smiled, politely.

Returning to his notebook, von Bulow continued: 'I could not find a report by the medical officer . . . Doctor Liebermann?'

Rheinhardt coughed nervously.

'Doctor Liebermann is not a medical officer. That is why he hasn't filed a report.'

'Then what is he?'

'An unofficial consultant,' said Rheinhardt authoritatively.

'Even so, you might have taken the trouble to commission a report.'

'I didn't think it was necessary.'

'Well, it is. How am I to come to any conclusions concerning his findings?'

'I'm sure the good doctor would consent to an interview.'

'I'm sure he would — but that doesn't help me right now, does it, Inspector?'

For the next hour, von Bulow worked through his notes, asking questions that invariably highlighted one or other departure from 'procedure'. As he did so, Rheinhardt's head filled with a whistling emptiness. A sense that he was teetering on the edge of a deep, dark abyss. He found himself staring vacantly at the portrait of Franz Josef — and curiously fascinated by the whiteness of the general's uniform that he was wearing and the deep red sash that fell diagonally across his chest. On a table beside the Emperor was a field marshal's large black hat with a thick plume of peacock green feathers.

'Rheinhardt?'

It was Brügel's voice.

'Would you please pay attention . . .'

64

'I GOT YOUR note, mother — is everything all right?'

'Yes, yes — everything is fine. Come in.'

Liebermann entered the drawing room.

'Where's Hannah?'

'Out with her friend — she said she wanted a new hat. They've gone for a walk down Karntner Strasse.'

Liebermann handed his coat to the servant who had followed him in from the hall.

'Do you want some tea?'

'No, thank you.'

'Then sit down, Maxim.' Addressing the servant, she added: 'That will be all, Peter.'

'Mother . . .' Liebermann hesitated. He was already beginning to suspect that he had been manipulated.

Before he could continue, Rebecca said: 'I know — I know exactly what you're thinking. Why did she say it was urgent? But if I hadn't said it was urgent would you have come? No. You would have sent me a note saying that you were too busy at the hospital. Am I wrong?'

Liebermann sat down on the sofa.

'No, mother, you are not wrong. However, the fact is . . . I *am* very busy at the hospital. To tell the truth—' He thought of telling his mother about Gruner and his pending dismissal but quickly changed his mind: 'Oh, it doesn't matter.'

'What doesn't matter?'

Liebermann sighed. 'Why did you want to see me today?'

Rebecca sat down on the sofa beside her son and took his hand in hers. She looked at him and her eyes creased with affection. Yet her gaze was also investigative, probing. Liebermann found her close attention a little unnerving.

'Maxim, I wanted to talk to you — alone.'

'What about?'

'Clara.'

'Very well, mother. What is it that you wanted to say?'

'She's a beautiful girl. So very pretty. And the Weisses — such a good family. You know, her father and yours—'

'They go back a long way,' interrupted Liebermann. 'They went to school together in Leopoldstadt, and grandfather Weiss helped grandfather Liebermann start his first business.' He placed a hand over his mouth and enacted a theatrical yawn.

'Yes, yes,' said Rebecca. 'You've heard it all before, I know.' She rubbed his hand with her thumb.

'What is it, mother?'

'Are you—' She smiled nervously. 'Are you sure that she is the one? Are you sure that she will make you happy?'

Strangely, the sentence that Liebermann had been composing for the benefit of Professor Gruner came into his mind: *Professor Gruner, much as I would like to retain my position at this hospital, I cannot act against my conscience . . .*

An odd coldness seemed to spread through his chest. Liebermann dismissed the thought, irritated at its intrusion.

'Yes,' he said, rather tentatively. 'Yes — I think we shall be happy together.'

'And you love her? Really love her?'

'Of course,' he said, laughing. 'I wouldn't have proposed if I didn't love her.' Yet, as he said these words, they seemed curiously light and airy, lacking in emotional substance. He did not feel the weight of affection compressing his heart. 'Mother — I'm not absolutely certain, how can I be?' He remembered the uxorious Rheinhardt: *My dear fellow, of course I had doubts. Everyone does.* 'I . . . I don't know what sort of a life we shall have together — I don't have a crystal ball. But I am *very fond* of Clara and when we're together she *does* make me happy. And she is very pretty.'

'That doesn't last, let me tell you,' said Rebecca sharply. 'They used to say that I was beautiful once.' She reached out and tucked a strand of hair behind her son's ear — as though he was still an infant. Liebermann frowned and pulled away.

'You're sure, then?' asked Rebecca, smiling.

'I'm as sure as I can be, mother.'

With that, Rebecca got up and went over to the chest of drawers on the other side of the room. She came back and, sitting down, handed her son a small black box.

'Take it,' she said.

Liebermann took the box and opened it. Inside, on a bed of silk, was an engagement ring. A cluster of little diamonds flashed around a deep blue sapphire.

'It was my grandmother's — your great-grandmother's. God knows how they came by it. I suppose you've been too busy to go out and buy a new one.'

65

The room was lit by candles, most of which had burned down to flickering stubs of wax. A line of abandoned hookahs obscured Záborszky's view; however, the grotesquely distorted images of two unconscious gentlemen could be seen through the glass cylinders. As Záborszky moved his head, his oblivious companions seemed to expand and shrink.

'My dear Count.'

Záborszky turned. A soberly dressed middle-aged woman was standing close by.

'Frau Matejka . . .' Záborszky sneered as he said her name.

'There is a matter that I wish to discuss with you.' Záborszky remained inert. 'In private.' Záborszky stood up, swaying slightly. 'Careful now, you don't want to fall.'

'I would never be so undignified.'

The madam led him down a dark passage into a dilapidated room that smelled of damp. The floorboards were bare and the wallpaper had begun to peel near the ceiling; streaks of black mildew dribbled down either side of the shuttered window; a paraffin lamp stood on a scratched and battered writing bureau in front of which were two rustic chairs.

'Please, do sit down.'

Záborszky pulled a chair across the floorboards, making a scraping noise so loud that it pained his sensitive ears. He collapsed on the chair, slumping and letting his arms dangle.

'Well,' he said, 'what is it?'

'As you know,' said Frau Matejka, 'you are a much-valued patron of our little business . . .'

'I've paid — I paid Olga for everything last week.'

'Yes, of course. I wasn't suggesting—'

'Then what is it? Get to the point.'

Frau Matejka looked like a provincial schoolteacher. She was not wearing make-up and her greying hair was tied back in a loose bun from which several unruly strands had escaped. The silver crucifix that hung from her neck reinforced a general impression of spinsterish propriety.

She smiled patiently.

'I like to think of our regular patrons as friends. Gentlemen I can talk to.'

'You can't have any more money, Frau Matejka. I don't have any.'

'It isn't a financial matter that I wish to discuss. It is a matter of conduct.'

Záborszky laughed — a slow, mechanical cackle.

'Conduct? But this is a *brothel!*'

The madam reached for the paraffin lamp and increased the length of the wick. The effect was not flattering. The sagging skin under her eyes looked bruised and the vertical creases that scored her upper lip were thrown into sharp relief.

'The girls are my responsibility — you do appreciate that, don't you? I'm like a mother to them. They come to me when they're worried — when they've something on their minds.'

'What has this got to do with me?'

'There have been some complaints.'

'Complaints?'

'Yes.'

'What complaints?'

'Roughness. It won't do, dear Count — you're frightening the girls.'

Záborszky rolled his eyes at the ceiling.

'Nonsense.'

'Amalie showed me her neck. She thought you were going to strangle her.'

'Heat of the moment . . .' mumbled Záborszky.

'You know,' Frau Matejka leaned forward, 'there are some who are willing to indulge gentlemen of irregular habit. Specialists. If you wanted, I could make some enquiries. Although, naturally, it would cost a little more. Let's say four — possibly five krone.'

'I'm going . . .'

Záborszky got up and left the room. He was feeling steadier, and marched briskly down the corridor and through the vestibule where his companions were still sleeping. In a small antechamber he collected his coat and cane.

Outside, he paused and allowed the cold night air to clear his head. The door had opened directly — and discreetly — onto a narrow and poorly illuminated alleyway. Bare bricks peeped through gaps in a decaying poultice of plaster. He set off immediately, noticing a figure coming towards him from the other end. The man advanced, a featureless silhouette against the diffuse yellow glow of the street lights.

There was not enough room in the alley for them to pass comfortably, and neither of them gave way when they met. As a result their shoulders banged together with considerable force.

Still fuming from his encounter with Frau Matejka, Záborszky wheeled around: 'Watch where you're going!'

The other man stopped and turned. Now that it was lit by the street lights Záborszky could see his face.

'Braun. What are you doing here?'

'The same as you, I imagine.' The younger man took a step forward. 'Not a very spiritually enriching place — Frau Matajka's house.'

Záborszky said nothing.

'You know,' continued Braun, 'I'd always suspected that your interest in our circle was superficial.'

'What do you mean?'

'You were never really interested in communicating with the dead — were you?'

'You're drunk, Braun. Good night.'

Záborszky turned and started to walk away. Then he felt Braun's hand come down heavily on his shoulder.

'No, dear Count. I think you should stay and talk a while.'

Záborszky remained absolutely still.

'It was all trickery you know — she wasn't genuine . . .' continued Braun. 'And I think you knew that.'

'Remove your hand.'

'So why did you keep on coming, week after week. Was it you?'

'What are you talking about?'

'Did you *have* her — did you?'

'Remove your hand,' Záborszky repeated.

'She was always impressed by foppery and promises.'

'I will not ask you again.'

'Were they your children? The ones she was carrying? *Were* they?'

Záborszky pulled on the gold jaguar-head of his cane. There was a rasping sound and the glint of light on metal. Braun jumped back, clutching his hand and nursing the deep cut that was already bleeding profusely.

'Test my patience again, boy, and I will slit your throat, not just your hand.'

Záborszky dropped the slim-bladed sword back into its unconventional scabbard and pressed down. Braun heard a gentle click — the locking of a mechanism. Without looking round to face Braun, Záborszky began walking again. When he reached the end of the alley, it seemed to Braun that the Count did not turn left or right but simply dissolved into the night.

Part Five

The Pocket Kozy

66

Haussmann was getting breathless. Von Bulow seemed to walk faster than most other people ran.

'What did you think when you first entered the room?'

'I thought it was a suicide, sir. What with the note on the table.'

'Yes, the note. I was reading Rheinhardt's report. He consulted that doctor — what's his name?'

'Liebermann, sir.' Their precipitate departure from the security office was still making Haussmann feel uneasy. 'Do you think we should have waited a little longer for Inspector Rheinhardt, sir?'

'No, he was late.'

'He is usually very punctual, sir.'

'Well, he wasn't on time today, Haussmann. If Inspector Rheinhardt has chosen to indulge in a leisurely toilette this morning, that's his business. I have work to do. Jewish, is he?'

'I'm sorry, sir?'

'Liebermann — is he a Jew?'

'I presume so.'

'Can't you tell?'

'Well, I . . .'

'Never mind. He — Liebermann — he worked out that she was pregnant from a mistake in the note. What did you think of that, Haussmann?'

'Very clever.'

'Or lucky?'

'He *was* right, sir.'

'Do you know him?'

'Not very well — but he has assisted Inspector Rheinhardt on a number of occasions.'

'What's he like?'

'Agreeable . . . intelligent.'

'Trustworthy?'

'As far as I know.'

An omnibus rattled by and von Bulow raised his voice: 'He's a follower of Sigmund Freud, I believe.'

'Who?'

'A Jewish professor. I'm not sure that his principles, his psychology, can be readily applied to the general population.'

'Very good, sir,' said Haussmann, without turning to make eye contact. Von Bulow quickened his pace even more.

'The door was locked from the inside.'

'Yes, sir.'

'And there were no hiding places — places where a man could have concealed himself while you were in the apartment?'

'No, sir.'

'Did you check?'

'Not at the time. But in due course I did, sir — and none were found.'

'How thorough was the search?'

'The floorboards were all secure. There were no compartments behind the shelves. Not enough room up the chimney.'

'And you were present when the examination took place?'

'Yes, sir. With Inspector Rheinhardt and constables Wundt, Raff and Wengraf. Besides, sir—'

'What?'

'The Japanese box. No one could have locked the Japanese box from the inside.'

'So, it was a demon, was it?'

For the first time, Haussmann allowed himself to smile.

'No, sir. But given our failure to come up with an alternative explanation it might as well have been.'

'Indeed.'

'Sir?' Haussmann pointed across the street. 'Café Zilbergeld. The maid, Rosa Sucher — that's where she went before going to Grosse Sperlgasse.'

Von Bulow nodded.

When they reached Fräulein Löwenstein's apartment building, von Bulow stopped and surveyed the square.

Market tables had been left out, and loose canvas awnings flapped in the light breeze. The surrounding buildings were relatively large, some of them up to six storeys high, and painted in bright colours — orange, yellow, lime and pink. However, the overall impression was not one of gaiety but of dilapidation. The buildings had lost their festive sheen beneath a coating of grime.

Von Bulow shook his head in apparent disgust, pushed the door open and entered the dingy ground-floor hallway.

'The courtyard is down there, sir,' said Haussmann, pointing ahead.

'Does the room where she was found overlook the courtyard?'

'No, sir — a backstreet.'

'Then I'll take a look at it later. Let's see the apartment first.'

'This way, sir.'

They began climbing the narrow spiralling staircase.

'Who else lives here?'

'The first- and second-floor apartments are empty — the landlord is having them redecorated. The ground floor is occupied by the Zucker family.'

'I didn't read anything about them in the paperwork.'

'Herr Zucker is blind. His wife works as a correspondence clerk in a shop.'

'Even so, Rheinhardt should have recorded their details.'

They came to the top of the stairs and Haussmann stopped abruptly. There were two items propped up against Charlotte Löwenstein's door. The first was a desiccated bunch of dead flowers. The second was a small parcel. Haussmann advanced slowly, and on reaching the door hunkered down. He prised the tangled brown stems apart — a shrivelled head of dry petals fell and rolled across the chipped tiles.

'There's no card,' he said softly. Then, picking up the parcel, he handed it to von Bulow. 'It's addressed to Fräulein Löwenstein.'

The Inspector broke the string and unfolded the stiff paper, exposing a flat cardboard box. He opened it carefully. Inside was a stack of photographs. The first showed a very attractive woman seated at a café table. She was wearing a turban-style hat decorated with a cluster of flowers and a stylish white dress. A middle-aged man sat opposite her — he was leaning forward and held her hand in his.

Von Bulow shuffled through the stack.

All the photographs were of the same scene — and the pictures were not of the highest quality; one was particularly blurred. It showed the man raising the woman's hand to his lips. Her moving forearm had left a vaporous trail — like the loose sleeve of a semi-transparent gown.

Haussmann stood up and von Bulow handed him the photographs.

'I know who the woman is, of course,' said von Bulow. 'But who is the man? Do you recognise him?'

'Yes,' said Haussmann. 'Yes, I do.'

67

It was by accident rather than design that Liebermann found himself walking down Wieblinger Strasse. Professor Freud had been quite correct. This was clearly the place to come if one wished to purchase antiques. Liebermann examined the various window displays and tried to muster some enthusiasm for the exhibits. But he remained unmoved. It was difficult to discriminate between true antiquities and worthless rubble — between Biedermcier and junk. The bronze, china, filigree and flock made him long for simple lines and restrained geometry, the clear, polished spaces of a modern interior.

The window through which he was looking had not been washed for a while — and at eye level a wrinkled *Neue Freie Presse* article had been stuck to the other side. The print was faded and the yellow paper cracked. Even so, Liebermann could still make out the content: a report on the findings of a British archaeological expedition to the Aegean island of Crete.

Among the tarnished silver, cracked vases and copper bowls — cloudy with verdigris — his attention was drawn to two small Egyptian figures, one a vulture, the other a human body with the head of a falcon. The second reminded him a little of the Seth figure found in Fräulein Löwenstein's Japanese box.

Why not? he thought. *What harm would it do to make a few enquiries?*

Liebermann opened the door and a bell rang. He was not, however, greeted by the proprietor but by the screeching and agitated fluttering of a mynah bird. Hanging from the raised arm of a weather-beaten Aphrodite was a bamboo cage, the night-black occupant of which squawked in a shrill falsetto: 'Pretty things, pretty things.' Next to the bird was a large canopied wicker chair, within which a wizened old man was ensconced, as snug as a whelk in its shell. He was wearing a Moroccan fez, and a heavy tartan blanket covered his legs. Tufts of grizzled hair sprouted out above his ears, and his long, peppery beard was streaked with remnants of colour — biscuit and beige. He was fast asleep, and neither bell nor bird could wake him. Liebermann noticed that the old man's pipe had fallen to the ground. He tiptoed across the cluttered floor space, picked it up, and placed it gently on the old man's lap.

It was insufferably hot and stuffy. Behind the Aphrodite a large stove was radiating heat.

Liebermann looked around. The shop was a strange emporium — a haphazard collection of lumber and ancient treasure. Among the battered chairs, old curtains, picture frames and silverware were items that appeared to be bona fide antiquities. Liebermann bent down to examine a terracotta Greek amphora decorated with a crude winged figure. A label attached to its neck and written in brown ink read *Classical period, 20 krone*. Next to it sat a sphinx. Its features were almost worn smooth, but its posture was resolute — sitting solidly on its haunches and staring ahead. The label declared that it was of Italian origin. There was no price.

Liebermann picked up the sphinx and was reminded of her giant cousins in the Belvedere gardens.

'Pretty things . . . pretty things.'

It was where they had always gone — the Belvedere. At first he had escorted both sisters, but eventually Clara was permitted to go with him on her own, without Rachel. Herr Weiss had voiced no objection. Why should he? They all trusted him . . . How many times had he and Clara walked through those gardens? Once she had insisted on touching the head of every sphinx.

He had always looked forward to her company — her laughter, the endless chatter, her mischievous observations. He loved the way she dressed — so fastidious, so careful with every matching colour. He was captivated by the subtle slant of her eyes, her inviting lips, her smile. She was *his* Clara. Yet something had changed. He didn't feel as he should . . .

'Pretty things, pretty things.'

Liebermann placed the sphinx back on the floor.

'The sphinx is worth at least eighty krone. But I'd let you have it for thirty.'

Liebermann very much hoped that he wasn't being addressed by the mynah bird — but he couldn't be absolutely sure. The words had been spoken in an equally shrill voice. He stood up and turned.

The old man's eyes were open and glimmering with unusual brightness.

'Good afternoon, sir,' said Liebermann.

The old man acknowledged the greeting by raising his pipe. Then, turning to the bird, he cried, 'Giacomo, you rogue!'

The bird squawked and preened its feathers.

Liebermann stepped forward.

'Are all of the antiquities authentic?'

'Authentic? Of course they're authentic,' stated the old man in his querulous screech. 'Roman, Etruscan, Persian, Greek, Egyptian . . . you couldn't find a better selection — not even in Paris! Not even in London!'

'I was wondering if you could help me? I'm trying to trace a particular item, one which you might have sold.'

'What kind of item?'

'An Egyptian figurine, about so big.' Liebermann indicated the size with his hands. 'A representation of the god Seth.'

The old man leaned out from beneath his wicker canopy.

'Come, come closer.' He beckoned with a gnarled finger.

Liebermann stepped forward. The old man squinted at him.

'Seth — what do you want him for, eh?'

'For a friend, a collector.'

'Word of advice,' said the old man. 'Let your friend find Seth for himself . . .'

'Why?'

'Because those who seek him usually find him.'

There was something rather chilling in the old man's delivery. A certain authority — in spite of his eccentric appearance — that made the hackles rise.

'What do you mean?' asked Liebermann.

But the old man did not reply. He smacked his lips, closed his eyes, and sank back into his chair. He seemed to have slipped back into sleep and was mumbling softly to himself: 'The mountainside . . . covered in bushes — and wild fruit trees. I'd been riding for eleven hours. They said the distance was nine *farsakhs* — but it was more, I tell you, much more. Beneath one of the bushes was a dead wolf. The road was almost impassable — slippery shale, a rock fall — but I reached the top: the Muk pass. I followed a stream . . . down to the Zanjiran gorge — narrow between two cliffs: a famous place for robbers . . .'

'That's enough, father — that's enough!' From behind a screen at the back of the shop came a plump middle-aged man wearing a tight suit. He immediately went over to the somnolent storyteller and straightened his blanket: 'Honestly, father, I can't leave you alone for five minutes.' He removed the old man's pipe and replaced it with a plate of sausage and sauerkraut. Looking up at Liebermann, the son said, 'I'm so sorry — I'll be with you in a moment.' Then he turned back to his father: 'How many times have I told you: when people come in, tell them to wait. They're not interested in your nonsense.' The old man opened his eyes, picked up a fork, and stabbed a slice of sausage.

'Good afternoon, sir,' said the proprietor, clicking his heels. 'My name is Herr Reitlinger, Adolph Reitlinger — how can I help you?'

'I'm trying to trace an Egyptian figure — a small effigy of the god Seth. I was wondering if you had sold it . . .' Liebermann's sentence trailed off.

Herr Reitlinger paused for a moment. 'Seth, you say?'

'The god of storms, boy — the god of chaos,' the old man called out.

'That's enough, father!' said Herr Reitlinger.

'Pretty things,' said the bird.

'No,' continued Herr Reitlinger. 'I don't think that was one of our acquisitions. But let me show you this . . .' Herr Reitlinger reached up to a shelf and offered Liebermann a small bronze figure of a walking man. 'Amon-Re — in human form. Late period — possibly 700 BC. I think you'll agree that it's a charming piece. Notice the detail.'

Liebermann turned the figure in his hands and whispered to Reitlinger.

'What was your father talking about — the mountains, the gorge . . .?'

'He travelled a great deal when he was younger.' Reitlinger made a stirring motion next to his ear. 'It all gets mixed up now.'

Liebermann handed the bronze back to Reitlinger.

'It is certainly a charming piece, but not really what I'm looking for. Good afternoon.'

The old man, his son and the bird watched in silence as Liebermann left.

68

THE HEAVY EMBOSSED wallpaper, thick red curtains and polished ebony floorboards of the Schelling parlour combined to create an oppressive atmosphere. Even the engraved silver plates, suspended on either side of an aureate Biedermeier mirror, seemed dull and patinated: large grey-green discs that absorbed rather than reflected the weak sunlight.

Beatrice Schelling was seated by a lamp stand and was embroidering Adele's name on to a quilt. Although the task should have been restful the speed with which she executed her needlework suggested urgency. Her lips were pressed together and her brow was deeply furrowed. She had been there for some time, and the fronded pattern she was working on was almost complete.

Marie — her younger sister — had taken Edward and Adele to Demel's (the imperial and royal confectioners) for a treat. She had urged Marie to keep a close eye on how much chocolate the children were consuming. The last time they had all visited Demel's, Edward had returned with a stomach-ache and had eventually been sick. He had eaten four praline busts of the Emperor.

Beatrice's mind emptied on hearing the slow, ponderous step of her husband in the hallway. The doors opened and Schelling entered. He was wearing a gold smoking jacket and a bright blue cravat. In one hand was the stub of a cigar and in the other a sheet of paper.

'Beatrice, I have received a letter from Amelia.'

'Is she well?'

'She has left the hospital.'

'She has escaped?' There was a note of shrill alarm in Beatrice's voice.

'No. She was discharged with her doctor's approval.'

'Then where is she? Are we to collect her?'

'She is not coming back.'

Beatrice's face became animated by a series of contradictory expressions — oscillating between hope and anxiety.

'She says that she's found another post,' Schelling added. He advanced slowly and, looking down, absent-mindedly observed: 'You're doing your embroidery again.'

'Yes . . .' said Beatrice. 'Where has she gone?'

'I don't know. It's an address in Alsegrund.'

'But how could she . . .?'

'I have no idea.'

'Such ingratitude.'

'Dreadful. Perfectly dreadful.'

Schelling reached for the lamp switch.

'You must have the light on, my dear. Otherwise you will strain your eyes and get a headache.'

Then, walking to the fireplace, he drew on his cigar and threw what remained of the stub on to the unlit coals.

'She has asked for her books to be sent on — and requests that special care be taken with respect to her microscope. She does not even mention her clothes.'

'I will get Vilma and Alfred to pack them.'

'Yes, of course.'

Beatrice picked nervously at her embroidery. Without looking up she said: 'What did Amelia say . . . about . . .' Her voice cracked. 'What were her reasons?'

Schelling took a step forward and offered his wife the letter. Beatrice shook her head with excessive vigour. It was as though he had offered her poison.

'She does not give any reasons,' Schelling replied. Then, folding the letter and slipping it into his jacket pocket, he added: 'I must write to her mother.'

'Yes,' said Beatrice, becoming agitated. 'This evening, otherwise she might—'

'My dear,' Schelling interrupted. 'You have overexerted yourself with the children. You are tired, do not fret.'

Beatrice had begun to breathe faster and her cheeks were glowing.

'The girl was very unwell,' continued Schelling, smoothly. 'Right from the beginning. Whatever poor Amelia says will immediately be recognised as fantasy. Delusion. It will be so distressing for Greta and Samuel . . . I pity them. I'm sure the doctors have tried their best — but inevitably . . .' Shaking his head, he began walking towards the door. 'There is only so much that they can do.'

Suddenly Beatice reached out and caught her husband's arm. It was an unexpected movement and Schelling's practised composure was momentarily disturbed. A nervous tic appeared under his right eye — the heavy rubicund flesh suddenly galvanised into life. Even though his wife's hand was shaking, her grip was surprisingly firm.

'No more now,' she said, grasping his sleeve tighter and speaking with a breathless intensity. 'This must be the last time. I cannot . . . it is . . . we must—'

Slowly, Schelling pulled his arm away. His wife's hand lingered but finally released the smoking jacket's sleeve.

'Do carry on with your embroidery,' he said softly. 'It looks very pretty. How clever you are.'

He continued on his way.

Beatrice heard the doors to the hallway opening and closing. Biting her lower lip, she returned to her needlework, her fingers working with furious dexterity.

69

THE SHOP WINDOW contained a terraced display of family portraits: husbands and wives, mothers and daughters, fathers and sons. Newly wedded lovers stared into each other's eyes, and children — in lederhosen and rustic aprons — posed against a painted canvas of rolling hills and distant mountains. The upper terrace, however, was bedecked with famous singers, a Valhalla of warrior princes and Valkyries, spear-shaking tenors and busty sopranos, who gazed beyond the limits of the picture frame at feasting gods and apocalyptic fire. And amid this heroic company was a large picture of the mayor, a dapper man wearing a white Homburg and leaning on a cane, surrounded by a coterie of admirers.

Von Bulow read the poster pinned on the door. The Camera Club was exhibiting the landscapes of Herr Heinrich Kühn (under whose name ran the informative legend 'Inventor of multiple rubber-plate printing').

'An exhibition of photographs,' said von Bulow. 'Whatever next?'

Haussmann thought it best not to express an opinion.

Von Bulow pushed the door and a bell rang.

The shop was a forest of tripods. Most were empty, but several supported cameras: large wooden boxes with extended leather concertinas. A low glass case was packed with cylindrical lenses, each labelled with mathematical figures and a price tag. The air was filled with an unpleasant odour that von Bulow found impossible to identify. It was like a blend of floor polish and cheese.

A curtain behind the counter parted and a small man in shirt-sleeves emerged, drying his hands on a towel. His hair had been plastered down and his well-trimmed beard and moustache made him look like a Parisian.

'Good morning, gentlemen.' He waved the towel in the air to clear the dense cloud of smoke that had followed him. 'I do apologise — I've been experimenting with a new recipe for flash powder.'

'Herr Joly?' von Bulow asked.

'Yes.'

'Fritz Joly?'

'Yes.'

'My name is von Bulow — Inspector von Bulow — and this is my colleague, Haussmann.'

Herr Joly looked from one policeman to the other and the gap between his eyebrows narrowed.

'How can I help?'

Von Bulow placed the parcel on the counter and unfolded the paper wrapping.

'Do you recognise these?'

Joly opened the box and on seeing the first image started. Then, raising his head, he looked quizzically at his questioner. He found no comfort in von Bulow's expressionless, colourless eyes.

'Yes,' he replied tentatively.

'Your card was inside,' continued von Bulow. 'Do you know who she is — this woman?'

'Yes. Her name is Löwenstein ...' Joly lifted the photographs out of the box and flicked through the images. A wistful smile softened his anxious expression. 'Not a face you'd forget, Inspector.'

'You took them?'

'A month ago — maybe more. Is there a problem? Has she done something wrong?'

Herr Joly placed the photographs back in the box and searched von Bulow's eyes again for a clue. The Inspector said nothing. Disconcerted by the silence, Joly added: 'She paid me in advance but never came back to collect them. My assistant cycled them over to her apartment: a Leopoldstadt address, I think.'

'They are somewhat unusual,' said von Bulow. 'Unlike the portraits in the window.'

'Indeed. I believe the gentleman is Fräulein Löwenstein's fiancé. Apparently he hates having his photograph taken. She wanted a portrait — of both of them, together — but insisted that the photograph should be taken without his knowledge. Candid, as it were.'

Von Bulow turned the box and stared at the first image. 'How could you have taken these without his knowledge? Surely he would have seen you erecting the tripod?'

Herr Joly smiled.

'Oh no, I didn't use one of those.' He pointed to one of the large wooden boxes. 'I used one of these.'

He opened a drawer under the counter and produced a small rectangular object covered in black leather.

'What is it?'

'A camera,' said Joly, his voice brightening with amusement.

Von Bulow and Haussmann were obviously not convinced.

'It's called a *Pocket Kozy*.'

'English?'

'No. American. They're getting remarkably good at making things — the Americans. It opens like a book — see?'

Herr Joly pulled the covers apart and, where von Bulow might have expected to see pages, red leather bellows appeared.

'Here's the meniscus lens, and the single-speed shutter is located here on the spine.' Herr Joly pointed to a small aperture. 'It's very fast, though, more or less instantaneous. This one's a few years old now, but I think they're developing even smaller models. The Kozy can take eighteen exposures on roll film, which produce three-and-a-half-inch photographs. It performs better under conditions where—'

'Yes, yes,' von Bulow interrupted loudly. 'That's all very interesting, Herr Joly. Where were they taken?'

'Outside a small café on the Prater,' Joly said, his voice now neutral. 'I forget which one. Fräulein Löwenstein told me when she and her fiancé were meeting — and I sat down at the next table after he'd arrived. You see, it looks like I'm simply reading a book . . .'

Herr Joly lifted the camera and looked into the open bellows. Then, raising his eyes, he peered over the leather covers.

'Can you remember how they greeted each other?' asked von Bulow.

Joly closed the camera and placed it on the counter with great care.

'How do you mean?'

'Did they kiss?'

'Umm — no, I don't think they did. But I can't be sure as it was some time ago now. Why is this important? Why are the police involved?'

Von Bulow fixed the birdlike photographer with a contemptuous stare.

'Do you read the papers, Herr Joly?'

'Yes. The *Taglatt*, the *Zeitung* . . . Why?'

'Then perhaps you don't read them very thoroughly.'

The little man shrugged.

'Herr Joly, Fräulein Löwenstein did not collect these photographs in person for the simple reason that she is dead. Murdered, I imagine, by our friend here.'

Von Bulow allowed his finger to drop on the small stack of photographs. Pressing down on the gentleman's image, his lips parted to form a wide, predatory smile.

70

ALTHOUGH AMELIA LYDGATE's rooms were still rather cheerless, signs of occupation had begun to appear. A modest fire sputtered in the grate, fresh flowers had been placed in an old blue vase, and some mezzotint prints were now hanging on the wall. The first showed the Royal Observatory in Greenwich, the second St Paul's Cathedral in the City of London, and the third cattle grazing by a circle of trees in a place called Hampstead.

Above the fire, a fortress-wall of encyclopaedias dominated the mantelpiece and miscellaneous volumes were piled and scattered across the floor. On the landing, an open trunk showed that Miss Lydgate had still not finished unpacking her library. Clearly, before embarking for Vienna she had already resolved to sacrifice her wardrobe in exchange for the companionship of several Greek and Latin authors.

While inspecting Amelia Lydgate's possessions Liebermann felt distinctly uneasy. There was nothing irregular about his presence, nothing improper. It was customary, expected even, for doctors to visit their patients once treatment had been successfully completed. However, Liebermann had chosen to make his house call not through duty but from curiosity. He wanted to know more about the erstwhile governess and was aware of his suspect motivation. She was, by conventional standards, an extremely unusual woman. Minister Schelling had been correct: Amelia Lydgate *was* abnormal, but her abnormality aroused in Liebermann fascination rather than repulsion.

Outside, the stairs creaked as she made her ascent, the tea things rattling on the tray. Having made a surreptitious study of the mezzotints, Liebermann guiltily returned to his seat at the table.

Miss Lydgate appeared at the door and Liebermann rose at once, intending to assist. But she demurred. He was her guest, she insisted.

While pouring the tea, Miss Lydgate talked freely about her domestic plans. She asked where she might purchase a sturdy bookcase, and pondered the feasibility of getting a laboratory bench up the stairs without causing damage to the banisters. Finally, she hoped that Frau Rubenstein would not object to her modifying the gas taps in order to fuel a Bunsen burner.

As usual, Amelia Lydgate maintained a certain English reserve. But as the evening progressed Liebermann found her formality, her upright posture, precise speech and impeccable attention to good manners less like coldness and more like the embodiment of a unique charm.

Liebermann's attention was captured by several unmarked volumes on the table. The spines were blank and the yellowing paper marked with brown maculae.

'Are these—?'

Before he could finish the question Miss Lydgate confirmed his suspicion.

'Yes, they are my grandfather's journals. Or at least some of them. Please, you are welcome to examine them.'

Liebermann felt privileged. He gestured towards the tea things.

'I couldn't possibly — I might . . .'

'Doctor Liebermann, my grandfather's journals have survived two fires, the flood waters of the Thames and abandonment in a bat-infested attic for nearly thirty years. I can assure you that they are robust enough to endure a spot of tea — should you accidentally upset your cup.'

Liebermann smiled and picked up the first volume. It was bound in what he presumed had once been pristine black leather but which was now much faded, cracked and scuffed. In spite of Miss Lydgate's confidence in the volume's robust constitution, Liebermann felt obliged to treat the journal with the utmost care. As he opened the first page, he was aware of a subtle fragrance — an odd combination of scent and mould, as through corruption had imbued the paper with a certain sweetness. The first page was blank, but the second was inscribed with the author's name in large Gothic capitals: *Buchbinder*.

Each subsequent page was dense with script, and occasionally illustrated with very fine pen-and-ink line drawings. Most were illustrations of microscopic slides. The overall effect suggested the operation of a fastidious mind and a close attention to detail.

'That volume,' said Amelia Lydgate, 'contains my grandfather's writings on the transfusion experiments of the Royal Society. It also contains records of his own research into the nature of blood. It is the sixth volume of my grandfather's journal, although I think of it more simply as the "blood book".'

Liebermann asked the young governess some questions concerning the purpose of the transfusion experiments: what diseases, for example, were the transfusions supposed to cure?

'The principal interest of the virtuosi,' replied Miss Lydgate, 'was therapy for the mind rather than treatment of the body.'

'How very interesting.'

Miss Lydgate hesitated and seemed unsure whether or not to continue.

'Please, do go on,' said Liebermann, closing the journal.

'They believed that there was a relationship between blood and character — an idea, of course, that dates back to classical times. Thus, they speculated that a change of blood might cure madness.'

'And they tested this hypothesis?'

'Indeed, my grandfather details the circumstances and method of the very first experiment. The subject was a madman called Coga. Employing an apparatus constructed of pipes and quills, the physicians of the Royal Society were able to transfuse some ten ounces of sheep's blood into Coga's body.'

'Sheep's blood?'

Liebermann wanted to laugh but suppressed the urge. Amelia Lydgate's expression was entirely serious.

'Indeed. The sheep is an animal famed for its docile and timid nature. I can only assume that the virtuosi believed this would pacify the deranged Coga.'

'And was the operation successful?'

'Yes. Coga's madness was cured and thereafter he was said to be a more sober and quiet man. He also received an honorarium of one guinea. Would you care for another cup of tea, Herr Doctor?'

'No, thank you,' Liebermann replied. 'That's extraordinary. I wonder why Coga didn't suffer any ill consequences?'

'Perhaps the transfusion was not as successful as the virtuosi believed. Perhaps the quantity of sheep's blood was too small to cause any significant harm.'

'In which case the benefit was probably psychological.'

'Indeed.'

'Did the virtuosi continue these experiments?'

'Yes, with both animal and human subjects. However, my grandfather writes that they eventually stopped because of fatalities.'

'I'm not surprised.'

'Even so, Doctor Liebermann, they succeeded in their efforts as frequently as any contemporary physician. Transfusion is still extremely dangerous and only attempted by the most enterprising — some would say foolhardy — surgeons. The procedure kills as many as it saves. For many years, specialists have speculated about the

inconsistency of results, and many theories have been proposed by way
of an explanation. But the most convincing of these theories concern
differences in blood type and their varying degree of compatibility. In
the past, the greatest obstacle to progress has been identification. How
does one go about identifying different blood types? The great surgeon
Theodore Billroth posed this question right here in Vienna some
twenty years ago.' Miss Lydgate paused and sipped her tea. 'My
grandfather discovered that blood cells taken from different individuals will either mix freely, or clump together. He concluded that
clotting — or its absence — might be the reason why some of the early
transfusion experiments failed while others succeeded.' The young
woman reached over and picked up the "blood book", opening it at
exactly the right page. 'Here are examples of his microscopy.'

She turned the journal towards Liebermann. It looked at first like a
work of astronomy — sketches of a planet at different times in its
rotation cycle. But each 'world' was, in fact, a view of blood cells in
different states of agglomeration.

'Of course, Doctor Landsteiner has progressed far beyond my
grandfather's work,' continued Amelia Lydgate. 'He has found that
clumping depends on the presence of two other substances that can be
found on the surface of blood cells, the antigens A and B—' She
suddenly stopped, blushing a little, and closed the book. 'Forgive me,
Doctor Liebermann: you are already familiar with Doctor Landsteiner's publications.'

'No — not at all. Please continue.'

'I fear you are merely being courteous, Doctor Liebermann.'

'No, I'm very interested.'

But in spite of these and subsequent protestations by Liebermann,
Miss Lydgate refused to be drawn any further.

Liebermann chose to walk home. He set off in a southerly direction
and found himself on Währingerstrasse. When he reached the

Josephinum — the old military college of surgery and medicine — he paused and looked through the high railings at an imposing representation of womanhood: a large cast of Hygieia, the goddess of healing. It was one of the few classical figures in Vienna that he actually recognised.

The goddess towered over Liebermann, her powerful hand gripping the neck of a huge snake which coiled around her arm and dropped over her shoulder in a series of diminishing involutions. She was feeding the great serpent, thus embodying the dual virtues of strength and compassion. As sunlight filtered through some low cloud, her eyes became mirrors of pewter.

71

Rheinhardt opened the door of Commissioner Brügel's room.

'Ah, Rheinhardt,' said Brügel. 'Do come in.'

Von Bulow was sitting by the Commissioner's desk. He stood and performed a perfunctory bow.

Rheinhardt did not reciprocate. He was too angry.

'Von Bulow. Where were you this morning?'

'Waiting in my office with Haussmann — as arranged,' said von Bulow.

'I arrived at five minutes to eight and you weren't there.'

'That's because we were supposed to be meeting at seven. You were late, Rheinhardt.'

'I was not. We had arranged to meet at eight!'

'Then there must have been some misunderstanding,' said von Bulow, smiling with perfidious confidence.

'Gentlemen!' Brügel said loudly. 'Please sit down.'

Rheinhardt was quite certain that there had been no misunderstanding.

'Well,' said Brügel, looking at Rheinhardt. 'I have some splendid news. It would seem that after only one day on the Löwenstein case, Inspector von Bulow has been able to make an arrest.'

'I'm sorry, sir?' Rheinhardt was flabbergasted. He shot a glance at von Bulow, whose rigid features betrayed no emotion.

'Take a look at these.'

Brügel passed his hand over a small stack of photographs and spread them out across the desktop like a card-sharp. Rheinhardt leaned forward. There was Fräulein Löwenstein, dressed in a turban-style hat and an elegant white dress — her monochrome image reiterated, with minute variations, on every one of Brügel's arc of 'cards', occupying every suit and every value. In almost all the photographs, Fräulein Löwenstein was smiling — a broad, radiant smile that occasionally became laughter. But her eyes, wide with interest and glittering with early spring sunshine, were always fixed on the same object: her companion — Heinrich Hölderlin.

Rheinhardt slid one of the photographs out of the splayed stack and examined it closely. The couple were seated in a restaurant. Although the horizon was smudgy and out of focus, it appeared to be parkland. Hölderlin was kissing Fräulein Löwenstein's fingers. The expression on his face was eager and lascivious.

'Where did you get these?' said Rheinhardt, stunned and feeling slightly light-headed.

'Perhaps you had better explain, Inspector,' said Brügel to von Bulow.

'Of course, sir,' said von Bulow, tugging at his jacket sleeve to expose a diamond cuff link. 'I found these photographs at Fräulein Löwenstein's apartment this morning. They had been delivered by a photographer's assistant a few days earlier. The photographer's card was in the package. His name is Fritz Joly — he has a shop on Bauermarkt.'

Rheinhardt was still staring at the images of Fräulein Löwenstein and Hölderlin.

'I went to the shop immediately,' von Bulow continued, 'and discovered that Fräulein Löwenstein had paid Herr Joly to take these photographs. She had claimed that Herr Hölderlin was her fiancé, and that he would not usually permit his photograph to be taken —

thus, Herr Joly would have to perform his task secretly. This was easily accomplished using a new miniature camera from America, something called a Pocket Kozy. Fräulein Löwenstein did not go back to Joly's shop, and Herr Joly was unaware of her murder. When she failed to return to his premises Herr Joly instructed his assistant to deliver the photographs to Fräulein Löwenstein's apartment. It is clear,' continued von Bulow authoritatively, 'that Hölderlin and Löwenstein were lovers. I suspect that, once she became pregnant, she planned to extort money from the banker using these photographs.'

'But they weren't in her possession when she was killed,' Rheinhardt objected. 'How could she have shown them to Hölderlin?'

'She didn't have to,' said von Bulow. 'As soon as she was satisfied that Herr Joly had completed his task, she could have revealed her scheme.'

'Carry on, Inspector,' said Brügel to von Bulow.

'Thank you, sir,' said von Bulow. 'Hölderlin killed Fräulein Löwenstein to escape his predicament, but became fearful of discovery. He suspected that the locksmith, Karl Uberhorst, had information that might implicate him, Hölderlin, in the murder. In your report, Rheinhardt, you mention that Uberhorst behaved strangely at Cosima von Rath's seance. He appeared to know something of value to the police. I think it is safe to assume that this concerned Fräulein Löwenstein's pregnancy. At that time, Hölderlin — like everyone else in the circle — was unaware of the results of the second autopsy. Thus, from Hölderlin's point of view, special knowledge of Löwenstein's pregnancy must have represented a significant threat, particularly if it made the police more inquisitive. Of course, he wasn't to know that even armed with such information, Rheinhardt, you would do precious little to justify his fears.'

'With respect, von Bulow,' said Rheinhardt, 'that really wasn't—'

'Rheinhardt!' said the Commissioner. 'Let von Bulow finish, then you can have your say.'

Rheinhardt folded his arms and hunched his shoulders.

'When Hölderlin visited Uberhorst's shop,' continued von Bulow, 'and found the locksmith engaged in experiments that might reveal Fräulein Löwenstein's murderer was human rather than demonic, he resolved to dispatch the troublesome fellow immediately. Remarkably, Rheinhardt, that sham seance you arranged to smoke out the killer actually succeeded. Hölderlin feared that he would be exposed and subsequently disrupted the evening's proceedings. Had I been in your position, Rheinhardt, I would not have hesitated at that juncture to make an arrest. These photographs,' said von Bulow, gesturing, 'are final confirmation of Hölderlin's guilt.'

Brügel was nodding his head approvingly.

'A compelling analysis, don't you agree, Rheinhardt?'

Rheinhardt was extremely irritated at his superior's attitude towards von Bulow. The man was an impressive detective, certainly, but on this occasion he had been plain lucky. Also, there was nothing 'compelling' about his 'analysis'. Anybody with a detailed knowledge of the case who stumbled upon such photographs might speculate in the same way. Moreover, von Bulow had made extensive use of paperwork that he had derided only the day before.

'These photographs certainly suggest,' began Rheinhardt, 'that Herr Hölderlin and Fräulein Löwenstein were lovers.'

'Suggest?' interrupted Brügel. 'Why else would a married man be kissing the hand of an attractive woman on the Prater if she were not his mistress?'

'Indeed, sir,' Rheinhardt replied, 'and Inspector von Bulow should be commended for his exceptionally clever find.' Rheinhardt's sarcasm escaped Brügel, but produced a minute tensing of von Bulow's neck muscles. 'But we are still frustrated by the main problem that has dogged this case from the very beginning. In principle, I agree that Herr Hölderlin looks to be our man — I have said as much myself in the report of the sham seance. Even so, we are left with the uncomfortable fact that Fraulein Löwenstein's murder is as inexplicable today as it was over a month ago. How can Herr Hölderlin be successfully prosecuted for a murder, the method of which cannot be explained?'

'Rheinhardt,' said von Bulow, 'your objections emphasise the difference in our respective approaches. I am sure that we shall learn how Herr Hölderlin engineered his theatrical coup in good time. The villain has been discovered — and I am confident that a lengthy period of confinement in a small, preferably windowless cell will encourage him to make a full confession. You will not have to wait very much longer for your explanation, I assure you.'

'Here, here,' the Commissioner chuckled. 'I'll wager we'll have our confession within the week!'

'I'm sorry?' said Rheinhardt, looking at von Bulow. 'You intend to extort a confession out of Hölderlin by keeping him in solitary confinement?'

'A period of isolation and hardship is sure to focus his mind.'

'Sir,' said Rheinhardt to his superior. 'I believe that there may be an alternative, more humane way of encouraging Herr Hölderlin to confess. I request that he be permitted an interview with my colleague Doctor Liebermann.'

'Out of the question!' said von Bulow.

'Why?'

'It'll spoil everything. Put the man under pressure and he'll talk.'

'Put *anyone* under pressure and they'll talk,' Rheinhardt retorted.

'Sir, Doctor Liebermann isn't a police medical officer,' said von Bulow, appealing to the Commissioner.

'With respect, von Bulow,' said Rheinhardt, before the Commissioner could respond. 'Your current mentor, Professor Gross, suggests that the wise investigator should make use of *all* talents at his disposal — official and unofficial.'

Von Bulow was surprised that Rheinhardt appeared to be conversant with the works of Hans Gross, but was stalled for only a fraction of a second. 'Indeed,' replied von Bulow. 'However, I am not altogether convinced that Doctor Liebermann is a man of talent. Nor do I agree with his methods.' He trained his bleached eyes on the Commissioner. 'Liebermann is a disciple of Sigmund Freud, sir. A man whose ideas are highly suspect, and whose psychology is peculiarly Jewish.'

'Sir,' said Rheinhardt raising his voice. 'There is nothing peculiarly Jewish about Doctor Liebermann's methods. He is an astute observer of human nature and was able to determine that Fräulein Löwenstein was pregnant from a single error in her death note. His talent is inestimable.'

Brügel slapped his hand on the desk. The report was as loud as a gunshot.

'Enough of this petty squabbling — both of you!'

The two Inspectors fell silent.

The Commissioner pulled at his chin, looking from Rheinhardt to von Bulow and back again.

'All right, Rheinhardt,' said Brügel. 'You can call your Doctor Liebermann. He can have one hour with Herr Hölderlin, but not a minute more. After that, Hölderlin is exclusively in the charge of Inspector von Bulow.'

'Thank you, sir,' said Rheinhardt, feeling as though he had won a small skirmish in the course of a generally doomed campaign.

72

ABOVE THE COMPANY of Tritons, sea nymphs and frolicking cherubs the roof of the Belvedere peeped over the lower cascade. The couple turned right, passing a demonic face with a large nose and long curled horns. The creature's mouth was wide open, giving the impression of laughter, but its sunken eyes seemed to have rolled back into its head. The effect was rather disturbing — it reminded Liebermann of an epileptiform seizure.

'I wore my new crêpe-de-Chine dress for the first time,' said Clara, 'and looked very sophisticated — even though I say so myself. I can't wait for you to see it. Frau Kornblüh spent months working on the lace collar — and you wouldn't believe how much it cost. One hundred florins! The bodice is tapered — very severely — and it has an old-fashioned bustle.'

They ascended the stairs and passed an irate-looking putto wearing an alpine hat that was tilted to one side. The figure was supposed to represent April, but the infant made a curiously ill-tempered-looking and oddly attired harbinger of an Arcadian summer. He looked utterly ridiculous.

'What an entrance I made,' Clara continued. 'Frau Baum came to greet me and led me through the room. Everyone was looking, but I kept my nerve. I managed to appear unperturbed — even haughty — though my heart was pounding. In fact, I felt quite dizzy . . . the stays are awfully tight . . .'

'Can't you loosen them?' asked Liebermann.

'Of course I can,' Clara responded, a hint of tetchiness creeping into her voice. 'But that would ruin the effect. The tapered bodice!'

Liebermann nodded. 'I see.'

The Belvedere had turned pink in the evening light. It looked like an enormous piece of confectionery — with icing-sugar masonry and a marzipan roof.

'Well, Frau Baum introduced me to some people — the Hardy family and the Lichtenheld girls — and we talked for a while. But Flora had to find her cousin, and I found myself standing alone. Suddenly, out of nowhere, Herr Korngold appeared.'

'Korngold?'

'A business associate of my father's — and of your father's too, I think.'

'Oh...'

'Well, Max, you wouldn't believe his impertinence. "Ahh — he says — I wouldn't have recognised you, young Weiss. The caterpillar has become a butterfly."' Clara's impersonation of a pompous roué was rather good. 'And so I had to stand there, pinned into a corner, listening to him talk rubbish while he leered at me over his champagne glass. It was interminable — and he has false teeth, I'm sure of it.'

Liebermann smiled — amused by the way Clara shivered, her shoulder trembling against his arm with disgust.

'Then who should appear but Frau Korngold. Now, I'm quite well acquainted with Frau Korngold. Mother and I are always bumping into her in town, and we always stop to talk. But she swept past — her nose in the air — without so much as a smile. "Whatever is the matter with Frau Korngold?" I asked. "Jealousy," replied Herr Korngold. "But of whom?" I asked. "You, of course," he said. And then he actually winked — can you believe it?'

'How did you get out of this difficult situation?'

'Fortunately, Frau Baum came to my rescue.'

They continued walking up the path, towards the palace. Another couple, on their way down, passed them, and everyone felt obliged to exchange modest pleasantries. The young man tipped his hat, prompting Clara to exclaim: 'Do you know, Max, I don't think I've ever seen you wearing a hat.'

'No,' Liebermann replied laconically.

'Do you have one?'

'Yes — several, in fact.'

'Then why don't you ever put them on?'

'I'm not sure, really . . .' But even as Liebermann said these words the image of the absurd vernal putto came into his mind and he smiled inwardly. Clara shrugged and, losing interest in her fiancé's indifference to hats, pressed on with her account.

'The following day we visited Frau Lehman. She lives in a very nice house — eleventh district. The dining room is entirely of wood. She very nearly cancelled, because her son — Johann — had fallen off his bicycle.'

'Was he badly hurt?'

'They were worried at first — he'd cut his hand and knee. But he made a remarkably quick recovery and Frau Lehman was happy to entertain us. Anyway, Mother and Frau Lehman were talking about the Kohlbergs—'

'Who are they?'

'Max, sometimes I wonder whether you and I live in the same city! Herr Kohlberg is a tea supplier — and a very wealthy one at that. He had been happily married to Frau Kohlberg for over a year when all of a sudden she ran away. Just like that — left the home, forsaking her husband and child. Well, naturally, Herr Kohlberg instructed his lawyers to proceed with a divorce — intending, of course, to retain custody of his son.'

'How old is he? The boy?'

'A baby — nine months, I think. Then, guess what happened? Frau Kohlberg returned and begged her husband — pleaded with him — to take her back. Said that she couldn't live without her child — and would end it all if he didn't let her return to the household. Which — believe it or not — he did. Mother said this showed remarkable strength of character — the ability to forgive. But Frau Lehman said it showed stupidity. She implied that Frau Kohlberg had taken a young lover who had promptly deserted her when he'd discovered that she had no money of her own.'

Ordinarily, Liebermann found Clara's tittle-tattle pleasantly diverting — but he was now finding it irritating and hurtful. Her rumour-mongering could sometimes be quite thoughtless, even spiteful.

'One shouldn't believe everything one hears, Clara.'

Their gazes met, and Clara produced an exaggerated pout in response to her fiancé's gentle reprimand.

Liebermann shook his head and studied the sphinxes. They crouched in pairs, facing each other on casket-like pedestals. Each was different, showing a unique expression. One member of the Belvedere's sisterhood was particularly striking. In spite of her regal appearance and ram's-horn hair braids, she looked close to tears. The subtle downturn of her lips seemed to presage the trembling that accompanies a welling-up of emotion. Liebermann wondered, fancifully, what kind of sadness might have insinuated itself into the cold, leonine heart of a mythical beast.

Clara soon tired of pouting, and cheerfully resumed talking: 'My aunt Trudi took me out on Wednesday — fetched me in a rubber-wheeled phaeton. Let me tell you, it was simply hideous. We drove to the Graben, had high tea, then hailed the smartest fiacre we could find and went on to the Prater.'

'Did you go on the Riesenrad again?'

'Yes. I never get bored of it.'

'Many people — especially young women — find it frightening.'

'I don't. I find it—' Suddenly, Clara stopped speaking.

'What?'

'I find it . . .' Her brow furrowed with concentration. 'Dreamy.'

'Dreamy? In what sense?'

'It's such an unusual experience. You know, like when you find yourself flying in a dream. Do you ever dream of flying, Max?'

'I think everybody does.'

'And what's it supposed to mean — when you fly in a dream?'

'It doesn't mean anything — specifically. Its meaning will depend on the person's character and circumstances. However, such dreams probably derive from very early memories. Professor Freud says that there cannot be a single uncle who hasn't shown a child how to fly . . .'

'That's interesting.'

'What is?'

'I think Aunt Trudi used to do that with me. She used to pick me up and rush around the room. I used to scream with laughter.'

'Well, there you have it. Perhaps, when you ride on the Riesenrad, you are unconsciously recreating the happy experiences of childhood. Perhaps that is why the Riesenrad doesn't frighten you.'

Clara paused for a moment and then said, with naive wistfulness, 'She's fun — Aunt Trudi — and so generous. She bought me some perfume and two boxes of sugar candy.'

Before Clara could continue, Liebermann interrupted.

'That reminds me. I have something for you too.'

Clara broke away and faced him, her cheeks red with excitement.

'A gift?'

'Yes.'

'Where is it?'

She pressed her hands against Liebermann's coat.

'Not in there . . .'

'Show me!'

'Just wait a minute.'

Liebermann winkled the ring from the fob-pocket of his waistcoat and held it up for her to see. Clara looked at it for a moment, somewhat bemused.

'Give me your hand,' said Liebermann softly.

Clara, suddenly silenced, offered him a slim white finger.

Liebermann slid the ring over her knuckle and kissed her forehead.

She stretched out her arm and rocked her hand from side to side. The movement was gauche but endearing. The diamonds flashed and glinted around the sapphire heart-stone, making Clara laugh with innocent pleasure.

'It fits perfectly,' she gasped.

And it did.

Clara threw her arms around Liebermann's waist and pressed her face into his chest. His arms closed around her and he gazed across the gardens, beyond the brooding, melancholy sphinxes and out over the city towards the distant blue hills.

73

A scabrous chin, bloodshot eyes, and a necktie hanging from his trouser pocket all suggested that Heinrich Hölderlin had spent an uncomfortable and sleepless night in his cell. The banker's former gravitas had deserted him. He no longer appeared dignified and well groomed but shabby and irresolute. Even though Rheinhardt accepted that this pathetic figure just might be a ruthless and brutal murderer, his miserable countenance evoked only pity.

At Liebermann's request, Hölderlin had been removed from his cell and escorted to a room with a divan. This was not to von Bulow's liking but the Commissioner had overruled his objections. Hölderlin was now supine, staring at the ceiling with hollow, frantic eyes.

Liebermann had assumed his usual position, seated at the head of the divan just beyond Hölderlin's view.

'I swear to you,' said Hölderlin, 'I met with her once — and once only. I was a fool, I admit it, a stupid fool. She made an appointment at the bank — declared that she would soon be receiving a large inheritance and asked if I would be willing to give her some financial advice. She was a cunning little minx, believe me. She said things calculated to flatter my vanity. Things about my office, my position and—'

'Yes?'

'My appearance.' Hölderlin sighed. 'As if a young woman like her . . . it's ridiculous, I know. What an idiot! Yet at the time I didn't so much as pause to question her motives. When she suggested that we should meet for lunch on the Prater the following day I agreed. You must understand this was most irregular. Exceptional, in fact. I'm not like *that* at all. I have never had such an assignation before. But Fräulein Löwenstein . . .' He shook his head. 'When she offered me her hand, I was powerless to resist . . . I felt . . . I felt bewitched.'

He glanced at Rheinhardt.

'The other Inspector, von Bulow, he's wrong, I tell you. We weren't lovers. The babies she was carrying — they weren't mine! And before yesterday, I'd never seen those dreadful photographs. She hadn't threatened me with blackmail — I don't know what she was up to.'

'Did you see Fräulein Löwenstein again, after that meeting on the Prater?'

'No, it was the last time I saw her. Within the week she was dead.'

The banker suddenly fell silent, but his breathing was loud and wheezy.

'And anyway,' he began again. 'Even if she had threatened me — I wouldn't have killed her, for God's sake. I'm not insane.'

Liebermann crossed his legs and sat back in his chair.

'Why did you interrupt Madame de Rougemont, Herr Hölderlin?'

'Isn't it obvious?'

Liebermann remained silent.

'I didn't believe I was going to be accused of murder — if that's what you're thinking. However, I did believe it possible that Madame de Rougemont might receive a flirtatious or affectionate communication from Fräulein Löwenstein. Something that might arouse my wife's suspicion. That de Rougemont woman was uncanny . . .'

'But your relationship with the Fräulein had not become very intimate?'

'No, Herr Doctor, it hadn't. But if your conscience is ordinarily clear, then even a relatively minor transgression acquires considerable significance. Please, Herr Doctor, I beg of you, make sure that my wife hears nothing about this. She is a good woman and it would break her heart. She is beside herself already.'

Liebermann pressed a crease from his trousers and made a steeple with his fingers.

'Herr Hölderlin, how did you sleep last night?'

'Not very well — as you can imagine.'

'And did you dream?'

Hölderlin paused for a moment.

'Yes . . .' he said, slowly and uncertainly.

'What did you dream?'

Hölderlin looked towards Rheinhardt quizzically. The Inspector responded with a polite, muted smile but he stopped smiling when he noticed Liebermann frowning and shaking his head.

'Herr Hölderlin?' asked Liebermann, raising his voice slightly.

The banker rolled his head back and said: 'You want to know what I dreamt? Last night?'

'Yes.'

'I don't know — some nonsense about my mother.'

'Go on . . .'

Hölderlin sighed, too exhausted to quibble.

'I was in a nursery — on a rocking horse.'

'Were you a child in this dream?'

'Yes, I suppose I must have been.'

'Was the nursery real? Did you recognise it?'

'Yes, it was in the house where I grew up: a big house in Penzing. I was on my rocking horse — pretending to race — and I noticed a box on the floor.'

'What kind of box?'

'It belonged to my mother.'

'A jewellery box?'

'Yes. Ivory — with mother-of-pearl inlay. I remember that when it was opened it played a tune. *Für Elise* — or something like it.'

'What happened next?'

'I got off the horse, picked up the box and tried to open it. But the lid was stuck. Then my mother appeared and — and reprimanded me — scolded me. Are you sure you want to hear all this rubbish, Herr Doctor?'

'Very sure.'

'Even though the box was in my hands, I protested. Which seems absurd now — but in the dream it seemed to make sense, seemed reasonable. Then I woke up.'

Liebermann paused for a moment. Then, turning to Rheinhardt, he said: 'That will be all, Inspector.' Gently touching Hölderlin's shoulder, he added: 'Thank you, Herr Hölderlin.'

The banker sat up.

'We're finished?'

'Yes.'

Hölderlin got off the divan and took a few uncertain steps into the middle of the room. He looked feeble and confused. The necktie fell out of his pocket and Liebermann picked it up for him.

'Thank you,' Hölderlin whispered, looping the tie loosely around his neck.

Rheinhardt opened the door and ushered him into the corridor, where two constables were waiting for him.

'Well?' said Rheinhardt. 'What do you think?'

'He's telling the truth.'

Rheinhardt returned to his chair and Liebermann lay down on the divan.

'How do you know that?'

'His fluency. The absence of significant hesitations. He made no slips or errors. And the dream — the dream was extremely interesting.'

'Was it?'

'Oh yes — it was entirely consistent with his story, and the unconscious never lies.'

'Perhaps you could explain?'

'With pleasure, Oskar. In order to preserve sleep, the mind must work certain transformations on the content of dreams, particularly if the dream is likely to promote anxiety. Otherwise that anxiety would constantly wake us up, which would not be very good for our general health. Thus the dream that we remember is an adulterated version of an original. Think of it as a coded message, a language of symbols in which relatively innocuous images replace those of a more challenging or disturbing nature. Herr Hölderlin found himself in a nursery — which suggests a wish to return to the world of childhood. A simple world, free from sexual intrigue. Most dreams conceal a wish of sorts . . .' As Liebermann spoke, he addressed the ceiling, punctuating his explanation with expressive hand gestures. 'But his assignation with Fräulein Löwenstein is still very much on his mind and his mental defences could not keep her out of the idyllic world of the nursery in Penzing.'

'Max, he didn't mention her once!'

'No, but she is still the principal subject of the dream. Take the rocking horse, for example . . .'

'What about it?'

'Are not horses a symbol of potency? Stallions and suchlike?' Liebermann's clenched fists closed around the imaginary reins of an equally imaginary galloping steed.

'They are, but—'

'And where do horses race in Vienna?'

'The Prater.'

'Which was where—?'

'He had his assignation.'

'Very good, Oskar.' Liebermann let his hands drop. 'And at that time, he would no doubt have been excited by the prospect of enjoying Fräulein Löwenstein's sexual favours. I hope that I don't need to spell out the obvious associations between Herr Hölderlin's expectations, connections with riding, and the motion of a nursery horse.'

Rheinhardt raised his eyebrows.

'He observed,' Liebermann continued, 'a jewellery box on the floor.'

'Which belonged to his mother.'

'One step at a time, Oskar. Can you think of what a jewellery box might represent?'

'I know that the term is sometimes used by uncouth individuals to mean . . .'

'Indeed. There is no need to be coy, Oskar. It is a common term, a slang word for the female reproductive organ. Now, in the dream Hölderlin is discovered attempting to gain entry into the box, which is more or less what actually transpired. He was discovered during an assignation. However, the dream tells us that his sexual exploits were frustrated. He didn't get very far. He may have propositioned Fräulein Löwenstein — in fact, he probably did — but she refused him. Thus, in the dream, the lid remains closed.'

Liebermann glanced at his friend. Observing an expression closer to horror than surprise, he added: 'Oskar, if you think this a little far-fetched, you might want to take another look at those photographs. The box was ivory, with mother-of-pearl inlay. Fräulein Löwenstein was wearing a white dress and a double string of pearls. I am absolutely convinced that Hölderlin is telling the truth about his relationship with Fräulein Löwenstein. He did not make her pregnant — they were not lovers.'

Liebermann's tone was positive.

Rheinhardt grunted his assent, and the young doctor continued his analysis.

'Herr Hölderlin described himself protesting, even though he had been discovered with the box in his hands. I think it safe to assume, given his mother's reprimand, that he was doing something that was supposed to be wrong. At first sight, this seems to make little sense. How could he justify himself when he had been discovered — and I use these words knowingly — *in flagrante delicto*? But in dreams, meanings are conflated. He was not protesting about the assignation. His protest concerned the more significant accusation of murder. That is why the inconsistency of his position aroused no emotional conflict. His denial was experienced in the dream as acceptable. Which would suggest that, with respect to the allegation of murder at least, he is indeed innocent.'

'But why was he discovered by his mother? In reality he was discovered by von Bulow. Surely, Max, you aren't going to tell me that Hölderlin's mother represented von Bulow?'

'Professor Freud has suggested that significant dreams often reproduce scenes from infancy. It may be that the whole edifice of Hölderlin's dream is founded on a real memory of discovery involving his mother but now deeply buried in his unconscious. However, to uncover the secret of what really happened in the nursery all those years ago would necessitate many hours of psychoanalysis.'

Rheinhardt shook his head.

'This is all very well, Max, but I can't see Brügel being very sympathetic to your interpretation.'

'Perhaps not,' said Liebermann, sitting up and turning to look at his friend. 'But I can promise you now, Oskar, that von Bulow will not extract a confession from Hölderlin, no matter how long he keeps the wretched man locked up!'

74

'The Mayor's absolutely right,' said Councillor Schmidt, dabbing his lips with a table napkin. 'Doctors, lawyers, teachers, opera-house directors — they're everywhere. Something has to be done.'

'Indeed,' said Bruckmüller. 'People have become so complacent. I tell you, Julius, we need another Hilsner. That would get people talking.'

Cosima von Rath, who had been staring wistfully at the last of the chocolates, turned to face her fiancé.

'Does he work in the town hall too?'

Bruckmüller and Schmidt looked at each other for a moment and then laughed.

'Good heavens, no, my love. He's not one of us — he's one of them. Surely you've heard of Leopold Hilsner?'

Cosima shook her head and the pendulous rings of flesh around her neck wobbled like blancmange.

'Hans,' she cried, pursing her lips together and producing a rather ugly moue. 'You know how unworldly I am.'

'Do you never read the papers, my dear?' asked Schmidt.

'Never,' she replied.

'I've seen you read the society pages,' said Bruckmüller.

Cosima ignored him.

'I would have thought,' continued Councillor Schmidt, 'that as a connoisseur of arcane rituals and practices the Hilsner case would have interested you a great deal.'

'Oh? Why's that?'

Cosima extended her hand towards the solitary truffle, seduced by its alluring sprinkle of cocoa powder.

'Hilsner was a ritual murderer,' said Schmidt.

Cosima's hand stopped above the chocolate where it hovered like a bird of prey.

'Was he?' She turned to look at Schmidt, her piggy eyes glinting in their pink pouches.

'See?' said Schmidt to Bruckmüller. 'I knew we'd get her interested in politics one day.' He raised his glass in a mock toast and sipped his brandy.

Bruckmüller smiled and placed a patronising hand on Cosima's shoulder.

'He was a Jew, my love. A shoemaker's apprentice. He was tried for killing a girl — she was only nineteen, I believe.'

'Yes, nineteen,' Schmidt asserted.

'Her body was found near the Jewish quarter of Polna. Her throat had been cut.' Bruckmüller dragged his forefinger across his Adam's apple. 'And every drop of blood had been drained from her body.'

Cosima's hand swiftly withdrew from the chocolate and clutched her jeweled ankh.

'Oh, how dreadful,' she piped. 'But why did he do it?'

'He needed Christian blood for that bread of theirs.'

'Matzoh,' said Schmidt, with an exaggerated expression of disgust. 'Dreadful stuff.'

'They've been doing it for centuries, apparently,' said Bruckmüller, pouring himself another brandy.

'Ahh yes . . .' said Cosima, suddenly making a connection between the subject of the conversation and her pool of abstruse knowledge. 'I've read of such things. I think it used to be called the blood libel.'

Schmidt shrugged: 'I wouldn't know.'

'But I had no idea that these rituals were still being performed in the modern world,' said Cosima. 'It is quite extraordinary.'

'Indeed,' said Schmidt. 'Hilsner's behind bars now, thank the Lord. But by rights he should have swung.'

'He wasn't sentenced to death?' said Cosima, theatrically placing both hands over her mouth.

'No, my dear,' Schmidt replied. 'Thanks to the vociferous liberal minority — mostly Jews — he was tried again. The business of the ritual murder wasn't even mentioned the second time around! It was all suppressed. Even so, they didn't have it all their own way. Hilsner was found guilty again, of course. He was sentenced to life imprisonment — but he should have swung.'

Cosima tutted and looked from Schmidt to Bruckmüller. Again, her features puckered to form a disgruntled pout.

'What is it, dear?' said Bruckmüller.

'I don't understand.'

'What don't you understand?'

'Why on Earth did you say that we need another Hilsner?'

'Politics, my dear,' said Bruckmüller, tapping the side of his protuberant nose with a thick, big-knuckled finger. 'Politics.'

75

Liebermann had completed the C-major fugue and had begun to pound out the C-minor Prelude. Playing Bach's 'forty-eight' was an exercise he performed with increasing regularity. Somehow, the purity and elegance of Bach's counterpoint helped him to think. He was so familiar with Bach's epic circumnavigation of the tonal world that his fingers arrived on the correct keys without conscious effort. For Liebermann, performing the forty-eight was like a spiritual discipline — a Western equivalent of the transcendental devotions practised in the East.

Liebermann was confident that his interpretation of Hölderlin's dream was correct. The banker was not Fräulein Löwenstein's lover — nor had he murdered her. There would be no confession.

Melodic lines chased each other at different intervals, and became entangled in dense episodes of invention.

So who, then?

His left hand began to toll the repeating tonic of the D-minor Prelude — above, the semiquaver triplets fell like lashing rain.

The god of storms!

It seemed to Liebermann that the Löwenstein case was like a labyrinth. He and Rheinhardt had been blindly stumbling through its dark corridors, occasionally grasping clues and following them for a short while, only to find themselves rudely deposited beyond the structure's walls. And at the centre of the labyrinth was the personification of an ancient evil, mocking their ineptitude. Whoever had killed Fräulein Löwenstein — and very probably Uberhorst too — had succeeded in sustaining a prodigious disguise. As long as the mystery remained, the case would not be brought to a satisfactory conclusion. The crime might as well be imputed to Seth.

Doors locked from the inside.

A gunshot wound — but no bullet.

How did the illusion work?

As Liebermann played on, it occurred to him that Bach's keyboard works were also a species of illusion. They sounded spontaneous, improvisatory and inspired, yet every fugue was driven by a ruthless internal logic. The magic, as such, could be reduced to the diligent application of musical rules and mathematical principles. Be that as it may, although Liebermann could lift the veil of Bach's enchantment he could not penetrate the illusion of Fräulein Löwenstein's murder. The machinery of deception remained invisible — its levers and gears thoroughly concealed.

The investigation had reached a sorry impasse.

Liebermann was forced to confront an unpalatable but self-evident truth. Neither he nor Rheinhardt could determine the solution alone. They needed help. By the time he had reached the fifteenth prelude, Liebermann knew what he had to do. He did not stop playing but remained at the keyboard and completed the whole of Book One. Then, closing the lid of the Bösendorfer, he stood up and walked to the hallway where he collected his coat from the stand. He would tackle Book Two on his return.

Outside it was still quite light, and the evening was pleasantly warm. The air was fragrant with lilac. He set off briskly, crossing Wahringstrasse and walking downhill towards the Danube. He slowed as he passed Bergasse 19 and was tempted to go in. Professor Freud would be happy to offer him an opinion on Hölderlin's dream, and might even comment on the mental state of the murderer. But Liebermann already knew that this would not be enough. The Löwenstein mystery required a different approach. He quickened his step.

When Amelia Lydgate opened the door, her eyes widened slightly with surprise.

'Herr Doctor.'

Liebermann bowed.

'Miss Lydgate. I am so sorry to disturb you — I was passing, and thought I might pay you a visit.'

'How very kind of you, Herr Doctor. Do come in.'

Before ascending the stairs, Liebermann paid his respects to Frau Rubenstein. He discovered her dozing in an armchair, a volume of poetry resting on her lap. The exchange of pleasantries did not detain him long. Liebermann accepted Miss Lydgate's offer of tea, and they were soon seated in her small reception room.

Liebermann began by asking the young woman some questions about her health. She responded in a matter-of-fact way, describing her progress with clinical detachment: her appetite had returned, she was sleeping well, her right arm remained responsive and her fingers had suffered no loss of dexterity. Liebermann felt slightly uncomfortable in assuming this outward show of concern while secretly wishing to move the conversation on to areas closer to his purpose; however, a transition was not difficult to achieve. When he invited her to talk about a recent visit to the Pathological Institute, she was soon detailing the methodology of a possible research project that she had discussed with Landsteiner: a microscopic analysis of haemophiliac blood plasma.

'Miss Lydgate,' Liebermann ventured, with more timidity than was usual, 'I was wondering — could I ask for your opinion? On a technical matter?'

Amelia Lydgate registered the equivocation.

'Technical?'

'Yes. You see, it is my good fortune to be a close friend of Inspector Oskar Rheinhardt of the Viennese security office . . .' He briefly explained his association with Rheinhardt and then attempted to introduce the topic of murder without alarming his companion: 'Forgive me for raising such a distressing matter, but six weeks ago the body of a young woman was found in a Leopoldstadt apartment. The circumstances surrounding her discovery were extraordinary — and the results of her autopsy were unlike anything anyone has ever seen before. You are a woman possessed of remarkable analytic skills, Miss Lydgate, and I would be much interested in your view of the facts. However, if the subject of murder is one that you find distasteful then I fully understand . . .'

As Liebermann's faltering enquiry stalled, the young woman proudly stated: 'Herr Doctor — I intend to study medicine. The fact of human mortality does not disturb me. I have conducted many animal dissections under my father's guidance and I fully expect to repeat these procedures on human corpses, should I gain a place at the university.'

'Of course,' said Liebermann. 'Please accept my apology.'

'I am perfectly happy to hear more of this remarkable case. Indeed, you have already aroused my curiosity. I fear, however, that you have overestimated my knowledge and deductive powers.'

Amelia Lydgate's pewter eyes glowed in the dying light.

Liebermann graciously accepted that he might be mistaken and then set about describing the crime scene: Fräulein Löwenstein, reclining on the chaise longue, her heart ruined by an impossible bullet. The note on the table, and the Japanese box with its demonic occupant. He did not describe any of the suspects, nor how the investigation had proceeded to date.

When he had finished, Miss Lydgate remained silent. Then, noticing the failing light, she rose from her chair and lit the nearest gas lamp. She performed these actions without speaking to or so much as glancing at Liebermann. She seemed wholly absorbed, her forehead lined by a customary frown.

'I could take you to the apartment,' said Liebermann, 'if it would help.'

She sat down and poured herself another cup of tea.

'What kind of lock was it?'

'On the sitting-room door?'

'Yes.'

'I don't really know.'

'A warded lock? A lever tumbler? A detector?'

'I'm sorry. . .' Liebermann raised his hands helplessly, indicating that he had no further knowledge to declare.

'Never mind,' said Amelia Lydgate. 'You noticed nothing remarkable about its design? There was nothing odd about it?'

'No. It was just an ordinary lock.'

'Good.'

'Inspector Rheinhardt would not object to our visiting the apartment, I'm sure we could—'

'No, Doctor Liebermann,' the young woman said firmly. 'That won't be necessary. But I'd be most grateful if you would bring me both keys — the key to the sitting-room door and the key to the Japanese box. I would like to examine them.'

Her face was impassive and, in a way that resisted analysis, tempered by a subtle beauty.

76

BEATRICE SCHELLING TIPTOED up the stairs, past the hissing gas lamps, ascending into the upper region of the house where light gave way to shadow. She fumbled in her dressing gown for a candle and, having lit it with a match, continued her journey. The sound came again — indistinct but undoubtedly real. Beatrice held her breath so that she could hear better, but found that her heart was thumping in her ears.

Creeping across the landing, she came to the last flight of stairs. They were uncarpeted and she had to negotiate them with even greater care. Stepping out of her slippers, she grasped the banister and pulled herself upward. The wood protested, groaning under her weight. Beatrice froze, paused, and gingerly placed the ball of her foot on the next step.

On reaching the attic area she heard the susurration again. It sounded like sobbing. Beatrice approached the door ahead and pressed her ear against one of its panels. She imagined the girl on the other side, sitting on her bed, her knees pulled up against her chest, abundant tears soaking her cheap nightdress. The new maid had recently arrived in Vienna from the country. She was slight, with curly brown hair — little more than a child.

The whimpering increased in volume.

Beatrice's instinct was to turn the door handle and enter the room — to place her arm around the poor girl's shoulder and console her.

You miss your mother and father, of course you do. But you will see them again in the autumn. Don't fret, my dear.

She had done the same when the previous maid had been tearful, and the maid before her — a beautiful creature from Croatia with jet-black hair and bright blue eyes. But Beatrice could no longer play her part. She was weary of the role, and knew that her lines would be delivered without conviction. Moreover, she was perfectly well aware that the ponderous step that had descended the attic stairs some thirty minutes earlier had belonged to her husband. Far below, in the entrance hall, a clock struck the second hour of the morning.

The whimpering subsided, to be replaced by a pathetic sniffling.

A drop of hot candle wax fell on to Beatrice's foot. She did not flinch but remained still, allowing the burning sensation to increase briefly in intensity. She found it perversely satisfying. The pain was in some obscure way redeeming. It seemed to purify her soul.

Behind the door the girl seemed to be drifting into a fitful sleep. All that Beatrice could hear now was a continuous *sotto voce* grizzling.

Beatrice straightened her back and walked — perhaps less cautiously now — to the edge of the landing. She paused for a moment, sighed, and blew out the candle.

When she reached her husband's study, she switched on the lamp. From his desk she took a sheet of creamy paper. Staring at its blankness, she began composing a letter. It began: *Dear Amelia . . .*

77

Nurse Rupius and Stefan Kanner approached each other from opposite directions. Both were wearing their outdoor coats.

'Good evening, Sabina.'

'Herr Doctor . . .'

They turned along the main corridor and continued walking side by side.

'Please call me Stefan.' He made a show of looking at his pocket watch. 'We are no longer at work.'

Nurse Rupius's cheeks coloured a little at his familiarity.

'Do you have far to go?'

'Josefstadt.'

'Not very far, then.'

'No.'

Kanner was desperate to keep the conversation going, but could not think of anything else to say. Sabina Rupius came to his assistance.

'And you, Herr Doc—' she broke off. 'Stefan?'

'Oh, Mariahilf.'

'Have you lived there long?'

'No. I moved from Döbling in January.'

'I have fond memories of Mariahilf. My father used to take me to see *The Magic Flute* there — every Christmas, or so it seemed.'

'The Am der Wien?'

'Yes.'

'A lovely old theatre. It's just been done up, you know.'

'Has it?'

'I go quite often. Do you still go to the theatre?'

'Not as much as I should, or would like to.'

She turned her head. Her eyes glistened.

Is she expecting me to ask?

It certainly looks that way.

Kanner swallowed nervously; however, as he prepared to speak, the opportunity that had presented itself was suddenly lost. Ahead, he noticed the approach of Brunnhilde Grützner — the surliest of hospital matrons. He watched as Nurse Rupius's expression changed from anticipation through dismay to disappointment.

Matron Grützner greeted them from a distance: 'Good evening, Herr Doctor.' Then, looking at Sabina with undisguised disapproval, she added curtly: 'Nurse Rupius.'

'Good evening, Matron,' they replied in unison while unconsciously moving apart. It was common knowledge that the Matron took a very dim view of young nurses socialising with doctors. The woman seemed to possess an almost preternatural gift for detecting nascent romance.

Kanner waited for Matron Grützner's footsteps to fade before attempting to pick up the threads of their broken conversation.

'Did you know,' said Kanner, 'the very first performance of *The Magic Flute* took place in that theatre.'

'Yes,' said Sabina Rupius, thinking that it might have been more advantageous to feign ignorance. 'Yes, I did know that.'

They both managed to smile but neither could ignore the undercurrent of shared embarrassment. Fortunately, they were rescued from this conversational quagmire by the unexpected appearance of several men outside Professor Gruner's room: porters, dressed in brown aprons and carrying large boxes towards the staircase.

'Is he going?' whispered Rupius.

'It looks like he's gone,' said Kanner, glancing into Gruner's room. 'Your friend will be pleased.'

Stefan laughed: 'Yes, he will. Gruner and Max never got on — it has to be said.'

'I wonder what happened?'

'The inquiry — he must have been dismissed.'

'Or he could have resigned.'

'Extraordinary.'

'Will we have a new professor?'

'Indeed— let's hope the new one is an improvement on the old one.'

Nodding to some porters at the head of the stairs, they made their way to the ground floor. Although they did not speak, the silence was no longer uncomfortable.

When they reached the foyer, Kanner felt a curious sense of urgency. They would step outside and go their separate ways — she to Josefstadt, he to Mariahilf. He must do something, say something.

The evening was pleasantly warm and they both paused on the hospital steps. Sabina Rupius looked up at her companion — the look of expectation had returned.

'Sabina . . .' said Kanner. 'Would you like to go to the theatre? Tomorrow evening? Of course, I would understand if—'

'I would be delighted, Stefan,' said Nurse Rupius, her face glowing.

'Well . . . that's excellent. Excellent,' said Kanner.

They stood looking at each other for a few moments before Sabina Rupius said: 'I must go.'

She glanced quickly around the courtyard and, seeing that it was empty, offered Kanner her hand. He took it and kissed her fingers.

Nurse Rupius smiled, turned and walked away — her hips swaying with each unhurried step.

78

AMELIA LYDGATE STOOD by her newly acquired laboratory bench. An umbilical pipe of red rubber dropped from a gaslight fitting to a battered Bunsen burner, and a conspicuously large microscope stood next to a row of empty test tubes. The surface of the bench was heavily scored, suggesting to Liebermann that Miss Lydgate had purchased this bulky piece of furniture from one of the junk shops near the hospital.

The curtains were open and the attic room was filled with light. The young governess's hair was pinned back but its colours were particularly vibrant — streaks of ochre, rust and gold. As usual, she was dressed plainly but effectively: a simple white blouse and a long grey skirt. She looked slender and willowy, in possession of a disarmingly fragile hauteur.

'I have the keys,' said Liebermann.

Reaching into his pocket, he took out two envelopes and handed them to Miss Lydgate. She opened both and tipped the keys onto her work bench.

'The larger is the key to the sitting room,' continued Liebermann. 'The smaller is the one for Fräulein Löwenstein's Japanese box.'

Amelia Lydgate picked up the larger key and seemed to be judging its weight in her right hand. She then raised it above her head and turned it in the sunlight. Her expression was particularly intense.

'What are you looking for?' asked Liebermann.

Miss Lydgate did not reply. She was completely absorbed in her task. Carefully placing the larger key on the laboratory bench, she picked up the smaller one and repeated the weighing and inspection procedures.

Liebermann could not prevent himself from admiring her figure. Anorexia had narrowed her frame, but now, as her recovery progressed, she was becoming more shapely. Her small bosom and the curvature of her hips was more pronounced. As his gaze wandered over her body, he felt a frisson of arousal, which immediately curdled with guilt. He remembered Katherine — the clinging hospital gown — the suggestion of her sex straining against constricting fibres — her naked feet and the ivory-white skin of her ankles . . .

'Very interesting,' said Amelia Lydgate.

'What is?' asked Liebermann, his voice humbled by a prickling sense of shame.

Again the young woman did not reply. But Liebermann was not offended. She was obviously lost in thought. Moreover, he was satisfied, at that moment, not to become the focus of interest of those enquiring eyes.

Miss Lydgate pulled a high stool from under the bench and, standing on tiptoe, managed to push herself up to sit on the elevated wooden seat. She then reached for the microscope — a beautiful instrument made from lacquered brass and black enamelled iron. It was obviously heavy, and she held her breath as she moved it. Placing the larger key on the silver viewing plate, she leaned over the eyepiece and turned the revolving turret of lenses. While adjusting the coarse- and fine-adjustment wheels, she tilted the mirror to get more light. Her movements had a certain fluency — an ease that indicated many hours spent in scientific study. It was unusual to see a woman so comfortable with a piece of optical technology.

She removed the larger key and replaced it with the smaller one.

'Doctor Liebermann? Are you carrying any keys?'

'Yes.'

'May I see them, please?'

Liebermann handed her two bunches.

'These are my apartment keys — and these are from the hospital.'

'Thank you.'

Amelia Lydgate systematically examined each key, occasionally changing the lens to increase or reduce levels of magnification. While she was still looking into the microscope, she said: 'Doctor Liebermann, would you be so kind as to fetch the key from my bedroom door — the second on the right as you leave this room.'

'Of course.'

Liebermann left the room and opened the second door, as instructed. The curtains were drawn and the room was filled with a dusky half-light. His gaze lingered on the bed, the cover of which was half off. The sheets were rumpled in a pattern of concentric loops — like sand on a beach at low tide. The mattress was depressed slightly, retaining in its tired springs the impression of her body. He removed the key from the lock and closed the door softly behind him.

When he entered the 'laboratory' Miss Lydgate was still bent over the microscope, her fingers deftly exchanging keys and rotating lenses. Hearing Liebermann approach, she extended her open palm. He placed the key in her hand.

'Thank you,' she said, without looking up. Her fingers closed around the key, which she immediately placed under the microscope.

'Yes,' she said. 'Just as I thought.'

Then, raising her head, she beckoned Liebermann closer.

'If you would care to look at this key first.'

Liebermann looked into the eyepiece and saw a slightly flecked metal surface.

'It is the key to my bedroom. And now, the key from Fräulein Löwenstein's apartment. What do you see?'

Liebermann adjusted his glasses and squinted.

'It looks like . . . it looks like the metal is marked. With a pattern?'

'Indeed.'

The key was ridged with minute parallel lines.

'The pattern appears on both sides,' continued Miss Lydgate.

She was standing very close and her proximity was somewhat distracting. Her dress material rustled loudly when she moved.

'And now — the small key from the Japanese box.'

Amelia Lydgate placed the smaller key under the objective.

'Another pattern,' said Liebermann.

'No,' said the young woman, rather petulantly. 'The same pattern, Herr Doctor. Only smaller. It does not appear on any of the other keys — and I suspect that we should not find anything similar even if we had a much larger assortment to examine.'

Liebermann stood up straight and looked into Miss Lydgate's eyes. Her expression was still calm and unemotional. She did not appear self-satisfied and there was nothing in her bearing that suggested she was in need of a compliment.

'What does this mean?' asked Liebermann.

'I think,' replied Amelia Lydgate, 'that it means we can confidently reject a supernatural explanation.'

79

THE LETTER FROM England had been placed among his other correspondence. She had wanted to ask about it — and had even dropped some hints — but her husband had not been forthcoming. He dismissed her enquiries and assumed a somewhat patronizing air.

'My dear, how tired you look. Perhaps you should leave the children with Marie again. Go out and buy yourself something — a new pair of gloves, perhaps.'

Before leaving, he had said, almost in passing, that he was interviewing another governess: a fine, virtuous young woman — recommended to him by Schmidt, one of the Mayor's colleagues. Nothing like poor Amelia. A hardy German. Healthy, stolid, someone who would set a good example for the children.

The door closed and Beatrice Schelling was left standing in the hallway, feeling dizzy and confused. It was as though she had become lost in her own home, and did not know where to go or which way to turn. A clock struck the hour. The day would proceed, with her or without her.

The children were delighted to see their aunt again. They threw their arms around Marie's neck and kissed her plump, pink face.

'Children, children! How lovely to see you again.'

Beatrice felt something unpleasant stirring in her belly. The swelling of a dark emotion — a corrosive mixture of envy and hurt. When the bile had drained from her stomach, she felt dry and empty.

As she and Marie chatted, Beatrice felt entirely dissociated. She listened to her own voice as though it belonged to someone else. It was like eavesdropping.

'I need to go to the lingerie shop on Dingelstedstrasse and, if I have time, to Taubenrach's. We have to attend a function in a few weeks and I can't wear the same dress again. The navy-blue taffeta — you've seen it, I'm sure. Frau Förster never wears the same dress twice.'

Beatrice piped on like a church organist improvising around an inauspicious theme. When she felt that the performance had lasted long enough, she simply stopped and excused herself. It had been her custom to raise the contentious subject of Demel's just before her departure, but on this occasion, she said nothing. Today, Edward and Adele could eat as much chocolate as they liked.

'Say goodbye to your mother!' Marie called out to the children, who were already playing noisily on the stairs.

'No, it's all right — let them play,' Beatrice said distractedly, affecting a tepid smile.

She did not go to Dingelstedstrasse or to the ladies' outfitters. Instead, she wandered the streets, drifting, by degrees, in a southerly direction. Eventually she found herself standing by one of the new station entrances on Karlsplatz. Her husband had said that they were a disgrace and that the architect should be shot. Beatrice had agreed, but looking at them now she could not understand why some people found them so offensive. The green wrought-iron framework of the two pavilions reminded her of a conservatory.

Beyond the pavilions was the massive Karlskirche. Its huge Italianate dome was flanked by giant columns. Scenes from the life of St Borromeo, in relief, spiralled to the top of each, where gilded Habsburg eagles had made their eyries.

What was in that letter? What had the girl said?

Would there be a scandal? Would they accuse her, too?

A tram bell sounded and a gentleman grabbed her arm, pulling her back on to the pavement.

A flash of red and white.

'I beg your pardon, madam — but the tram . . .'

'Yes, of course, how silly of me.'

'You must be more careful.'

'Indeed. Thank you.'

Stepping backwards, Beatrice hurried off into the crowd.

At the tram stop passengers were climbing aboard. She joined the queue and, without thinking, mounted the vehicle's platform and found herself a seat. She was oblivious to the journey, and eventually found herself delivered outside the mock Renaissance edifice of the Süd-bahnhoff.

The booking hall was like a palace. A glorious stone staircase ascended and diverged, leading to two high arches: the banisters were festooned with artificial candelabra, as tall as apple trees, and an austere white light streamed through high windows.

Beatrice stood under the clear glass globes of the cast-iron lamp-posts, and watched the people coming and going, the busy throng of the concourse. After composing herself, she visited the post office and deposited the letter she had written in the early hours of Tuesday morning. She then returned to the booking hall, where she examined the destination board.

There were so many places.

Baden, Wiener-Neustadt, Semmering . . .

Bruck an der Mur (Klangfurt, Meran, Udine, Venice).

Graz (Marburg, Agram Trieste).

Beatrice glided towards one of the ticket booths where she purchased a single to Trieste.

The clerk looked at her.

'Single, madam?'

'Yes, single.'

Clutching her ticket, she walked to the platform area.

Two servant girls passed, giggling into their hands; a soldier in a long coat stood with a large pack on his back; three middle-aged men, looking remarkably similar, with turned-up moustaches and bowler hats, were discussing business. Beatrice continued her journey, and was no longer sure whether the Süd-bahnhoff was real or a dream.

A stationmaster caught her attention.

'No need to go any further, madam.'

She paused. But when the man had gone she continued placing one foot in front of the other.

The platform began to tremble. In the distance, she saw the approaching engine. A whistle sounded.

She stared at the sleepers, which were covered in sand and coal dust.

Shame pressed down on her.

It would not be difficult — and, if she landed in the right place, it would be painless.

80

THEY HAD DINED on caviar, sardines, goose liver, and pheasant's eggs in aspic, washed down with two bottles of Asti and followed by the sweetest pineapple. Coffee was served with cognac pastilles, each delicately wrapped in silver foil. They had intended to leave an hour earlier, but somehow satiety, slivovitz and cigars kept them seated. None of the other tables were occupied, and a hovering waiter suggested that they had overstayed their welcome.

'We had a splendid time,' said Kanner. 'The play was excellent, and afterwards we walked the length of the Naschmarkt . . . I couldn't take my eyes off her. You know, Max, I have to admit that I haven't felt this way in a long time.'

'But Stefan, you said much the same thing of that shop girl — what was her name?'

'Gabrielle.'

'And the singer?'

'Cora.'

'And, if I'm not mistaken, the actress?'

'Emilie.'

'So how is Nurse Rupius different?'

'She just is . . .' said Kanner, making a circle in the air with his cigar. A flake of ash traced a figure of eight as it floated down to the table. 'I can't explain it. Which makes me more inclined to trust the authenticity of my affection.'

'You are a romantic, Stefan.'

'There are some things in our nature that defy analysis, Max — and love is one of them.'

'Ahh . . .' said Liebermann, leaning forward and clutching the edge of the table with both hands. 'So you *are* in love with Nurse Rupius.'

'Well, put it this way — Cupid might not have landed an arrow yet but he's certainly emptied a quiverful in my direction.'

The waiter coughed.

Liebermann looked at his wristwatch and noticed that he was having some difficulty focusing. The hands blurred, making it difficult for him to establish the exact hour. He should have refused the slivovitz.

'It's not time to go yet, is it?' asked Kanner.

Liebermann shrugged and lifted his glass. He swilled the contents around and took a sip. As the warmth spread through his body, he felt his purchase on reality slip a little more.

'I wonder what *really* draws two people together?'

The question he posed was involuntary, finding expression as soon as the thought formed in his mind.

'Fate,' said Kanner, with mock solemnity.

'We need fate to bring us together, undoubtedly. If two people never meet, it's unlikely that they'll fall in love. But assuming that fate works in their favour . . .'

'I don't know why you're asking me, Max — you're the one who's engaged to be married!'

'Seriously, Stefan . . .'

Kanner drew on his cigar and grimaced: 'It has to be said, it isn't easy to fall in love with an ugly woman.'

'We fall in love with beauty, then?'

'Beauty certainly sharpens desire.'

'Then why don't we fall in love with every attractive woman?'

Kanner paused for a moment and, looking somewhat perplexed, exclaimed: 'Perhaps I do!' A beat of silence was followed by a quick burst of laughter. 'What does your friend Professor Freud have to say about love?'

'Not much,' Liebermann replied. 'He is more taxed by sexuality. But I gather he takes a rather dim view of romance. He believes that love is a kind of symptom that arises through the repression of libido.'

'Mmmm ... which implies that once one has become intimate with a woman, passion cools?'

'Bluntly, yes.'

'He has a point ... don't you think?'

Perhaps that was all it was, then: this dull ache, this longing to be with her — an urge, and nothing more. Something that he could master, like any other basic drive. If only he tried harder, it might be like skipping a meal or putting off sleep. But in truth Liebermann knew that this wasn't so. His attachment, for that was what it had become, was more complex.

'I don't agree with everything Freud says. I can't help feeling that the pleasure we derive from the company of a woman — a woman with whom one has formed an attachment — is more than just a frustrated animal instinct.'

'Now who is being romantic?'

'You misunderstand me, Stefan,' Liebermann continued. 'I am not referring to anything mystical or magical. What I mean is that there are more factors than just libido to consider. We are prone to desire, of course, but don't we also seek companionship, conversation? The comforting proximity of a kindred spirit?'

'Yes, but not all of us are lucky enough to have found her.' Kanner raised his glass. 'To the future bride!'

Liebermann could hardly bear the irony of their conversation, the cruel cross-purposes. The fug of his alcoholic stupor suddenly closed around him, making him feel cut off from Kanner, the restaurant, and, indeed, the whole of Vienna.

'Stefan . . .'

A note of desperation had entered Liebermann's voice.

'Yes?' his companion replied.

'I'm not always sure that . . . You know, sometimes I think . . .' He looked at Kanner, who was smiling foolishly.

What wise counsel could he expect from his friend now? If he had meant to take Kanner into his confidence he should have done so at the beginning of the evening. 'Oh, it doesn't matter.'

Kanner's hand dropped to the table, splashing the starched white tablecloth with slivovitz.

Liebermann beckoned the waiter and snapped: 'The bill, please. We're ready to leave.'

Part Six

The Riesenrad

81

AMELIA LYDGATE CLIMBED the steps of the university like a pilgrim, at once awed and giddy with excitement. The atmosphere of scholarship affected her being like a cleansing balm, emollient and soothing. In such a place she might leave the world behind, forgetting its vain preoccupations, empty chatter and tiresome emotional complexities, and seek solace in a universe of absolute values — the unquestionable certainties of science. Her destiny, she determined, was connected with these stones.

She paused and glanced upwards. The university was a beautiful construction, built in the style of a Renaissance palace. Its dimensions would have made a merchant prince envious. Along the rooftop, figures looked down on her like a detachment of guardian angels. Amelia took a deep, tremulous breath, and stepped beneath the shelter of three massive arches. If there were such things as benign protective agencies, they had been considerate of her fate.

Only a few months earlier, it had seemed that her ambition to study medicine in this Mecca of learning would never be realised. Yet now everything had become possible again. Doctor Liebermann had come by chance into her life, transforming her circumstances. Fear and shame had been replaced by hope and quiet optimism. Amelia suspected that she would never be able to repay Doctor Liebermann for his kind ministrations; however, she had resolved to show her gratitude by assisting him with his police work.

She pressed her palm against the heavy door of iron and glass.

The foyer was shrouded in perpetual twilight, an amber gloaming never relieved by sunlight or the sulphurous inadequacy of the artificial lighting. A forest of columns, like prehistoric tree trunks, ascended to a vaulted ceiling of bas-relief concavities. Although it was early evening the university was still buzzing with activity and conversation (lectures began before dawn and continued until eight o'clock in the evening). Knots of students gathered in the shadows, while others trailed behind frock-coated sages. One of the professors sported a long white beard that dropped well below his waistband. Amelia was amused by his retinue, all of whom had followed his example and had grown beards of similar length.

Among these masculine crowds Amelia caught sight of only one other woman, marching briskly through the sea of waistcoats, wing collars and pinstriped trousers. As the lone female passed they acknowledged each other, as two countrymen might in a foreign land. There was a flash of recognition, the registration of surprise, followed by a smile of solidarity. Encouraged by this encounter, Amelia approached the porter.

'Good evening, sir.'

The man looked up and examined her with a look on his face that could only be described as sceptical.

'I have an appointment to see Professor Holz,' Amelia continued. 'Could you please direct me to the department of physical sciences?'

The porter issued some peremptory directions but seemed disinclined to be anything more than minimally helpful.

The corridor that intersected the foyer led to a grand double staircase, the stone balustrades of which supported cast-iron gas-lamps. At the summit of each post a trio of opaque globes emitted a weak light. The walls of the enormous stairwell were high and, although decorated in baroque relief, had a pleasing simplicity. Black marble columns supported what looked like a gallery, and the remote curved ceiling captured the last remnants of the day's afterglow through high arched windows.

Amelia reached the top of the stairs, after which the porter's miserly directions became impossible to follow. Excusing herself, she asked a young man in a short cape for directions. He laughed and said that he had only just finished attending Professor's Holz's interminable class. He insisted on escorting Amelia to a small lecture theatre where the professor was still examining some equations on the blackboard.

'Herr Professor,' called the young man. The professor did not turn, merely pushing his hand back as if repelling an assailant. The young man grinned inanely. He tried again: 'Herr Professor, a young lady to see you.'

This time the professor pulled himself away from his work and looked up the aisle.

'You will excuse me,' whispered the young man to Amelia. 'The pleasure is now undoubtedly all yours.' He winked impertinently and scurried off.

'Yes!' demanded Professor Holz.

'My name is Miss Amelia Lydgate. You kindly agreed to see me this evening.'

'Ahh . . .' said the professor. 'Did I? Very well, come in, and sit there for a moment, will you?' He motioned towards a seat and added: 'I won't be long.' Amelia lifted her skirts slightly, and made her way down the precipitous wooden stairs. The professor returned his attention to the blackboard, which he attacked — violently — with a stub of chalk. A stream of Greek letters and relational symbols appeared, spreading across the dusty surface like a skin disease. Amelia sat on a bench in the front row and immediately applied herself to the professor's problem; however, she found it almost impossible to understand his purpose. Eventually the professor stopped, groaned and tossed the chalk on to the lectern. Amelia wanted to say something consoling but thought it better to remain silent.

'So, Miss Lydgate,' said the professor — still with his back to her and gazing at his fluxions — 'what can I do for you?'

'I have a question pertaining to your area of study.'

'You have a question concerning ballistics?'

'Yes, Herr Professor. I recently discovered your monograph on trajectory calculus, which I found most stimulating.'

The professor paused and, turning slowly, looked at Amelia properly for the first time. He peered through a pair of tortoiseshell pince-nez that balanced precariously at the end of his nose. His nostrils flared, like a wild animal testing the air for predators.

'Stimulating, you say?'

'Very much so, and I have a question — to do with projectiles and their integrity.' The professor continued to stare at her. 'I understand that you are a very busy man, Herr Professor, and I do not wish to waste your valuable time. For that reason, I have taken the liberty of expressing the problem in a formula — which I hope you will be kind enough to examine.'

Standing, Amelia took a sheet of foolscap from her bag and offered it to the professor. Holz condescended to look at her mathematics and almost immediately uttered a dismissive 'Pfha!'

Amelia paused respectfully before saying: 'There is an error?'

'My good woman,' said Holz, 'surely you do not mean to ascribe theta with these value parameters? An elementary mistake!'

Holz tossed the paper back at Amelia, who caught it before it fluttered to the floor.

'With the greatest respect,' said Amelia, 'it is not an elementary mistake. I have given theta these values for a very specific reason — because I am interested in answering a very specific question.'

The professor looked at Amelia again with renewed interest. He blinked, sniffed the air, and demanded: 'What sort of question?'

82

THE GIRL HAD fallen asleep. Before leaving, Braun paused to look at her. She was young, probably not much older than seventeen, and a Slav. Madam Matejka had said that she was originally from Gallicia. Wherever Felka came from, her German was terrible and Braun had had to mime his requirements. The girl had watched him with intelligent, serious eyes before carrying out his instructions with unexpected industry and imagination.

Felka uttered a few unintelligible words in her sleep, made some mewling sounds, and then rolled over. The blanket fell from her body, revealing a pleasing landscape of fleshy contours that swept towards a patch of tight black curls. She was still wearing her cotton stockings and garters.

Experiencing an odd and uncharacteristic combination of pity and gratitude, Braun found some loose change in his pocket — a pitiful clutch of ten-heller silver coins — which he left on the table. (The girl would see very little of the money he had given to Madam Matejka.) In the cold grate, he noticed a stick and a sponge lying in a bowl of cloudy liquid. Felka had forgotten to douche — but that wasn't his problem. Braun shrugged and crept to the door.

The floorboards creaked as he walked along the upstairs landing. A gust of wind rattled the casement and his candle flickered in his grip. With his other hand touching the mildewed wall, he made his way cautiously to the rickety stairs. Before he reached the bottom he peered over the banister. The room was, as usual, poorly lit, and a woolly haze of thick smoke hung in the air. Two gentlemen were occupying the deep sofas. The first was unconscious, scrunched up, looking like a pile of discarded rags. The other was sitting straighter, drawing on a bubbling hookah. The second man was Count Záborszky.

Braun felt a surge of anxiety, but his depleted body was too weak to sustain the emotion. His heart, after the briefest of accelerations, slowed to a more pedestrian beat and his breathing became regular.

He clumped down the stairs, walked to the low Turkish table and, placing the candle next to the hookah, slumped down next to the unconscious patron, whose form was no more discernibly human at close quarters. Braun squeezed the candle's flame out with his fingers, and watched the ascending thread of grey smoke wind upwards like the soul departing from a dead body.

Braun looked into Záborszky's eyes, which were dull and lifeless. The Count showed no sign of recognition — until he removed the hookah's mouthpiece and whispered: 'How is your hand, Braun?'

Braun smiled, and held it up. It was still bandaged.

The Count nodded, approvingly. Braun was unsure whether he was impressed by the dressing or pleased that the wound hadn't properly healed. The younger man produced a box of six handmade Egyptian cigarettes. The pale yellow wrapping papers were the same colour as the tobacco, threads of which protruded from either end.

'Which girl did you have?' asked the Count.

'Felka,' replied Braun, tamping the loose tobacco.

'The new one?'

'Yes.'

'Would you recommend her?'

'She was very conscientious.'

The Count inhaled and closed his eyes.

'That witch Matejka wouldn't let me have her.'

'Why not?'

'Thinks I'm too rough.'

'To be frank, I'm inclined to agree.'

The Count's eyes opened slowly and his lips curled upwards.

'I take it that you've heard about Hölderlin?' said Braun, finally lighting his cigarette.

'Of course.'

'It seems, then, that I owe you an apology.'

Záborszky executed a languorous benediction with crossed fingers — before releasing a deep, world-weary sigh. He drew on the hookah again and, after another lengthy silence, said: 'You were Fräulein Löwenstein's lover?'

Braun assented with a curt nod.

'And accomplice?' Záborszky added.

Braun nodded again, and let his body slide forward on the sofa.

'But the children were not yours.'

'No, they weren't mine.'

The Count brought his two hands together and, linking his fingers, made a dome. He was wearing so many rings that it looked as though he had magically conjured up a jewelled orb. A big emerald caught the light, producing a viridescent glimmer.

'Hölderlin,' said the Count. 'The bank manager. The devoted husband!' He began to laugh — a curious rapid barking that suddenly stopped dead. 'Who would have thought it?'

Their unconscious companion suddenly belched and sat bolt upright, looking around the room as if he had awakened from a nightmare only to find himself in the lower circles of hell.

83

LIEBERMANN TOOK THE letter and sat back in the armchair, letting his head rest on the antimacassar.

Dear Amelia — I know what he did to you. You were not the first and I know you will not be the last. I am truly sorry: forgive me. I should have done so much more but I did not have the courage to speak out. Beatrice.

'When did this arrive?' asked Liebermann.

'Thursday,' Miss Lydgate answered.

For a while, neither of them spoke. Outside, a church bell began to chime. The evening was drawing in.

'It is a tragedy,' said Amelia Lydgate. 'Especially for the children.'

'Indeed,' said Liebermann. 'I wonder what arrangements Minister Schelling will make for their care?'

'Edward and Adele are very fond of their Aunt Marie. I hope that he has the good sense to seek her assistance. She is a childless widow and will love the children as if they were her own, of that I am sure.'

Miss Lydgate rose from her seat, took a box of matches from the mantelpiece and lit a gas lamp.

'But what are your own feelings, Miss Lydgate? Concerning Frau Schelling? Her death is a terrible tragedy — but this —' Liebermann raised the letter '— is also a dreadful admission.'

The young woman sat down and stared directly at Liebermann. In the gaslight her metallic-hued eyes had turned a pellucid shade of blue.

'I pity her, Doctor Liebermann. By keeping silent, she undoubtedly colluded with her husband — but what else could she do? Had Frau Schelling petitioned for divorce, she would have encountered terrible disapproval. The Catholic church is not renowned for its liberal attitude to the dissolution of the marriage bond. Edward and Adele would have been stigmatised and Herr Schelling's political career might have suffered, which in turn would have affected the children's financial security. Even worse, Frau Schelling's complaints and grievances might have been misconstrued as abnormal symptoms. I dare say that during the ensuing conflict her voice might have become raised, her speech more excited, her passions more violent, and then what?' Amelia Lydgate smiled sadly. 'There are many, particularly in your profession, Herr Doctor, who would associate such unfeminine behaviour with mental illness. Frau Schelling might have found herself incarcerated in the General Hospital or even at Am Steinhof. Herr Schelling's behaviour was despicable, but I am not naive, Doctor Liebermann. Men like Herr Schelling are not so unusual in this city, or in any other European capital — nor is the silent suffering of the women whom they subjugate.'

'You pity her because you identify with her.'

'Of course. All women know what it is like to be caught on the horns of an impossible dilemma, and all women share a precarious fate. We tread an acrobat's wire, delicately weighing and balancing our own needs and desires against the needs and desires of men. And if we deviate from this narrow wire — we fall.'

Liebermann felt disturbed by her speech — even accused.

'Please excuse me, Herr Doctor,' Miss Lydgate continued, detecting his discomfort. 'You did not ask me for so forthright an opinion. And I may have caused you some offence.'

'No, not at all . . .' he replied. 'I . . . I have much sympathy with your view. Women are ill served by our society, and by medicine. There are some doctors in Vienna who still believe women are uniquely vulnerable to hysteria on account of their having a wandering womb. There is much to be achieved.'

Liebermann handed the letter back to Amelia Lydgate who folded it in two and placed it on the table. The chandelier hissed quietly.

'Perhaps,' said the young governess, 'when there are more women doctors, such risible ideas will attract the scorn they deserve.'

'I hope so,' said Liebermann with evident sincerity.

Their conversation progressed naturally to the subject of women's suffrage — a cause which seemed to have attracted more vociferous advocates in London than in Vienna. Liebermann acknowledged that his countrymen, particularly those who sympathised with the Pan-German movement, were violently opposed to women's involvement in politics or public life. As far as the Pan-Germans were concerned, the education of females should serve only one purpose: preparation for motherhood. Although the university had opened its doors to female medical students, the principle had been opposed by the entire faculty. It was only when old Franz Josef himself had insisted that the Muslim women of Bosnia must have female physicians that the concession had been made. Moreover, it was still impossible for a woman to study law and there seemed to be little prospect of change.

When the opportunity arose, Amelia Lydgate excused herself and returned with a pot of tea. Liebermann was conscious of a certain irony. After expressing such militant views concerning women's rights, the young Englishwoman was curiously compliant with respect to one particular gender convention. She would not permit Liebermann to pour his own tea.

Miss Lydgate tilted the pot and the hot liquid bubbled and steamed into his teacup. 'Oh, incidentally,' she said casually. 'I have given the matter of your murder inquiry some more thought.'

'Really?' said Liebermann, sitting up in his chair. 'And have you reached any conclusions?'

'Yes,' said the young woman. 'I have.'

Liebermann craned forward.

'Would you like some milk, Doctor Liebermann?'

'No, thank you, Miss Lydgate.'

'Are you sure? I always find that a splash of dairy improves the flavour of Earl Gray immeasurably.'

'I really am quite happy to forgo the pleasure — but thank you, nevertheless.'

Miss Lydgate's expression became earnest as she tipped the milk jug, allowing a carefully calculated quantity to spill out into her own cup.

'You were saying . . .' said Liebermann.

'Oh yes, forgive me, Herr Doctor. The murder . . .'

She placed the jug back on the tea tray.

'With regard to the autopsy results and that mysterious bullet wound . . . It seems to me that such an effect could be achieved in two ways. Firstly, by using an ice projectile. Ordinary water, frozen in a bullet-shaped mould, could be inserted into the chamber of a revolver and employed as conventional ammunition. The bullet would — of course — melt away. However, there are some obvious problems with this method. Although a frozen-water bullet might feasibly produce a wound identical to that inflicted by a metal counterpart, it might not be very . . . reliable. A frozen bullet could easily shatter in the chamber. And then there is the problem of refrigeration. I take it there was no means of refrigeration close by? There was no ice store? It had not been snowing?'

'No.'

'Well, then, it is most unlikely the murderer used this method.'

'You said there was another way?'

'Yes — a second, much simpler way. It is more reliable and does not require refrigeration.'

She picked up her teacup and took a sip.

'Miss Lydgate.' Liebermann clasped his hands together, his knuckles whitening. 'I would be most grateful if—'

'Indeed, I am being dilatory and you are impatient to hear my conclusion.'

What she said next was so extraordinary, so compelling, that Liebermann could barely suppress his excitement. Moreover, he now knew who it was who had killed Fräulein Löwenstein.

84

THE OMNIBUS HAD made surprisingly good progress. It had already crossed the Danube Canal and was rattling up the wide thoroughfare of the Praterstrasse. Liebermann glanced at his watch and realised that he would be arriving too early. The conductor, a short, jovial man with a military moustache, shook his leather satchel and took another fare.

Liebermann's euphoria had subsided, leaving in its wake a rising sense of unease. When he had explained his scheme to Rheinhardt it had seemed faultless. But now, as he came closer to his destination, he wondered whether it was such a good idea after all. He might be wrong, in which case the consequences would be awkward and embarrassing, particularly for Rheinhardt. The Commissioner was sceptical, and his equivocation had been exacerbated by von Bulow's insistence that Hölderlin was about to make a full confession. But, on reflection, Liebermann determined that he was worried not so much about being wrong as being right. His scheme, formulated in a moment of heady excitement, was not foolproof. Things *could* go wrong.

Rheinhardt had made it quite clear that his friend should not consider himself under any obligation. He might choose to abandon his assignment at any point and would still retain the respect of Rheinhardt and his colleagues: *You're a doctor, Max, not a police officer.* But in reality Liebermann knew that it wasn't so simple. Withdrawal was no longer an option. Now that he had embarked upon his task he must complete it. Failure to do so would be dishonourable — an abnegation of duty. It was precisely because he *was* a doctor, and not a policeman, that he had to proceed.

Should I have written a letter? To mother and father, to Clara? Just in case?

He chastised himself for being morbid — yet his exhortations were hollow. The unabated sense of foreboding folded the contents of his stomach like cream in a revolving churn. He found himself thinking about Amelia Lydgate. How would she fare in his absence? Would Landsteiner continue to help her? These were questions to which there were no answers. Yet the fact that he had posed them at all exposed the depth of his attachment — a factor that compounded rather than relieved his anxiety.

The omnibus slowed down.

'Not a very pleasant evening, is it, sir?' said the conductor.

'No,' Liebermann replied, standing up and flattening his coat against his trousers.

'Still, the rain might hold off — if we're lucky.'

'Perhaps . . .'

The conductor raised his cap, turned around and called out: 'Prater. Last stop. Prater.'

The other passengers — an ill-assorted assembly of young men — followed Liebermann as he jumped off the back platform. When the vehicle was empty, the driver, exposed to the elements in his open cabin, shook the reins and the horses moved forward.

The sky was indeed overcast, for which Liebermann was quietly thankful. There would be fewer people milling around the Volksprater. He looked up and caught sight of his destination for the first time: the awesome structure of the Riesenrad. It turned, like the principal cogwheel in a universal clock, ratcheting time, bringing Liebermann's fate steadily closer.

As he made his way down the Hauptallee, he could hear the sound of a barrel organ grinding out a simple, happy march — the bass part oscillating between a low C and its octave. The inane melody was soon competing with the cries of Prater folk who were trying to attract the attention of potential customers. The air began to smell of sausages.

Liebermann wandered into the labyrinth of marquees and pavilions: past the shooting hall, a wrestler's tent and the closed puppet theatre. Then he passed the double-arched entrance of 'Venice in Vienna' — a reconstruction of the famous canals, complete with singing gondoliers. Soon after, he came across a curious wooden cabin, its exterior painted with mystical scenes, the most striking of which appeared to be a mesmeric monk levitating a woman in white robes. A large board hung beside the curtained entrance, bearing a crudely painted upturned palm in a circle. The drapes suddenly parted and a man wearing a top hat poked his head out.

'Want to know your future, sir?'

'Unfortunately, I know it only too well.'

'No man knows his own fate, sir.'

'Then I am the exception.'

'The clairvoyant is very pretty . . .'

'I'm sure she is.'

'Face like an angel.'

'Thank you, but I'm afraid I must decline.'

The man shrugged and his head vanished behind the drapes as quickly as it had appeared.

Liebermann drifted away from the attractions and found himself standing on an open concourse. To his left was the Lustspieltheater, Restaurant Prohaska, and the four towers of the water chute. To his right were the low roofs of more entertainment buildings and the Café Eisvogel. Directly ahead, viewed from this angle, the Riesenrad had become an ellipse.

A gust of wind washed the concourse with a diaphanous veil of drizzle, sending a small group of men running towards the café. Luckily, the sprinkling was brief and light. Liebermann had neglected to bring an umbrella. He cleaned the rain off his spectacles and combed his damp hair back with his fingers. Looking at his watch, he took a deep breath and marched briskly towards the colossal wheel.

There was no queue at the kiosk. The Riesenrad was not a popular attraction on a dull evening — the damp haze would obscure the view. Even so, a steady trickle of thrill-seekers paid for their tickets and entered one of the thirty red gondolas, eager to experience the juddering ascent. While the wheel was stationary, the wind plucked a strange keening from its taut steel cords. Then, like a waking giant, the girders yawned and groaned as the wheel began to turn again.

Liebermann looked at his watch.

Ten minutes late.

He had expected him to be more punctual and hoped that this small error of judgement was not symptomatic of a more profound miscalculation. The red of the gondolas suddenly reminded Liebermann of blood-caked muslin — the horror of Karl Uberhorst's ruined face and exposed cortex. His adversary was not only clever but capable of inhuman brutality.

'Herr Doctor — forgive me.' Liebermann flinched. 'There was an accident on the Schweden-brucke and I was delayed.'

He turned slowly and was obliged to shake the new arrival's hand.

85

AN ATTENDANT CLOSED the gondola door and the two men stood on opposite sides of its cabin-like interior.

'I must say, Herr Doctor,' said Bruckmüller in his resonant bass, 'although I appreciate that the information in your possession is sensitive, was this *really* necessary?'

'I could think of no better place in which to have a wholly private conversation,' said Liebermann.

'Indeed,' said Bruckmüller. 'But I would have been perfectly happy to entertain you at my club. The rooms are excellent and the staff exemplary — the model of discretion.' The steel cords vibrated and the girders groaned as the wheel turned and the gondola lifted. 'On the telephone, you said that this new information concerns me directly.' Bruckmüller removed his bowler hat and placed it on a seat.

'It does,' said Liebermann. 'There have been a number of developments in the Löwenstein investigation.'

'Really? It was my understanding that the police have their man. Isn't that so?'

The gondola lurched as the wheel came to an abrupt halt and both men stumbled to retain their balance. Liebermann looked out of the window and saw that a soberly dressed man was being helped into the next gondola.

'Is there a problem?' asked Bruckmüller.

'No, I don't think so,' said Liebermann.

Bruckmüller repeated his original question: 'Well, Herr Doctor — isn't it so? Isn't it true that the police have their man? It said so in the *Zeitung*.'

'That is certainly Inspector von Bulow's opinion.'

'And mine, indeed. God in heaven! You were there — at Madame de Rougemont's. You saw how Hölderlin reacted.'

The gondola lifted again. This time the movement was more smooth.

Liebermann did not respond and Bruckmüller shifted uncomfortably. The big man's eyes narrowed with suspicion.

'Tell me, Herr Doctor — are you acting in an official capacity this evening?'

'Yes, I am.'

'Then why are you not accompanied?'

'As I said, the information in my possession is extremely sensitive.'

Bruckmüller was obviously dissatisfied with Liebermann's answer. But, after a moment's tense hesitation, he decided not to quibble. He nodded and produced a disingenuous flat smile.

'In which case, Herr Doctor, I would be most grateful if we could proceed.'

'Of course.'

Liebermann walked to the opposite window. His breath steamed the glass and he wiped it clear with his hand.

'I must begin by sharing with you some of the facts concerning Fräulein Löwenstein's history . . .' Through the criss-cross lattice of metalwork Liebermann watched the water chute produce two walls of high spray.

'It would seem,' continued Liebermann, 'that Fräulein Löwenstein was not, as members of your spiritualist circle asserted, a talented medium. Rather, she was an unsuccessful actress who in partnership with her lover sought to exploit the gullible for financial gain.'

'That is absurd, Herr Doctor! Hölderlin is a man of means.'

'Hölderlin was not her lover, Herr Bruckmüller.'

'But of course he was.'

'No, Herr Bruckmüller, her lover was Otto Braun — not an artist, as he would have you believe, but a stage magician. He very probably did his apprenticeship down there.' Liebermann glanced down at the Volksprater. 'The relationship between Charlotte Löwenstein and Braun had become strained and unhappy. Braun was becoming increasingly dissolute — you may have noticed some changes in his appearance yourself — and was amassing substantial debts. As a result, Fräulein Löwenstein realised that she could no longer depend on Braun to sustain her livelihood. An unreliable accomplice would inevitably jeopardise their little enterprise. Being a perceptive woman, she also recognised that her principal asset, her beauty, could not last for ever. In the fullness of time, Charlotte Löwenstein began to devise a plan that would provide her with long-term security. It involved the use of blackmail.'

Liebermann turned to catch Bruckmüller's expression. His veneer of bluff affability suddenly hardened and flaked away like dry scales. A ridge of muscle tightened beneath his jaw.

'She was a very attractive woman — wasn't she?' said Liebermann.

The wheel stopped to admit more passengers. The gondola rocked in the buffeting wind.

'Yes, she was.'

'I only saw photographs of her, and not very good ones at that. Even so, it was obvious that she was a woman of quite exceptional beauty. In the flesh she must have been . . . irresistible.' The Riesenrad creaked and groaned like the ropes and timbers of an ancient galleon. A string of electric lights suddenly flashed into brightness outside one of the restaurants on Austelungstrasse. 'Did you find her attractive, Herr Bruckmüller?'

The big man turned away and appeared to be admiring the view. He seemed to have vanquished his emotions again and was now quite composed.

'It would be a strange man who did not appreciate Fräulein Löwenstein's beauty. Yes, of course I found her attractive.'

'Attractive? Or, in truth, would it be more accurate to say irresistible?'

Bruckmüller laughed.

'Herr Doctor, are you really insinuating—'

The wheel began to move.

'She seduced you, Herr Bruckmüller.'

'That is an utterly ridiculous accusation.'

'And you would have been happy to retain her as your mistress indefinitely—'

'Herr Doctor!' Bruckmüller interrupted. 'You are testing my patience.'

'But unfortunately she became pregnant, at which point the nature of your relationship changed. She began to ask you for money — substantial sums, I imagine — which you obligingly provided. She was, after all, in quite a strong position. If she chose to announce that she was carrying your child, the ensuing scandal would have ruined your chances of marrying into the von Rath fortune — to say nothing of your political ambitions. And even if you did manage to survive the initial scandal, the likelihood of your marriage and reputation surviving the appearance of an illegitimate child — or children, in this case — would have been vanishingly small.'

Bruckmüller shook his head: 'Aren't you forgetting something rather important, Herr Doctor?'

'Hölderlin?'

'Indeed.'

'Fräulein Löwenstein was not entirely sure that she would be able to succeed with her plan. You might, for example, have become resigned to your fate. Disgrace does not kill a man. There is nothing stopping an entrepreneurial spirit from transferring his assets to another capital, where he might start an entirely new life. And where would that have left Fräulein Löwenstein? No, she was determined to have financial security for the rest of her days at whatever cost. I dare say that the few months in which she enjoyed the benefits of your . . . patronage, merely strengthened her resolve. Poor Hölderlin was simply an insurance policy. A safety net that would catch her if, ultimately, you failed to comply with her demands.'

As they gained height, the landscape of the city was being slowly revealed. A few early gas lamps had been lit, and smudges of yellow light began to gleam through the mizzle.

'Of course,' continued Liebermann, 'you knew nothing of Fräulein Löwenstein's contingency plan, and the pressure on you was mounting. You needed to resolve this difficult situation — and quickly.'

The wheel juddered to a halt.

'Do you know something, Herr Doctor . . . I must confess, I have never been on the Riesenrad before. The view is quite extraordinary.'

Liebermann was unnerved by Bruckmüller's uncharacteristically quiet delivery and the incongruity of his statement. Yet it was symptomatic of a dissociative process that he was eager to encourage.

'You visited Charlotte Löwenstein and at gunpoint forced her to write a note suggesting that she had made a Faustian pact with the devil. Halfway through, she realised that she might be writing her own death certificate, paused, and got up abruptly. You pressed the revolver to her chest and pulled the trigger. Inside the chamber was a modified bullet. It was made not of metal but of compacted meat and bone. Such a bullet would be strong enough to punch a hole in Fräulein Löwenstein's chest but would ultimately disintegrate. Tiny fragments of — let us say — a pork chop would be completely undetectable in an autopsy.

'Charlotte Löwenstein died instantly. You then arranged her body on the chaise longue and placed the Egyptian statuette in the Japanese box. The key was left on the inside, and locked from the outside using minute surgical forceps — made by Bruckmüller & Co. The same technique was used to turn the larger key in the sitting-room door. Correct me if I am mistaken, but the subsequent deluge was sheer good fortune, reinforcing the idea that Fräulein Löwenstein had been visited by the devil in the person of Seth — the god of storms, chaos and mischief.'

Over the distant hills, a cloud break allowed the setting sun to peek through. A ruddy haze spread across the horizon, and for a moment the sky acquired the texture and colour of beaten bronze. Under this vengeful firmament, Vienna appeared like a biblical city, a decadent sprawl ripe for retribution and the cleansing lick of holy fire.

Bruckmüller was entirely motionless.

'Your ruse worked remarkably well, Herr Bruckmüller. The police were baffled, mystified, bewildered. The Löwenstein murder seemed to have been perpetrated by a supernatural entity. The police were so distracted by the bizarre circumstances of Fräulein Löwenstein's death that they almost forgot to conduct a proper investigation! And even when the police did start to ask pertinent questions you remained unconcerned. You were confident that your clever illusion would never be unravelled. And you knew that no one would ever be successfully tried for committing an impossible crime. I congratulate you, Herr Bruckmüller: it was a brilliant plan.'

The wheel groaned and the gondola continued its ascent. Bruckmüller turned his large head.

'But then your fiancée, Fräulein von Rath, organised a seance, during which it became obvious to you that Herr Überhorst was in possession of some very important information. Information that he was considering disclosing — very probably — to the police. Perhaps Fräulein Löwenstein had confided in him? Perhaps he knew that she was pregnant? Perhaps he suspected — or even knew — the name of her lover? These must have been some of the troubling questions that you began to ask yourself. Soon after, you might also have learned — although I'm not sure how — that Herr Uberhorst was trying to work out how the illusion of the locked door was achieved. If he determined that such a trick could be performed by using surgical forceps, then he would become doubly dangerous to you.

'Perhaps you imagined the von Rath fortune slipping through your fingers? Or was it the dead weight of your body, swinging from the gibbet? Whatever image it was that played on your mind, you panicked. In the early hours of the morning you entered Uberhorst's shop, again using forceps, and crept into his bedroom. He was, I believe, asleep when you bludgeoned him to death.'

The wheel ground to a halt. The gondola had reached the very top of the Riesenrad. It was the strangest sensation to be suspended in such a high place. Looking directly out of the window, it indeed felt like flying. More lights were appearing below, like the majestic stellar revelation that accompanies dusk in winter — a general twinkling of stars, the constellations of which were the streets and squares of Vienna.

'It is such a beautiful city,' said Bruckmüller. 'Wouldn't you agree, Herr Doctor?' But before Liebermann could answer he began talking again. 'No, I suppose you wouldn't agree. Being Viennese . . . I dare say it would offend your urban sensibility to make such an admission. You would prefer, no doubt, to make some cynical remark about its excesses.'

A firework, launched from the Prater, shot into the air and exploded — a starburst of blue and yellow stars.

'But what a prize . . .' continued Bruckmüller reflectively. Then, shaking his head, he repeated: 'What a prize.'

The gondola was slapped by a gust of wind, rocking it backwards and forwards like a cradle.

'You wanted to be Mayor,' said Liebermann, recognizing the reach of Bruckmüller's ambition.

The big man's face swung around. Perspiration was trickling off his forehead.

'He's got some good ideas, has Lueger — but he never goes far enough . . .' The four hundred tons of iron on which they were perched began to revolve again. 'He'll never do what's necessary.'

'And what's that?'

'To get rid of the vermin. The journalists, the subversives, the intellectuals . . . I pray that someone has the good sense to do what needs to be done. Before it's too late.'

They had begun their descent.

'Vienna,' said Bruckmüller again. 'The jewel of the empire . . . but it won't hold, you know. All these people. All these different people. They are too numerous, and too varied. It'll need a strong arm to protect the honest, decent folk when it all begins to unravel. Do you believe in destiny, Doctor Liebermann?'

The young doctor shook his head.

'I didn't think you would,' said Bruckmüller.

Liebermann's clinical sensibility had not deserted him. He examined Bruckmüller as if he were a patient. He saw a man who believed that he was, in some way, chosen. A narcissist who subscribed to a suspect Pan-German philosophy in which the threads of mysticism, prejudice and a folkish idealism, had become hopelessly entangled. It was little wonder he could kill so easily. A man like him would kill anyone who got in the way of his lofty ambitions.

Bruckmüller puffed out his cheeks and exhaled slowly. Then,

bracing himself, he stood up straight and took a step towards Liebermann.

'Well, Herr Doctor, you must be feeling very pleased with yourself. I feel almost obliged to return the compliment that you paid me earlier. Yes, and why not? I think I will. Congratulations, Herr Doctor: a brilliant exposition. I can only assume that when we reach the ground the police will be waiting to arrest me.' Bruckmüller's smile was broad and humourless. 'Which makes me wonder: are you so very clever, after all? Sly, cunning, slippery — as one would expect from a member of your race — but clever? Maybe not.'

Liebermann took a step back and shifted to the other side of the gondola.

'You have left me very few options, Herr Doctor. But I can still exercise some choices. I take it that you now realise your mistake.' Bruckmüller reached for the door and yanked it open. A gust of damp air blew into the cabin.

'Don't jump!' cried Liebermann automatically.

Bruckmüller laughed.

'I don't intend to, Herr Doctor.'

The big man moved towards Liebermann, his fists held up like a pugilist's. Bruckmüller's bulk made him appear more squat than his true height but now that he was up close Liebermann realised that his antagonist was disconcertingly tall.

The young doctor was able to dodge the first punch but there was nowhere to run. A second swipe cuffed Liebermann on the side of the head and he stumbled towards the open door. The gondola rolled and Bruckmüller lurched forward, clawing the air before his heavy paw landed on Liebermann's shoulder, his grip tightening as he pressed down. Bruckmüller's fingers dug into Liebermann's flesh like the teeth of a Rottweiler. The sheer weight of his arm threatened to snap the young doctor's collarbone. Liebermann flailed around helplessly before Bruckmüller landed an eviscerating punch. It felt like a cannon ball tearing through Liebermann's stomach and scorching his innards. Unable to breathe and wanting to vomit, he was still bent double when a second punch lifted him off his feet and deposited him inches from the door. Dazed, Liebermann managed to stand for a brief moment before losing his balance and falling backwards.

He grabbed the door frame but found himself hanging out of the gondola, his feet barely keeping their precarious purchase on the cabin floor. He looked down at the vertiginous drop.

'That's it,' shouted Bruckmüller. 'See where you're going!'

Bruckmüller smacked his palm against the fingers of Liebermann's right hand, producing a white-hot shock of pain. The fear of death was suddenly superseded by a lesser anxiety: it occurred to Liebermann that his fingers might be crushed and that he might never play the piano again. A helpful gust of wind allowed him to pull himself forward a little. But again, Bruckmüller's palm slammed against his grasping fingers like a mallet blow. This time, the incandescent pain was short-lived and was soon replaced by a terrible numbness. Liebermann's hand had become insensate and he watched with detached resignation as his fingers slowly began to slip away from the door frame.

Bruckmüller raised his arm, ready for the final blow.

Suddenly there was a loud report and the noise of glass shattering.

The big man spun round, bewildered. A stain had appeared close to his shoulder — a dark circular stain that spread quickly, fed by a small bullet hole from which blood was bubbling. Liebermann scrambled back into the gondola and threw the weight of his body against Bruckmüller who lost his footing and stumbled backwards — grabbing at the lapels of Liebermann's coat.

Liebermann found himself being dragged after Bruckmüller. The big man's shoulders hit the cabin's woodwork, bringing his bulky body to an abrupt halt. Bruckmüller leaned against the cabin wall for support and drew Liebermann's head up so that it was level with his own. Liebermann struggled to get away but found that he could not move. Bruckmüller's superhuman grip held fast. Glancing down at the expanding stain, Liebermann said: 'Herr Bruckmüller, you have been shot.'

Bruckmüller's jaw began to move, as though he was chewing. Then, after clearing his throat, he hawked into the young doctor's face. Liebermann flinched as a ball of bloody mucus hit him and splattered across his cheek.

'I know I've been shot,' said Bruckmüller. 'And I don't want to be shot again.'

Liebermann realised that Bruckmüller was using him as a shield.

'There is no escape, Herr Bruckmüller.'

'Not for you — Doctor Jew.'

Bruckmüller's basso profundo vibrated in Liebermann's chest. Before Liebermann could respond, Bruckmüller's free hand closed around his neck. An instant later, Liebermann could not breathe. Instinctively, he tried to prise Bruckmüller's thick fingers apart — but his right hand was still numb and each of Bruckmüller's digits was slick with blood.

Liebermann was horrified by the look in Bruckmüller's eyes. Malice had been replaced by something far more sinister: detached concentration. Bruckmüller was like a scientist observing a creature expiring in a vacuum jar. He seemed to be willing Liebermann dead — dispassionately consigning him to oblivion. As the world began to darken around him, Liebermann became aware of a thought forming in his mind — a small voice, striving to be heard amid the noise and confusion.

I am not ready to die.

It was the closest that he had ever come to praying and even though he had not requested the intervention of a higher power this assertion — resentful and pathetic — was still an appeal. An entreaty. And, against all expectations, it appeared to have some effect.

Bruckmüller's serious, studious gaze clouded. His lids fell and then lifted in a sluggish blink — and, miraculously, Liebermann found that he could breathe again. He gulped the air hungrily, sucking it deep into his lungs through his painfully restricted windpipe. Bruckmüller's grip weakened and his fingers peeled away from Liebermann's throat one by one.

The big man's coat was soaked with his own blood. He blinked again and this time his lids remained closed for longer. Then he swayed and fell sideways, toppling to the floor.

Liebermann rested against the side of the gondola and tried to catch his breath. Looking out of the window, he experienced a curious illusion. The ground seemed to be rising up to meet the gondola. He glanced at Bruckmüller, whose supine body looked like that of a slumbering giant.

Bruckmüller pushed himself up with his left hand and then clasped his shoulder. Blood was gushing out between his big white knuckles. With his mouth wide open he was panting like a thirsty bulldog.

The wind whistled through the smashed window. In the next gondola, the soberly dressed bourgeois — clearly a police marksman — had his revolver at the ready for a second shot, should it prove necessary.

Bruckmüller shifted and immediately winced.

'If you get up,' said Liebermann, 'I have reason to believe that you'll be shot again. I would strongly advise that you remain exactly where you are.'

Bruckmüller closed his eyes and let his body fall back on to a bed of broken glass.

'May I ...' Liebermann paused. 'May I attend to your wound, Herr Bruckmüller? You are losing a great deal of blood.'

The big man tried to open his eyes.

'Stay away from me ... you filthy ...'

But before the insult was complete Bruckmüller's eyelids flickered and he lost consciousness.

Liebermann crouched beside Bruckmüller and did what he could to staunch the flow of blood. But his right hand was still insensate and Bruckmüller was lying in an awkward position. He applied as much pressure as he could. The big man was still breathing but each breath seemed more shallow and difficult. His chest and stomach were hardly moving.

A chorus of metallic voices filled the air — the demented strains of the great wheel coming to a halt. The gondola had returned to the ground.

The door flew open and Rheinhardt stepped into the cabin.

Liebermann looked up from his patient.

'I believe he'll live,' he said softly.

86

THE SONGS THAT they chose were necessarily slow. Liebermann's right hand was better but his fingers were still bruised and stiff. He did not feel ready to play anything with a tempo marking faster than *allegro moderato*. As a result their buoyant mood was not reflected in their music-making and what might have been an evening of carefree *Ländler* and popular songs became instead a programme of wistful ballads and soulful meditations. Yet, as he plumbed the darker sonorities of the Bösendorfer, Liebermann recognised that this valedictory concert was more fitting. It was, after all, a murder investigation that had been brought to a successful conclusion.

After some dignified choral-like Beethoven they decided to end with 'Der Leiermann' from Schubert's *Winterreise*. The piano part was so sparse, so frugal that Liebermann had no trouble producing an entirely faultless performance. Bare fifths in the left hand imitated the sound of a drone, while the right hand picked out a sad, desolate melody. It was chilling music — stark and emotionless. Even the scarcity of notes on the page suggested the open, blank whiteness of a frozen landscape.

Rheinhardt's voice was sweet and true — each note produced with hardly any vibrato.

Druben hintern Dorfe steht ein Leiermann.

'Over there beyond the village stands an organ-grinder . . .'

Numb with suffering, Schubert's narrator follows blindly:

'Strange old man, should I come with you?'

As the final chord faded, with its promise of redeeming cold and oblivion, Liebermann lifted his hands off the keyboard. Reverently, he closed the piano lid, allowing the sustain pedal to amplify its beat, the hollow echo of which dissolved into the vastness of an imaginary icy waste.

'Well, Max,' said Rheinhardt, 'that wasn't too bad at all, considering. You acquitted yourself rather well.'

'Thank you,' said Liebermann, raising his right hand and rubbing his fingers together with a swift scissoring movement. 'Another week or two and I'll be ready for the *Erlkönig*.'

Rheinhardt laughed and slapped his friend on the back.

'You might be, Max, but I'm not sure that I will.'

Without further delay the two men retired to the smoking room where, between the leather armchairs, a new table had appeared — a simple, empty wooden cube, the upper plane of which was a square of polished ebony.

Rheinhardt stared at the new acquisition and tilted his head from side to side.

'You don't like it — do you?' said Liebermann.

'Was it expensive?'

'Yes. It's from Moser's workshop.'

'Who?'

'Koloman Moser?'

'No, can't say I've heard of him.'

'Never mind. Regardless of its aesthetic properties, I can assure you that this table will serve our purposes as well as the old one.' Liebermann gestured towards the brandy and cigars.

The two men sat down, Rheinhardt to the right, Liebermann to the left, and stared at the glowing embers in ritual silence, puffing and sipping. Eventually, Liebermann shifted his position and said, somewhat sheepishly: 'You want to know everything, I presume.'

'Yes, I do.'

'Well, I must say, Oskar, that you have exercised admirable restraint this evening. A lesser man might have insisted that we should forgo some of our musical pleasures.'

'Indeed. And having shown such admirable restraint, I feel bound to advise you that any further equivocation on your part will test our friendship to the limits of endurance.'

'Yes, of course, Oskar,' said Liebermann, smiling. 'Forgive me.'

The young doctor turned to look at his friend. 'You know, I've told you most of it already.'

'I should hope so, too,' said Rheinhardt with justified indignation. 'Even so, I am curious to know how it all came together — in your head, I mean.'

'Very well,' said Liebermann, 'kissing' his cigar to sustain the burn and producing great clouds of pungent smoke. 'I am happy to satisfy your curiosity. But I must begin with a confession. It was not I who solved the mystery of Fräulein Löwenstein's impossible wound, but Miss Lydgate.'

'The microscopist?'

'Indeed — although her talents extend well beyond the novel employment of optical devices: she is now registered with the university and will begin studying for a medical degree in the autumn.'

'But she's—'

'A woman — obviously. The university has recently changed its admission policy.' Rheinhardt assumed a benign but perplexed expression. Liebermann's cuboid table had been enough modernity for one evening. 'She's quite remarkable, Oskar, and endowed with extraordinary intellectual gifts. I simply told her the circumstances of the crime, and after a few days she had the answer, claiming — quite rightly — that a bullet made from meat was the only solution. Such is her predilection for rational thought that she wasn't distracted or tempted in the least by supernatural considerations.

'Once Miss Lydgate had explained how the illusion of the vanishing bullet had been achieved, I had what can only be described as a . . . a moment of revelation! I remembered that Bruckmüller started life as a provincial butcher. I also remembered seeing him with Mayor Lueger at the Philharmonic — Lueger has always received strong support from butchers and bakers — and it occurred to me that perhaps Bruckmüller's origins were much more significant than any of us had guessed — and in more ways than one. Bruckmüller, by virtue of his original occupation, would have been very familiar with the properties of meat, in much the same way as I, being a psychiatrist, am familiar with the properties of the human mind. Who else but a butcher would recognise the ballistic possibilities of his supper!'

'It is extraordinary,' said Rheinhardt, 'and yet—'

'So simple,' said Liebermann. 'I couldn't agree more.'

They both raised their glasses at the same time.

'Go on . . .' said Rheinhardt, eager for his friend to continue.

'Of course,' said Liebermann, 'as soon as I had identified Bruckmüller as the likely perpetrator other things about him started to acquire greater significance — his business, for example. You will recall that Miss Lydgate's microscopic examination of Charlotte Löwenstein's keys revealed unusual indentations. She had suspected that some instrument or other had been employed to rotate the keys.' Liebermann sipped his brandy and shook his head. 'Had I been a surgeon, Oskar, I think I would have linked Bruckmüller with the crime immediately. Even though Miss Lydgate's results suggested the use of a specialised tool I simply failed to think of forceps. My mind was fixed on some train of thought to do with locks and locksmiths . . . However, when Miss Lydgate suggested that a bullet could be constructed from meat, and I remembered that Hans Bruckmüller was a butcher, the significance of his business became obvious. Armed with a microscope, I went to the department of surgery and discovered that the indentations on Fräulein Löwenstein's keys corresponded exactly with a gripping pattern found on forceps manufactured by Bruckmüller & Co. We have since, of course, found the very same pattern on the key to Uberhorst's shop.'

'Why didn't you want to see that key too — before suggesting your meeting with Bruckmüller?'

'I didn't need to and anyway we were running out of time. There was always a possibility that von Bulow was going to succeed in extorting a bogus confession from Hölderlin, which would have complicated matters a great deal. When I tried to lock the door of my own apartment using Bruckmüller's forceps, I found the task extremely difficult. Turning keys in this way requires considerable strength — the kind of strength that had already betrayed itself in Bruckmüller's memorably firm handshake (which I had the pleasure of experiencing on the night of the seance) and the depth of Uberhorst's wounds.'

'Indeed,' said Rheinhardt, shuddering as he recollected the carnage. 'And I presume you had also already visited the antique dealers?'

'There are only a few establishments on Wieblingerstrasse who sell Egyptian artefacts. Apparently, they aren't very collectable at the moment. I soon learned that an Egyptian statuette with a forked tail had been sold to a big man with a strong handshake some time in March.'

'Thus,' said Rheinhardt, 'we had in our possession — at this point — some extremely good evidence. So why . . . why on Earth were you so insistent that your meeting with Bruckmüller should take place?'

'Extremely good evidence, you say? But was it really? Anybody can purchase forceps from Bruckmüller & Co. And he isn't the only big man in Vienna!'

'Yes, that's true.'

'And Bruckmüller is very well connected — and potentially very rich: a friend of the Mayor, no less. Sadly, I am not convinced that our judicial system always reaches the correct verdict under such circumstances. We had collected some *incriminating* evidence, but it was not *decisive* evidence.'

'All right, but why the Riesenrad? You told Brügel that you needed to be completely alone with Bruckmüller to extract a confession. Yet there are many secluded places in Vienna. I'm afraid I can't help feeling that you're concealing something, Max.'

Liebermann knocked the ash off the end of his cigar.

'It was necessary to meet Bruckmüller on the Riesenrad because of its peculiar effect on the mind.'

'Oh?'

'Have you been on it lately?'

'No, but I did take Mitzi last year.'

'Did you not find the experience . . . unreal?'

'It is certainly very odd, being taken to such a great height.'

'Exactly. It detaches the passenger from everyday existence and suspends him in an environment that is usually the exclusive province of birds. Now, think, Oskar: when else does one experience something similar?'

'Well, I don't know that there is somewhere similar. Still—'

Liebermann interrupted: 'Are you sure?'

'Yes, quite sure.'

Liebermann swirled his brandy round in its glass and tested the aroma.

'What about when you dream?'

Rheinhardt twirled his moustache and frowned.

'Isn't it just like flying in a dream?' Liebermann persisted.

'Yes,' Rheinhardt replied. 'Now that you mention it, I suppose the two experiences are not dissimilar.'

'You see . . . it is my belief, Oskar, that a ride on the Riesenrad blurs the boundary between reality and unreality — the conscious and unconscious divisions of the mind draw closer together.'

'Which means . . . ?'

'Did you read that book I gave you?'

'The one on dreams? Well, I started but—'

'Never mind,' said Liebermann. 'In the dream-world, our inhibitions break down. Forbidden wishes are frequently dramatised. Even the most devoted husband cannot avoid assignations during his sleep.' Rheinhardt shifted in his chair and looked faintly embarrassed. 'When Bruckmüller learned that I had discovered his method and understood his motives he had one wish, and one wish only: to kill his adversary, an adversary who (at least for him) embodied all of his irrational prejudices. Bruckmüller's political ambitions had been thwarted, and in the dreamlike atmosphere of the Riesenrad, his forbidden wish found expression all too easily. He attempted to kill me — and in doing so as good as confessed to the crime.'

'In which case, it was never your intention to extract a verbal confession. You always meant to provoke Bruckmüller!'

Rheinhardt's voice had risen slightly.

'Now, Oskar, do you see why it was impossible for me to be entirely candid? Brügel would never have accepted a psychoanalytic rationale for the operation—'

'And nor would I — particularly if I had known all the details of your thinking!' Rheinhardt shook his head. 'You do realise, don't you, that the police marksman was instructed at the very last minute? It was an afterthought.'

'Yes,' said Liebermann. 'I am extremely lucky to possess, in your person, such a conscientious friend, and I owe you both an apology and a debt of gratitude.'

'I can't believe you didn't tell me!'

'It was absolutely necessary.'

'To provoke him — knowing that he would probably attempt to kill you!'

'There was no other way. I had hoped that by the time Bruckmüller responded to my provocation the wheel would be nearing the end of its descent. I thought I would be relatively safe . . .'

'Relatively safe! I can't believe you didn't tell me!'

'Well, to be frank, Oskar, I still can't quite believe you didn't tell me that the seance you arranged was a sham!'

'That was different.'

'Was it?'

Rheinhardt grumbled something under his breath and sustained a mask of disgruntlement — which gradually, and grudgingly, softened by degrees towards resignation.

'Still . . .' he finally murmured. 'It all worked wonderfully, and it was good to see von Bulow squirm for once!'

The two friends looked at each other and simultaneously burst out laughing.

For several hours they continued to savour their triumph. The room had filled with cigar smoke and the fire had long since died down. As Liebermann poured the last of the brandy, Rheinhardt chanced to remark that Charlotte Löwenstein's fate would no doubt serve as an example to others of her kind. But instead of agreeing, Liebermann found himself not judging the dead woman but defending her.

'Without question, Fräulein Löwenstein was a femme fatale — a siren worthy of a place in a work of romantic fiction; however, I cannot condemn her, Oskar. In modern Vienna there are few opportunities for intelligent, spirited women to make their way in the world. The majority either relinquish their ambitions and resign themselves to marriage and motherhood — or, alternatively, they protest and attract a diagnosis of hysteria. Charlotte Löwenstein should be pitied. She was, after all, only trying to protect her interests.'

Rheinhardt did not always share his friend's liberal sympathies but this analysis prompted him to consider the future world that his daughters might inhabit. He thawed a little. On reflection, he hoped that Therese and Mitzi would not have to accept an unhappy destiny through want of opportunity. Rheinhardt finished his brandy and prised his watch from the fob pocket of his waistcoat.

'Good heavens, Max, it's almost eleven. I must be getting home.'

As he was leaving, Rheinhardt stopped for a moment and looked at his friend. His eyes expressed a great deal: pleasure, amiability and even, perhaps, amusement.

'Well done, Max,' he said softly. Liebermann did not reply, but simply increased the pressure of his handshake.

87

Miss Lydgate picked up the card and read aloud: 'To Miss Amelia Lydgate, with heartfelt gratitude for services rendered to the security office of Vienna. Please accept this small token of our esteem. Sincerely, Inspector Oskar Rheinhardt.'

Liebermann was seated at the gateleg table and tapped the large mahogany box.

'For me?' she said, her voice uncertain.

'Yes,' said Liebermann.

Miss Lydgate released the hasps and opened the lid. As she did so, the metal object inside lit her face with a reflected warm, golden light. She did not gasp or smile. The only visible response was a slight creasing of her brow; however, Liebermann was not offended. He understood that the young Englishwoman's impassive exterior belied the depth and authenticity of her appreciation.

'Thank you,' she whispered.

Inside the box, among folds of blue velvet, was a large brass microscope.

'It was made by Eduard Messter of Frerichsstrasse, Berlin. The case is signed by the maker — see here.' Liebermann pointed to the manufacturer's signature. 'I believe this instrument is more powerful than the one you currently employ — and the lenses are ground more finely. You will experience less distortion at higher levels of magnification.'

Amelia Lydgate lifted the microscope from the box with a gentleness that was almost maternal. It was obviously too heavy for her to manipulate with ease, yet she held it aloft and admired it from every angle. The brass gleamed triumphantly.

'You will be so kind as to thank Inspector Rheinhardt — it is a gift I do not deserve,' the young woman said in a level voice.

'Oh, but you do deserve it, Miss Lydgate!' Liebermann exclaimed. 'The Löwenstein murder would not have been solved without your help.'

Amelia Lydgate lowered the microscope carefully to the table's surface. Then, sitting down, she said: 'I would like you to tell me more of what transpired, Doctor Liebermann. I read in the *Zeitung* that the "Leopoldstadt demon" had been caught, but the article contained very little detail.'

'Very well,' said Liebermann, and he proceeded to give a full account of the investigation, from Rheinhardt's presentation of Fräulein Löwenstein's note to his own almost fatal encounter with Bruckmüller on the Riesenrad. As he was describing the point at which he was forced out of the gondola and his grip was failing, Miss Lydgate reached across the table and touched his sleeve. The moment of contact was so brief, so inconsequential, that it could easily have been missed. Yet this simple sign of concern had a profound effect on Liebermann. He felt as though his thoughts had become like dewdrops trembling on a cobweb. He felt insubstantial — weightless and airy.

'You were very brave, Doctor Liebermann,' said Miss Lydgate. Her gesture had been apparently unconscious. She showed no sign of embarrassment or self-awareness.

Liebermann cleared his throat and, after managing to utter some self-deprecatory remarks, gradually recovered a sufficient degree of composure to complete his story.

'It is strange, Doctor Liebermann, that the two murders were so different. One meticulous and clever — the other crude and brutal.'

'It is of course possible,' said Liebermann, 'that this was part of Herr Bruckmüller's plan. Perhaps he intended that the police should think that there had been two different murderers, in the hope that they would also conclude that the killings were unrelated. But I do not think this was the case. Fear is a very fundamental emotion. It strips away our sophisticated veneer and reduces the person to his or her core elements. Bruckmüller feared discovery, and in a state of panic his true, savage self found expression all too easily.'

Miss Lydgate seemed extremely interested in the workings of Bruckmüller's mind, and prompted Liebermann to speculate about the man's personal psychology.

'He wanted to be Mayor of Vienna, almost certainly — but I suspect that his ambition was even more far-reaching. When he was dissociating, he began talking about the Empire unravelling, the need for leadership. I believe that he may have seen himself as some kind of Messiah. The German people have a highly evolved mythology in which a semi-mystical hero figure almost always appears to usher in a new dawn. When Herr Bruckmüller's house was searched by the police, a horoscope was found with an attached commentary suggesting that his birth was in some way auspicious. It was both Fräulein Löwenstein and Herr Uberhorst's misfortune to threaten his appointment with destiny.'

'And it was almost your misfortune too,' said Miss Lydgate pointedly.

Liebermann smiled.

'Yes,' he replied. 'I am lucky to be alive.'

When Liebermann glanced at his wristwatch he realised that he had stayed for several hours longer than he had originally intended. Evening had given way to night, and it was no longer proper for him to be alone with Miss Lydgate. He stood to leave. Amelia Lydgate requested again that he should thank Inspector Rheinhardt for her gift, and escorted him to the door. They descended the dark stairs, and the sound of her skirts rustling behind him made a sensuous music — teasing and haunting.

Liebermann did not attempt to hail a cab. He felt like walking. In due course he passed the Josephinum, where he paused in order to admire the statue of Hygieia. Elevated and unattainable, eternally feeding the great serpent that coiled around her arm, the goddess looked down at him with regal indifference.

Bracing himself against the chill night air, Liebermann marched through Alsegrund and down Bergasse to the Danube Canal. There he stared into the dark water and enjoyed a cigar in solitude.

When he returned to his apartment he still felt restless, and contemplated playing some Bach — something undemanding, like the two- and three-part inventions — but remembered the time. Such was the level of music-making in Vienna that there was a general edict banning the playing of musical instruments after eleven o'clock. He needed something to occupy his mind.

Liebermann drifted from the piano to his writing bureau where he switched on the electric lamp. He collected some loose papers from the bottom drawer, sat down, filled his fountain pen with ink, and began writing:

It was the day of the great storm. I remember it well because my father — Mendel Liebermann — had suggested we meet for coffee at The Imperial. I had a strong suspicion that something was on his mind . . .

Acknowledgements

I WOULD LIKE to thank my agent, Clare Alexander, for taking me out to lunch in September 2002 and suggesting that I might want to think about a detective series; Hannah Black and Oliver Johnson for providing indispensable editorial guidance, Steve Matthews for his finely honed critical faculty, Sarah Liebrecht for translating various documents from German to English, David Coffer for alerting me to the existence of the inestimable Raymond Coffer (a walking encyclopedia of early twentieth-century Viennese lore), Eva Menassa in Berlin for yet more help translating correspondence, Sonja Busch and Fabrizio Scarpa for being splendid hosts in Vienna, Wolfgang Sporrer for recommending some very useful books, and Antonia Nagel and Anna Maxted for advising on Jewish observances. I would also like to thank Maria Käfer of the Austrian Embassy in London, Bruno Splichal and Herr Winter of the Bundespolizeidirektion Wien, Harald Seyrl of the Wiener Kriminal Museum, and Dr Ulrike Spring of the Historisches Museum der Stadt Wien. Finally, I would like to thank Nicola Fox, yet again, for helping in ways that really are too numerous to mention.

Frank Tallis
London, 2004